ALSO BY B. CELESTE

Underneath the Sycamore Tree

Lindon U
Dare You to Hate Me
Beg You to Trust Me

DARE YOU TO HATE ME

B CELESTE

Bloom books

Sourcebooks and the colophon are registered trademarks of
Sourcebooks. Bloom Books is a trademark of Sourcebooks.

Published by Bloom Books, an imprint of Sourcebooks
P.O. Box 4410, Naperville, Illinois 60567-4410
(630) 961-3900
sourcebooks.com

Originally self-published in 2021 by B. Celeste.

Cataloging-in-Publication Date is on file with the Library of Congress.

Printed and bound in the United States of America.
VP 10 9 8 7 6 5 4

*To those who asked me if I'd ever write a
sports romance and I told them no.
Maury detected that was a lie.
You're welcome.*

PLAYLIST

"Lego House"—Ed Sheeran

"Little Toy Guns"—Carrie Underwood

"Bad at Love"—Halsey

"Get Stoned"—Hinder

"One Step Closer"—Linkin Park

"That's What You Get"—Paramore

"Love Again"—Dua Lipa

"Let Me Down Easy"—Billy Currington

"Lasting Lover"—Sigala and James Arthur

"Again"—Sasha Alex Sloan

TRIGGER WARNING

This book deals with self-harm and thoughts of suicide, though neither are graphically shown in this story.

Prologue

IVY

THEY SAY I'M LUCKY.

Less than two millimeters to the right and I would have been gone before they found me on the bathroom floor.

But I'm not lucky at all.

I have nothing—not a cent to my name, a future to work toward, or a family who knows their daughter nearly bled out on the grubby, cold tiles of a public bathroom at a truck stop.

The rich-haired doctor looking over my chart regards me with questionable caution as he delivers yet another, "You're very fortunate, Ms. Underwood." There's a distant smile on his face, full of curiosity over the eighteen-year-old propped up on the hard stretcher with wrapped wrists and hollow eyes in front of him.

That girl doesn't feel like me. She feels distant and cold, lost mentally and emotionally somehow.

"Out of your head, Underwood," my best friend always told me when I'd lose myself in it, waiting for the trained "Head in the game" reply he got from me every time.

I'm not her anymore though.

Because I'm not fortunate at all.

I was two millimeters off.

Chapter One

IVY

Two Years Later

THE POUNDING HEADACHE IN my temples matches the loud thumping of my housemate's headboard smacking into the wall above me. Covering my face with the stained, flattened pillow does little to drown out what's going on upstairs. What's *always* going on. That's what you get when your rent is dirt cheap—four hours of sleep a night in a party house that I heard had a spare room through the grapevine at work.

I didn't realize when I showed up with two measly bags and the clothes on my back that I'd be shoved in the dank, musty, half-finished basement that smells like old socks and lavender Febreze and brushed off with barely a second look from the six other girls I live with. Or that most of them like to party, drink, and screw, usually in that order, whenever they get the chance to.

But I'd endure. I have nowhere else to go in this godforsaken town thanks to my spontaneous decision to get my life together, and I have no room to judge what Sydney is currently doing in the confines of her bedroom. I've done far worse, far more times, I'm sure of it.

Groaning when I drag myself out of bed, I throw on my typical Bea's Bakery attire, blue jeans and a black long-sleeve shirt that has the business's cartoon bee logo flying around a cupcake across the chest, and slide a brush through my faded blue hair. I'm lucky Beatrice Olsen, the elderly woman who owns the bakery here in Lindon, New York, hasn't asked me to dye it back to my natural color. The copper-brown color my hair used to be had natural red and caramel highlights in the sunlight, a unique mixture my mother used to tell me she envied because it took a lot of money at salons to produce the same results.

No longer is my hair a mixture of my parents'—my mother's pretty copper and my father's chocolate brown. The long locks I desperately need to cut soon are one of the few things I can change about myself. It's a chance to be someone else even temporarily, an identity of my own, unattached to my past or the people I walked away from.

It's barely seven in the morning when I slip upstairs, ignoring the moans coming from the only other door off the kitchen besides mine, and focus on grabbing my Starbucks iced coffee from the fridge and leaving before my housemate and her hookup are done.

People have rarely bothered me since I moved in back in July. The large white two-story Victorian is well known around campus as the place to party. Unfortunately, that means a lot of guests stay overnight; hookups, people too drunk to drive, and the occasional significant other pop up from time to time when I'm not locked in my room.

Raine, the only girl here who acts like I don't have fleas, and her boyfriend, Caleb, are two people I tolerate. The few times I've been hassled by one of my roommates' hookups, it's always Caleb, the laid-back but charming running back for Lindon University's football team, who gets them to leave me alone. Since words aren't my forte, I thank him with homemade baked goods that he takes to his place, which is rumored to house a handful of other football players.

I never ask for confirmation, and he never remarks on the double batch of desserts I send his way figuring there are other massive men to feed. He simply brings back the clean dishes for the next time he has to fend off some asshole who can't take no for an answer.

My shift at the local bakery is like any other when I clock in, tie a small white apron around my waist, and help Bea's granddaughter Elena get the pastries out for the day. There are early morning regulars, older couples who love the Sunday specials, that I get to greet and make easy conversation with, and a few grad students who don't totally piss me off when they hang around using the Wi-Fi.

In Lindon, everyone knows everyone even though the college brings in over three thousand students each semester. It's what I imagine a real-life Stars Hollow from *Gilmore Girls* would feel like if it were a small city. The customers who come in the bakery always have a new slice of gossip to share, and you're never safe from being one of the topics.

The sixteen-year-old sitting on the back counter with her legs dangling over the side in a swinging motion pokes at my hair. "When are you going to redye this?"

I make a face as I pour myself a cup of coffee since the one I brought didn't cut it. I'll need the extra caffeine after the last hour and a half turned into a nonstop morning rush. "I don't know. I'm not sure what color I want to do next."

And I'm broke, I silently add, blowing on the steam

billowing from the cup. No matter how hard I save up what little extra money Bea not so subtly sneaks into my paychecks each week, it's still not enough to justify buying pointless little things.

"I can do it," Elena, or Lena as I call her, offers, sipping on some disgusting concoction that only she drinks.

Setting my cup under the counter so I don't accidently spill it, I say, "I'm good, Lena."

Lena is sweet enough. A little too talkative and bubbly for my liking, especially first thing in the morning, but I've worked with worse—spoiled teenage brats and older people who are asses. My biggest problem with the social butterfly is how much she reminds me of what could have been before I messed everything up. It's not her fault that her tender age and obvious naivete trigger something dark inside me that I prefer to bottle up.

It's something I have to deal with every time she complains about things like her mother refusing to extend her curfew, let her date, or wear certain types of clothing when she's out. Her nose always crinkles when I say, "I don't see why you're so upset. Your mother loves you. That's why she's hard on you."

Lena's about to say something when her eyes get big and she kicks me a little too hard in the back of the thigh with her favorite checkered platform Vans. "He's back!"

I know instantly who she's talking about before I even turn to scope out the entrance. The little bell on the door goes off at the same time every Sunday, and Elena feels the need to point him—and his staring—out each week. He'll wait to order until the line is down before he gets the same thing as always—a small coffee, no cream or sugar, six milks, and half an everything bagel.

All the bagels are homemade and probably the best things I've ever eaten. Bea makes them herself, never trusting anybody else to get them right. She stays late, makes the dough, bakes them, and leaves them for us to heat whenever they're ordered the following day. They sell out every time.

The only reason I don't raise a fit about the not-so-mystery-man's order is because I get to eat the other half, since nobody in their right mind would only order half of the delicious doughy treat.

I manage to roll my eyes without the person I'm cashing out seeing. "Calm down. And no kicking. Your excitement gives me bruises."

She scoffs behind me, and I'm sure if I glance over my shoulder, I'll see her arms crossed and her pink glossy lips sticking out in a pout. Sure enough, when I steal a look, she's doing just that. "It's not hard to make you bruise when you're barely a shade darker than white."

I grin to myself and pass the man his change, coffee, and bag of pastries before turning to her. "Whatever. And he's just another customer, so chill."

Now *she* rolls her eyes, disbelief evident in them like always when I brush off the appearance of Lindon U's star tight end. He's a guy who excels at what he does, I'll give him that. But he's still *just* a guy—a guy who orders half a bagel like some kind of carb-hating demon while still paying full price for it.

"He's coming over," she squeaks, cheeks turning red like they always do in his presence. It's why, as much as I want to pass him off to her to avoid any conversation, I have to handle it so she doesn't make a fool of herself.

I know some of the guys on Lindon U's football team from my intro classes this semester, making it easier to handle the mostly overbearing team members better than some when they come in. Biological anthropology is where a lot of athletes wind up because of the professor's reputation for giving out easy As. I guess it makes sense that sports team members would flock to classes like that since their GPAs are required to be over a 2.5 to stay on any team here, but their presence makes it harder to concentrate. They're all stupidly attractive, and considering their cocky smiles and flirty winks at the female (and male) students who notice, they know they are too.

I've seen some of the players use the attention to their advantage, making me scoff every single time they convince some poor victim to help them with homework or papers or buy them something here at Bea's.

Maybe if I were any other person, with any other experience, I'd succumb to their looks as well—give them free things when they approach me at the counter or agree to study and wind up with my shirt up and jeans down in the stacks at the library or pinned between a wall and a bulky body in the locker room. Attractive people make you do stupid things out of human need, but it's the ones who have the whole package that are the most dangerous.

Especially the one stopping in front of the cash register right now.

According to ESPN, the man towering over my five-nine stature is close to six six. Tall. Powerful. Authoritative. I'll never forget the day he walked into Bea's with his normal group of friends all bellowing over something stupid. His head was down, his shoulders hunched, his hands stuffed into the pockets of his red Lindon U sweatshirt like he didn't want anybody to bother him, but somehow I knew.

I knew I'd be met with electric blue eyes when he looked

up—the kind impossible not to be enamored with. And if I looked close enough, I'd see a formation of freckles on the right side of his face that resembles the Big Dipper.

What I didn't expect was how defined his jaw became, slightly squared and clean of any scruff most of the time, a patrician nose free from any breaks despite his aggressive sport, and a set of lips that are enviously fuller than mine.

He's the perfect type of football player in my eyes. Tanner from the summer sun, built but not overly so despite all the training he does, and a smile that's so white I hear Crest reached out to him on his Instagram to be featured. Whether that's true or not, I don't know. I don't have social media these days, just housemates who love to gossip. Especially about the football players who have made a splash on ESPN and local news stations with talk of going pro.

"Your usual?" I greet him, careful to keep my tone even despite the way my skin tingles as he towers over the register.

One of his brows, dark brown like the hair on his head, quirks. "Am I that predictable?"

It's Elena who chirps out a "Yep."

He chuckles, swiping one of those huge hands through the tresses of thick hair that are longer on the top versus the sides. "The usual then."

I try not to focus on the low, husky tone of his voice, which causes bumps to rise over my arms. He's twenty-one, but he doesn't sound it. Before I settled for a half-renovated basement, I couch surfed with strangers. Most of them were men older than my twenty years with every intention of making me pay them in some way, and usually not with money.

Aiden Griffith doesn't give me the same vibes those guys do though. I've had limited interactions with him since the day he walked in and stared in my direction until every inch of me felt the lick of flames from his burning blue gaze. He'll order, I'll tell him it's ready, and he'll give me a generic "have a good day," knowing I'll never offer an opportunity for more. One time, he told me my shoe was untied, which I'd already figured out after almost falling on my face with a tray full of breakfast for table three—who happened to be his buddies. Most of them besides Caleb and DJ, a guy from my anthropology class, laughed at my clumsiness until Aiden shot them a look. They shut up quickly.

It makes no sense to me why a player so sought after would be at a school like Lindon. We're not Division I. If anything, we're the misfit college—once thriving, now barely making ends meet if not for the championships the football team wins. I've heard people say that athletes who blow it at other schools come here to redeem themselves. Some of them make a future for themselves in the pros after their second chance, and others fizzle out.

I wonder which the man in front of me is.

I've been to a few games in the last year when I was squatting near campus and checking out my financial options for enrollment. Thanks to having nothing to my name and a decent GED score, financial aid pulled through for me when I was accepted. I know a little bit about the game but not what each position is called or what the scoring system is like. Most of what I do understand comes from the sixteen-year-old I work with, who feels the need to read out sports stats from online that are more like code to me than English. But because I want to understand, to learn after he walked in the first time, I try piecing together the little tidbits she always babbles about—who's the best, who's going pro, who won't get the chance. Lena and her grand-mother have predictions for the entire team, and like most of

Lindon, they're in agreement that Aiden Griffith can make it to the top.

Elena is the conversationalist in this transaction as I prepare Aiden's coffee because my tongue is too heavy. "Grandma Bea said the Dragons are going to kick butt all the way to the championships."

From the corner of my eye, I see the tight end's lips twitch upward, like he doesn't want to be cocky but can't pretend it's untrue. "That's the plan. Are you coming to support us?"

According to some of the locals who come in for coffee, the university has broken the records for most wins at home and away because of the team they've had the last two years.

"Are you kidding? I wouldn't miss it! Bea was going to shut down early until Ivyprofen here said she'd stay and close." Lena snorts while I roll my eyes at her nickname for me. "I don't know why. Nobody will be here except her."

A new set of eyes focuses on my face, but I busy myself by spreading the olive oil and sea salt butter he likes over his bagel. "Ivyprofen?" There's amusement in his tone, but he doesn't let either of us explain that Elena calls me that because she says I'm a pain and she needs medicine after dealing with me. Instead, he proceeds to ask, "Not a fan of football, huh?"

All I give him is a stiff shrug, and even the smallest upward movement feels draining. I know better than to believe it's from exhaustion but refuse to acknowledge the real reason behind the tightness consuming my body.

I remind myself I'm here to work, not make conversation with every customer who comes in. Especially not him.

As Elena goes to answer for me, her grandmother walks out from the back. "Lena, I need you to help me take out the bins of dough from the back and set them in the kitchen for me. We have a lot of baking to do today for the week."

I usually help with the week's preparations, but Elena expressed interest in learning her grandmother's recipes, so I took a step back. I want to believe Bea sees me as another grandchild—one of the twelve she lays claim to. But I know I'm not and that I shouldn't try so hard to be.

You're here for a paycheck, I tell myself again silently. *Not a family.*

Feeling my throat close up as I wrap up the bagel and stick it into a bag, I begin folding the top to complete the order when I hear, "Ivy."

It doesn't roll off the tongue like he's testing its sound.

It's in familiarity.

You're here for a paycheck, I tell myself once more as I turn on my heels and pass him the white bag and coffee cup without meeting those bright blue eyes. "That'll be $4.25 please."

"Ivy," he repeats, and I wonder if he can hear how hard my heart thumps with the sound of my name coming from his lips again.

"Cash or credit?" I press, staring at the machine's buttons, ignoring the pumping organ in my chest.

"Iv—"

"We also take Dragon Dollars," I say, cutting him off, gesturing toward the new promotion. Any college student who comes in can pay by scanning their student ID card.

He cusses under his breath. "You're just going to keep pretending then?" Even though his words are barely more than a hushed murmur under his breath, I feel them deeper than that. They sweep under my skin and squeeze my heart until I hear it crack from the pressure.

All I give him is, "Yes."

Because pretending is all I can do to get through today without remembering the past or the girl who confided in a boy before he left her to her demons four years ago.

I don't blame Aiden.

And I've never forgotten him either.

That's the problem.

Chapter Two

IVY

FOR ALMOST TWO WEEKS, I busy myself with school and work until I'm too tired to care that there's another party going on when I get home. I ignore the red plastic cups and abandoned half-empty beer bottles, step around the mass of bodies gyrating in the crowded halls, and collapse in a heap on my bed downstairs, tuning out the music thumping and people laughing above me as best I can.

Unfortunately, lulling myself into a peaceful oblivion is nearly impossible. Not only because the bass from upstairs rattles the windows but because my thoughts run rampant in my head, bouncing to the beat of the techno music. Trapping myself in my thoughts is dangerous territory because I always wind up in the same spot.

Two years ago.

The cold tile.

And every single moment leading up to it.

~

The small green establishment with an Underwood's Grocer sign hanging crooked from the side became the center of all our problems.

My father spent every second he could at the store while my mother stayed home full-time to take care of me and my little brother, Porter. Every night when Dad got home from the store, there'd be bags under his eyes and a new strand of white in his hair, and nothing I, Mom, or Porter could do ever got those tight lips to form even the tiniest smile like we used to be able to.

Whenever I asked Mom if Dad was okay, she'd pat my back, pass me a plain sheet of construction paper and a box of crayons, and tell me the same thing. "Your father is just stressed."

But every resounding explanation came with a heavier delivery, timid pat, and demand for distraction. When drawing wasn't enough, Mom's tired honey-brown eyes would look to me after a hushed conversation with Dad after dinner, and she'd tell me to check on Porter and then go to my room.

She never failed to come in later, pick out my favorite book from the small shelf of fairy tales and fables we collected, and read until I fell asleep.

The moment the atmosphere changed was when I looked up from the TV Porter and I watched our favorite Saturday morning cartoon on to see Mom gaping at a piece of paper she took from the mailbox earlier. The lips she always painted pink were parted, her hand holding her head up with her wedding ring I'd always been obsessed with glinting in the light, and her copper hair fell messily over her shoulders because she hated doing things with it.

When I slid off the couch and tugged on her shirt, she

took a few moments before setting the paper down to look at me. "I'm just stressed, Ivy. Don't worry."

I'm not sure when I realized that I hated those two little words. *Don't worry.* How could I not worry when hushed conversations in the kitchen turned into heated phone calls in the living room? Or when their voices rose in their bedroom and Dad would storm out and slam the front door behind him and be gone all night?

I didn't know what was going on, but Dad stopped coming home for dinner at his normal time, Mom stopped reading to me at night, and soon it was just me and Porter at the kitchen table while our mother took calls in other rooms. Sometimes I'd hear her talk about Grandma Gertie and a trip to visit her, but most times I'd hear the store brought up and listen to the muffled cries my mother tried hiding behind closed doors.

It came time to worry when Dad came home late at night to find Mom waiting for him with a face void of emotion. I snuck out of my room to listen to their conversation and heard him tell Mom we'd have to sell the house and find something smaller. Mom had asked, "Why can't you let the store go, Fred? I'm tired of it not going anywhere."

And even at the tender age of eight, Dad's response sliced through me like I knew it wasn't right. "I can say the same about us, Kate."

Their voices became louder as they moved down the hall, their argument becoming heated until I heard something loud in the kitchen crash.

Mom yelled.

Dad yelled back.

For the first time, I took refuge in my closet and burrowed into the line of ugly dresses that I hated wearing.

The material may have been scratchy against my skin, but it served as a barrier that drowned out some of the noise.

From the outside, our home was what one would expect a blue-collar family to live in. My parents were the American stereotype—husband and wife, two kids, and a small store they ran with big dreams of success. Dad had a business degree and used to work at a bank until getting the loan approved for Underwood's Grocer, and Mom helped out until she had Porter and decided to be a stay-at-home mother.

On the inside was a different story than the one people seemed to envy.

I refused to think about the nights I spent huddled behind a row of clothes, using them to soak up the tears and whipped words while Mom and Dad argued about another pointless topic. Dad worked too much. Mom spent too much money. The house needed work. Porter ruined another pair of sneakers and needed new ones. It was always something.

"Why don't you go play?" Mom suggested, breaking me from the memory of falling asleep in my closet until a mixture of bright blue and red lights flickering underneath the door woke me up.

I thought of the one thing that always made me happy on Saturdays and wondered if it'd work on Mom too. "Want to watch cartoons with me and Porter?"

Her smile didn't take right away, and when her lips curled upward, it was slow and nothing like the warm one she used to flash me. "I've got adult things I need to handle right now, but maybe next time."

It wasn't until sometime later when Porter and I went to our rooms to play that I realized something wasn't right.

When I went to ask Mom about it, the landline was held up to her ear as she shook her head at whatever paperwork she was going through.

"I wish I'd never married Fred and had the kids sometimes," I heard her say into the phone receiver. I stared down at a picture of four badly drawn stick figures surrounding a house that looked like ours with a nipping feeling taking over the pit of my tummy.

When she looked over to the hallway and saw me standing there, her eyes widened before closing for a few seconds, blowing out a deep breath. "I've got to go, Janet." Hanging up, she rubbed her eyelids with her fingers and turned from the paper scattered table to me. "It's grown women talk, Ivy. That's all. I'm just—"

Stressed. She's stressed. Dad's stressed.

"Don't worry," she finished, patting my arm before gesturing toward my room. "Why don't you go make sure Porter is napping and then hang out in your room for a while?"

Her dismissal came naturally, a common occurrence etched into everyday routine.

As I turned back to my room, I noticed an empty space on the wall where our family portrait used to hang. Mom made sure we all dressed nicely and smiled for the cranky woman behind the camera. I wasn't sure why, but I glanced at the garbage can and saw the broken frame and shattered glass with the very picture still between the two destroyed pieces.

Mom didn't say anything about it.

~

I don't often let myself linger in memories, pretending instead everything that led to my poor decision was simply a nightmare. The long sleeves I wear hide the reminder well enough where it's out of sight, out of mind, but the thick pink scars are there to taunt me when I need reminding of the reality I gave myself.

Seeing *him* again doesn't help. Aiden was the one good thing in my life before it turned to shit. His neighboring house was my happy place when mine was a war zone. His tiny bedroom closet was my escape when mine couldn't filter the noise—the screaming, the crying, and the blue and red lights.

Maybe I don't mind the noise my housemates create because there's a bite of familiarity in the loudness they produce. Even after packing a single bag and sneaking out of my childhood home in the middle of the night, I still think about that house and everything that went on inside, wondering what would have happened if I stayed.

To this day, I don't understand why my parents never got divorced. The one time I asked my mother about it, she'd looked at me and said, "Where would we go?"

Maybe my obscured notion of love is why I never felt the need to fall into it. Not if it meant being trapped without anywhere to go like my mother seemed to believe she was. She had no degree, no job experience, and no money of her own.

My ventures after leaving home are worse. Instead of proving I could handle it, I had to sleep on men's couches and floors and let them between my legs for a roof and food. After a while, I didn't mind it. They were a pastime. A means to an end. But I'd be lying if I said I didn't keep my anxiety under lock and key every time I got close to a guy. Intimacy has always been less about feeling good and more about survival. And if I keep that acknowledgment buried deep, deep inside the back of my mind, then it doesn't bother me as much as it should.

I'm not sure how long I've been stuck in the past when I hear the basement door open. I sit up quickly, realizing I must have forgotten to lock it when I got in.

"Occupied," I call out. I learned the hard way that if I don't close off my space, horny partygoers will try hooking up down here. After depositing my first paycheck from Bea's, I went to Anders Hardware—the local hardware store owned by Caleb's dad—and bought a dead bolt, installing it as soon as I got home.

The footsteps keep coming in heavy thuds on the creaky wood. I slide out of bed quickly, grabbing my phone and slipping my feet into the closest pair of shoes. I've invited my fair share of guys down here by my own free will. I know what people on campus say about me because of the hookups I've kicked out after the deed is done, but what those people probably don't know is that I'm empowered by telling the men who I let inside my body to leave because it's *my space* and *my right* to do so.

I don't find out who's lurking before I climb onto the broken washing machine stuffed in the corner and shimmy out the narrow window leading to the front yard, brushing off the dust, dirt, and wet grass when I stand up. I hear drunken murmuring coming from the basement and quickly round the front of the house to see what I'm working with. The party is in full swing still, and I don't feel like going back inside.

Maybe I should feel bad about not trying harder with my housemates, but they don't put any effort in with me either, besides Raine. As far as the others are concerned, I'm the person who gives them the last of the rent they need to keep the house and occasionally cooks them dinners when I get bored and feel like utilizing their otherwise neglected kitchen.

Sighing, I hug my arms to my chest and start walking down the driveway. The night breeze is chilly against my bare arms, and I regret changing out of my work clothes in favor of a pair of worn leggings and form-fitting T-shirt. Normally, I don't step outside my room unless I'm dolled up—face full of makeup, colored hair styled, and clothes painted on. I like clothes that hug my hips and cling to my narrow hourglass curves and makeup that fills my lips, extends my lashes, and adds a little color to my otherwise porcelain skin.

I struggle enough liking who I am knowing the things I've done, so I refuse to let anyone else make me feel less than the voice in my head already does by judging me for it.

With the sound of the party fading behind me, I glance down at my phone and frown when I realize it's going to die soon.

"Great," I murmur to myself. It wasn't a hard day at work, but it still dragged enough to make me grouchy at the smallest things. Elena must have caught on to my foul mood because not even she pushed my buttons when she came in after school. When Bea caught sight of my baggy eyes, she almost sent me home, but I refused. It isn't like getting sleep midday is any easier than at night. The girls like to talk, gossip, and do God knows what else at the loudest volume possible.

I'm a block away when the wind picks up, and goose bumps pebble my skin. I curse and teeter on my feet, covered in only flip-flops, and almost trip when I try avoiding a tree limb that flies at me from the sudden strong gust.

A pair of headlights blinds me as a large truck passes. I don't think much of it until I hear the tires brake suddenly. My muscles lock when I look over my shoulder and see the reverse lights flick on. It isn't the first time some guy has tried picking me up on the side of the road. And once, when I was really desperate, I even got in. But I learned my lesson then and don't plan on making the same decision now.

I have something to lose.

When the newer-style truck stops beside me and the passenger window rolls down, my lips part.

"What the hell are you doing outside like that in forty-five-degree weather?" Aiden barks at me.

Crossing my arms over my chest, more for warmth than anything else, I sneer. "Taking a walk. What does it look like?"

He cusses and throws the truck into park before climbing out. I back up when he rounds the front and comes toward me. "Get in." Aiden throws open the passenger door and stares at me with hard, expectant eyes.

"No."

"Ivy. Get. In."

My jaw ticks. "I'm not getting in the truck with you, Aiden. I said I'm fine."

I get a few feet away before an arm hooks around my waist and yanks me into a hard body, just like he used to do when we were younger. He'd never let me storm off angry before stopping me to talk about it. It pissed me off just as much then too, but I'd be lying if I didn't feel the tiniest tinge of comfort in his warmth. Not that I'm planning on admitting that.

I try not to focus too much on the obvious muscles he has now compared to the past. I'm by no means a small woman. I've packed some meat on my bones over the years, and I wholeheartedly enjoy the pastries at Bea's any chance I can. Employee discounts are good for the wallet but bad for the body—evident in the way my thighs fill out my tight pants and love handles like to peek out the top of the squeezing waistband.

"Put me *down*!" I demand, thrashing in his hold as he hauls me into the cab of his truck like I weigh nothing. I smack his arm away uselessly, since he's already withdrawing it to reach for the door. "What the hell, jackass!"

He has the nerve to roll his eyes as he makes sure my feet are out of the way before slamming the door shut and jogging around to the driver's side. Before I can even think about jumping out, he's already inside and putting the vehicle into drive.

"Do you manhandle everybody?"

"Yeah," he deadpans, fingers wrapping tightly around the wheel. I can't see well because of the dark, but I'm sure they're white from the grip. "My teammates especially love it." He catches the glare I cast him but only scoffs at it. "Christ, Ivy. No, I don't manhandle anyone. Because *they're* smart enough not to be in goddamn summer clothes in upstate New York in fucking October."

I am not playing this game. I pop the lock and open the passenger door. He slams on the brakes in the middle of the road, not even looking to see if anyone is behind him. I've got one foot out the door before he's yanking me backward onto the seat.

By the time I right myself again, he's suddenly in front of me with a deathly look on his face, and I have no idea how the hell he got out of the truck so quickly. "What the fuck are you doing?" he growls, blocking my way out.

Isn't it obvious? "Getting out."

"I was driving. Are you nuts?"

My teeth grind. I hate that word and all its variations. Nuts. Crazy. Insane. Psycho. Maybe they're all true, but nobody but me gets to decide that. "I told you I didn't want to get into your truck. You forced me in. We're not kids anymore, Aiden. I don't answer to you."

"I was just trying to—"

"What?" I challenge. "Was helping me? I don't need, nor do I want, your damn help. Thanks anyway."

I go to climb out again, but he won't let me. His arms keep me caged in. "I don't care if you hate me. I'm not letting you walk in the fucking dark when it's below fifty in that outfit. You're wearing sandals."

Ignoring his "hate" comment, because it's the last thing I feel toward him despite how much easier it'd be if I did, I wiggle my toes, which are half-numb from the cold. "Gee, am I?"

His jaw ticks. "Let me drive you home, smart-ass."

Before I can stop myself, I blurt, "No." When his dark eyebrows raise a fraction, I stifle a sigh and try appearing calm. "I don't want to go home. That's why I was taking a walk."

This time, he says nothing. I can see the contemplation in his eyes though. He's wearing a long-sleeve black Henley that fits his body a little too well. He was never the type to show off when we were younger, so I doubt it's on purpose that the material clings to his huge biceps, but he also didn't look like this back then. Gone is the lanky boy and in his place is a man who grew into his body. I don't know how to feel about either of those things, because watching him stand before me means everything is different now.

He's still the same driven boy I remember, but it seems

22

dangerous now. Because he's capable of making moves he couldn't when we were younger.

He's capable of stopping me.

"Please?" I'm ashamed of the soft-spoken word that escapes my lips, but it sends him into action. He gives me one subtle nod, gently repositions my legs back into his truck, and closes the door again.

This time when he gets behind the steering wheel, neither of us says a word. Biting down on my thumbnail until it snaps, I watch the scenery pass and listen to the low hum of the country station playing on the radio. He still listens to the same stuff, quietly humming along to the lyrics. I even recognize one of the early 2000s songs that we used to sing along to together when I spent time at his house. He has a nice voice but never used to let anyone besides me hear it. Has that changed?

We're heading toward the busier side of town where a lot of the local businesses and bars are located when he asks, "Why?"

I cautiously shift in my seat, daring a peek at him through the shield of fallen hair. "Why what?"

His lips flatten. "You were never stupid, Chaos. Don't act like it now."

"Don't call me that." Memories flood back, and I squash them out of habit. Being this close to him makes something stir in me that I don't like.

Now *he* plays dumb. "What? Chaos? You never minded when we were younger. Remember all those times you said you wanted to be a superhero?"

"Chaos was never meant to be a superhero." Chaos wasn't a self-appointed nickname or some antihero to cheer on. It's what I became—what my mother called me until I started believing it was what I was too. Unlike him, who was always obsessed with comic books and superheroes, I had no interest when I always felt like the villain in my household. Like the person to blame for the tension when all I wanted was to make it better. I used to tease Aiden about him being my own personal savior, which he'd blush over and deny every time. It was true though, no matter what he thought. I was Chaos and he was the person who mellowed me.

My gut tells me that's still true.

I know his love for superheroes is still strong because one of his arms is covered in a tattoo sleeve, including one of Captain America's shield. I'd seen it when he came into the bakery when it was warmer, showcased in a T-shirt that highlighted the masterful ink on his skin and the bulging muscles beneath it. He must have gotten over his fear of needles, because I remember his mother sharing the time he blacked out after seeing a nurse pull one out for the blood donation he agreed to.

Aiden snorts as he stops at a red light and watches a group of students, all better dressed than I am for the weather, walk in front of us to get to one of the popular bars. "I would hardly call you the villain."

I look out the window again. "Well, you can't really say that now considering we haven't seen each other in years."

The wait in the cab of his truck is tense as we sit at the light. He mumbles something when it turns green, turning off the main drag. "Are you going to hold that over me?"

Wanting nothing more than to tell him *yes*, I force myself to shake my head. What good does holding on to past grudges do? He hurt me by not coming with me, but he was young. We both were. There was a lot we couldn't control, and I couldn't hold his choice against him. If I were him, I wouldn't want to go either. "No."

"Then what's your deal?"

The laugh that escapes me is cold. "My deal," I repeat dryly, more to myself than not. Where do I even begin? "I have a lot of *deals*, but none of them that I expect you to understand. Like I said, I'm not holding anything against you for staying behind. It was smarter that you did." Sighing, I turn to him, noting his tight one-hand grip on the steering wheel twist while the other hand rests in a fist on his thick thigh covered in dark denim. "I'm a bitch. That's really the only thing you need to know about the new me if you haven't figured it out already. I do what I need to do in order to survive and get what I want."

His jaw ticks like that somehow irritates him, but the truth isn't meant to be pretty. "And what is it that you want?"

What everybody does. "To succeed."

The noise rising from his throat makes me narrow my eyes at him, but I remain silent. If he wants to doubt me, then so be it. Like I already surmised, he knows nothing about who I am now. The little girl who'd sneak in his window and cower in his closet doesn't exist anymore.

Eventually, I ask, "Where are we going?"

Wherever our destination is, it's outside town. There isn't much out there besides some spaced-out residences, cow pastures, and a few farms that produce the crops for the Saturday farmers market Main Street has every week as long as the weather is decent.

"My place."

My muscles lock. "Wait—"

"Relax, Chaos," he grumbles, and I do little to stop the scowl over the name from forming on my face. "I don't live there on my own, so you won't be stuck with just me. And unlike where you live, we're not usually huge on parties or bad shit goes down. We have to keep it low-key and stay out of trouble to stay focused on the field."

He doesn't see the way my uneasiness only intensifies from his attempt at reassurance. I do my best to look impassive about it, forcing my knee from bouncing. "And who is 'we'?"

Aiden glances at me with the kind of dumbfounded expression on his face that makes me want to grind my teeth. "Me and some guys from the team. We house together. It's easier."

It's a confirmation to what I already know, and my nerves are still through the roof as he slows down in front of a large white house that's in far better condition than the one I live in. There's even a huge wraparound porch with seating that looks brand new. "You live here?" I murmur as he parks his truck in the driveway.

There are a couple of guys on the front porch chatting and smoking, and when they see us in the driveway, one of them lifts a hand in greeting.

There are a few cars lined up already, and almost every light in the home seems to be on. But there's no music or mass of people like I'm accustomed to. *Wait.*

"How do you know about where I live?" I question suspiciously, recalling the remark he made.

He turns the keys and pulls them out of the ignition, leaning back in his front seat. "I know people who know people. All I had to do was ask."

My stomach does something it hasn't done in a long time. It *flutters*. And I don't like it. "I don't think I appreciate that," I inform him uncomfortably. It's more than likely that Caleb is his source of information. When I found out they weren't just teammates but friends, I felt a sense of betrayal— from Caleb for probably reporting back to him and from Aiden for replacing my place at his side.

You left first, the taunting voice of reason reminds me.

One of Aiden's shoulders lifts. "It's a good thing I didn't ask if you'd care." I shoot him a glare, and again, he brushes it off. "Let's go. You can get out. The child locks should be off now."

I gape. "You put the child locks on?"

I'm really starting to dislike his *you're kidding me* look. His brows pinch and his lips flatten, and those stupid blue eyes narrow at me as if to call me an idiot without verbalizing the insult. "You tried getting out of a moving vehicle. It seemed appropriate."

"I'm not a child!"

He blinks.

My nostrils flare.

He opens his door, looking over his shoulder at me. "You're not a bitch either. Come on. I haven't eaten yet."

"It's almost eleven." I pause. "Where even were you? Aren't football players on curfew so they don't royally screw up on the field?"

His responding snort is all I get as he climbs out of the truck. I freeze when he says the words I haven't heard in a long time. "Out of your head, Underwood."

Unlike the past, he doesn't wait until I give him the typical response of "head in the game"; he just closes his door until I have no other option but to follow when I see him walking around the side of the house. He throws a wave to the guys who call out his name, and I can feel their curious eyes move to me. I ignore their stares and the way my nervous heart thumps in my chest over the unknown that I'm walking into and quicken my steps to match his fast strides until we stop at a side door.

I've never been scared when I'm with Aiden, and not

even time has seemed to change that. Does that mean I appreciate him dragging me into truck? No. In the back of my mind, I'm fantasying myself smacking him upside the head for thinking he has the right to. I'd have to appreciate the little things though, like him not taking me home when I didn't want to go.

It's the only reason I shake off the nerves as I follow behind him.

"My room is in the basement. It was fully renovated after we moved in since so many people live here," he explains, unlocking the door and holding it open for me.

Hesitantly, I walk inside.

"It's only me down here right now. The guys mentioned moving someone else in. Newbie on the team who's known to party. Better to keep an eye on him so he doesn't mess up his chances." His voice echoes slightly behind me as I descend the brightly lit staircase, and I can't help but hear the roughness in his tone. As I reach the bottom, cinnamon and pine needles fill my senses and goose bumps pimple my arms. It's the same scent that always surrounded his house growing up.

If he knows what I'm thinking, he doesn't say anything. He passes my still body and waves me forward with his hand, hooking into a large room with a couch, a few chairs, a huge flat-screen TV, and doors on the back wall.

Trying to keep my face neutral even though I'm both impressed and jealous that this is where he lives, I examine the rest of the room. The wood paneling reminds me of the design in my old childhood home—the bottom halves of our living room walls were paneled the same way, and the top halves were a pale yellow that my mother always asked my dad to help her repaint. To my knowledge, it never happened. Trailing my fingers along the wood crevices, I shake myself from the thought.

When I glance down at the beige carpet, I notice mud stains from my sandals and cringe. Sliding them off my feet, I pick up my dirty shoes and let them dangle from my fingers. "Sorry. If you let it dry, vacuuming it should take out most of the mud, and then mix dish detergent and warm water to help get out any stain left."

It isn't until I look up that I notice him staring at me.

I move my weight from one foot to the other. "Quit it." He doesn't. "Stop looking at me. I mean it." I walk around the communal space, running my fingers along everything. "How long have you lived here?"

At first, he doesn't answer. I can feel his eyes on me as I slide my fingertips along the walls. Eventually, he answers, "A couple years. Transferred here after freshman year, moved in my second semester of sophomore once I got to know the guys better."

He's a year older than me, yet here I am a twenty-year-old freshman. "Fresh meat" as a group of guys yelled after my orientation group during a campus tour. A few of the boys in my group rolled their eyes; others grumbled. All the girls blushed and avoided their gazes. But not me. I kept my head held high and cast them the nastiest glare I could conjure, then flipped them off with a little extra swivel in my step, knowing their gazes wouldn't last long on my finger as soon as we passed.

I've come too far, been through too much, to feel lesser because of other people. Screw them and their ridiculous words. I shouldn't have made it this far after what I'd done, yet here I am. Nobody is taking away my chance to prove I can become something.

"Why did you bring me here?" Turning around, I finally meet his distant eyes. "You could have brought me anywhere or ignored me and took me home since your spies told you where that was."

He evades my eyes for a moment before sighing and walking over to the couch, dropping onto the farthest cushion, and draping a long arm over the back. "That isn't what you wanted."

"I didn't want to get into your stupid truck either, but look at where that got us. So who cares what I want? You clearly don't."

Aiden stays silent, but his gaze pierces mine like he's trying to figure me out. I always hated how blue those orbs are—how they captured everybody's interest in school, especially the girls. Growing up, I'd always get approached by them because they thought I was their in with Aiden. Be nice to me, get information about the boy they wanted, and make their move.

I walk over to the couch, studying the many open spaces. Instead of sitting on one of them, I stop in front of Aiden's slightly parted legs. "Why did you bring me here?" I repeat.

"I already told you." His eyes pin me to my spot before they leisurely slide down the length of me. I've changed since the last time he saw me, that's for sure. Gone is my too-lean sixteen-year-old body, gangly limbs, and blemished face. Now I have curves in *mostly* all the right places, legs that fill out my clothes nicely, and when I'm not too stressed, clear skin.

There's a lot of uncertainties in life that I tend to question. What I do know is that Aiden Griffith is looking at me with *that look*. Hunger. It's far from the friendly way he'd watch me with his huge smile and dorky laugh.

Without thinking, I drop my dirty shoes onto the floor

and move to straddle his lap. His body tenses under me as I rest my hands on either side of his head, gripping the top of the couch cushions behind him. Despite his tense frame and eyes widened with surprise, I can feel him harden under me when I purr, "Is this why you brought me here? Two old friends reuniting after so long."

He bites back a groan when I settle deeper onto his lap, his obvious erection pressing against the center of me. Still, he says nothing. Has he ever thought of this? Ever wanted to be more than just friends? The old me never would have dared cross that line, not if it meant losing the one stable person in my life. It didn't matter though.

I lost him anyway.

"Most guys," I press, "would give me a sign. It's usually the way they look at me. I stayed with a guy once whose eyes were plastered to my ass more than my face. But it was somewhere to sleep."

His hands fall to my hips, whether consciously or subconsciously. I feel his fingertips dig into the fleshy part of my legs, but I don't make a move to get off him, and he doesn't say a word. Is he afraid to?

I shift again, rubbing our bottom halves together until his lips press together in a firm line, while mine curl upward. "Not going to say anything? How very unlike you."

Something in his eyes sparks. Lust. I study one blue orb, then the other, while he watches me silently. If I hadn't already heard him speak, maybe I'd be worried he's gone mute over the years.

I lean forward, teasing his jaw with my lips. They graze his smooth skin lightly, and I feel him let out a harsh breath. Pulling back, I whisper, "Is this what you wanted when you brought me here? It's okay if it is."

His nostrils flare at my challenge, and it makes me smirk. The version of me he used to know would have died of embarrassment for even thinking of making this move. Does he like this version of me better? The bolder one? The girl who isn't afraid to cross lines or risk ruining anything?

After all, what's there to ruin?

He murmurs a defeated, "Christ," under his breath, his hands gripping my hips harder and rolling his pelvis into me.

One of my hands cups his jaw, my thumb stroking dangerously close to his bottom lip. Instead of making that move, I move my palm down the column of his throat until it's wrapped around the front of his neck. As soon as I squeeze, I feel his cock turn to steel against me.

Pressing my pelvis down, I lean forward again until my lips hover over his. "Is this why you brought me down here and away from your friends? Didn't want to share Chaos with your little football buddies?"

He exhales through his nose, not bothering to confirm how much he hates sharing. He was only ever good at it when he had to be. "I thought you said you didn't want to be called that."

I shrug, acting like I don't care. Even if Chaos is what I became in the long run, I still don't like being called that. Not by him. Not by anyone. "I'm just giving you what you want," I taunt him, squeezing his throat a little more.

He tips his head back, giving me more access. He doesn't tell me to stop; his hands barely even move on my hips. He only stares at me through his lashes like he's trying to figure me out.

Good luck.

"Who said I want this?" he asks, his throat vibrating against my palm with each word.

I crack a grin, wiggling in his lap to emphasize the size of the erection demanding to be let out. "Your cock does, seeing as it's rock-hard right now."

He arches upward, not showing an ounce of shame at his body's reaction. "You climbed onto my lap and started grinding on me. What the fuck did you think would happen?"

My grin widens as I lean forward, my lips dangerously close to his. One movement, a single jolt forward, and they'd be touching. I can feel the way his breath caresses my parted mouth, and I try not to let it get to me, but it does.

Once upon a time, I pictured this moment.

Kissing Aiden Griffith.

But I'd long since given up that little fairy tale when I realized Cinderella wouldn't have gotten Prince Charming without her fairy godmother, and fairy godmothers don't exist. As far as I'm concerned, neither do the Prince Charmings of the world. The books my mother read me were all made-up bullshit to give children false hope that finding love and happiness would be easy.

There are footsteps coming fast down the stairs before a deep voice says, "Hey, Griff, the guys are ordering—Oh, shit."

"We're a little busy," I tell the new guy in the room, looking over my shoulder and silently groaning when I recognize DJ from class.

"I can see that." His gaze moves from me to his unmoving teammate still pinned by the throat. With a small, amused grin, he holds up his hands and starts backing toward the stairs. "It's about time, Griff. That's all I'm saying."

With that, our mutual acquaintance disappears.

Chapter Three

IVY

WHEN IT'S JUST US, I return my focus to the boy I used to make faces at for picking his nose and scratching himself in public. He never seemed to care what people thought, and it doesn't seem like that's changed any now.

"Was that necessary?" he asks in a low tone that lacks offense.

Biting down on my bottom lip to fight a smile, I raise my eyebrows. "Would you prefer he stayed and watched?"

I can feel him swallow, his Adam's apple bobbing beneath my touch. "What would he be watching exactly?"

Reaching between us, I use one of my hands to palm between his legs. He groans when I rub his hard length, stroking it up and down over his jeans. "It seems DJ thinks it's been a while for you. Maybe you were trying to kill two birds with one stone tonight by bringing me here. You know what the storybooks leave out when the knight saves the damsel?" My lips curve wickedly. "They get their dick sucked in the end as a way to say thank you."

His eyelids flutter as he arches his hips into my hand. "Why do you think I have an ulterior motive?"

"Because everybody does," I state matter-of-factly.

"Fuck," he breathes. He closes his eyes when I squeeze his cock gently, the denim rough against my skin, then opens them again to meet my gaze with midnight-blue hues. "What's *your* motive then?"

"To prove a point," I whisper, closing the distance between us and brushing my lips against his in a ghostly caress. I don't want him questioning my point because I don't even know what it is. To show I can have him? To show that I *want* him?

He eagerly meets my lips like he's been waiting for years for the opportunity, parting them with his and instantly teasing my tongue. I'm not sure how I feel about that. Normally, I like when men react this way to me. I can use my body to get what I want, but I don't need to now. Yet it's not something I can turn off. With Aiden, I don't need to do this to survive.

But I *want* to.

And isn't wanting something more than needing it the kind of threat to my self-control that I promised I'd never risk giving up?

We fight for who controls the kiss, battling until he bites down on my bottom lip and sucks it into his mouth before letting it pop free. The sensation makes every concern leak from my brain until all I can think about is him. Aiden doesn't feel like any of the others. He's safe.

The hand teasing his cock moves upward until my fingers find the button to undo it, then the zipper to pull it down. His sharp breath paired with the metallic teeth of his fly gliding down is a melody to my ears. When I reach in and touch the hardened shaft in his pants, the warmth between my legs intensifies. He drops his head backward and groans the second I wrap my fingers around his thick, hot length to pull him out.

"You're going commando," I remark, smirking wider as I guide him free of the denim. I stroke upward to his tip, then back down to the base of him until he's bucking against me. There has to be close to nine inches in my hand, and I try not to look impressed, but I probably fail. He's big. Bigger than most of the guys I've been with, which says a lot. "I never understood why men do that. Doesn't it hurt rubbing against your clothes?"

"Are you really asking me that while my dick is in your hand?"

I stop my languid strokes, making him groan again. It only empowers me. "I don't know. Would you rather we talk about something else?"

Waiting for his reply, I already know I'm not getting one. Slowly, he rolls his head back and forth, still resting on the top of the couch cushions behind him. I squeeze his throat and cock at the same time, getting a choked noise in return as he grows in my fingers.

Without another word, I begin working him with my hand, feeling his smooth, hard skin twitch under my grip with every pump. My thumb grazes the underside of his tip, teasing the sensitive nerve endings there, before tracing the thick vein downward and listening to his hiss of breath. I relish in the noises he makes, the way he lets me do whatever I want to him. In a way, it's like we're younger again and he'd follow my lead because he never wanted to push. Except then, I never anticipated seeing what Penelope Case claimed she did behind the bleachers at Haven Falls High School.

This version of Aiden isn't anything even my sexiest fantasies could have conjured in my weakest moments when I wish my life were different—when I wish I'd stayed instead of running. Maybe then this could have happened sooner. Everything would be different. I definitely would have been.

After all, there's nothing hotter than watching the man under me come undone by my touch.

He curses under his breath, his eyes trained on the ceiling as he thrusts into my palm the faster I jerk him. The bead of precum that leaks from his tip dribbles down the side, and I use it as lubricant as I twist my palm under the tip of his shaft and build him closer to the brink.

"Condom," he rasps, hips meeting my hand to get more friction.

Something in my stomach tightens over him wanting to go further. Isn't that what I want?

"No," I find myself saying. I'm not sure to who—him or me.

His head snaps forward but his neck is still restrained by my hand. Hair falls into his eyes as he narrows them at me. "What do you mean *no*?"

I meet his challenging stare, my hand movements never faltering as I bring him closer and closer to climax. He's steel under me and only getting harder with every tug. I want to watch him come and know it's because of me. No more. No less. "You know damn well what no means, Aiden."

He moves his hand to my wrist, wrapping those long fingers around me and halting me from getting him off. It takes me by surprise. Doesn't he want this too? "What game are you playing?"

"The game of life." I go to kiss him, to shut him up, but

he turns his head to the side in rejection. "Why don't you want this? You're almost there. I know you are."

He gently peels my hand away from his cock, then does the same to the palm that clenches his throat. "Because you don't want it."

I snort, eyeing him in disbelief. "I'm the one in control here. I'm making the move. I'd say I want it enough."

He reaches between us and tucks himself back in his jeans. I notice the slight wince when he zips up his fly, leaving the button undone to give himself some room since he's tenting his pants. "If you really wanted this, you wouldn't have told me no. What the hell are you doing, Ivy?"

I try sliding off him, but his hands catch my hips. His fingertips dig into my flesh again, making me stay straddling him. "Jesus, Aiden. What are *you* doing?"

The look he plasters me with is one of fury and disbelief and something else. Longing? He leans forward to get in my face. "You want to know the reason I brought you here? It's because you said you didn't want to go home."

I'm about to retort with something snarky when he pins me with a look that basically says *shut the fuck up*.

My hips sting with his demanding grip, but I don't dare move when he asks, "How many fucking times did you tell me that when we were younger, huh? That you didn't want to go home. I always found us something to do, a reason to stay at my place longer, because you didn't want to face your parents. I would have done anything for you, Chaos. That hasn't changed."

I bite the inside of my cheek so hard over his question that I taste blood.

"I brought you here because I may not have a goddamn closet big enough anymore—" Once again, his eyes pierce mine until there's a hole in my chest that I thought I'd patched up a long time ago. "—but I have a couch and bed you could sleep on if you ever needed it."

Before I can stop it, a tiny breath escapes my lips at his heavy yet heartfelt admission. The delivery of each word stabs me with a brutal truth until my heart threatens to bleed out. I'd thought about this moment in the past—wondered what it would be like if Aiden had tried to keep me around or begged me to stay. But this...this isn't what I expected. Not this feeling.

It's hard to swallow.

To breathe.

To look at him.

Why is it so much harder now?

Because he doesn't know what you did to survive, that annoying voice in my head answers for me.

His nostrils flare as he studies my face, except this time, in disgust. When his hand wraps around my wrist again, his thumb traces upward over the scar without even looking at it.

He must have seen it before, but the question that escapes him in a rough tone takes me by surprise. "Who the hell are you anymore?"

He finally lets me slide off him, and I find my footing and hold my head up high despite how badly I'm shaking internally. "I don't know," I tell him with as much honesty as I can summon in the moment. I slide my sandals back on, not meeting his hard gaze that burns me. "But I'm working on figuring it out."

I walk toward the stairwell that leads to the door we entered when he calls out, "Where are you going?"

"Don't worry about it," I say, fighting back a sudden

onslaught of tears as I ascend a few steps. I take a deep breath, grind my teeth, and add, "Enjoy your blue balls."

When I'm outside, my arms go back around my torso as a tear escapes. To the wind, I whisper, "Out of your head, Underwood."

And the wind whispers back, *Head in the game.*

Chapter Four

IVY

THERE'S NOT ENOUGH CAFFEINE in the world to prepare me for classes on Monday. I'm barely able to stay awake during English composition and have no recollection of dragging myself across campus to get to biological anthropology. The room is abuzz when I settle into my normal seat in the back of the lecture hall, closest to the doors for a quick escape once the fifty-minute class ends.

I'm getting out my worn black notebook and pen when a body drops into the seat beside mine—something that hasn't happened in the two months since class started. When I glance up from my messy scrawl on the notebook paper in front of me, I gape at the boyish smirk that's staring back, belonging to someone who usually sits across the room.

"That's not your seat," I point out, as if DJ doesn't already know. We've had class three days a week for eight weeks.

He settles in despite my obvious statement, dropping his backpack onto the ground by his feet and spreading his long jean-clad legs out to get comfortable. I find myself scowling over how much space he's using until he chuckles over my reaction. "You're not very friendly, are you?"

I scribble the date in the corner of the page and reply, "That's not very nice to say."

He lifts a broad shoulder, one that I've heard can do some damage to players during games, looking unapologetic in his true assessment. "I'm DJ, by the way."

My eyes turn from DJ—who has a slight Boston accent—to the front of the room, where the elderly professor lays out his materials on the front table and logs into the computer. Professor Relethford makes class interesting. When my adviser suggested the elective, I wasn't sure I'd like it. Learning about people who died a long time ago seemed boring, but I quickly learned that they have even better stories than we do. It makes me wonder what they'll say about me when I'm gone, and the thought takes me back to a dark place. That could have easily become a reality nobody would have expected.

What would my parents have said if someone knocked on their door saying they'd found my body? I'd be known as the runaway, nothing else. Would Mom cry? Would Dad? I know they'd be sad because they're not bad people, just not great parents. Mom teared up when our cat Button had to be put down from all her strokes, so it wouldn't be far off to say she'd do the same for me.

DJ nudges my arm playfully like we're old buddies, pulling me away from the depressing thoughts swarming my mind. "What? Only willing to talk to our tight end?"

My cheeks heat before I can stop them. I'd hoped he wouldn't bring up walking in on Aiden and me the other day. DJ and I never had many interactions before now, but I know who he is. If Lena isn't yammering on about

Aiden, it's someone else on the football team—Caleb, DJ, or their quarterback and captain of the Lindon Dragons, Justin Brady. DJ gets more airtime dancing on the field after touchdowns than any other player gets for playtime. He can't stand still, always walking along the sidelines when he's not on the field, smacking his teammates, and messing with the fans. There are videos I've seen on the university's YouTube channel thanks to Elena shoving them in my face to watch in between customers.

The fidgety boy beside me snickers over my silence. "I'm just messing with you. Griff doesn't talk to many people, so you must not be a total nutcase if he's willing to have you around. And let's be real. Nobody wants a nutcase near their junk, so you can't be that lethal. Plus, you've seemed chill when I've seen you around."

He's seen me around? One of my brows raises when I look at him again. "Thanks, I think." His lips kick up higher at the corners at my dull reply. "Why are you sitting here?"

Propping a dirtied boot on the back of the chair in front of him earns him a scathing look from the dark-haired girl sitting in it. That is until she realizes who it is. Her eyes light up and a small, flirty smile stretches across her lips when she makes eyes at the school's wide receiver. Unlike mine, they aren't painted a bright color.

My makeup is my war paint.

The girl batting her lashes clearly doesn't notice me until I snort at her typical reaction to Lindon's athletes. She catches me rolling my eyes and her smile drops into a scowl. Whatever. I have to watch and listen to my housemates become fools whenever most athletes are involved, so it's nothing I haven't seen before. In hindsight, DJ *is* one of the more attractive players in a goofy boy-next-door sort of way. It's no surprise that he gets a lot of attention. I've heard through the grapevine, though, that his attention is locked on one specific girl with a reputation of her own around campus. Not that I believe everything I hear.

"See?" DJ says, tipping his chin at the girl, who wiggles her fingers at him before turning back around and whispering with her giggling friends. "That's what I'm used to. Same with Aiden. Except the attention pisses him off for some reason. Me and the guys don't get why. More chance of him getting lai—"

I shoot him a look, causing his cheeks to pinken slightly before he picks up his hands in surrender.

"Well, you get my point. I'm only stating facts. Women like football players. You know, jersey chasers."

Doesn't mean I want to hear about them, I grumble to myself.

Professor Relethford starts the lecture, skipping roll call as usual since there's over a hundred people crammed in the room. When I walked into the room on the first day, I nearly had a panic attack when I saw the massive number of people taking up the seats. But I quickly realized it was the exact class I needed to keep the attention away from myself. I blend in, drown in dutiful silence as I take notes. My other classes are much smaller, more intimate, which is no fun for somebody who hates attention.

When the professor announces our next exam is on Friday, it gets a collection of groans and mumblings in reply. He gives us a study guide that has every question word for word that will be on the test, so all we have to do is fill in the blanks and study the answers throughout the week. It's the only class I'm doing well enough in because he basically hands us the A.

"You know," DJ whispers ten minutes later despite

the cold shoulder I've given him to take notes, something he hasn't done once since class started. "We could study together at my place."

I blink, taken aback. Usually that offer isn't *actually* about studying. "Excuse me?"

He cocks his head, rolling his eyes in a playful manner. "You. Me. Studying. For the test we have. Naughty girl. Were you not listening to our professor at all? No funny business, promise."

Frowning, I gesture pointedly toward the notes, still not sure I believe his intentions are innocent. I've already got half a page of lecture notes written, proving I'm the one out of the two of us who's clearly been listening. "The only reason you want to study is because you're not even paying attention to what he's saying about Neanderthals."

He shakes his head instantly. "Nah, I happen to like you and your sass. Wouldn't mind seeing more of it. Though I wouldn't mind using your notes either. And before you get all girl power and all that, I'm not trying to use the lame studying excuse as a way to get into your pants. I'd just ask if you wanted to sleep with me if that's what I was after."

I blink. "And that works for you?" It shouldn't be surprising to me. I've been in situations where it took a lot less to get me to unbutton my pants.

He gives me a cocky smile. "Every time." A weird look crosses his face. "Well, usually. I'm working on it."

Which means he's working on *somebody*.

The professor clears his throat loudly in warning, his eyes cast in our direction. I sink into my seat and shield my face with my hand since my faded blue, nearly white, hair is pulled back in a messy braid today.

That doesn't stop DJ though. Only moments after

Relethford goes back to his lesson, he's back at it again. "Plus, I want to see how Aiden reacts."

I can't pretend that doesn't interest me. I have no idea what he thinks of me after storming out, and it irritates me that I care so much. I never wanted to complicate things with Aiden before because he was my safe space, but ever since I left the football house, I've been playing our little foreplay moment on repeat in my head.

He didn't sleep with me, and I'm not sure why I'm so confused over how to feel about it. "I don't see why that matters," I lie. Whether DJ believes me or not, I don't know. Maybe if he were Aiden, he'd know my tells.

DJ leans in. "He was pissed, you know. Would have thought finally getting some would calm him down. He's too tense all the time. I don't know what you did, but it only made him worse."

My lips snap together. There's not much I can say to that. Whatever happened between us is nobody else's business, and I walked away that night knowing it was better for both of us.

That's not true.

I walked away for *me* because running away is all I know how to do.

DJ bumps my knee with his. "What do you say? You know where we live. Come over. We can get this guide done and study for the test. Maybe order some food. I won't even try copping a feel, though I'm sure you'd like it."

I snort over his certainty, starting to shake my head over his offer when he does something I haven't seen since I was at least seven. He gives me the puppy-dog look.

And for some reason, it works for him.

"Give me an hour," he pleads, sticking his lip out and batting his lashes.

His theatrics make me sigh. "It'll take longer than that to get all the answers down, much less study them."

His eyes light up. "Is that a yes?"

I shrug. If I want to keep my grades up, I need a quieter place to study than my house. I usually hide out in the library on the third floor, but I've learned that's where a lot of people like to go to hook up, and the noises I've heard from the periodicals are almost traumatizing.

"Fine."

"I'll give you my number," he says, starting to take out his phone.

My nose scrunches before I can stop it, making him snicker. "No. I'll swing by tomorrow at five. We need to start ASAP if either of us stands a chance."

He sticks his hand out. "Deal."

I don't shake it and ignore him the rest of class.

~

Bea's is almost closing when I get called into the back by the namesake herself. Her white hair is chopped short into a pretty pixie cut that only someone with her lean facial structure can pull off. She's smiling like usual when I walk in, gesturing toward the counter with ingredients covering it.

"What's up, Bea?" When Elena tried calling her that, Bea lectured her on how she'd always be Grandma or Grandma Bea to her. Lena smacked me later when it was just the two of us again because I'd laughed, cementing her Ivyprofen nickname for me.

Bea picks up an apron and passes it to me. "I'm going to teach you how to make my famous pumpkin cheesecake bars like we discussed. Don't think I forgot about it."

My stomach growls over the sound of them, which she smiles at. I tie the apron around my waist and look at all the ingredients. "Are they new? I don't remember seeing them on any fall list from last year."

One of her wrinkly hands, aged and scarred from all her kitchen mishaps in the past, waves at me. "I always change up the fall menu. These kids always want pumpkin something or other this time of year. Might as well play around and profit from it. Before now, only my family has ever had these."

That makes me smile wider. "You could always cave and start offering pumpkin spice—"

"Don't you dare say it, missy." She eyes me in warning, making me bite down on my bottom lip to suppress the amused laugh that wants to come out. "I swear if you say it even once, it's like they show up in herds. That damn drink is like the Bloody Mary to mirrors."

In this moment, I remember why I'm always jealous over not being related to Bea. Elena doesn't appreciate her sassy-mouthed sixty-something-year-old grandmother. I'd met my grandmother Gertie a handful of times when I was younger. She's more subdued than Bea, their personalities polar opposites from one another. I have nothing against the woman personally, but if I got to choose, I'd prefer Bea taking the grandmotherly role because of everything she's done for me in the short time I've been in Lindon.

It's why I considered going to her place, somewhere I've only been once or twice since moving here, after storming out of Aiden's house. Instead, I sucked it up and walked home. I didn't want to be a bother to her, even if I knew she'd welcome me with wide arms. Thankfully, the party was quieter and whoever was in my room didn't trash it or take anything. Not that I have anything of value most people would want. To be safe, I changed the sheets, double-checked the door was locked, and fell asleep for a few measly hours.

I let Bea guide me through the recipe like she's done with her other favorite treats. It's not that complicated on paper, but I've always been more of a wing-it girl, which explains why most of my own attempts at baking usually fail. Only one time had I messed up so bad the smoke detectors at the house went off, and the girls who were home at the time freaked out and called the fire department before I could tell them it was just smoke from a new kind of cookie that I'll never try again.

I finish closing after a few batches of the bars are made, count the register, and double-check that the front door is locked with the CLOSED sign showing and then head into the back again. "Can I ask you something?"

Bea is drying the last piece of bakeware when she turns to me. "Anything."

"Why don't you teach Elena more? I think she wants to learn."

A small smile graces her lips, making the corners of her eyes crinkle more than they already do. "She's eager to learn because of you, dear. My little Lena looks up to you."

All I manage to do is gape at her.

She nods once. "I'd love for my granddaughter to be more invested in the bakery, but I know it's not her main interest. Not like yours. Your eyes light up every time I ask if you want to help, and I see the way you study things even when I'm not looking. You're like me. Happy creating in the kitchen, experimenting, being in control of things. Lena is young. Perhaps one day she'll decide she wants to learn, but right now, she only wants that because she's copying her idol."

"I'm the last person she should be idolizing," I admit sheepishly. There isn't anyone here who knows my past. My résumé didn't require it. I was honest about my experience in retail work—I worked at a few different seedy gas stations for a hot minute—but had to talk my way into convincing Bea that I had the type of smile that could make even a rattlesnake grin back.

Her hand reaches out and pats my forearm lightly. "I don't believe that for a second. Whatever makes you think so is all in your head."

My fingers go to the spot on my lower arm that's covered by a sleeve. I rub my scar, feeling it heavy under my touch. "I'm sure. Next you're going to tell me you hired me because of my charming wit and glowing personality."

Amusement flickers in her eyes. "Your wit and personality certainly make this place livelier, that's for sure."

I can't help but grin at her reply. "Is that why my paychecks are always more than they should be? You're paying me for the entertainment too?"

She doesn't acknowledge my comment, but I'm not surprised. Bea never admits to paying me over my hours. She tosses the wet towel into the little hamper in the corner that she takes home every night to clean. "Elena is awful at listening. Trying to get her to follow directions will kill me long before my age does, so I don't bother putting more effort in than I do. She nearly burned my bread the other day because she was on that dang phone of hers. Probably looking up that Face chat app or football website."

Her confusion over Snapchat and Facebook makes me smile, but that quickly fades when I realize she meant what she said. "You're being serious about Lena looking up to me, aren't you?"

She knows what I mean. "As a heart attack. You're far too talented and good-hearted to think so poorly of yourself, Ivy."

I snort. "Talented?"

"There you go again." Her hands go to her hips as she *tsks*. "I see the way you take on a project here. It's not just what you do in the kitchen, it's how you handle the business. You enjoy yourself. You're at peace. I hear more about a recipe you tried at home than how school's going or anything else in your life. That's quite telling."

I flush from the acknowledgment. "I've always enjoyed baking," I admit. My mother never had time to teach me, but Mrs. Griffith would give both Aiden and I lessons. Cookies, pies, and a few of her favorite Italian dishes to cook that weren't too complicated.

Plus, there's nothing to say about school. I get a mixture of Cs and Bs because I struggle with listening to lectures. My mind wanders if I'm not interested, and I find myself thinking about anything other than the material we'll be tested on.

Bea smiles and bats me away. "Maybe you should focus on culinary instead of taking all those silly classes the school requires you to. Now go home. It's past your shift. And you're sure you'll be okay closing again on Friday?"

For the game. I've told her at least twice already that I was more than capable of running the place on my own. It worked last time Lindon had a home game, and it'll work this week. "Yes. Most of the town will be at the game supporting the Dragons anyway, so it'll be easy to handle."

I can tell she wants to push the issue, but she's learned it's pointless with me. I could use the money, and so could she. Especially since she's saving for a new high-tech oven that'll offer more space for baking. "Fine, but one day you'll tell me who it is you're so adamantly trying to avoid by not attending. Don't think I haven't seen the way your eyes go to the TV when it's playing something on the team here. I'm old but I'm not stupid."

Halfway home after bidding her goodbye in the brisk breeze, my phone buzzes against my butt cheek, and I pull it out of my pocket to figure out who's bugging me so late when rarely anybody does these days.

Unknown: Hey

I falter on the sidewalk for a moment at the number. Another text comes through.

Unknown: It's me

"That's helpful," I mutter to myself, tempted to text the person back. But the few contacts I do have are the only ones I need, so I turn it on silent, deposit it back into my pocket, and go home to a surprisingly quiet house.

Knowing it won't last, I take a quick shower in the downstairs bathroom, change into my pajamas, and start my study guide. DJ's offer still comes as a surprise considering we've barely talked until today, and I have no intention of getting into drama if he thinks he can mess with Aiden by having me around. If I'm going to prove to anybody that I can make it through college, I need the grades to back me up. Drama is a distraction, yet I can't ignore the temptation to show back up at that house no matter what greets me.

There are some people I don't want to mess with for

a lot of reasons, and I already crossed that line with Aiden once. He doesn't need me crossing it again or else I won't be able to stop. There's a reason I didn't fight for him harder to come with me when I ran away. He was always better off without me in his life. I've proven that's true now more than ever, no matter what the stubborn tight end seems to think.

Chapter Five

AIDEN

I'm BEAT WHEN I walk in the front door, ready to raid whatever is in the fridge before going downstairs and hopping in the shower. I have homework piled up, two exams to study for, and a paper to finish writing for econ, but I have no intention of doing any of it until I get a stomach full of food and at least an hour nap.

I slap my best friend's hand as I pass by the couch. Caleb is a chill dude—quiet like me, more reserved than the others. He's not into going out every weekend like some of the other guys on the team, mostly because he's hung up on the girl he's been with for years and spends a lot of time at Anders Hardware, his father's hardware store in town. He's being groomed to take it over one day, so unlike my aspirations to train and utilize my football skills, he'll be graduating with a business degree and keeping the family business up and running.

"Another long day?" he asks, pausing the TV on the ESPN coverage they're playing. A guy I recognize from

Wilson Reed University is on the screen, his Raiders jersey on full display during their power play in last week's game against the Lions. I have to peel my eyes away before the glowering starts from remembering the bullshit I was put through there my freshman year.

Because you were reckless. Desperate.

I rub the back of my neck, not wanting to think about how I was willing to trust anyone if it meant having a friend again. Someone to rely on like I could Ivy. Except I trusted too easily and got fucked in the end twice over. I didn't have Ivy or Wilson Reed anymore. "Something like that. Barely passed one of my papers and the professor won't let me do extra credit to make up the grade."

"Mercer?" he guesses.

I frown. "Yeah."

He shakes his head. "Told you not to take her class. She was, like, burned by some big-time baller in the past. Hates everyone who plays the game now. And I know you, man. You won't report her for misconduct even if she deserves it for grading poorly."

"I—" My words are cut off by a loud, pitched laugh that I know all too well coming from the kitchen. "What the hell?"

Caleb opens his mouth, but before he can comment, I'm stalking to the kitchen with clenched fists. As soon as I walk in, I see two people sitting a little too closely at the table. The tiredness deep in my bones is long forgotten when those annoying honey fucking eyes glance up and meet mine.

It's the dipshit I live with who says, "Hey, dude. You remember Ivy, right?" The grin on DJ's face isn't that different from any other day, and it doesn't falter when I narrow my eyes at him.

Rubbing a closed fist over my sternum, I slowly focus

back on the girl who's purposefully staring at the notebook in front of her instead of me. "Yeah. I remember her." I have to bite my tongue from adding, *gave me the nastiest case of blue balls, so watch out.*

Just because she's a self-proclaimed bitch these days doesn't mean I need to stoop to her level. That's not who I am, and I know damn well it isn't who she is either. It's a mask she's wearing, and I have every intention of finding out why she feels the need to be here for DJ when she couldn't even text me back.

"Not going to say hi?" I prod her.

She finally looks up, makeup caked on her face even though she sure as hell doesn't need it, only to mutter, "Hi."

It's more than I thought I'd get, dry tone and all. "What are you two doing?" DJ is usually handsy with the women he brings by, but the small distance between them is safe enough for sanity. Since the girls he usually messes with are jersey chasers, they don't care who's around to witness it as long as they're getting attention from someone on the team. Ivy isn't like that. At least not from what I've heard.

It's obvious based on the scattered textbooks and notebook paper between them that they're doing something for school. A few of the guys share a class with her and make sure I know it every time they come home.

Ivy let Marks borrow a pen.

Ivy flipped off one of the Kappa-O's.

Ivy ignored DJ's advances.

Up until now, the last comment always made me feel relieved. DJ flashes chicks a smile and shoots them a wink and they practically throw their panties at him. I've heard plenty about Ivy since opening the can of worms, but nothing I could discern as truth or rumor.

I regret filling my schedule with core requirements for my business major instead of easy gen eds like the others tried convincing me of. It was Caleb who convinced me not to go into sports therapy like I planned, so I mirrored his courses until I realized I liked the idea of business management more than I would have training to be a physical therapist. I could still coach and train like I plan to and even make my own business out of it if for some reason playing doesn't work.

By the time I realized Ivy was in class with the guys after seeing her at the café, it was too late to add it. And the assholes make sure they mess with me every time I ask if anything happened, knowing it's her I'm really inquiring about.

And the other night...

Shit. The second I realized what Ivy was going to do, my brain shut off and my dick took control. My mother would have smacked me upside the head and told me not to think with that head, especially if she knew it was Ivy I'd fooled around with, but I did.

The problem is that I would have screwed her right there. I would have let her control every goddamn second of us fucking on the couch, when I've never let anyone have that same courtesy. I played her game until I realized it wasn't real and stopped anything from going further. My ego and dick are still bruised over it, because the truth is, I *wanted* it to be real. There's no bigger bitch slap to the face than having your teenage crush use you like you mean nothing and having to act like it doesn't bother you.

"Studying," Number 81 says casually as I walk farther into the room and start digging through the fridge for things to eat. "If I'm going to ace this thing, I need to use my secret weapon. Did you know Ivy is a closet nerd? She *enjoys* school. Takes notes every single class."

I turn on my heel, bread and deli meat in hand, and eye Ivy as if to say, *since when?* She never liked school. Every time we'd get into trouble, it was because she was cutting class and I was dumb enough to follow her.

I notice the slightest way she sinks into the wooden chair, as if she doesn't want the attention. Mine or anyone else's. Too bad. "I like the structure," she corrects him, picking up her pen and jotting something down on the stapled packet off to the side. "And are you even filling this thing out? That's the whole reason I'm here."

DJ's hand shoots to his chest, a palm flat over his heart. "And here I thought it was to see me."

I snort as soon as I see the way she stares at him—deadpan yet deadly. He's smart enough to back off, sighing, and reaches for his pen and much emptier paper.

"So," I press, laying everything I need for a sandwich out on the counter. "You still planning on skipping the game?"

Clearly, our wide receiver didn't know that, based on the way he dramatically drops his pen and gapes at his study partner. "What? Why wouldn't you come to the game?"

Ivy doesn't even bother glancing up at him. "Because I don't like football. Or any sports for that matter." There's a slight pause. "I'm partial to soccer, I guess. Plus, I like making money. Taking Friday night shifts means a bigger paycheck, not that I'd expect you to understand."

My lips curve up slightly as I open the mayo. She used to play soccer in middle school. Goalie. She got pulled in eighth grade during one of the last games because the ball broke her collarbone, and she never joined again. Her parents couldn't afford another hospital bill.

She's right to assume DJ comes from money too. His family has a big place in Boston, and he tends to wear nicer clothes, brands I've never heard of until hanging around him. My family is middle-class, but it never stopped us from settling for something from a Target clearance rack back home.

"Are you a heathen?" my roommate asks.

Ivy doesn't miss a beat. "Are you a hermaphrodite?"

I choke on my own saliva as I spread mayo on one of the slices of bread. When I look at DJ, he's sputtering out, "What the fuck? No. Why would you even ask that?"

Her shoulders lift. "I thought we were just throwing out random questions that make no sense. Unless there *is* some truth to it." This time, she looks behind her shoulder right at me. "You've seen him in the locker room. Is there?"

I snicker when I notice the way DJ's face turns red, all the way to his ears. "Unfortunately, I can confirm he's all male. I've seen him whip it out one too many times to be uncertain. Including that one time he got so drunk he flashed—"

"That was one time!" DJ instantly cuts me off, standing up and glaring at me.

My grin grows over his agitation. Sophomore year, he hit Captain Morgan a little too hard and ended up not only flashing a male cop but woke up spooning Number 14, who's since graduated, in the living room. They'd both been hammered and vowed not to speak of it to anyone. But there are pictures.

Taken by yours truly.

Ivy clears her throat. "As fun as this spat is to watch—"

Her tone says the exact opposite, which makes me shake my head in amusement as I go back to making dinner for myself.

"—I have places to go after we're done here, so can we please finish this?"

DJ drops back into his chair obediently. Can't say I'm too surprised. Ivy has that touch, that edge to her that people usually listen to when she means business.

"Hot date?" I press, stacking some of the roast beef onto the bread and slapping a few slices of cheese on next. "I'm sure the guys are lining up at your door to experience that shining personality of yours."

Through my lashes, I see her shoulders straighten. It's an asshole thing to be sarcastic about, but I am curious. The guys say nobody sits by her in class because she scares them off with her expression. DJ looks slightly curious too, which I'm not as enthused about.

Ivy ever so slowly turns around, resting an arm on the back of the chair. "Not that it's any of your business, but I do have a hot date. Tangled sheets and all."

My nostrils flare when we lock eyes, and she smiles innocently at me. "With whom?"

"None of your damn business," she snaps back quickly.

I stop what I'm doing and lean my palms on the edge of the counter to hold myself up. "I'd say it is considering you had my cock in your hand only days ago."

DJ quietly murmurs *oh shit* under his breath but otherwise stays silent as he looks over his notes.

"Well, tonight is somebody else's turn." Again, she shrugs, unabashed over the simple statement. Her eyes show no mercy, no shame, and I don't know what to think. Gone is the girl I used to know, and in her place is a total stranger with a fiery personality she could have only gotten from the shit she's experienced in the last few years. "Don't be greedy, hotshot."

A slow smirk stretches across my face, and I won't lie when I say the next words out of my mouth make me cringe. "Everybody gets a turn with you, huh?"

Even my teammate winces at that.

Ivy clicks her tongue and turns back around, closing her notebook, then the textbook in front of her. "I think it's time I left. Apparently, I have a busy night of fucking the entire campus, so I need to get an early start."

DJ tries stopping her. "Iv—"

"Bye," she says, cutting him off, collecting her things and walking out the door without a look in my direction. I hear Caleb tell her goodbye and get a muffled response in return.

I drop my head forward between my shoulders and heft out a sigh. "Don't," I warn the only other person in the room when the front door slams shut.

"Dude," he says anyway.

"She pissed me off."

"So you say *that*?"

"She was egging me on!"

"And she won," he points out matter-of-factly, eyebrows raised. "Damn, Griff. Never seen you like that with anyone before. That was…something else. Kinda hurt to watch."

I shake my head again and angrily finish making my sandwich, even if I'm not hungry anymore. "You don't know shit about her or me, 81. I suggest you stop butting into my business for once. I haven't been butting into yours lately, no matter how badly you need it."

He catches on quickly. "There's a 'her and me' suddenly? Didn't seem that way to me. It'd make sense why you've been in such a mood lately, I guess."

I cut him a look, causing him to raise his hands in surrender. He doesn't want to play this game.

"Fine," he says. "All I'm saying is that you owe her an apology. Might get you out of the doghouse if you ever want to act on that little proclamation."

Do I? I put all the ingredients back into the fridge and pick up my sandwich. "And you're an expert on pissing women off, I suppose."

He grins at me. "Voted most likely to get divorced by the time I'm twenty-five. My mom was so proud."

Sarcastic douche. "I'll be downstairs. Tell everyone not to bother me."

He chuckles as I start walking out of the room. "Going to jerk your frustrations out of you? Good luck with that!"

I flip him off and jog down the stairs.

He's right about one thing.

I need to apologize to Chaos.

~

Matt Clearwater and DJ horse around in the athletic adviser's office as she gathers paperwork for them. I smack them both upside the head as I pass by the chairs they occupy before dropping onto the small sofa off to the side. "Quit it. Rach doesn't need your bullshit today."

The woman in question is a twentysomething new addition to Lindon's athletic department. Coach Pearce told HR he didn't care who was hired as long as they got the job done. And if for no other reason, the guys show up when Rachel Holloway sets a meeting because she's petite, has big tits, and doesn't take any of their crap.

"Thanks, Aiden," she muses, passing the boys two separate pieces of paper. "But I'm used to it by now."

DJ looks around Matt at me. "Yeah, lighten up. Not even Brady is this uptight about having a little fun."

My lips flatten. "That's because Justin is more focused on

62

getting into med school than dealing with your dumb asses all the time."

Our adviser stifles a laugh. "Matthew, you're all set. Pick up that Spanish grade if you want to keep playing. Got it?"

"Yes, ma'am," he says with a wink, standing up and shoving DJ one last time. "And consider that one-on-one tutoring. I'd love all the help I can get."

I'm trying to hold back from rolling my eyes at his cheesy line when I notice Rachel's cheeks tinting red. She tries hiding it, but unlike the two idiots who high-five over the remark, I'm paying attention. Rachel moves a piece of hair behind her ear and looks at Matt through her lashes like she's considering it.

You've got to be kidding me.

Matt and DJ work well together on the field because they're basically the same person: dedicated wide receivers but easily distracted when it comes to women. And the last thing Matt needs is to get involved with the damn adviser because he's got loose lips about his conquests.

As if he knows what I'm thinking, he shoots me a devious grin that I return with a warning shake of my head. Because he and I don't get along as well as I do with the others, he looks back to Rachel and purrs, "I'll see you around, *Ms. Holloway.*"

He smacks a laughing DJ on the shoulder before leaving the room without a second look in my direction. I move over to the seat he took and bump fists with DJ, who turns to me and asks, "I haven't seen any bags of dog shit lit on fire on our front step, so should I assume you made up with Ivy?"

Rachel perks up. "Aiden, did you get a girlfriend?"

The asshole beside me howls. "That's classic, Rach.

63

This guy? He barely even lets the jersey chasers near him, even when they're throwing themselves his way. More for us though."

Our adviser shakes her head but can't help but smile. "Some people want more than that, Daniel."

DJ makes a face at her. "Aw, c'mon. You know I hate when you call me that."

She crosses her arms on the edge of the desk and gives *Daniel* an amused look. "That is your name, isn't it?"

DJ grumbles under his breath.

I snort and drape an ankle over my opposite knee and prop my arm up on the back of DJ's chair. "Could be worse, Danny Boy."

My friend huffs. "Don't start."

Grinning, I remember the first time I heard his mother call him that when she visited for our championship game last season. She yelled out his childhood nickname and made him groan while I laughed from the sidelines where I was grabbing water and a towel. "Can't help it. It's fitting somehow."

He glowers, and I grin.

Rachel shakes her head at us. "Well, I think it's nice if you found a girl who isn't going to throw herself at you."

That pulls DJ out of his stupor. "If anything, he'll wind up on a case of *Forensic Files* because of this chick. She's awesome but intense as hell."

I can't refute him there, but I don't offer any information on my old childhood friend like they're both expecting. "Coach said you wanted to see me," I redirect instead.

DJ rolls his eyes and looks to Rachel. "I can go now, right? Pass classes or else blah blah blah. I feel you. I'm hungry."

"When are you not?" I remark.

He shrugs. "I'm a growing boy, Griff. I need the proper

nutrients to dominate on the field." When his sly eyes focus on Rachel, I already know his next line is going to make me groan. "And off the field."

Unlike with Matt, Rachel offers a small, uninterested laugh at the flirt and gestures toward the door. "You're free to go. You know what we talked about."

One more fist bump later, it's just me and Rachel left in her office. I lean back in the chair, resting my elbows on the armrests. "Matt is persistent, you know. He doesn't give up easily when he puts his mind to it."

Her eyes go from the file in front of her to me, a flush back on her face. "I'm not sure I know what you mean, Aiden."

We both know she's full of shit, so I don't bother calling her out on it. "My grades have been good this semester, so I'm not sure why I'm here. Coach mentioned a check-in."

She seems appreciative of the subject change. "It's mandatory to meet up a few times a semester to make sure everything is okay. Bill asked me to talk to you about next year since you were invited to the combine." Her manicured fingers open the file folder and her eyes scan the page. "Your stats this year have been stellar, and your grades are perfect. You want to be drafted, right?"

When she meets my eyes, I offer a tip of my chin in confirmation. "Coach says the combine will open that door for me. He suggested ending after this semester."

"Is that what you want? You're on top of your courses and in the top three of your class. It'd be a shame to see you stop right before getting your degree."

"It's just a piece of paper" is my reply, even though I think of Mom's face when I say it. She wants me to earn it because she knows I enjoy school. And with one semester left after this one, it seems stupid to drop out now. But

Coach Pearce wants me to train hard to be on my A game for the combine. "I've never cared about college that much. It was only about football for me."

Her nod in understanding doesn't ease the crawling feeling under my skin. Wilson Reed would have gotten me on this path sooner, but Lindon was still offering me the same opportunities even if it was later than I'd planned.

She leans back in her chair. "I saw what ESPN was saying about you after your last game. They seem optimistic that you'll be a first pick."

I lift a shoulder. It's old news.

When I don't offer her a reply, she chooses another topic. "What about this girl you're supposedly into? Bill seems to think you're one of the few he can invest the most time in because you're never distracted by the wiles of college. Is she going to change that?"

Wiles of college. "Clearly, experiencing college like a normal guy didn't work out so well for me when I tried it the first time. I was booted and brought here, which is why Coach is so willing to invest his effort. He knows I won't fuck it up again. Not even for—" I don't say Ivy's name, which makes one of Rachel's brows go up.

"Ahh. This is about Wilson Reed," she concludes.

She knows the story. It's all laid out in the file in front of her. "I fucked up and refuse to repeat the same mistakes. The girl…" I want to say *she doesn't matter* but I'd be lying. "She won't be a problem."

Rachel lifts her hands. "I never said she would be. And we both know that Bill wants what's best for you."

"He wants what's best for the team," I correct dryly. "And so do I."

The sigh she lets out is soft. "Aiden, you do understand

that it's okay to have more than football in your life, right? There's more than playing the game. Dating, especially at your age, is perfectly natural. It won't mess you up as long as it's a healthy relationship."

I give her nothing in return.

Her head shakes in defeat. "Fine, we won't talk about it. It looks like Wilson Reed will be one of your competitors this season with how you're both playing."

"So?"

"You didn't come here on the greatest terms. It may be hard to see some of your old teammates. I know a few of them graduated—"

I grip the armrests. "Can we just tell Coach we had this talk? I don't need a therapy session. No offense, but I have better stuff to do with my time than gossip about my old college or personal life."

Her frown makes me feel a little bad, but I brush it off because the last thing I want to be doing is getting lectured by another woman in my life telling me that *it's okay to be upset*. Mom has that handled on our weekly calls when she checks in.

It's okay that I'm pissed over Wilson Reed.

It's okay that I'm irritated with Ivy.

It's okay that I'm stressed over my future.

But it's not. Because all those feelings will ravage my mind if I let them take over. With Ivy back in my life, I know it's only a matter of time before my family worries about how I'll react to my past colliding with the future I'm building. They know I'll want Ivy to be part of it in any way she can be.

Closing the folder, Rachel puts it on the pile with a few others. "I only want to help, but if that's all you want to say today, then head out. I know you're busy."

Rubbing my lips together, I grab my bag from the floor and haul it over my shoulder. "I didn't mean to be a dick."

"You weren't. I get it."

"And about Matt..." I'm the last person to tell someone what not to do with their lives, but it wouldn't be pretty if they got involved and shit hit the fan. "He doesn't always think about others when he goes after things. Keep that in mind. You both have a lot to lose."

There's a long pause between us before she nods once and forces a tight smile. "Thank you, Aiden. Have a good day."

I hum and walk out, not feeling bad for planting that in her head. We can't afford to lose Matt to an impossible endeavor like screwing school faculty. She may not be that much older than us, but the school won't see it that way. His bragging record will get her canned and him kicked off the team for misconduct, and then we'd be fucked. Most second-string players are nowhere near as good as first, and we need a steady winning streak to keep us getting noticed.

As I pass by Coach's door, I see him on the phone with somebody through the narrow window. Whatever conversation he's having looks intense, and as if he knows I'm walking by, he looks up to lock eyes with me.

Tipping his head once, he turns his chair to face the wall and scrubs his face over something the other person is saying.

I promised not to let him down when I transferred here, and he's never doubted me. But there are other people I made that promise to in the past who I failed.

There's no way in hell I'm making that mistake again.

Chapter Six

IVY

It's been almost a week, and I'm still grinding my teeth over my encounter with Aiden. The only date I had that night was with my bed, and I slept even shittier because of what he said to me. I'm usually good at ignoring what people think.

Until Aiden.

Since the day I met him, I've always held a high regard of what Aiden thought. Anything he liked, I quickly followed suit—watching the clouds in the large yard behind our houses even though I could never figure out the shapes, playing basketball even though I rarely got the ball into the hoop, and exploring in the woods even though I hated bugs.

But having his attention meant not having my mother's or dealing with Porter when he threw temper tantrums. Instead of being trapped inside my pink room with stuffed animals taking over the twin bed and dolls scattered on the floor, I was able to listen to the crunch of sticks and leaves under my dirty shoes while Aiden pulled me to some new destination where we could hide out, just the two of us.

Whenever he'd ask why I never wanted to hang out at my house, I'd give him the same, mundane answer: *I like yours better.* And over the years, he stopped asking why and made his own conclusions, especially when I found myself sleeping in his room more often than mine.

After another poor night's sleep thanks to a leak in the basement that soaked the rest of my clean clothes, I realize I'll have to use what little money I have to go to the laundromat to have something to wear. Though based on the poor perception of Lindon's tight end and probably half his teammates by now, he wouldn't be surprised if I walked around town without clothes.

I'm still exhausted when I double-check the time on my phone to see when the laundromat opens. It's only after I close out of Google that I see the newest message waiting on my phone.

Unknown: You going to pretend you don't see these?
Got your # from a friend. We need to talk

That message is from three hours ago, shortly after I fell asleep. Knowing whoever the person is, because it could be anyone, is probably asleep by now, I send them back a text.

Me: Most people mention who they are before sending dickish messages. I don't have time for that anymore. Blocking you now

And I do just that.

I've had to change my number three times over the years

70

because the people I stayed with liked to harass me. Blocking their numbers on my older cells was never an option, but since I saved up enough money to buy a decent phone with the capability of putting people in my past without a second thought, I'd utilized the feature more times than I can count.

I'm only half-awake when I realize I'll have to go around town wearing what I fell asleep in, which is nothing more than a ratty pair of black joggers and an off-the-shoulder green sweater that has moth holes all over it. At least I'm covered. The last time I showed off my scarred arms, the boy whose blue eyes would always see through my barriers looked at me in a new light, like he was seeing the real me for the first time.

I could handle the stares and whispers from strangers whenever a piece of my deformed flesh showed, because they were easier to brush off. But there are two types of strangers in the world—ones you've never met before and ones you share memories with.

Aiden Griffith is the second. He's grown into the man who everybody at Haven Falls would be proud of. A man they can cheer on when they see him on the television screen on Superbowl Sunday and brag about. There's no denying he's someone who people look up to, and no matter what Bea says, I'm the opposite. I'm the woman people tell stories about so their kids *don't* follow in my footsteps. I'm the example, he's the idol.

Shaking it off, I slide into my warm boots and count the money in my wallet, thankful I'll have enough for one big load of laundry.

I slip my wallet into my backpack, shove a few notebooks and textbooks inside, and throw one of the straps over my shoulder. Thankfully, the Center Street Laundromat is open when I finally get there, having to stop a few times to readjust the heavy basket in my hands.

The owner is a cute little Indian woman named Hiya who's always smiling whenever I come in. She makes easy conversation, asks everyone if they need help, and tidies the place whenever she can. It isn't like the other laundromats I've been to that you wouldn't want to be caught dead in, especially when the sun goes down.

Finding a seat at one of the corner tables in a quiet end of the room, far away from the machines and flat-screens playing news reels, I dump out my backpack and frown at the cold Starbucks drink in front of me. It's my last one until I get paid next Friday, which means settling for what I can make myself at Bea's.

Thirty minutes into my study session, a shadow blocks some of the natural light from the large floor-to-ceiling windows. When I look up from my notes, I expect to see Hiya, though she can't be more than four eleven even with a pair of platform shoes on.

Instead, it's Aiden.

"What are you doing here?" My heart jumps when I lock eyes with him, not expecting to see the person I've been thinking about all morning standing right in front of me. Is my voice harsh? Sure. But I don't have the time or energy to hash out any more insults like last time we interacted.

His large arms cross over his chest, stretching out the material of his jacket. It's a far cry from the leather one he used to wear when we were younger because he thought it made him look cool. This one looks cheaper, no more than a windbreaker for the fall weather, but well worn. "I always do laundry on Saturdays. The guys keep fucking up the machines at home by overloading them, so I come here to do mine."

"No, you—" I stop myself. Shaking my head, I scratch behind my ear and tap my pen against my study guide. "I've never seen you in here before."

"Because you don't come in here first thing in the morning. I would have noticed," he replies easily, glancing down at the table and all my belongings spread out in front of me.

I shift, hiding my face in fear he'll see what those words do to me.

"The semester I stayed on campus freshman year at Wilson Reed, the RA told us that the best time to do laundry is Friday night or Saturday morning when kids are either partying or hungover."

My lips part, then close. That actually makes a lot of sense. I'm tempted to ask him about his time at the prestigious Massachusetts school but opt not to because that'd give too much away. That I care. He's better off thinking I don't.

Leaning my arms on the edge of the table, I look over my shoulder at the machine still spinning my load. "Huh."

To my surprise, he pulls out the chair next to mine and sits down. "He also said not to take a shower without shower shoes and to avoid Red's on Tuesdays because it's half-priced everything night. Red's is a bar, by the way. In Northern Mass. Went to college there for a while before transferring."

I grip the pen a little too hard in my hand. Did he forget I encouraged his enrollment at Wilson Reed knowing he loved that college? Does he not realize how big he is here? How everyone talks about him? Even if I didn't know him before, I would have heard his name the second I stepped onto Lindon's campus and realized he's a huge deal here. I knew he'd be big no matter where he wound up. That's just who Aiden is.

All I come up with is, "I'm not sure any of that is useful information for me. I only have to share a shower with a few girls and avoid most public places."

His lips threaten to rise. "Doesn't surprise me. You were never a people person, Chaos."

I choose to ignore that comment, focusing back on my papers. "I'm busy. Lots to do today."

From the corner of my eye that can't seem to ignore the bulky figure, I see one of his elbows drape across the back of his chair. "We need to talk."

"I disagree."

"You blocked me." His face is suddenly serious, expression darkening as he scopes me out. "I've had the same number ever since my parents agreed to let me have a phone, and you blocked it. We used to text all the time when I snuck you your first cell, knowing your parents couldn't afford one for you. How didn't you recognize it?"

He...? "That was *you*?" My tone is incredulous. Hurt flashes across his face only for a microsecond before he masks it with irritation instead. I shake my head, not willing to explain that I barely remember my phone number now, much less the one either of us had then. "Who has the same number for seven years?"

"I don't let go of things easily," he states pointedly, leaving the phone on the table where he dropped it between us. It's an upgrade from the ones we used to have—changed with the times. When he gave me the box containing the prepaid phone one night, I'd been speechless. He showed me how to use it, where he programmed his number, and how to text.

Slowly, my eyes lift to his. "We both know that's not true."

His fingers grip the table as he bends forward, eyes never

leaving mine as they narrow at me. "For someone who isn't holding it against me, you definitely seem to have a grudge."

Doesn't he get it? "I'm simply stating a fact. That doesn't mean it's a hostile one."

Now he scoffs, a sound I'm becoming a little too familiar with. "Don't lie. You were never good at it."

"Excuse you, asshole. Just because you don't like when I'm telling the truth doesn't mean you can be a dick to me."

"Then how about you actually tell the truth for once?" he spits, eyes hard as they focus on me.

"You want the truth?" I whisper, laughing slightly to myself. I lick my lips, only slightly self-conscious that they aren't covered in lipstick. I only bothered with basic makeup, forgoing my bright lipstick and dark eye liner in favor of something that simply covered the exhaustion from insomnia. "Fine. The truth is, when I asked my seventeen-year-old best friend if he'd run away with me, I hoped he'd say yes. But I didn't expect him to. He had a good home and a good life in general. Football. Friends other than me. Loving parents. That annoyingly adorable dog that yapped all the time whenever we tried doing something without him.

"Maybe part of me wanted him to try convincing me to stay, but I also didn't expect that. Because he knew why I hid in his closet and how many times I locked myself in mine to avoid the bullshit I always had to hear. He knew about the missed birthdays and the cop calls and the police reports. That boy telling me *no* was the only gift I'd ever gotten in life. He let me leave."

Aiden's nostrils twitch, and there's a blanket of something damp forming in those icy eyes I used to be obsessed with.

"I'm not angry that you didn't come along with me, Aiden. Not really. I was okay with that. Happy even. It meant that you were going after your dream to play football. You didn't risk messing up your life like I did mine because I was sick of being stuck in a rut." My throat gets thick, cramming with emotion that I swallow. "So no. I'm not holding anything against you. The only grudge I have is that life couldn't have given me a better home that I wouldn't have wanted to run away from."

With that, I lift my shoulders dismissively and stand up when the washing machine stops spinning. Walking over with a rolling basket to transfer my things to the dryer, I try ignoring the eyes I feel on me and the heat when footsteps near my back as I throw in a dryer sheet, close the door to the large machine, and shuffle through my wallet to gather change.

Before I can put any in, I hear the telltale sound of quarters being dropped into the slot in front of me. Peeking through my lashes, I see long, tan fingers sliding in each coin slowly before he says, "I waited. I remembered when you'd locked yourself in your room for a day and a half before your parents ever knocked to check on you. So after two days passed from when you'd said goodbye, I told my parents you'd left, and they went and told yours. I waited."

He gave me time.

Almost so quietly I can barely hear myself, I say, "Thank you."

He inserts the last coin and watches me play with the settings until I have it on what I want, then press the button to start the load. It isn't until then that he takes my arm closest to him, slowly lifts the sleeve, and flips it around to face him.

My heart pounds when his thumb runs over the scar, and it's a sensation I can't describe. I don't like the touch, but I don't hate it either. I'd rather pretend the markings aren't there, and Aiden makes it impossible when he does stuff like this.

"My parents grounded me. Said I should have told them sooner because"—his voice grows hoarse—"something bad could have happened to you. Something bad *did* happen, didn't it?"

I can't look him in the eye, and my energy is low, so I don't even try yanking my arm back even though he's close to discovering all the other marks if he moves the sleeve higher. They're the same ones that coat my inner thighs, outcomes of every stupid choice I made since getting on that bus instead of listening to Aiden or my mother. "What *didn't* happen to me?"

"Tell me."

"No."

"Iv—"

"You don't want to hear it," I snip at him, this time finding the effort to jerk out of his hold and lower my sleeve back down. "You don't want to hear about the places I stayed and how I afforded it." I stop myself, realizing that's exactly what he needs to hear if I want him to leave me alone. He'll see I'm not a worthy cause anymore—not the same Ivy he took under his wing all that time ago. "I slept with people. Lost my virginity to a thirty-three-year-old when I was only sixteen because I thought *why not?* Not everybody wanted something from me, but I rarely ever fought the ones who did, because I had nothing to lose. I've had a lot of sex with a lot of people and done things I'm not the proudest of. Pot, ecstasy. Sometimes I'd be offered harder stuff by the people I stayed with and I'd be so tempted to take it if it meant getting out of my head for a while. I managed to say no though.

"But this?" I gesture toward my wrist with my distressed gaze. "This was all me. It wasn't the drugs or the guys that led me to making this decision. It was desperation. The doctor called it a cry for help."

His throat bobs. "Nobody told me."

"I was eighteen," I explain, wrapping my arms around myself. "I didn't have to tell them anything, so my parents weren't contacted. I wasn't even in New York at the time."

I'd been in Vermont, and the hospital I was brought to only asked the questions they needed to. My ID had confirmed my age and the fact that I had no insurance or way to pay for the care I'd received. I had a plan to run in between nursing shifts, but then one of the hospital counselors walked into my room and handed me a pamphlet all about a program that helped cover the cost of hospital visits for people with no insurance. I'd qualified, stayed an extra day, gotten fluids, gotten my bandages changed, but by day three, they'd walked into my room to find nothing but an empty bed, a discarded gown, clean bandages missing, and my personal belongings gone. I wasn't about to risk anybody finding next of kin to collect me or let them haul me off to some sort of asylum to get help I couldn't afford.

"I shouldn't have let you go" is what he finally says to break the silence that's thickening the atmosphere around us.

I shrug. "But you did. And I'm glad."

He goes to reach for me, but I take a step back, halting when he states, "I won't make that mistake twice, Ivy."

Blinking slowly, I gape at the massive man built on lean protein and hard work. "That's not up to you, Aiden."

"You didn't miss me?"

Every day.

But I say nothing.

"You didn't regret leaving?"

Stop talking.

He manages to grab a hold of my hand, threading our fingers together like he needs the connection more than air itself. "You don't hate me?"

This time with my silence comes a hand squeeze that causes me to look up at him with a wary expression weighing my lips downward.

I'm not sure what's going on in his mind, but his jaw moves back and forth and the tendons in his neck tighten. "I have no fucking clue what's going on in that stubborn head of yours half the time. One second, you look like you hate me, and the next, you look at me like you did back then." His head shakes, clear confusion on his face as he processes it all. "*Do* you hate me?" he asks again.

Once again, I give him nothing because I want him to think I do. Maybe then he'll give up on me. Finally.

Instead, he does the opposite. "I dare you to hate me, Ivy. Because we both know you don't. You couldn't even if you tried."

Because he gave me time.

I let out a tiny breath and unwind our fingers. "Thanks for the change," I murmur, distancing myself from him again.

His lips twitch into a frown before they settle into a flat line that shows his feelings about the matter. Hurt and anger—they're there in the narrowed blue eyes lined with thick, long lashes that make the bright tones pop that much more.

"We're not finished," he informs me.

But we are.

We have been for a while.

Chapter Seven

AIDEN

COACH PEARCE SCREAMS AT us to reel it in after another bad practice, leaving us all in shit moods by the time we make it to the locker room drenched in sweat and bitter as hell. Half of us are dragging, and the other half are bitching about the newbies on the team.

DJ and Caleb are grumbling over Justin Brady's ACL injury that's going to leave us with the second-string alternate whose team spirit is about as nonexistent as Ivy's is these days.

By the time I'm showered, dressed, and grabbing my shit from my locker, Caleb is on his way out too. "You good, man?" he asks, knowing damn well I'm not.

"Can't stand that kid," I murmur, looking over my shoulder at Ricky Wallace. He's a year younger than most of us and has the skill to be a great fucking quarterback, but he's stuck-up because he knows he's good.

As if he knows I'm talking about him, the kid looks up and flashes a cocky grin. "You talking about practice? It's okay, Griffith. Maybe you'll be better next time."

My teeth grind.

It's Caleb who murmurs, "Ignore him."

Jaw ticking, I grumble, "I dropped three fucking passes."

"But you've never done it before," he reasons like he always does to disperse the tension building. "It was a bad day. Tomorrow is a new one. Just gotta focus better."

Shaking my head, I gesture toward the door to leave. I don't feel like listening to the asshole inside gloat about his new position. Somebody needs to remind him that he wouldn't have this chance if Justin's knee hadn't gotten fucked up.

Caleb's expression looks contemplative as we push open the door and head out to the hallway. "Brady is going to be pissed off once he hears about Wallace."

"What's he going to do? He's out. There's no way he's playing the rest of the season with that knee. Not since it's a repeat."

My friend's face turns grim. "I know."

We walk silently for a while, stewing in the possibility of our winning streak being over. Wallace is good, better than good, but that doesn't mean he'll help take home our next victory while we're away this weekend. If practice is any indication, we're fucked.

"Things going okay with Everly still? I know he can be a pain in the ass, but he's got real talent."

The teen in question has a killer arm on him. When Caleb mentioned Everly was looking to be mentored so one of Lindon's college scouts would scope him out in another year or two, I was more than happy to check out what he had going for him. Now I go over to his house for a few hours every week, throw a ball around, give him some tips on how to build more muscle, run faster, and eat better, and go home when his mother tells me it's time to. She doesn't seem as enthusiastic over him pursuing a contact sport, or any sport for that matter, especially since his grades need major help. She works an extra part-time job to pay for a tutor for him so he can stay on his high school team, since he's determined to get an athletic scholarship like a lot of the Dragons did. He could get into any school he wants with the talent he already has, and I'm determined to drill that into his head.

"He does," I agree easily, shifting my bag higher onto my shoulder. "I'd rather deal with his ass over Wallace's."

The snort that comes from my friend makes me crack a grin. "Yeah, Everly's a good kid. Always was growing up."

"If he stays focused like you did, he'll get his pick of the litter."

Caleb gives a small laugh. "He wants in Lindon. I doubt he'd consider anything else even if scouts offered him a full ride. He doesn't talk about it, but he wants to help out his mom since they've struggled after his dad died."

Sounds a lot like Caleb. I know he'd do anything for his family, which is why he's pursuing his degree to learn how best to run the family business one day. He could get far in the NFL if he wanted to, but he won't listen to anyone who tries telling him as much.

It'd be a shame to watch Everly hold back to stay close to his mom, just like it's a shame to watch Caleb stay behind, but I get it. I'm close to my parents, talk every week with them, and would do about anything if they needed me to. They supported me through everything when I fucked up at Wilson Reed and got sent to pick up the pieces here, and they still believe I have a shot at a real future in the league.

When we make it to the parking lot, we slow at Caleb's

truck. It's an older Ford that his father passed down to him. Rust coats the bottom, the interior is torn and worn, with a musty, aged scent, but he loves the thing.

"You know," I say, "it's not too late to talk to Coach about the draft. He's brought up the combine a few times hoping you'd bite since you got the invite. You've got the talent to make it." I kick his front tire with the edge of my boot and watch some rust fall off the bottom of the cab. "Could buy you a new truck if people like what they see."

He makes a face at me before opening the passenger door, which creaks so loud I wince, and throws his bag onto the bench seat. "That isn't what I want to do, and you know it. Plus, I know I don't have the same skill sets as everyone else who will be showing off there. The scouts watching will want someone to take them to the top. I'd be fourth or fifth pick at best if I even get a chance at the draft."

You'd think someone who was born and raised in Lindon would want to leave it at some point, but not my best friend. He loves it here, and the people love him. Not just because he's a badass on the field but because he has roots. He wants to be involved in the community since they've always cheered him on growing up. He's loyal.

"Raine coming over tonight?" I ask after he slams the door shut, knowing the conversation is over.

He grunts and pushes on the door, since it never latches right the first time, before turning to me. "Nah. I have plans to go over to her place. Her and the girls are doing a movie night."

"All the girls?"

Caleb knows who I'm really asking about and fails to hide his smile. "Your girl doesn't participate. Hell, I barely even see her when I'm there." He's *always* there. "It doesn't help that only Raine makes an effort to involve her in anything."

My lips twitch.

A head nod, not that I'm surprised. "Ivy prefers staying in her room. Sometimes she'll be in the kitchen making something, but usually she likes avoiding everyone. Those brownies I brought home were from her, by the way." He gives me a sheepish smile. "DJ demolished most of them. Anyway, the girls gave her the basement there."

He makes a face, causing my eyes to narrow at him in silent question.

He goes on, "Dude, the basement is gross. I know I brought it up before, but I didn't want to admit how bad it was. There's mold and it's not even finished. Nobody should be living down there. When Raine told me that's where she was placed, I couldn't believe it. Remember last summer when I had to help them move some shit down there because there was a huge leak? It hasn't changed, and it was nasty even then."

My nostrils flare. "And Ivy didn't say anything? Didn't put up a fight?" I imagine living in a moldy basement is better than some guy's house who wants sex from her as compensation for the roof he's supplying, but still.

Our conversation last weekend comes back full force, and I want to punch something. I took it out on the guys at practice all week and it barely helped. How could Ivy think she deserves to be treated like that by men? By anybody? Hell, did she think *I* only wanted to use her that way when I brought her back? It would explain the way she acted.

My anger had increased tenfold over the possibility of what Ivy went through that Coach asked what I'd been thinking about because he hadn't seen me play like that in a long time.

"Whatever it is, son, keep thinking it."

Obviously today all those pent-up feelings got the better of me. Not only did I drop three passes, I got taken out by one of the smallest damn members of the team like an embarrassment.

"Like I said," Caleb sighs, pulling me from my thoughts, "she doesn't say much. Keeps to herself. I know she works at the bakery and spends as much time out of the house as she can. Heard one of the guys mention seeing her at the library a lot working on homework. I think she only really comes home to sleep if she can help it. And, well, I've told you some of the shit the girls gossip about."

My jaw ticks. About the guys.

I don't let myself think about that.

I swipe a palm down my jaw. "If something happens, can you let me know? You're over there because you have a reason to be. There's not much I can do unless someone keeps me informed. I want her to be…" *Safe.*

Another wavering smile is what he graces me with in reply. "You know I will. If I knew what she meant to you before, I would have told you about shit at the house sooner. And the brownies. Damn good. Worth fighting DJ for. You've got it bad, huh?"

Truthfully, I already knew who made the brownies. They tasted exactly like the kind my mother makes, which makes sense considering she's who taught Ivy the recipe. It was the hint of coconut that gave it away.

Caleb's known Raine his whole life, which is the only reason I admit, "We were neighbors. Became best friends. Got separated a few years back. When I saw her at Bea's the first time, I almost couldn't believe it was her. Thought I was imagining a ghost."

It was the eyes that convinced me she wasn't some sort of mirage. The honey tone is brighter than anything I've seen on anyone, even when she's in a mood—something she's been in since the day I approached her at Bea's. That unique gold color told me all I needed to about the girl I'd missed for too damn long.

His eyebrows dart up. "No shit? How long has it been?"

"Too long." My jaw ticks again, not wanting to think about what she said. "She left when she was sixteen. I'll leave it at that. The past doesn't matter. We've somehow landed in the same town, at the same college, and trust me when I say that shit shouldn't have happened."

I think of the scars.

"But it did," he says slowly, knowing the reason I got hauled here.

I got distracted.

I let people under my skin.

I forgot what I wanted most.

And Ivy? She went through shit I can't even pretend to imagine.

"But it did," I confirm, cementing an old belief that things happen for a reason. Dad always tells me there's no such thing as coincidences in life.

"DJ said you asked him to keep an eye on her in class," he remarks.

My chin dips. "It's not like I'm asking anyone to follow her around. Only to let me know if something goes on. She's been through a lot, man. She doesn't need anything else happening. If I can make things easier for her here while I'm around, then I'll do it."

"Does she know about the combine? That this is your last semester here?"

A dark feeling rises inside me. "No."

He reads my mood and grabs my shoulder. "I've got your back. So does DJ, even if he's a flirt. Not like you have to worry about him anyway now that he's got his hands full with the blond he's been drooling over." Looking away, he sighs again and glances at a group of girls giggling and waving as they pass us. "Those girls at the house can be real bitches. Raine hates most of them, but it's a place to live. I imagine it's how Ivy feels too since Lindon doesn't have a lot of off-campus housing."

I don't confirm or deny my agreement.

When we part ways, I'm left sitting in my truck knowing I should go home. Instead, I find myself driving toward the bakery.

The younger girl who's usually talking Ivy's ear off sees me before my old friend does. It gives me time to check out Ivy's curvy figure while her back is to me. Her long legs are wrapped in tight blue denim that's formed to her hips and perky ass, and her arms are covered in sleeves that go well past her wrists for reasons I now know well. I know that there's a huge cupcake on the front with Bea's written in big font across her chest and a bee buzzing around it. I'd be lying if I said one of the first things I noticed, besides her eyes, was anything other than how big her tits had gotten. Last time I'd seen her, a few guys at our high school had pointed out how they barely filled out her bra.

I'd punched one of the dickheads who'd made the comment and nearly got suspended. Mom scolded me when she got the call to pick me up but quickly changed her tune when she found out I'd only hit him to defend Ivy.

Bea's granddaughter catches me staring and grins, her cheeks turning pink when I shoot her an unashamed wink, and then she bumps Ivy's arm, tips her head toward me, and heads in the back to leave me alone with her.

When Chaos turns, surprise flickers across her face. "It's not Sunday," she blurts, wiping her hands off on her thighs.

I crack a grin. "I'm aware."

She glances down at the floor, hesitates a moment, then walks over to the counter closest to me. "Did you want your usual? Or is that only your Sunday order?"

I can't help but wonder if that's an invitation to make dropping in at random a common occurrence. "I wouldn't mind a coffee," I admit. "Practice was rough, and I have homework to do still."

She probably doesn't care, but she at least pretends she does as she goes about preparing my regular.

While she's busy, I look around the empty bakery. "Slow day?"

"It's usually slower this time of day."

"Oh."

We go silent again. The sound of liquid pouring into the cup is the only thing between us. I shift on my feet, slide my hands in my pockets, and watch her pour in my shots of milk.

Eventually, I say, "How has your day been?"

She pauses what she's doing for a moment to glance over her shoulder at me, the colored hair falling down her back, then puts the lid on the cup and walks back to the counter. "It's been fine. Do you want anything else? Bagel?"

"Are you asking just so you can eat the half I don't?" I swear her cheeks color. "I noticed, by the way. You're welcome."

She rolls her eyes and punches in the order before giving me an amount. "You can't pretend you do it for me."

All I do is smile and then pass her the money I owe. "Keep the change."

"I don't need your pity," she grumbles under her breath, even though she doesn't try to give me the remainder.

Fighting a smile, I pick up my coffee.

She clicks her tongue. "Did you come in here for coffee?"

I play along, sipping my drink. "What other reason would I come in here for?"

Her brightly painted lips part to answer, then quickly close. Ivy has never been the shy type when it comes to me, so catching her off guard is a little amusing. Though there's a bittersweet tug in my chest over her new reaction to me. She'd always been content when we were around each other, but I have a feeling that the day on the couch officially changed that. I'd take it back if I could—if it meant seeing her smile effortlessly like she used to around me.

"I wanted to see you. Though the coffee really is needed. I've been procrastinating with my assignments, so they're piling up in my room."

She toys with the hem of her shirtsleeve, avoiding my eyes. "Are you still a brainiac and pretending not to be for the sake of your reputation as a meathead jock?"

I lift a shoulder, not confirming or denying that I break more than one of the stereotypes tied to football players. "Maybe."

Her eyes narrow, the honey-brown color filling with skepticism.

Relenting, I smirk. "4.0 GPA."

Not that she says so, but I can tell she's impressed. Something clouds over that though, and I cock my head when she murmurs, "Is there anything about you that's changed besides your appearance, or are you still perfect?"

Pride swells in my chest despite the urge to tell her I messed up plenty of times in the past, leaving me far from how she views me. After all, I let her walk away. There's nothing I'll regret more than that. "You been checking me out, Chaos?"

"Chaos," a voice coos breathily from behind her.

I look over at Bea's granddaughter. Elena, I think. Before I can say anything, Ivy shoots the young girl a look, making her disappear around the corner again, her laughter fading as she goes. When she turns back to me, she says, "No. Years tend to change people, that's all. Hard not to notice. I gained weight. You gained…muscle."

"You look good," I tell her honestly.

She doesn't say anything, only squirms on her feet.

I lean against the counter. "This is where you tell me I look good too."

"Oh, do I?"

I nod, waiting for her to say it.

She doesn't.

"That's okay," I yield. "I know you're thinking it. It's in your eyes. Caught you staring at my ass a time or two."

Now she's casting a glare at me that I'm finding endearing more than anything. "You mean like what you were doing when you walked in here? Felt like my butt cheeks were on fire."

My eyes flash. "If you really want your ass to burn, I can—"

"Don't finish that sentence," she warns.

I push off the counter and stand to full height, shrugging nonchalantly. "Guess you'll have to fantasize the rest on your own. Thanks for the coffee, Chaos." Her eyes roll as I wink and start backing away. "Are you coming to the game this week?"

"What do you think?"

"I think that I'll convince you to eventually," I answer casually, twisting to push open the dosor. "Unblock my number and text me sometime. Until then, I'll see you around."

I don't hear her answer before I'm back in the truck, grinning over the one conversation we've had that didn't involve insults or regretted words.

It's a baby step in the right direction.

~

"My name is Ivy, like the plant" was how the new girl next door introduced herself when she walked over to me and my friends as we played basketball. We dragged the hoop out to the street to play two on two until Ivy walked over with a big smile on her face and asked if she could join.

Captain, my golden retriever, trotted over to her and nudged her hand until she started petting his side, giggling as he licked her. Cap didn't like many people and usually growled at most of the boys from school I invited over. Mom said animals are good judges of character, so it seemed like Ivy passed the test.

It was my friend Judd who stuffed the ball under his arm and looked at my neighbor. "Are you lost?"

Our other friend Zach joined in. "Need us to call your mommy?"

They both laughed as I rolled my eyes and walked over to pet Cap. "Ignore them. I'm Aiden."

Those two words somehow made the smile on her face

grow five times bigger than it was before, and that smile was all it took.

When I told her she can shoot hoops with us, my friends groaned in complaint and said they were going to Judd's house to play video games instead.

Ivy frowned as they walked away, the ball dropping to the pavement and bouncing a few times as it rolled toward the hoop. "This is why I'm called Chaos. You know, kinda like how ivy spreads everywhere. That's me." Cap nudged her again, bringing her attention from my loud friends disappearing down the street on their bikes to my dog.

I didn't let her dwell on Judd and the others because that was who they are. They annoyed me half the time and Mom didn't like most of them, but they were people to hang out with when I'm bored. "My mom just made cookies. Want to come in and have some?"

When the sun hit her eyes, they looked almost golden. She glanced over her shoulder at the house they recently moved into before looking back at me. "I like cookies."

I started walking toward my house before I stopped, remembering the stranger assembly we had at school. "Do you need to ask your mom if it's okay to come over?"

She started to say something before stopping herself, her eyes darting back to her house before she quickly shook her head. "My mom is busy, and my brother is napping. Do you have any siblings?"

"Only child."

Ivy followed me to the front door. "I'd probably be sad if Porter didn't exist, even if he annoys me sometimes."

I hold the door open for her and see Mom come into view from around the corner. Her eyes widened when she saw Ivy trailing behind me before they went to me. "Who's this? Where are the boys?"

It's Ivy who murmured, "I chased them off."

A small laugh comes from Mom as she walked over. "Well, that must mean more cookies for you two then. Do you like chocolate chip?"

My neighbor's head picked up to look at my mother before slowly nodding. "I'm not supposed to take food from strangers, though."

"I'm Emily Griffith, and you've obviously met my son. Your family just moved into the Averys' old house next door, didn't you? We saw the moving trucks there last week."

"Yes, ma'am."

"We're hardly strangers then," Mom commented, holding out her hand for Ivy to take with the same warm smile she gave everybody stretched across her face. "Aiden's father and I shop at your parent's store sometimes. I've spoken to your father a time or two."

I'm not sure if Mom saw it, but Ivy winced at the mention of the store. I'd heard about Underwood's Grocer. My parents said it's important to shop local and support local business, but they never came home with more than a few items.

I get the milk while Mom directed Ivy to the kitchen table and grabbed some of the fresh cookies, and I sit beside Ivy, whose legs kicked back and forth on the wooden chair after putting glasses down in front of us.

I tell Mom, "Cap went up to Ivy."

Mom passed us napkins and smiled. "He likes you then" is what she tells the timid girl staring at the melted chocolate in the baked dough.

It's a moment before we hear, "I keep asking to get a dog, but my parents say they're too much work."

Pouring us cups of milk, Mom capped the jug and put it back in the refrigerator. "It can be, I suppose. You're more than welcome to come over anytime and play with Captain."

My neighbor smiled as she picked up a cookie and took a bite. "I want to learn how to bake," she declared after half of it is gone. "My mom used to let me help her bake Christmas cookies, but we didn't do it last year because she said Santa was on a diet. Can you teach me?"

I hadn't seen Mom's face get so bright since the day Dad and I surprised her with a ring with my birthstone on it for Mother's Day a few years ago. "I'd love to teach you. We'll have to schedule a time with your parents to make sure it's okay to come over. And it's the perfect time of year because Santa won't have to eat what we make."

Ivy gets quiet.

Mom studied her closely.

I filled the silence. "Can we play outside after we're done? I want to show her the old fort by the creek."

With Mom's permission, I lead Ivy through a thin patch of trees leading to a creek that winds around town. Dad told me the stone foundation left in the middle of the trees used to be an old fort from the French and Indian War, and when I relayed that information on to Ivy, her eyes widened in wonder instead of boredom like my other friends when I showed them.

And that's when I knew.

We were going to be good friends.

Chapter Eight

IVY

I'M WALKING INSIDE AFTER a long day of classes and work, my feet throbbing in the cheap pair of knock-off Chucks I bought at Walmart, and I tense when I hear deep sets of laughter coming from the living room. When I walk past the open room, Caleb sees me first, then Raine, who's cuddled up beside him on the couch.

"Hey," I greet them tiredly, about to ask how their days were since they always give me the same courtesy, before my eyes go to DJ sitting on the couch across from them by himself.

To my recollection, he's never been here before. I don't attend parties if I can help it, and I've never heard the girls talk about the football team making many appearances—least of all the big flirt who's using that charming smile on me again. When they do show up, it's always big news. The girls dare each other to make moves on some of the players, which usually winds up with a lot of colorful public displays of affection and morning-after walks of shame out the front door.

"Long time no see, Ives," DJ says, jumping up from the couch with a wide smile on his face. He's in his usual jeans and college sweatshirt, red with a black-and-white embroidered dragon across the front, and the same pair of dirty boots he always wears. I asked him if he owns more than those, and he said he has an entire closet full of shoes but is too lazy to break any of them in.

I'm taken back at the nickname. "You just saw me this morning in class."

He grins, all boyish and dimpled as he approaches me with outstretched arms. "And it's been far too long since I've seen that pretty face of yours. C'mere."

Before I can object, he's wrapping me in a tight hug. My body locks up from the contact, knowing he doesn't smell right. Not bad, just not like the cinnamon and pine that encompasses the one football player I wouldn't object to touching me. Instead, he's wearing some expensive-smelling body spray that takes over my senses. I can't find it in myself to return the hug, so I keep my arms to my sides until he backs away.

He doesn't seem offended by my stillness. "We'll have to work on your hugging skills. You're not supposed to stand there acting like you're being held captive."

Debatable.

Before I can ask what he's doing here, Raine and Caleb walk over to us hand in hand. I used to envy the way they always feel the need to touch one another. I haven't had that in a long time, and the desperate, rushed touches I'm used to are nothing in comparison to the obvious love they have for each other.

It's Raine who says, "We thought you'd like to go out with us for food. Syd mentioned that there was a party here tonight, so…"

When isn't there a party? This house has become known for them around campus. "Er, I'm not sure." My eyes go to the kitchen, where the door to my room is. Despite the plumber never coming, there haven't been any more leaks. Caleb fixed Sydney's tub and said he could find some new tile to redo the pieces damaged on my ceiling from his dad's store. Hesitantly, I look back at the three expectant faces and see them all waiting. "What did you have in mind exactly?"

"Malvin's Place," DJ pipes up, slinging an arm around my shoulder. I never liked touchy-feely guys, but I refrain from shaking his arm off like I want to because it's innocent. "You can't say no to pizza, can you?"

"I've got a lot of work to do," I try, despite the stuck-out lip the blond is giving me.

Caleb laughs, playfully smacking DJ's arm. "I think she just told you no, bro."

Raine gives me a small smile. Seeing her pressed against Caleb, both of them with warm, genuine expressions on their faces, makes it hard to turn them down. "We won't be out long. Caleb and I wouldn't mind getting away from here, and Malvin's has the best pizza in town if you haven't been yet."

"I'm paying," her boyfriend adds, eyeing me like he knows that's a deciding factor in my decision to agree or not.

And sadly, it is. At least he doesn't look judgmental about it. Plus, if he's offering… "Can I change first?" I tug on the clothes I'm wearing, covered in flour and other food from the bakery.

They all nod, and Caleb yanks DJ back when he tries following me, DJ saying, "I can come help if you need me to."

I silently laugh at his theatrics like I have since he's taken over the seat next to mine in class. What's worse is that his buddies have all followed suit, taking other peoples' seats around us. There's an unspoken rule about seat assignments once the semester passes the first week—nobody takes different spots. Yet nobody has complained about the sudden change, probably because most of the football team is double the size of everybody else. A few peers cast me accusatory glances when they see me surrounded by the burly men like I'm to fault for their eviction, and I can't say they're unwarranted. It's hard to refute when all the guys greet me with a short "hey, Ivy" or head nods every time they take their seats as if we've been friends all semester.

When I asked DJ why everyone switched spots, he'd simply shrugged and told me, "The team is a family. Where one goes, we all go."

And even though I have a feeling it's more than DJ's friends taking his lead on the changeup, I don't let myself think about it harder than necessary.

By the time I'm in a pair of decent leggings without any holes and a sweatshirt that I bought on sale at the campus store, a few of my housemates are setting up the kitchen with drinks for the party. They pay me no attention when I emerge from my room, so I offer them a meaningless wave and meet the three people who actually seem to want me around by the front door.

Malvin's is one of the three pizzerias in Lindon and also the priciest. The brick building sits between a hair salon and thrift shop that I've spent more money in than I like to admit. But Raine isn't wrong when she says it's the best, which makes me feel less guilty about Caleb paying for a meat lover pie that I dive into once the busty waitress sets it down on the stand, shooting the two boys a wink despite Raine and I sitting here.

"So," DJ says, popping a piece of sausage into his mouth. Raine giggled earlier when she saw what I was wearing, saying I matched the dirty blond currently staring me down. "Are you hung up on our tight end, or do I stand a chance at all?"

I choke on the piece of pepperoni I'm swallowing, grabbing ahold of the water Raine passes me as she glares at the team's wide receiver.

He shrugs at her innocently. "I'm asking a fair question. Griff barely says a word to anyone but your boy toy here— oh, don't give me that look, Anders. You're a long-term boy toy, but still a boy toy. Anyway, Griff only tells Caleb here shit. So I'm in the dark wondering what your deal is."

I set down my pizza and try not to let the heat spread from where it prickles the back of my neck. "There is no deal. And don't pretend like you're actually interested in me."

Even Caleb chuckles at that, but I refrain from glaring in his direction.

Raine passes me a napkin before grabbing one for herself. "Ignore DJ. He's just being nosey. He's like a puppy. Totally innocent."

"Until he starts chewing the drywall and pissing on the rug," Caleb remarks, flashing his teammate an amused smile.

The man beside me grumbles, "I've done neither of those things."

"But the stray you took in did," Raine reminds him.

I watch the three of them go back and forth on the matter in amusement. By the time I'm done with my first slice of pizza, I've learned that DJ is a big softy—especially when it comes to animals.

"...scratches everywhere. Grandma Meadow always told me I was more of a dog person and I guess that thing knew when I tried smuggling it in from the cold. I was trying to do the right thing, but maybe it had a family somewhere in Boston it wanted to get back to."

I snort over his troubled feline story. It's sweet he wants to help animals, but it sounds like he's batting zero for any of the attempts being successful. "Maybe you should flash them that pretty-boy smile of yours and they'll retract their claws."

A sly half smirk stretches across his face as he leans toward me. "But the claws are the best part, Ives. Haven't you figured out by now that I like a little sass?"

"Oh, brother," Caleb groans, throwing a balled-up napkin at him.

Raine picks up her water, her eyes widening from over the plastic Coke cup at something behind me. Before I can figure out what, a hand comes down on my shoulder and squeezes once, and the faintest scent of cinnamon wafts around me, bringing me back to happier times.

"Just got your text, man," Aiden says, hand still on my shoulder as he towers over me. He must be close because I can feel his body heat radiating into my back.

Caleb gives me a sheepish smile when I eye him knowingly. He quickly looks away and gestures toward the empty chair at the end. "We just finished eating, but take what's left. I don't think we were planning to leave anytime soon."

"Actually, I—" My voice gets cut off with a yelp when Aiden drags my chair with his foot closer to the empty one and drops down beside me. I glare at him while Caleb fails at hiding an amused snort. "Was that necessary?"

Aiden simply shrugs and reaches for one of the few remaining slices on the tray.

I make a face. "You hate meat lovers."

"No, I don't." To prove it, he takes a hearty bite while I

watch with surprised eyes. "I only used to say that because you always liked the boring shit."

"No, I didn't!"

He deadpans. "Yes, you did."

"No."

Skepticism cements his hard features as he lowers his slice. "The shitty-ass Hawaiian pizza doesn't count. You only ate two bites before you threw it away when you thought nobody was looking."

I feel other sets of eyes on us and try ignoring them. "Well…" I have nothing to say to that, so I sink down slightly in my seat. One of my few birthday parties growing up was tropical themed, so I begged my mother to order a Hawaiian pizza. She told me I wouldn't like it and that I'd waste money when she'd have to throw it away. When I realized it tasted like shit, I had to hide what I did with the rest of it so she wouldn't get mad.

Aiden grins and takes another bite of his pizza, victory evident in his eyes. I glance at Caleb, trying to ignore the gaze locked on me from my side. It's obvious Aiden isn't going anywhere, but that doesn't mean I have to give in easily. "Thanks again for the food. It saved me from heating up leftovers."

His smile comes easily. "No problem. When Raine suggested inviting you along, I was more than happy. Could have done without DJ hitting on you every two seconds though."

From the corner of my eye, I see my old childhood friend tense in his seat. He doesn't say anything though as silence takes over the table. Instead of drowning in it, I shift again and smile at Raine. "Thank you for thinking of me."

There's sadness in her eyes. "I know the girls aren't very welcoming, and that's because of Sydney, but if you ever want to hang out, I'm usually free. You don't need to stay in the basement. Caleb just mounted a nice TV on the wall. It's better than the one in the living room."

"Speaking of," Aiden cuts in, voice gruff as he turns to me. "What's this shit I hear about the basement not being finished? You could get sick down there from what Caleb told me."

Once again, I shoot my narrowed eyes on the man in question across the table. The snitch chooses not to look at me. "*Caleb* was just exaggerating. It's not that bad."

"I call bull," Aiden retorts. "When you get sick, I'm saying, 'I told you so.'"

My nostrils twitch. "It's a place to sleep. I've stayed at worse."

The tick in his slightly scruffy jaw tells me it wasn't the right thing to say. "You're not helping your case right now, Chaos."

"Chaos?" DJ repeats, eyes bouncing between his teammate and me in interest. His eyes land on me as his head cocks. "I thought you said you two didn't have a deal?"

"Oh, we have a deal," Aiden informs him.

I cross my arms. "Oh, do we?"

He forgets his food and leans on the edge of the table with his arms, bending toward me so we're unapologetically close. "What did we tell each other in the fort we made our own in the woods all those years ago?"

His stare penetrates me, and I refuse to blink first. I level his gaze, lean forward to match his stance, and say, "What we told each other doesn't matter because we were kids. Kids always fail at the things they promise."

"You never fail until you stop trying," he counters immediately.

I think back to the summer we met. It was a month or

more after I'd walked over to him and his friends to introduce myself. We always found ourselves back at the fort, climbing over the leftover stone foundation and camping out during the day. After an hour of lying on the ground surrounded by the old fortress's fallen walls, he'd said, "We should make a deal to always go to each other when things get tough. To always have each other. Like a pact."

I hadn't truly understood how serious the ten-year-old boy beside me had been at the time. I wasn't even sure what a pact was then. But I'd agreed nonetheless because he'd proven to be the person I could come to for an escape whenever I needed. I'd always find him outside riding his bike or playing with Cap, and he'd make time for me no matter what.

At nine, I'd made a clueless pact with the boy who'd become my fast friend to always come to him when things got rough. And I did. Shortly after we agreed, I began crawling into his room. The first time he asked what was wrong, and I admitted my parents were arguing. I wouldn't tell him any more than that. But when it became a reoccurring reason to climb through his window, he'd pass me an extra blanket and pillow and wouldn't fall asleep until he knew I was situated in the makeshift bedroom I'd made in his closet, hidden away in case either of his parents checked on him in the middle of the night.

As we got older, the closet got too cramped, and I'd sleep beside him in his bed instead. It wasn't until I was thirteen when Aiden had started sleeping on the floor because he thought it was too weird to have me beside him.

Looking back now, maybe the small crush I had on him by then was obvious. Maybe that was his way of drawing a line. But he never, ever forgot about the pact regardless of how I started to feel. Not until he told me he couldn't go with me. While that'd hurt for a while, longer than I liked admitting, I know everything happens for a reason. Some pacts are meant to be broken in order for us to grow into the kind of people we're supposed to be.

Aiden breaks the train of thought I become lost in to say, "Deals are meant to be broken sometimes, but loyalty never is."

His low tone has me clenching my hands into fists and squeezing. "Who says I'm loyal to you, Aiden Griffith?"

The slowest, most calculated smile forms on his face, making an eerie feeling creep into my chest and wrap around the beating organ that drums in my rib cage. "Baby, I don't think you've ever stopped."

My throat closes up at his purred *baby*.

We face off like that until someone clears their throat, and even then, neither of us wants to break the staring contest. It's Aiden who rips his eyes away first, yet I feel no sense of victory or accomplishment from the small win.

Because Aiden may be right.

I'm not sure if that pisses me off or scares me more, but something tells me I'll find out soon enough.

~

It's drizzling again as I speed walk through campus to get to my last class of the day. I had to miss the first two because I barely had any energy to get out of bed. Usually, I can push past the exhaustion and make do, but I couldn't even shove the blanket off me when my alarm squawked bright and early.

I know I'll regret not attending morning courses since there's nobody in them I can ask for notes. I'll have to email my professors about what I missed, which I already know won't go over well. We all got the same "you are adults now" lecture on day one. If you miss a class, you're responsible for making up the content.

I'm glancing down at my phone when all of a sudden, a hand hooks around my arm and yanks me under an awning between two academic buildings. Instantly, my opposite arm reacts in defense. I swing it as fast and as hard as I can toward the person responsible until a strong hand stops me mere inches from his face.

"What the fuck, Aiden!" I drop my arm once I realize it's him, my heart not calming any from the rapid beating it's doing in response to his move. It's a good thing he has killer reflexes, because I've learned how to pack a punch. "You never grab a woman like that."

"I called out to you," he says, gesturing toward my phone. "But you weren't paying attention. And where the hell is your umbrella?"

My...? "I don't have one. And you still don't grab people. I know your mom taught you better than that."

He deadpans over the mention of his mother. I've always loved Emily Griffith for putting him in his place. She never shied away from scolding him if he did something she didn't approve of. "Life is about learning," she always told us. "Even if it means messing up and making mistakes in order to figure things out."

And I've definitely made plenty of those.

Aiden says, "DJ mentioned you weren't in class today. I was worried."

He was *worried*.

About me.

"And you're pale," he notes, scoping out my face, then

the rest of me. I didn't even bother with much makeup other than lipstick. Trying to keep my shaky hands steady enough to apply my liner and mascara was too much.

I sigh, knowing he won't relent. "I'm a little worn down. Haven't been sleeping well. And before you get your panties in a twist, it's just insomnia." He goes to speak, but I cut him off before he does. "Don't you have somewhere else to be? Or were you randomly lurking here hoping I'd show up? Because that's pretty creepy if you were."

His eyes go to the passing students, some walking in raincoats and boots without a care for the weather, and some speeding like I was because they're not well equipped. At least it's not too cold. There's nothing worse than a chilly rain icing everything over once the sun goes down.

Aiden leans against the wall of the brick building behind him. It's the first thing I noticed about Lindon. Everything is styled the same. Brick, wood, and cobblestone make up most of the buildings, and they're all structured to conform to the designer's whims. It's a cute little campus, warm, small, and easy to navigate, but nothing special. Maybe that's why I like it so much. There are no surprises here. Well, at least there weren't until Aiden walked into Bea's Bakery.

"I was on my way to the gym when I saw you walking, so I figured I'd wait to see if everything is okay."

He always does that. Concerns himself with me when I've proven time and time again I'm not worth his time. "Aiden..."

"Can't I do that? Check in?"

My gaze drops to the ground. Rock salt and dirt cover the broken pavement where there clearly used to be a pathway before one of these buildings was put in. "You can. I just don't understand why you'd want to."

Two fingers tilt my chin up to meet a set of deep blue eyes. They burn as they lock with mine, making it hard to break contact. "When are you going to get it through your head that we're always going to have a past, Ivy? We were friends for a long time, and I swore I'd be your friend for life."

Pain strikes me, weaving into every possible nook and cranny it can. "But people lose touch all the time. Friendships fade. I've done things that—"

"I don't care about what you've done." There's an edge to his voice that says he's lying, but he doesn't address it. "I care about what you do now that we have each other again. I'm determined to prove that to you."

A moment passes. "How?"

"However I can." His answer is instant, making me blink slowly a few times as if his determination will somehow disappear with the flicker of my lashes. "You never questioned me when we were younger. Why start now? Why not believe in me?"

My emotions threaten to choke me, but I manage to swallow them. "Because I know what people are capable of now. I'm not naive anymore. You said no to me before, Aiden."

Hurt drowns his eyes as if I've personally wounded him. "I'm not going to hurt you, Ivy. I never have. You said you were happy I didn't come with you. Which is it?"

All I manage to do is shake my head, uncertain of my reasons.

"I. Won't. Hurt. You. What makes you think now is any different?"

Because now I don't think I'd be able to walk away from you, and I'm scared of what that means for me.

I've always mapped an escape route. I like having a plan,

knowing where to go if the time arises. It's how I've survived the past four years—fight or flight.

I fight the feelings that take over my stomach and wrap around my rib cage and wait for the moment I bolt before I can let them win.

Aiden makes me feel that way.

Anxious.

Needy.

Unsettled and settled at the same time.

Seeing him after all this time hasn't changed that, and it should have. Four years has molded who I am, what I believe in, and how I view the world.

So why hasn't it changed how I feel about the boy who used to be my best friend?

"I'm protecting myself," I tell him honestly, knowing there's no room for lying if he wants to understand. "You should do the same. I'm Chaos, remember? I mess every-thing up. I hurt you. I left. I—"

He steps toward me, crowding my space with his large body and making the words lodge in my throat. His arms go to the wall on either side of my body, caging me between him and the building against my back. The brick is scratch-ing my head as I look up to see his serious expression pinning me to my spot in a challenge, like he's daring me to try moving away.

I don't.

I stay there, locked in a stare down with the person I've always admired and wanted to be like. What does he see? Someone broken? A ghost? A disappointment?

The last thought fills my heart with darkness. It'd be a deserved title knowing what I've done—who I've had to be in order to make it where I am today. I shouldn't be ashamed, but I am. And shame welcomes a downward spiral that I can't afford right now, so I shove it away with as much mental strength as I can muster.

"I want to be your friend," he declares.

A stuttered breath releases from my parted lips, surprise evident in the way my eyes widen at his firm statement. There's no question or doubt like there should be, knowing how unpredictable I am. Doesn't he get that?

Aiden doesn't stop there. "I want to be the person you can rely on if you need someone, even if you can do it on your own. I want to cheer you on like you always did for me. To support you with whatever makes you happy. And I want that to be me."

Thump. Thump. Thump.

"You want to make me happy?"

"I miss your smile." A hand raises and I freeze as his fingertips brush my bottom lip like he's exploring it in wonder. "You don't do it nearly as much as you used to. Even when your parents fought, even when you crawled into my room at night, you found reasons to smile."

I blink.

He blinks.

I move my hand so it rests on his abdomen and feel his muscles contract under my palm.

His hand moves to brush fallen hair out of my face so there's no obstruction of view. I see the intensity in his eyes as they take me in.

All of me.

My past.

My present.

"Let me be a reason to smile," he whispers so quietly it's almost drowned out with the pitter-patter of rain around us.

My eyes close for a moment as I collect my rampant emotions, but I already know I'm done for with that plea spoken in seven tiny words.

All I can manage to say through my choked voice is, "I missed smiling too."

It's not a yes.

It's not a no.

It's not me pushing him away like my default is. He's been warned already, and if there's one thing about Aiden Griffith, it's that his determination is his strongest trait.

I hope it doesn't backfire on him.

Someone whistles close by and yells Aiden's name, breaking the trance I'm in. I shake my head, duck under his arm, and walk into the rain again, not willing to see who caught us in the intimate-looking standoff.

"Ivy," he calls after me.

I stop, letting the rain run down my face to hide the panicked tears that start doing the same.

He says, "Out of your head, Underwood."

Letting out a surprised laugh, I look over my shoulder at him in disbelief. He's waiting like he always did. "Head in the game," I call back, trying to convince myself of its power even though my voice wavers with doubt.

Out of your head.

Out of your head.

Out of your head.

Nobody wants to be stuck there, least of all me, so I nod once to myself until I think the reminder is engraved in my mind.

"Head in the game," I whisper as I finish my trek to class.

Chapter Nine

AIDEN

WHEN COACH PEARCE TURNS the lights on after watching game day footage, we get the same spiel as always before a big game. Kick ass, take names, come home with something to add to the trophy case. We're holding a record for Lindon U's longest winning streak this season, and he doesn't want us to fuck it up. Especially since our original QB is out and a few of us have trouble trusting the new one to level up and be what we need to keep the good luck going.

"Griffith," Coach barks as everyone starts gathering their things to move on with their day. "Stay behind so we can talk."

A few of the guys shoot me smirks, and a couple dipshits drag out long "oohs" as they pass by. I roll my eyes at them, smack Caleb's hand that's outreached to me, elbow DJ as he shuffles around my seated body, and nudge Justin as he claps my shoulder and teeters on his crutches.

Leaning back in my chair, I cross my arms lazily and stretch my legs out in front of me. "What's up, Coach?"

"Don't play stupid with me, boy," he says, arms mimicking

mine with his playbook still firm in his grasp. For someone in his midforties, he looks older. Dealing with our asses has definitely contributed to the white sprinkled in his beard and wrinkles evident on his face. "I don't know if it's a girl, a guy, or whatever the hell you're into that's making you zone out on me. The only way we can beat Delmar this week is if you let go of whatever is holding you back. They've got strong players this season."

"I know they do."

His eyes turn skeptical. "They won't be easy to beat when their defensive linemen can take down a goddam tank."

Again, I say, "I know."

His graying eyebrows raise. "I'll have to handle the little punk ass on the field who's starting for the first time, and I'm not sure what will happen. You're the glue, son. You need to make this season the best you've ever had even if our alternate screws us. I've seen how distracted you've been, and the only person who can pull you out of it is yourself. It's a team out there, but you're one of the few members who can carry it."

No pressure there.

I press my lips together and nod once.

There's always been a lot of pressure on my shoulders since I admitted that I wanted to make this into a career. Showing up at Lindon and becoming a starter is my shot to make shit happen for myself. "I understand, sir."

"Anything you need to tell me?" he prods, something firm in his eyes as he pins me to my seat.

"No, Coach."

"Nothing you need off your chest?"

My nostrils twitch. "No, Coach."

He watches me for a moment, waiting to see if I'll

squirm or break. I do neither. I remain stoic, waiting for my dismissal. When he gives me a single nod, I collect my shit and stand.

"I've always liked you, Griffith. You remind me of some of the greats. But everyone has a weakness, and you have to decide if you're willing to cave to whatever yours is or to let it go and be selfish."

Dad used to tell me that the greatest accomplishments were done by being selfish, but I don't want to act for my own convenience if it means forgetting others. Mom didn't teach me to be selfish, no matter how much Dad encouraged it. I never thought twice about working my ass off to get what I wanted until now, because there was only ever me once I started college. Now I have someone else to think about again.

Before I can exit, he asks, "What did Sanderson say after your appointment?"

I roll my shoulders. "He gave me some stretches to do and told me to come in after game day so they could help loosen the knots."

"You stressed?"

When am I not? "No more than usual."

He grumbles under his breath. "Good thing you'll be done soon then. You don't need the extra bullshit that comes with college."

Instead of giving him a verbal reply, I shoot him a wave and head out. I think about what Ivy said in the laundromat and can't help but fight off a frown. *I'm not angry that you didn't come along with me. It meant that you were going after your dream.*

Ivy's weakness is selflessness—it always has been. It's her fatal flaw.

And mine is undoubtedly her.

But the two can't seem to coincide in Coach's eyes, and I'm not sure how I can convince him otherwise.

~

When I walk out of the rain into the café, I brush off my jacket, swipe a hand through my damp hair, and glance at the counter. My shoulders drop slightly when I see it absent of the person I'm here for.

Bea Olsen, the owner and avid football fan, turns the corner with an empty tray in her hand and gives me a wide smile. "There's Lindon's star player. A bunch of your boys just left. Missed them by a few minutes. How are you, honey?"

Sliding my hands in the pockets of my jacket, I lift my shoulders. "I'd be better if this rain would stop, but otherwise I'm all right. I'm actually not here to meet up with the guys."

"It's supposed to dry up tomorrow just in time for your game. Ready to kick Gator butt?" On cue, someone a few tables back starts hooting like fans always tend to when our rivals are mentioned.

Lindon is a loyal community, filled with people who always have the team's back. "You bet." My eyes trail back to the empty counter. "Is Ivy working today?"

Something sparks in the old woman's eyes before the corners of her lips curl. "She was feeling under the weather, so I sent her home. Had to fight the girl. Always stubborn, that one."

I huff out a laugh. "Got that right."

Her head tilts. "You know my girl?"

My chest tightens over her careful choice of words as I

study her features. *Her* girl. I nod slowly, grateful Ivy has her, since she hasn't had anyone else in a long time. "Is she okay?"

When I saw her a few days ago on campus, the washed-out color of her skin alarmed me. She's always been pale—envious of the way I could be outside for an hour and have a tan while her skin does nothing—but paired with her glassy eyes and faded lips, I knew something wasn't right. It's more than being worn out like she insisted.

"Why don't you see for yourself? I told her to get some rest, but I'm sure she's doing anything but. In fact—" She holds a finger up and walks over to the counter, snatching up a bag and filling it with a few pastries from the case. By the time she's done, I'm balancing a white bag, container of soup, and drink carrier in my hands. "Bring her this. They're all her favorites. Homemade cream of broccoli soup, my famous hot chocolate, and a few fresh cookies."

I'd bet a kidney that the cookies are chocolate chip. It's always been Ivy's go-to ever since my mother taught us how to make them. We'd spent more time making a mess of the kitchen than making edible cookies, but it never stopped Ivy from trying again. Mom encouraged her to keep practicing, always keeping an open invitation to the girl who clearly needed it.

I clear my throat, fighting a wavering smile at the small woman in front of me. "How much do I owe you?"

Her hands go to her hips. "Don't you dare insult me, Aiden Griffith. I'm doing this for her. All I ask is that you treat her right."

My lips part, but she eyes me into silence. Pressing them together again, I find myself nodding and walking toward the door that she points at in dismissal.

She calls out, "You have her address?"

"Yes, ma'am."

A scoff comes from the small woman that makes me snicker slightly to myself. "*Ma'am.* I'll let it pass because you're going to take the team to the championships. I'll be rooting for you someday on the big screen too. But call me ma'am again…"

I shoot her a wink from over my shoulder, amused by her theatrics. "Sorry, Bea."

"I don't want her getting cold soup, so hurry along. And don't think I won't be asking for details from her later on."

Good luck getting them, I want to tell her, but something tells me she already knows.

It doesn't take long to get from the bakery to the house from hell. Caleb has told me horror stories about the parties held here, and I hate knowing Ivy has to deal with the girls who run the place in addition to the entitled frat fuckers and players who always try making moves.

But I also know she won't accept any help unless she has no other choice.

Knocking on the front door of the infamous house, I wait in the rain with a scowl on my face as I try shielding the food until the front door opens. The petite brunette standing in front of me looks vaguely familiar as she gapes at me. I've probably seen her around, but the way her eyes go down my body with a glint in her eye tells me she's more than likely a jersey chaser.

Her tongue trails along her lips. "Um…"

"I'm here to see Ivy."

Her lips part in obvious surprise. "*Ivy?*"

I refrain from sighing, not patient enough to deal with this. "Yes. Ivy Underwood. I was told she's here. You mind letting me in? I'm getting soaked."

She moves aside and watches me step over the threshold. "If you could point me in the right direction…"

The brunette stares at me after closing the door. "Are you *sure* you're here for Ivy? Sydney is upstairs helping some of the girls with a project, but I can get her."

Teeth grinding, I look around the room, hoping a sign will appear telling me where to go, since she's no help. "Don't you think I'd ask for *Sydney* if I wanted to see her? Where is Ivy?"

Slowly, she shakes her head and then gestures toward the room to the right. "Basement. It's the first door in the kitchen."

I don't give her another response before heading in that direction. When I knock on the door and try turning the handle, it's locked. Groaning to myself, I set down the food on the counter closest to me and say, "Ivy? It's Aiden. Can you open up?"

For all I know, she's sleeping. I'd feel better knowing she is if she's as sick as Bea implied. It isn't often Ivy would succumb to someone telling her to go home unless she needed to.

After a few seconds of silence, I knock again with no luck. I pull out my phone and text the only person who's been downstairs before.

Me: Any way to get to the basement of the house on Madison?

Almost instantly, bubbles appear at the bottom of the screen.

Caleb: There's a key hidden under the third plant on the counter. Fake bottom

117

I'm not sure I like that he knows that. I find the key and unlock the door before grabbing the food and heading down. My nose is hit with thick, musty air and what I can only think is mold. It reminds me of the abandoned house Ivy and I snuck into once on a dare. She wouldn't back down when I told her it was haunted, and I couldn't watch her go in by herself, so I followed a few feet behind. That was in better shape than the bullshit room I'm entering.

A form on the bed quickly flips over and sits up, nearly toppling off the mattress. "Get out!" she rasps in a hoarse voice.

"Relax, it's just me," I tell her, searching the dark room for a light switch. When I find it and flick it on, a groan comes from her direction.

Eyes snapping to her as she drops backward onto the bed, I walk over and examine the baggy clothes on her body and the blanket tangled around her legs. Her glassy eyes meet mine, face pale, and I fight a frown when she rasps, "Is that Bea's food I smell?"

Momentarily forgetting what I'm holding, I lift it with a nod. "Stopped by to see if you were there. She sent me on my way with a delivery. Said this stuff was your favorite. Don't think she packed bagels though."

She rolls her eyes, but even that movement is lagging. "I don't want a bagel anyway. My throat hurts. Is that cream of broccoli in the cup?"

Looking around, I find a spot to set everything down before grabbing the soup and plastic spoon Bea thought to pack. "What's wrong with you?"

She sits up and accepts the food with a glare, plucking the top open and watching the steam billow from it. "I know your mother taught you better manners than that."

I huff out a dry laugh and nudge her legs out of the way

so I can sit on the edge of the mattress. "You like pointing that out, huh? You're not wrong. Now answer the question."

Blowing on a spoonful of the soup, she peeks at me through her lashes. "I caught a cold or something. I'm just run-down, that's all."

"You sound like shit," I agree with a single shoulder lifting. "Odd. I seem to recall saying that this would happen not long ago."

She sips the warm liquid, but it doesn't hide the small smile that begins tipping the corners of her lips upward. "You always were a smooth talker."

I peel my eyes away from her to examine her room. If that's what you can call the shithole with only a few pieces of furniture. It's basically storage for all the trash they don't want elsewhere. "You don't belong down here, Chaos."

Remaining silent, she focuses even harder on the soup wrapped in her hands. Something on her face shifts, darkening as she slips into her thoughts.

I don't relent. "There's gotta be shit growing in here that you don't need to be inhaling."

"Stop talking."

"Start listening."

She levels with me. "I'm not leaving."

Figured as much. "Even if this place is making you sick? You can't go to work or school if you're feeling like—"

"Please don't," she cuts me off, eyes glazed but hard on my face. "Don't show that you care. That makes... It's hard for me, okay?"

My jaw ticks, but I nod in understanding. I don't know what's happening between us, but neither of us is stupid enough to believe that it's nothing. It means a lot more than we want to acknowledge.

She nibbles her bottom lip. "It's probably from the weather changing, that's all. Everyone gets sick this time of year."

"Do you need anything? Medicine?" My tone is rough from the rejection, but I know it's better that I ask even if I can guess her answer.

"No."

I stare at the soup she stopped sipping, thinking about what Coach said about distractions. I ignore his words though. "Keep eating."

"Don't boss me around."

"Don't be stubborn."

We stare at each other, her eyes narrowed into a glare, mine distant but firm. To my surprise, she backs down first.

I glance at the watch on my wrist that doubles as my fitness tracker and sigh at the time. I promised Everly I'd stop by this afternoon. His mother won't be happy if I bail like I had to last time because of the shit practice that left me in a bad mood.

"I need to get going soon, but I can run to the store for some—"

"Just go," she tells me roughly, spooning out more broccoli pieces and staring at them. "I don't need anything from you except for you to leave me alone. Get the hint."

I stand, stuffing my hands in my jacket pockets to hide them clenching. "Tough luck for you. I'm not letting you get your way that easily. If I didn't have somewhere else to go, I'd stay here and bug you until you fall asleep."

She deadpans. "Then what? You'd watch me snore?"

"Wouldn't be the first time."

Silence.

I know I'm not being fair, but when is life ever that way? We all have to come to terms with what we're given, and the nights I got to watch her sleep peacefully beside me in bed were some of my favorites, before I was afraid of making a move while we slept and ruining everything. When I dozed next to her, it was usually the best sleep I got. I wasn't going to tell her I slept like shit after she left and only recently managed to tire myself out until I'd pass out in exhaustion.

"I'll check in on you later," I tell her, grabbing one of the drinks Bea slipped into the carrier. I'm a few steps away when I turn to look at her again and ask what taunts me. "Did they ever do anything to you that I don't know about?"

Confusion twists her face as she lowers her soup again. "Who?"

I drag the tip of my tongue across my bottom lip and shift my weight. "Your parents. Did they ever… I don't know, did they hit you? Take things further than you let on?"

My blood boils from the thought alone and simmers when she quickly says, "Jesus, Aiden. Never. They just always fought and said…things. Some people are better off not being parents, that's all."

Nostrils flaring, I give her a few short nods before rolling my shoulders back. "Needed to be sure."

She's quiet, refusing to look at me.

I quietly add, "I'm glad the assholes decided to be parents, even if they sucked at it."

She doesn't get a response in before I'm walking back up the stairs. Instead of returning the key to its spot, I slide it into my coat pocket and notice a few girls in the kitchen watching me from where they're pulling food from the fridge.

Turning to the taller one, I ask, "Where is the head of the house at?"

The brunette from earlier smirks like she knows something nobody else does and points toward the door behind me. "You're in luck. Sydney's alone and I'm sure she'd love seeing you again after last time."

I say nothing and knock on the door.

When it opens, I slip in wordlessly until the door clicks shut behind me.

Chapter Ten

IVY

A WEEK OF AN all-liquid diet and as much sleep as possible left me fifteen pounds lighter. I barely left my room until the cold meds a football player left me helped fight off the virus.

In and out of my fever dreams, I vaguely recall Raine and Caleb checking on me. But it was Aiden who I'd wake up to sitting in a chair someone brought down for him, reading a textbook, jotting down something in a notebook, or sometimes forcing water and medicine down my throat despite my protests. Sometimes, I'd feel his eyes on me and refuse to acknowledge his presence, choosing to sleep off the nagging feeling in the pit of my stomach every time he was around. It never stopped him from sitting me up, making me eat and drink, or washing off my sweaty skin with a cold washcloth until the fever broke.

And when I finally came to and found myself alone, in clean, dry clothes that were too big to be mine, I found a note beside my table with scratchy handwriting I know is Aiden's that simply said *Raine helped change you so don't think I copped a feel. Unblocked my number in your phone. Text me when you're awake.*

I could block his number again and ignore his request, but as I push myself out of the lumpy bed that's been my prison for the past week and examine the Dragons football sweatshirt twice the size of me and pair of rolled-up gray sweatpants on my body, I know I can't keep pushing him away. How many times did he give me clothes to sleep in when we were younger? An extra blanket? One of his pillows even if he didn't have a spare? Here he is doing it all over again, no matter how shitty I treat him. I know the second I wake up that I have to be better. Not for me but for the person who's clearly never given up on me when he should have a long time ago.

I want to be your friend.

Aiden didn't have to spend his spare time taking care of someone like me, but he'll always be the little boy who took me by the shoulders after my mother said something hurtful and told me, "Out of your head, Underwood." The first time I heard those words, I stared at him with glassy eyes until he added, "This is where you say, 'Head in the game.'"

To this day, he doesn't want me being trapped alone in my thoughts, replaying old fights or moments that would leave me twisted in his spare blankets or bedding instead of the ugly pink ones I grew out of when I was twelve. Because now I don't have that escape—I won't let myself.

Pulling up his name, which he clearly programmed into my phone while I was out of commission, I type out a quick message before forcing myself up the stairs with clothes that actually fit and heading for the shower.

When I'm done drying off and combing my hair, I

notice the blinking light in the corner of my phone when I glance down at the counter it rests on.

Aiden: You're welcome

~

The whispers at the house get worse each time I find myself coming and going. Some of the girls who would barely pay me a second look now stare a little too hard like they're trying to figure something out, and the itchy feeling under my skin builds from the unwanted attention.

Sydney has been even worse to me since I recovered because of her latest boy toy, Remi, and his wandering gaze and Aiden's daily cameos to make sure I'm still alive. Her glares are more obvious after the tight end leaves, and her snipes are like whips against my skin whenever Remi tries making conversation with me.

They may only be words, nothing that can do any permanent damage, but even cat scratches hurt like a bitch for a few days before they fade.

Their words wouldn't be so bad if I hadn't overheard Sydney talking to a few girls when I was dragging myself to the kitchen for juice that Aiden bought for me. Normally I tune out their gossip, but as soon as the tight end's name was mentioned, I couldn't help but eavesdrop from behind the basement door. When I heard Paris Hilton 2.0 mention her candid history with my childhood friend, something heavy dipped in the pit of my stomach. But that feeling spread to my chest and gripped my heart when I heard the other girls asking what happened when Aiden slipped into Sydney's room the other day.

I have no reason to be jealous over what—or who—he chooses to do. I've been far from celibate over the years, taking what I want since moving in because I can and not because I'm obligated to, so there's no reason for me to feel betrayed that Aiden gets some too. Even if it's from the girl who's done everything to beat me down with her lackluster opinions and dirty looks.

Swallowing down the little green monster, I grip my bag a little tighter as I walk through campus. The brisk air is exactly what I need after holing myself up, and the nipping November wind against my skin distracts me from the thoughts that pop back up.

Unfortunately, Aiden and the she-devil still haunt me even when I get to my first class. By the time anthropology comes around, my mood is sour, my energy drained, and my patience ten times thinner than normal.

"You sure you don't need to go home?" DJ asks for the third time since I sat down, seeing the way my body slumps into the seat and eyes struggle to stay open through the lecture.

I've been ready to go home since I left my room this morning, but I have a shift at the bakery despite Bea telling me to take as much time to recover as I need. "DJ, I don't wake up and strive to be a hard-core bitch every day of my life, but you're about to see that side of me if you ask me that one more time."

One of the guys, Matt, snickers from the other side of him. When I lean forward and shoot him a look of warning, he sinks down in his seat and pretends to care about the lesson.

DJ nudges my arm. "I'm looking out for you, and not just for the tight end either."

I don't acknowledge what he's getting at and focus on my notes instead. It's bad enough I'm over three classes behind. "Did you take any decent notes while I was away?"

His lips twitch downward. "No, but—"

"You can borrow mine," another football player says from nearby. I give the guy, Wallace according to the others, a grateful smile before sitting back in my seat and scribbling halfway coherent notes across the page.

The persistent blond next to me sighs and murmurs, "Watch out for that one. He thinks because he's the new quarterback he can charm his way into anyone's pants."

I stiffen. "You don't need to worry about that. I'm not interested." There's a heavy pause between us. "In anyone," I add in vain.

My seat neighbor shakes his head, tapping his pen against my hand. "Griff told everyone to back off. He normally doesn't care who we go after. Take that for what it's worth."

I slide my focus to him. He's staring at the front of the room, acting like he cares about what the professor has to say for once. His profile doesn't give much away. "What did Aiden say?"

A shoulder lifts. "To keep our hands to ourselves and give you space. Got to be honest, though, not sure you'll get far with him even when you decide to stop pretending you don't like him."

My eye twitches. "And why is that?"

Exhaling, he rolls his shoulders and finally glances at me with sorrow in his eyes that makes my anxiety curdle my stomach. "He's going pro, Ives. Don't know if he told you or not, but he's supposedly leaving after this semester is over. I know you don't go to games, but you pay attention when someone brings up our stats so you know he's good enough to be snatched up by a major team."

Though the news about his future career is far from surprising, my heart clenches over the confident statement of his departure. I've heard people talk on campus and at the bakery, even if I try tuning out news of Lindon's best player. Aiden deserves to go pro from everything people have said. It's what he's always wanted, after all. Still, I wish he would have told me that our reuniting was short-lived if he is leaving Lindon in a matter of weeks. It feels like history is about to repeat itself, except he's the one walking away this time while I stand idly by.

Forcing a smile, I shrug as if the news doesn't squash what little hope remains inside me. "Good for him."

DJ looks like he wants to say something, his lips parting and eyes focused on me for a moment too long before shaking his head. Scratching his jaw, he faces forward again. "You two drive me nuts. Always fighting what other people would just let happen if you weren't both in your damn heads. Do something about the tension before he goes if nothing else."

Chest tightening, I stare at my notes absentmindedly. "You're being kind of an ass."

"I'm just saying you might regret not doing something about it while he's around. You're both into each other, and I'm not just saying that because of what I walked into that day. You can pretend all you want, but you're not fooling anyone but yourselves. Who knows what will happen when he leaves if you don't do something about it now. You're both here, Ives. You don't seem like the cowardly type."

I grip my pen a little too tightly until my fingers hurt. If he thinks calling me a coward will get me to act on feelings

I've had since I was a teenager, he's wrong. If anything, it's a reminder that acting on them will only hurt worse in the long run when Aiden's gone. "It doesn't matter because Aiden and I aren't even friends, much less anything else. Drop it, DJ."

I wonder how many times I have to say that out loud before I'll start believing it. Because acquaintances don't act like they care when you're sick, much less take care of you, and they certainly don't have your back without motives.

But friends do.

DJ hums out a noise but remains silent the rest of class, and his doubt bothers me more than his words do.

What does he know that I don't?

The irritating voice that likes to pop into my head at the worst times speaks up loud and clear, offering me an answer I can't ignore no matter how hard I try.

He knows how to be honest with himself.

~

I knew I was walking into a losing battle when I entered the kitchen and saw Mom looking at the empty spot on the wall where our old family portrait used to hang. She never replaced it or made us take a new one this year. It was like she wanted the emptiness as a reminder of how broken our household really was these days. Part of me was glad, because I hated dressing up and putting a fake smile on my face for people. But sometimes I missed that. Pretending like we were fine instead of accepting that none of us were.

The face-off I have with my mother ended with a long sigh as she set down the checkbook and shook her head. "I can't give you more money."

"It's only thirty dollars," I tell her, shoulders dropping at her firm decision. She used *the voice*, the one that said her mind was made up. "If I don't come up with it by the end of the week, I can't go on the trip."

Mom rubbed her makeup-less eyes before standing and walking over to the coffeepot. When she realized it was empty, she gripped the counter for a few seconds before searching for the grounds in the cupboard. "Ivy, I don't know what to tell you right now. I already gave you some money I scrounged up so you could get those baking supplies. You're almost thirteen. Maybe if you learned to manage your allowance better, you could have saved for this trip instead."

Her reasoning was logical, but that didn't mean I'm ready to give up. "Porter got all new sports equipment last week even though you guys just spent a ton of money on him for other things. Way more than the money I'm asking for to go to New York City."

Mom turned to me, filter full of fresh dark roast grounds in her hands, and said, "Your brother's situation is different. We're investing in a hobby that could lead him somewhere."

My lips parted. "My baking—"

Her laugh was abrupt. "You're only baking because the woman next door put it in your head that you can make it work as a career. I'm sorry, Ivy, but I don't see it happening. Most of the things you make end up in the trash anyway. That's perfectly good food wasted, not to mention money. A trip to New York City with your class isn't going to get you any further with that silly dream of yours."

Swallowing down the hurt, I fell back into the seat at the table and watched her finish prepping the coffee and turning on the machine.

When her eyes met mine, her head tilted in exasperation.

"Don't look at me like that. I didn't say that to upset you. I'm being realistic. Porter is good at what he does. He loves football and your father agrees he could get a scholarship someday to a good college."

"How come you don't believe in me like you do in him?" I asked, unable to keep our gazes locked in fear of what I'd see. "Mrs. Griffith says I can do whatever I want if I believe in myself."

My mother grumbled as her slippers shuffle around the kitchen and she grabbed a coffee cup from above the sink. "*Mrs. Griffith* obviously doesn't know what it's like to struggle. People who have the means can do whatever they want, but we are not those people. The sooner you realize that, the quicker you'll understand that life is not a Hallmark movie. You're fourteen, Ivy. It's time you start thinking about an honest future for yourself so you don't end up—"

My eye twitched at her abrupt stop. I stared down at the dirt on the floor I must have tracked in after meeting Aiden at our fort until I heard another sigh escape her.

"I want what's best for both of my children. Parents have to learn lessons to help teach their kids. I'm saving you from making my same mistakes."

When I finally found the courage to lift my head and face her, she wasn't even looking at me. Her eyes were trained on the coffee dribbling into the half-full pot in front of her. "And what mistakes are those? Having us in the first place? It seems like that's a recurring regret you like to remind us of."

The room grew eerily quiet save the *drip, drip, drip* of coffee as it fills to the top of the pot.

"I swear, I don't know how to handle you and your mouth sometimes," she replied sometime later. She poured herself a cup of coffee before walking over to the table without glancing at me once. "I don't need all this extra chaos right now, Ivy. And that's all you are when you throw these little tantrums. I'm sorry I can't be like your friend's mother, but you're stuck with me. If you don't like it, perhaps you should go to Grandma Gertie's for a little while."

The comment made me stiffen. "What?"

Mom set her cup down and picked up her checkbook again. Her eyes shifting to me. "I'm not saying I don't love you, but you create more chaos than I need. It seems like nothing I do is enough. I give you money for food and you complain about not having money to go to the city. I ask you to watch Porter while I go to the store and help your father and you act like I'm ruining your life. What do I need to do to show you I'm trying here? What do I have to do to get it through your head that life isn't fair?"

My lips opened to say something, but I realized I had nothing. No suggestion. No comeback. Not even an apology. Because I'd learned not even those could mend what distance was separating us further and further from each other with every conversation we had.

"Maybe going to Gertie's wouldn't be so bad," she admonished. Gertie lives clear across the state, close to the Canadian border. "She loves baking. I'm sure she could teach you a thing or two. And it's no big city, but she lives in a far bigger town than Haven Falls. There are opportunities for you that we can't offer here."

"Are you really trying to get rid of me?"

She closed her eyes and said nothing.

"You'd feel bad if I left," I informed her, standing up and waiting for a reply. "You'd miss me, especially because I wouldn't be around to distract Porter while you and Dad argue about something stupid."

Her voice is pained when she replied, "Go to your room please. I don't want to see your face for the rest of the day."

I did as she asks, but her words echoed in my head as I slipped on a pair of shoes, opened my bedroom window as quietly as possible, and threw a leg over the pane.

I don't want to see your face.

It wasn't the first time she'd told me that.

~

I know as soon as I walk in the house after a long shift at work and see all the girls stuffed into the small living room that there's some sort of house meeting going on. And since I wasn't invited, their cautious eyes as I enter say it's about me. I stop by the archway and look around, meeting Raine's eyes, which instantly drop to the floor.

"What's going on?" I ask.

Sydney flattens her shirt, which looks way too fancy for a night in. She always dresses to impress whenever Remi comes over. "We've been waiting for you. I have some bad news that I had to discuss with the girls to prepare them."

Dread fills my stomach.

She walks over and gives me the fakest sympathetic smile known to man. "I'm sorry to have to tell you this, but we can't let you live in the basement anymore. The owners came over and said we could get in a lot of trouble if anyone finds out you live in a room that isn't thoroughly inspected. I'm sure you get it."

My heart thumps wildly in my chest at the news that bitch-slaps me in the face as my eyes snap to the others, specifically Raine, who still can't look at me. "So, what?" I let out a sharp breath before gripping the strap of my bag until my fingers are white. "There's no other room I can take? I can sleep on the cou—"

"We all decided," the she-devil says, cutting me off and smiling at me with her intentions leaking out of her eyes. "We're sorry, Ivy. If you need help packing, I'm sure one of the girls can give you a hand."

A million thoughts swirl in my head as I'm dismissed, but none of them can be verbalized past the shock. Jaw tight, I walk downstairs and hear the sudden chatter from the living room fade into nothingness.

Sitting on the edge of the bed, I drop my backpack on the floor and look around. I shouldn't be upset, but now it's back to square one, and I'm staring at defeat in the form of stained ceilings, half-finished walls, and poor hospitality. Once the shock wears off, I won't miss the horrible smell, the leaks, or the parties.

I'll be better off.

Happier, even.

It isn't until hesitant footsteps come down some minutes later when I make myself stand and pretend not to care that any of this is happening. The aching feeling to release some of the stress in my body comes back full force when I see Raine pop up at the doorway. I've managed to push off the feeling before, telling myself not to go back to that place that demands relief. With every heavy blow I'm dealt, it becomes harder to ignore the need to succumb to old habits.

"Ivy?" Raine's quiet voice does little to ease my clenched fists as she walks farther in. All I can think about is which way to release the pressure crawling under my skin, how I can get back some semblance of control. "I'm so sorry. She sprung this on us out of nowhere. I mean, her godparents did come and look around, but none of us knew they told her you had to go. It seemed like they were just here to check in."

I don't want to fault her or anyone else here for what Sydney and her pretentious connections do. "She makes the rules around here," I murmur, squatting down and collecting my duffel bags from underneath the bed. "There isn't anything you could have done."

"I tried telling her you could stay in my room until we figured something else out. Caleb wouldn't have cared if he couldn't sleep over. He likes you. But…"

Sighing, I stand and drop the bags onto my unmade mattress. Unzipping them, I give her an unconvincing, "It's fine. Sydney never liked me anyway, so it was bound to happen. I'm sure this is her way of finally getting me out of the way so she can have—" I cut myself off abruptly, my bitter tone swallowed down when I remember who I'm talking to. The girlfriend of Aiden's friend. His new best friend.

I don't look at her when she says, "He doesn't like her, Ivy."

Throat bobbing, I shake my head and start stuffing clothes forcefully into one of the duffel bags and gesture toward the other. "Can you pack those shirts and jeans into that bag? I'll handle the other stuff. It'll be faster."

A small hand meets my arm. "Come on. Talk to me."

"There's nothing to say," I snap. Shaking her off, I continue packing, hoping she'll drop it.

But she's just like DJ. "You've got friends who care about you. I know we've only hung out that once, but I'd like to think we're friends. And I texted Caleb, who's probably told Aiden by—"

"Of course you did." I pause what I'm doing to shoot her an annoyed look while clenching a worn old band tee in my hands that I stole from one of the guys I stayed with a while back. "Listen, Raine. I like you. You're a nice person. But I'm at rock bottom right now, and if you keep talking, I'm going to lose it again. And I can't go back to that place because I don't know if I'll be able to pull myself out of it."

"What place?"

I go to answer but quickly press my lips together, grinding my teeth to refrain from admitting the truth. *Don't think about it*, I tell myself. Despite my silent chides, I shiver over the memory of cold, grubby tile under my bleeding body. The way the blade felt against my skin. How...freeing it was knowing the helplessness would go away once and for all until I realized I wasn't free at all.

That desperation is creeping its way back in, taunting me at another failed endeavor. I'm homeless again, but I still have more than I did last time I was booted out from under the roof sheltering me.

I have a job.

I have school.

I could ask Bea—

"Where'd you go?" Raine's voice cuts in, distant, but thick with concern.

When I look at her again, I feel nothing. No energy. No anger. Only emptiness. And I don't let myself go back to the days leading up to the ambulance taking me away because I know all too well what that would do to me.

I'm better now.

I've got something to work toward.

I have things to lose, which means they're things to fight for.

"Nowhere," I rasp, anxiety winding around my windpipe and choking me. "Are you going to help me pack or not? I want to leave."

Want. It's hard not to snort at the word choice, as if this is my decision, but it's better than facing reality and accepting that *unwanted* is the most accurate term that surrounds my existence. My parents proved that a long time ago, and in some ways, Aiden did too. Then again, I fed into that, made myself believe I was better off without any of them when that was the furthest thing from the truth. At least where Aiden was involved.

I think back to the first time Mom indicated I should go to Gertie's house. How she constantly reminded me it'd be better if I left by feigning false excitement, as if there were better things waiting for me at my grandma's place. How many times had she pushed me in that direction? Made it seem like it was the best option for everybody?

For a moment, I think Raine's going to tell me no, but eventually she helps get my things divided between my two duffel bags until there's no room for anything else.

I grab one and put it over my shoulder. "I don't need the bed or bedding, so someone else can have it. Or throw it away. I'm sure it's not quality standard around here and doubt it'll sell for anything."

Pain laces into Raine's features. "Ivy—"

"Don't worry about it." The smile on my face is effortless because I've had to mold one like it countless other times to show my sanity, as fragile as it may be.

I sidestep her and walk upstairs, refusing to acknowledge the people I pass. I'm sure Sydney is among them, looking smug like she just won a competition I had no chance at winning. My skin itches from the acceptance that this walk of shame is being witnessed by a houseful of people I never got along with, making it somehow worse than if they were complete strangers.

Hearing Raine call my name as I close the front door a little too hard, I keep my gaze forward as if I'm walking with a purpose.

You can break when you're alone, I tell myself bitterly, holding back the frustrated tears that well in my eyes. *Head in the game.*

When I'm halfway down the street, headlights come into view and blind me. I block the light with a raised hand as the fancy sports car stops beside me, the window rolling down until a familiar cocky smile fills the space. "Need a lift?"

I should tell him no. Sydney certainly wouldn't like me getting into Remi's car. But then again, since when do I care?

"Sure." When I hear the locks click, I open the back door to toss my things inside. Another vehicle rounds the bend, causing my stomach to sink when I realize who it is.

As soon as the black truck stops, I quickly drop my other bag into the seat and slam the car door shut, hoping to get away before anything is said.

Luck is never on my side though.

"Don't even fucking think about it," Aiden yells as he jumps out of his truck and storms toward me.

Opening the passenger door, I'm bending to get into the pricy set of wheels when a hand snakes around my arm. I snap my head toward the person holding me back. "If you don't let me go, I'll scream, Aiden."

He's openly glaring right back. "Don't go with him."

I yank my arm away. "It's none of your business who I get into a car with. I swear to god if you—*son of a bitch!*" My body is being thrown over a broad, muscular shoulder before I know what's happening.

Another door opens and Remi's obnoxious voice calls out, "What the fuck, man?"

"Sorry," Aiden says. "You're going to have to find another way to get your dick wet tonight, fucktard."

I smack his back with my fists. "You asshole! Who said I was going to sleep with him?"

When he opens his truck door and drops me onto the bench seat, I grunt on impact and do my best to show my displeasure with being thrown around. My face goes completely slack when he says, "Isn't that what you do, Ivy? How you pay them for somewhere to sleep?"

Before I can even think of a reply, he's moving my legs out of the way and slamming the door. I'm frozen in my seat with gaping lips when he confronts the snobby frat boy by his car. I don't know what's said and I'm not sure I want to. All I see is Aiden fishing my bags from the back seat before tossing them into the bed of his truck and climbing in beside me.

My arms hug my knees tightly to my chest, my feet propped on the edge of the seat in a protective stance. "I'm not a whore," I whisper, failing at patching the internal wall up as a tear slides down my cheek.

He turns the truck on, not looking at me once as he puts it into drive. "No, baby. You're a survivor."

Chapter Eleven

AIDEN

THE GUYS ARE ALL packed in the kitchen, arms crossed, shoulder to shoulder, in silence as they stare at me with a mixture of raised brows, stoic faces, and indifference. Nobody has said a word since I told them Ivy is going to stay downstairs with me.

Justin leans against his crutches and reaches for the closest pizza box I brought home as bribery. "I don't know why you called this meeting. The girlfriends stay here all the time anyway and nobody cares."

Raine does spend a lot of time here with Caleb, though she's absent for this conversation because of some school event, and a couple of the other guys have steady girlfriends or consistent hookups that spend the night a few times a week. "Ivy isn't my girlfriend though."

DJ hops onto the counter with his go-to energy drink in hand. He has enough energy on his own, but he doesn't go without one a day at the least. "You know I don't mind having a chick like that as a roommate, especially if she's up for dibs."

A few of the guys try hiding their snickers and choke them down behind their fists when I eye them. "Watch it, DJ. I can still take you down on the field."

He raises a hand, chortling. "Yeah, yeah. Hands off the goods. We got it. Can we eat now? I don't think any of us are going to bitch about the new addition to the house. Most of us already like her for putting people in their places in class, and now that we know she can bake, that means we have our own Martha Stewart living downstairs."

I roll my eyes. "She's not here to cook, bake, or do anything for you. Any of you." My eyes go to each one of them until my point is across.

DJ keeps going. "Plus, it isn't like any of us are going to start anything with her when you two will be going at it like— *umph*." Caleb smacks him in the chest, causing DJ to glower. "Jesus, dude. Fine. I'll shut up about it. I was making a point none of you fuckers can refute. Can we eat the pizza now?"

All the others watch with interest, some of them darting between me and the food waiting in front of us, others waiting to see what else I have to say.

Christ. "Eat. I'm going downstairs."

I push off the counter and turn to leave when Caleb stops me. "At least take some down with you. She might be hungry. Something tells me she won't be willing to come up and get any herself for a while."

I cuss and accept a couple pieces before nodding at him. When I make it back down to her, Ivy is sitting on the end of the couch with her legs curled under her and her arms crossed over her chest as she stares at the blank TV.

Dropping a slice of pepperoni pizza on a napkin on the table, I gesture toward the flat-screen. "That turns on, you know. It'll show you magic pictures with a click of a button."

Slowly, her fierce eyes peel away from it and toward me. She blinks once, the honey tone darkening, then drops her gaze toward the abandoned pizza. "I know what a TV is and how it works, ass. Just because I didn't have one of my own for years doesn't mean I forgot how one works." I try to say something to ease her irritation over the bad joke but before I can, she adds, "And I'm not staying here."

"The guys don't care."

"But *I* do," she states, dropping her legs onto the floor. "Christ, don't you listen? I don't want your charity or pity. I don't want your pizza or your teammates' opinions about me t—"

I bark out a laugh, realizing what this is really about. "Think with your head, not your pride. Who the fuck cares about what my teammates think?"

She stands and faces me, our height difference making it hard to find her as intimidating as she probably wants me to. I fight the smirk that wavers my lips, making her scowl harder. "I don't need your friends thinking that we're screwing. It's bad enough I've had to hear about you and Sydney. I'd like to be shown some courtesy about who I do or don't choose to hook up with and who knows it."

My face twists. "Sydney?"

"My former housemate" is her dumbfounded response.

When I was directed to her old housemate's room, I honestly wasn't sure who'd open the door. All I knew from Raine and Caleb in prior conversation is that Sydney rules the place with her catty commands and spiteful personality. The day she opened her bedroom door, I'd been surprised that it was the only girl at Lindon I'd messed around with to blow off some steam. We'd never exchanged names, and it never lasted long because I'd make an escape before certain lines were crossed. "I know who she is. I'm wondering what the hell there is to talk about. Her and I aren't anything."

"Not according to her."

Sydney has always been a clinger, which is why I should have never agreed to hang with her to begin with. It was DJ who introduced us and Caleb who warned me away. I hadn't spoken to her in months before knocking on her damn door that day. "Whatever you heard is bullshit. Don't let people like her get to you."

Her eye twitches.

"And," I add, stepping toward her without breaking eye contact, "don't let whatever shit my team gives you go to heart. They like to talk smack. It's nothing. You deal with a few of them in class, so you know that already. Quit making excuses as to why you can't stay. None of us are asking for rent or for you to do chores or cook us shit. There are no strings, only a place to sleep. Which, in case you've forgotten, you need right now. It isn't like you haven't taken me up on the offer before. The pact, remember?"

This time, she says nothing. Her eyes don't falter from locking with mine, the challenge to go as long as she can without blinking evident in her gaze. I succumb first, breaking contact and sighing.

"Being stubborn is going to get you nowhere, Chaos. I'm going to make that clear now before you try convincing me otherwise. Feel me?"

Bending forward, I hear the sharpest inhale of breath come from her as my face nears hers. The caress of her hot breath brushes my cheek as I reach around her and grab the food from the table, my lips grazing her jaw in the process. I wonder if she can hear how hard my heart is beating right now, all because of her. Her citrus scent, her hot breath, her warm body heat soaking into me. It drives me fucking crazy, and my cock hardens just being near her.

Returning to full height, I try to act like she doesn't affect me. "Eat up."

She stares at the food offering with a small frown on her face that I'd like to think is disappointment. Lips curling, I pick up one of her hands and place the pizza on her palm since she won't accept it on her own.

After she meets my eyes again, there's a glint in them that I can't quite read until she blows out a breath and says, "You're annoying as hell, you know that?"

I give her an easy shrug. "People who care will irritate you no matter if you like it or not. That's how you know they're legit."

Her head tilts. "Are you? Legit?"

Chuckling lightly, I tip my chin toward the food in her hand and back up. "Eat. I'll be in my room if you need anything. Let me know when you're ready for bed."

Another sigh. "Aiden—"

I wink and shut the door behind me, knowing she won't follow. Maybe I should be worried that she'll up and leave, but her bags are currently sprawled on my bed. If she does bolt, she'll have nothing but the clothes on her back, and something tells me she won't easily let go of what she's collected over the years.

It's hours later when I'm finishing up a few assignments and realize there's utter silence coming from the room outside mine. When I glance at the clock and notice it's past midnight, I grab a blanket from my tiny closet and check to see if she's still there.

Ivy is curled up on the couch, her hands under her cheek like a pillow, fast asleep, when I approach. I watch her for a few moments, seeing how her full chest rises and falls to a slow, peaceful rhythm before sighing to myself.

Instead of draping the blanket over her, I carefully put one arm under her knees and the other under her back and scoop her into my arms. She's as light as I remember her, but I try not thinking about how much I missed this. Holding her while she slept. Having her near me. It tightens my chest to think about the time apart when she experienced that with other men.

She murmurs and squirms but settles against my chest as I walk us back to my room and gently place her on the bed.

It isn't until I'm flicking the lights off, peeling off my shirt, and sliding down my jeans to crawl in beside her that her groggy voice penetrates the room. "What are you doing?"

I smack the pillow a few times before resting against it. "Go to sleep, Ivy."

She shifts when I cover us with the comforter and says something unintelligible that I don't bother trying to make out.

"Shh," I say, turning on my side so my back is to her. If I face her, if I inch closer, she'll feel how hard I am and the moment will be ruined. I'm not trying to fuck her, to give her mixed signals or expectations like her staying here has to mean something between us. I want her friendship back. I want *her*.

"Let me have this, Chaos. For old times' sake." My voice is hard, bordering desperate, as I deliver the statement.

For once, she doesn't fight me.

And for once, I can finally *breathe*.

Chapter Twelve

IVY

I'M WALKING INTO ONE of the bathrooms in Myers Hall after another crushing exam grade and stop in front of the water-stained mirror. My reflection is haggard, the makeup contoured on my face doing little to hide the exhaustion lingering even though I've been sleeping better than I have in a long time next to Aiden.

The body heat wrapped around me at night does little to chase away the things that resurface when my conscious is at its weakest though. I always get trapped remembering the choices I made, which led to some of my darkest moments. And every time I wake up in a cold sweat, Aiden is right there to pull me into his arms and tell me it's just a nightmare.

But it's not. Every time I wake up slick with sweat, chest heavy, and mind warped with anxiety, I know it's my own doing. I pretend to be okay, but I'm not. I pretend to be strong, but I'm not. How can I be when I've let my weaknesses get the better of me?

Sleep has always been hard for me. The few hours I get are the best I can do because I always force myself to wake up before something bad happens. You can never be too careful when there's a stranger sleeping next to you—you never know who invited you inside their home or what their intentions are past sex.

Yet Aiden's reassurance is the biggest reason I never fight being carried to his bedroom every time I fall asleep on the couch. I curl up on his suede sofa watching something mundane on the television knowing the next time I open my eyes will be in a room surrounded by the only person I've ever called friend.

Next to his strong body.

His kind heart.

He never complains when I take the blankets or hog his pillows, and that's *if* I'm not using him as my own personal body pillow. We don't talk about morning breath or the clear morning wood he sports or make a big deal out of it. We never used to then either, but there was never this tension—a tiny, invisible string attaching us that could break easily if we let it.

Blowing out a breath, I run the cold water and splash some on my overheated face. The poor exam grade isn't going to hurt my GPA *that* bad. I'll pass, which is a miracle considering I don't understand what's going on half the time. School has never been my strong suit, something I used to be reminded of when report cards were sent home to my parents' house when I was younger. The Cs and Ds always sprouted another argument between them until the end result would be me promising to raise my grades by the end of the year. With Aiden's help, I always did. Unlike me, he was a brainiac. Everything came so easy for him, and it made me feel embarrassed when he'd help me study for something and it'd take three times as long for anything to stick in my head.

Even now, I can tell little has changed. Knowing his perfect GPA, I suppose I shouldn't be surprised that he can wait until the last minute to do an assignment and still come home with an A when I'd spend weeks on a project and still barely scrape by with a B minus.

The biggest plus side to my new living arrangement, as temporary as I swear it'll be, is that Aiden's place isn't very loud. Yet I still find myself struggling to concentrate on my work if the famed footballer is in the same room as I am. If he's sitting on the other end of the couch while I'm studying, I find myself peeking at him through my lashes instead of absorbing the information in my lap. His presence interferes with my focus—he'll shift on the cushion, glance at me with those piercing eyes that see through a person, or simply *breathe*, and I forget what I'm doing.

Being around him has dug up old demons that stir up the memories of my presence being an inconvenience to my parents. I've let myself bury that feeling for the past four years, not letting myself get in anybody's way so I'd never have to feel it again. It's hard not to feel like I'm a bother now when I'm letting Aiden back in. Letting him help when everything in me wants to fight that. I do better when people aren't looking out for me because there's nobody to disappoint when things go south. And because I'm me, *Chaos*, they always do.

Letting the water run, I stare absently at it while trying to pull away from the slick feeling that still crawls just beneath the surface of my soul begging to be let out. I've felt it before. The cloudiness in my head, blurred focus, and tightening chest, and suddenly the only thing I can think about is the release of pain and lack of control creeping up on me.

Swallowing, I dig through my bag anxiously for anything that will do.

Don't do it.

Don't do it.

Don't do it.

I find a pen cap buried at the bottom of my bag that's jagged from being chewed with subconscious anxiety. I frown at the sharp plastic edges, knowing it won't do, but still lift the sleeve of my shirt anyway and find an unmarked piece of skin on my forearm. With a racing heart, I put the sharp edge against my flesh and begin digging it in just as the door swings open. I drop the cap with a startled breath into the sink basin and watch the ripples float it away.

A couple girls I've never seen before walk in and give me small smiles before disappearing behind the stall doors across from me, leaving me watching the blue pen cap and debating my next step.

I need relief but…

My throat bobs with a struggled swallow.

I turn off the faucets.

Grab my bag.

And walk out.

I don't want to see your face again.

Mom's words hold tight and squeeze.

But the pressure never bursts.

～

I'm absent-minded at the bakery, and Elena's persistence in making conversation makes it hard to sink into routine without notice. "What's going on with you and Aiden? He came in here all the time when you were sick to get you things like a boyfriend would or something."

As I finish making a hot chocolate for one of the customers waiting, I say, "Not that it's any of your business, but nothing is going on. Are you going to help me with this or not?"

"Are you going to quit lying?" she quips, walking over and grabbing a few requested pastries from the case with a grin.

"I'm not." I walk over to the young woman and her eager-looking little girl with the kind of curly hair my brother used to have when he was younger. I pass the mother her drink and give her daughter a small smile before focusing back on Lena perched against the counter. She doesn't need to know where I spend my nights, or she'll start planning some football-themed wedding. "Quit staring at me like that and get back to work, twerp."

She sticks out her tongue and flicks my hair before getting the rest of the order set. "You know you love me. And when are you going to let me do your hair? I'm sure Aiden would love to see something new."

I choose to ignore her. "Get the banana nut cookies out of the back, please. Your grandma wants to get the last tray sold before closing."

Like Bea, her hand goes to her hip in exasperation. "You can't avoid this conversation forever, Ivyprofen. I see the way he looks at you when he comes in. It's not the same way it used to be. It's…I don't know. Intense."

Ignoring the statement, I hip bump her out of the way and greet the next customer. When a middle-aged man walks up to the counter wearing a jacket that says COACH, a baseball cap with Lindon's logo on it, and a stoic expression on his face, I'm surprised when the first words out of his mouth are, "So you're the girl that's got my best player all twisted up."

I hear Lena's squeak from behind me. From the corner of my eye, I see her grip her drink and stare between me and the man I can only assume is Lindon's football coach based on his attire and brazen remark. "Can I get you anything?" I ask instead of entertaining his question.

The man crosses his arms over his chest, clearly uncaring of the people lining up behind him. "You can explain why you decided to make a move on my player right before *his* big move."

I blink at his dry comment, replaying it in my head before asking, "Excuse me?"

"I normally stay out of my players' business, but I think of Aiden as a son and want to see him succeed. Those boys gossip worse than middle-school girls, and the second your name popped up, I knew there'd be trouble."

My face heats as the young couple behind him start whispering. "Er…"

Elena clears her throat. "We're in the middle of a midafternoon rush, Coach Pearce. If you don't want to order anything, you should probably head out so everyone else can get something."

I give the teenager a quick, grateful look.

"I want no trouble for you two or your grandma," Coach Pearce tells us, looking directly at me as he says it. "I'm just here to say that if you really care about him, then you'll step away until he gets his life figured out. If it's meant to work out, then it will, but you're both young and I've seen a lot of men with great potential lose it because they've made untimely decisions."

Untimely decisions.

How many times am I going to be called that in my lifetime?

Elena's hand taps mine from under the counter, wrapping around it and squeezing once in comfort before directing a firm tone I've never heard from her at the coach. "You should probably go."

I count my breaths as the man tips his head once at her and steps out of the line, but not before digging into his pocket and stuffing twenty dollars in the tip jar on the counter.

For some reason, that's more infuriating than the insinuation I'm a gold-digging mistake. I pluck out the bill, walk around the counter to him, and shove it into his chest until he has no other option but to take it back. "I don't need whatever this is, because unlike your rude assumption, I don't like free handouts." Dropping my voice when customers start turning to us, I add, "And considering I've known Aiden since I was nine, I think I can confidently say he's the type of person who can make his own choices without his coach or anyone else butting in. If he wants me out of his life, I won't stop him from shutting the door in my face. Frankly, he'd be better off if he did, and I've told him as much already. But you and I both know he's not that kind of guy."

His eyebrows arch in surprise as he slowly wraps the twenty-dollar bill in his fingers and stares down at it. I take a step back and wait for him to say something, anything, but all he gives me is a cleared throat and a "No, he's not."

When he leaves, I walk silently back to my spot behind the register where Elena has already taken new orders for me to fill. She gives me a concerned look that I brush off as we work together to get the customers cleared out as fast as we can. It goes like that for half an hour before there aren't any more people coming or going.

Eventually, I pour myself a cup of coffee, slowly mix in some milk and sugar while my young coworker watches, and murmur, "Sorry about the money. You probably would have liked to keep it."

Her hand waves in dismissal. "It's okay."

I pause, staring at the steam coming from the hot liquid in the ceramic mug. "Maybe you can help me with my hair when we're both free one of these weekends."

The teenager bounces, her hands clapping a little too loudly. "Really? What color? I think you'd look amazing with rainbow streaks. Or what about unicorn—"

"I'm already regretting this," I groan, walking away from her with my drink. Her laugh echoes as I escape to the back and absorb the coach's words in silence.

It wouldn't be the first time someone has thought the worst of me, but it felt great for once putting someone in their place instead of taking it. How many times had Aiden told me to do that in the past? He'd get upset that I didn't stand up for myself even though I tried explaining it was easier to avoid confrontation.

I find myself smiling knowingly because Aiden would be proud of me, only trying to dull my wavering lips when Elena shoots me a curious look when she walks into the back room and asks, "What's the smile for?"

I simply shrug and say, "Mind your business."

~

Porter threw another tantrum over not being able to have friends over for his eighth birthday. Based on the way Mom rubbed her temples, she was seconds away from losing it. She'd been getting headaches a lot lately, and I tried doing whatever I could to make her stress less, but it usually never works.

I'm supposed to get ice cream with Aiden, so I did something I usually don't. "Want to come along with me and Aiden to Cones?"

My little brother's eyes quickly shot to Mom to ask in silent permission. Her head picked up to examine us, me longer than Porter, before pressing her lips together and nodding once.

She eventually replied with a firm, "Fine, but watch your brother carefully. Don't let him out of your sight. I don't want anything happening to him."

My lips twitched and I'm tempted to ask, *And what about if something happens to me?* But I choose not to poke the bear today. "I won't."

Hesitation crept into her eyes before she walked over to her purse and stifled through it. Her shoulders tightened and then dropped. "I only have three dollars on me right now."

Porter started to whine, but I didn't let him get far because Mom would only get irritated. "I have money. I'll pay for both of us." I wouldn't tell her that Aiden will probably get money from his mom that he'd most likely pay with. Mom didn't like it when Mrs. Griffith gave me things. She said we didn't take free handouts, that we worked for things in this household.

When Mom turned around, there was sadness in her eyes I didn't understand. But I also didn't feel like analyzing the dull gaze, so I tugged on Porter's hand and told him to put his shoes on so we could leave.

When it's just me and Mom, I'm surprised to hear, "Thank you for doing that. I know you don't like sharing time with your friend."

I liked that Aiden was all mine, but sometimes we had to sacrifice things for the greater good. If Mom wasn't stressed, she'd be happier. And when she was happier, she and Dad wouldn't fight. Well, not as much at least.

It was a win for everyone, especially me.

Aiden didn't seem fazed to see Porter trailing close behind me as we walked down our driveway where he was waiting. He was in a pair of cargo shorts and a loose T-shirt I'd seen him wear tons of times. It had some famous football team across the front, but the words were faded from all the wash and wear.

"Hey, dude," he greeted my brother, offering him a hand, which Porter smacked eagerly. Whenever I tell him I'm going to hang out with Aiden, he'd get angry with me when I said he couldn't go too.

They chitchatted as we walked down the street, talking about school and sports and other things that I slowly tuned out. One of the neighbors waved at us, which we all returned.

When Cones came into view, I took Porter's hand, but he fought me. "You know I have to hold your hand when we cross the street. There's a lot of traffic here."

"No!" he smacked my hand away as we stopped at the edge of the sidewalk. "I'm not a baby, Ivy! Just don't tell Mom."

"Porte—"

"No!" he yelled louder, making me cringe when people across the street turned to see what the commotion was.

My face blasted with heat as I exchanged a panicked look with Aiden. He turned to Porter and knelt in front of him. "You don't want your mom to be upset if you get hurt crossing the street, do you?" he asked my annoying little brother.

The brat twisted his face and crossed his arms in defiance, clearly not caring.

Aiden tried again. "Do you want Ivy to get into trouble if something happens? I'm sure she promised your mom to take care of you."

There was contemplation on Porter's face. A moment where his eyes peeked up at me through his lashes before he returned his focus to our neighbor. Slowly, his head shook.

My friend nodded once. "Okay, then. Hold her hand only until you get to the other sidewalk, and then I'll get us all ice cream." I went to argue, but he cut me off. "Mom gave me extra money when I told her what we were doing. It's fine."

It wasn't, but I didn't tell him that.

Hopefully, Porter didn't tell Mom.

Two ice cream cones later and a bowl for Porter because it was hot out and he was a slow eater, and we were taking up one of the last picnic tables. Porter was swinging his legs back and forth on the bench on the other side of Aiden, seemingly content.

"You're quiet," Aiden said to me, nudging my shoulder with his. "Are you okay?"

My eyes went to Porter for a moment, my best friend understanding my lack of conversation. I think I saw his jaw tick before he goes back to his vanilla ice cream. I'd tried getting him to try new flavors before, but he always hated the ones I offered him and said, "There are certain things that shouldn't be made."

Clearing my throat and lowering my voice, I leaned in and whispered, "I think my parents might get a divorce."

His eyes roamed over me. "I'm sorry." He didn't sound it though. "Maybe that wouldn't be such a bad thing."

My heart dropped into my stomach when I considered he might be right. "Maybe," I murmured, eyes peeking at my little brother again. I knew it'd be a good thing because then we wouldn't have to deal with the cops showing up at our house all the time. The neighbors wouldn't talk. But then I wouldn't be able to spend so much time with Aiden at his house. I hated when my parents argued but I loved my sleepovers with my best friend.

Thankfully, my little brother seemed oblivious to my conflict. He was happy people watching rather than worrying about what our mom and dad did. His face lit up when he saw a dog on a leash walking toward Cones with a family, and Aiden picked up on it.

"You like dogs?" Aiden asked him.

Porter quickly nodded. "I want one, but Mom and Dad say—"

"They're a lot of work," Aiden finished for him, shooting me a knowing look, having heard it before. "Do you know I have a dog?"

Porter suddenly started acting shy, humming out a confirmation of his knowledge about Cap. He'd asked me about him before, wondering if he could take him on walks. I told him no because Cap would pull him too much since he was so big.

"Maybe you can play with him," Aiden said, like Mrs. Griffith told me.

I found myself staring in awe, unsurprised by his kindness but still taken all the same. I was lucky to have him. I told myself that every single day. He was the first person I thought of when I woke up and the last person who crossed my mind when I went to sleep.

Mostly because he was close by.

It wasn't my parents I thought of.

It wasn't Porter.

It was Aiden Griffith.

I hoped that never changed.

Chapter Thirteen

AIDEN

"WE'RE TIED AT THE end of the third, but if Griffith keeps playing like he has tonight, the Dragons will take home yet another win," the sportscaster says as I grab water from the sidelines.

Coach Pearce walks over and slaps my back in praise. "Way to turn it around, son."

I'm nodding absently while looking at the packed crowd waving red-and-white school memorabilia at us. The person I want to see is probably serving coffee and pastries across town instead of front and center where I want her to be.

I left out an old jersey on the bed for her to wear today, but when I passed her on campus, she was in a pair of black jeans that clung to her long legs and a shirt that should be fucking illegal on her figure. She looked untouchable—her outfit screaming "fuck you" as a direct response to me.

I couldn't help but smile over it.

When I turn back to the crowd, I roll my eyes as DJ moves his hips to the music blasting like he's auditioning for

Magic Mike. The crowd cheers him on as he dances in his gear, and I watch as Matt and a couple other guys join him to do the electric slide along the sidelines.

Caleb walks over and bumps my shoulder with his, chuckling over our teammates. "That was crazy back there, man. You were dragging two guys as big as you all the way to the end zone and still wouldn't go down."

I shrug it off like it's no big deal, wiping my arm across the sweat that trickles down the side of my face before putting my helmet back on and fastening it. "It's whatever."

Justin comes over and stops short of us, using his crutches as leaning posts. "How the hell did you even catch that? I thought for sure we were fucked after Wallace tried running the play himself."

There's no doubt Coach is going to chew our asses out as soon as the game is done, especially after what Wallace tried doing on the field. "I don't even know, dude. Just happened."

He snickers. "And did you see the look on Erikson's face? Priceless. He was *pissed* his guys couldn't take you down. Beast, bro. Beast."

DJ walks over to us with his hands in the air, pumping as a group of girls from the stands scream louder at him. "We're all going to get laid tonight, boys. I can feel it."

"Don't get cocky," I warn, knowing damn well the game isn't over yet. "Anything can happen still. They almost took down Dicky and Lamar, and without Brady..."

DJ stops me with a hard smack to the back. "But we have you, me, and Caleb, so there's no way they can get us now. And as much of a fucker as Wallace is, he'll help get us the upper hand and round out the score."

My eyes go to the scoreboard. Being tied makes me uneasy with only fifteen minutes to go. We haven't tied all season, which means anything can happen. Two of our guys are being targeted since they're the strongest defense we have, and Wallace is still acting like his shit doesn't stink out on the field. "Only if Wallace plays by the books. I was lucky to even catch that pass. He made it out of desperation, which made it hard to figure out his move."

Justin nudges me. "But you caught it out of necessity. Fuck Wallace, dude. I sure as hell won't give him any thought after seeing that."

It's DJ who snickers at Justin's biting remark. "That's because you're still bitter he took your spot, J-Dog."

Justin ignores the remark and watches DJ run toward the nearest group of fans, climbing the fencing to start smacking some of their hands. When it's just the three of us again, our captain looks to Caleb with a hesitant expression before turning to me. "So, uh, I heard a couple of the guys talking about something that happened earlier."

I set the water down on the bench and cross my arms. "What?"

Caleb gestures toward Coach. "Ivy got a visit from Coach. We're not sure everything that was said, but you know how Coach is with your career. He always tries protecting it."

Justin nods. "Daria, Lamar's girl, was at Bea's and overheard him tell her to back off. I don't think he threatened her. It was more of a warning."

"And before you lose your shit," Caleb intervenes when I make a move toward where Coach is talking to the assistant coach beside him. "Your girl dished it right back at him like we all know she can. She handled herself."

"Daria and her friends said they'd never seen Coach look embarrassed, but nobody knows what Ivy told him," our QB confirms.

My shoulders tense as I eye Coach, who's oblivious to my pointed glare. "He shouldn't have approached her at all. What the hell is he thinking?"

The guys both shrug, but Caleb says, "You remember what supposedly happened to his son when he got drafted a few years ago? Got some chick pregnant and ended up getting bad press when she sued for child support when he wouldn't marry her. He's probably afraid to see you taken advantage of, since you're like a son to him too, and he doesn't know Ivy."

"Exactly," I growl.

"I shouldn't have said anything," Justin mumbles, sighing. "Whatever was said between them is done with. I figured you should know in case your girl is off tonight."

Before any of us can say anything else, Coach calls us to huddle. When we circle up, he looks at all of us. "You done gossiping, princesses? We've got a game to win." We all clammer up and hear out the next play, nodding along to his direction even if my teeth are grinding the entire time he talks. When he's finished, he eyes each one of us. "Don't fuck up. I ain't about to get my ass handed to me by goddamn Erikson or the missus tonight because you decided to let the last quarter get to you. I'm talking to you two, Wallace and Bridges."

I notice DJ flinch at the mention of his name. He may hate Wallace, but his attitude isn't that different from the newbie's. I've told him before to tone it down, and usually he listens, but on game days like this when we're playing a good team, it's even more vital he remembers what to focus on. Everything else is white noise.

When we break on three and run back out to the field, I can feel the adrenaline pumping in my veins.

Don't fuck up.

I drown out the crowd.

Shut off my brain.

And I give it my all.

By the final buzzer, we barely scrape by with a 27–24 win. A few of the opposing team members give us handshakes, others shoot off at the mouth, and Caleb has to hold back Wallace from going over and starting something that will get him kicked off the team. We may not like him, but we sure as hell need him if today is any indication.

Piled into the locker room and stripping out of our gear, Coach Pearce walks in and claps loudly to get everybody's attention. "Listen up, ladies, and listen good. You may have won today, but we still got our asses kicked out there. It shouldn't have been this close of a game when we had the upper hand in the first two quarters. Wallace," he barks, eyeing the stand-in quarterback. "You let them get in your head. Let them fucking *distract* you with their petty words. Bakersfield, you were running like Forrest Gump before his goddamn braces came off. I told you to go see the physical therapist, and I know for damn sure you skipped out twice in the last week. Lot of good that did you today. When I tell you to do something, you do it, and that goes for all of you. You're out next game, and I'm putting Rigger in your place."

My teammate gapes at him. "Coach—"

Coach doesn't let him finish. "Does it look like I'm leaving it up for discussion, boy? You all got a second chance by coming to play for *my* team, which means *I* get to say who I let play or not. If I tell you to take an extra ten minutes soaking in an ice bath, you do it. If I tell you to see the physical therapist for a checkup to make sure your body is good, you do it. If I think you need tutoring because your grades are sucking more ass than the Bulldogs this season, then you better see a tutor. See a pattern here?

"I'm not here to hold your hands and tell you everything is okay. I'm here to whip you into shape and win. Some of you have the talent to go pro, and you're wasting it by half-assing plays that should be easy to implement out there. You better believe the next practice we have, we're going ten times harder than normal until you know how serious I am. That includes conditioning."

The room breaks out in groans and murmurs that Coach chooses to ignore.

"We got lucky and that's the only reason I'm letting you off easy. Our next game is against Wilson Reed, and don't think for one second I'm going to let you screw that up."

Caleb elbows me, knowing what playing them means for me. My nostrils twitch at the thought of seeing the assholes who booted me to save themselves, all because they were pissed at how much airtime I was getting. Turns out some people don't do well with not being the center of attention. I learned the hard way what seasoned players will do to make sure you never outplay them.

I nod at him in reassurance before trailing my focus back to Coach while he looks around the room at his spent players.

He's right. We screwed up more times than I can count tonight. Dropped passes. Cracked defenses. These guys were good, but the Wilson Reed Raiders are better. They've always been the team to beat.

"I'm over it," Coach concludes, waving his clipboard at the team. "Clean up and get out of my face tonight. Rest up, fuel up, and we'll meet to watch tapes so I can rip into you about what the hell went wrong first thing Monday."

He exits, followed by the silent assistant coach, leaving us all to wash up and change. I'm waiting for Caleb outside the locker room when my phone buzzes. My parents reach out after games, but they usually give me time to get home. So when I see the name and the short text attached, I'm left staring at the screen in surprise.

Chaos: Heard it was a good game

I reread the text, then snort when a new one vibrates my phone.

Chaos: Still not wearing your jersey

A small grin curls my lips, and I only wipe it away when Caleb smacks my arm to indicate he's ready. His eyebrows raise as he looks at me, his eyes narrowing slowly before he snorts in amusement. "Let me guess. That look has to do with a blue-haired girl."

I say nothing, but I don't need to.

He shoves me.

I shove him back. "Let's grab some food before we head back."

After grabbing subs from our favorite deli in town, we go home to the girl in question where I find her studying on the couch. Her papers and books are scattered everywhere, and the laptop I told her she could use is sitting open on the coffee table in front of her, playing music.

Ivy may not say a lot to me when I'm home, but her roaming eyes tell me all I need to know when they linger in my direction.

I'm in serious fucking trouble.

"Whatever Coach told you today—"

"Don't, Aiden."

"Hear me out," I tell her anyway. "I don't know what Coach told you today, but ignore him. He's got his own problems and experiences that get in the way sometimes. He means well."

Her eyes stay on her paper for a full minute before she sighs and lifts her gaze, her face clear of makeup and her hair pulled back. "I realized something after he left the bakery."

I sit down next to her, picking up her legs and dropping them on my lap. "What?"

Her smile takes me by surprise, but not as much as when she says, "That I'm worth more than some washed-up former football player's opinion. He doesn't know anything about me, and he never will."

"Ivy—"

"No, listen. What he said sucked, and I won't lie, I wanted to throw something at him. But he knows nothing about me, so why should I let him dictate who I talk to? I can respect him for caring enough about you to warn me off, especially because Elena told me he used to be a pro player and probably has a lot of connections you can utilize."

"That shit doesn't matter to me."

A shoulder lifts casually. "It should though. You've wanted this for so long, so why not play by his rules? I'm not saying I'm going to run away because some middle-aged man with a serious attitude problem told me to. I'm ready to make something of myself for once. I'm done running, Aiden. It's going to take time when I've spent most of my life trying to blend in after being told how much of a bother I am, but I want to be better."

My throat bobs at her words. "And what about us?"

"What about us?" she returns quietly.

I look down at her bare legs, smooth and soft and slightly scarred from who knows what. I trace one of the white lines on her calf and wonder how she got it. "Are we okay?"

She barely pauses this time. "As okay as we can be. I'm far from perfect, Aiden. I'm going to say stupid shit and shut down. It's what I do. But I wouldn't mind..." Her lips rub together in hesitation. "I wouldn't mind a friend, even if you're only going to be around for another month."

My jaw ticks. "Coach told you?"

"Some of your teammates have loose lips," she murmurs, undeniable hurt slowly spreading across her face.

"I was going to tell you."

"You don't owe me anything."

"*Friends* tell each other everything." Or did she forget what that was like? Who's been in her corner for the past four years?

"If anybody gets a free pass, it's you," she teases halfheartedly, nudging me with her leg. "I owe you for taking care of me when I was sick, even if the medicine you gave me tasted like ass."

"How do you know what ass tastes like?"

All she does is grin.

It's a few moments of comfortable silence between us with nothing but the music playing on the laptop before I say, "You *are* worth more than anybody's opinions. I'm glad you know that now."

She fidgets with the paper on her lap. "It took me some time and a lot of bad experiences to realize it. But I'm kind of a badass."

I want to ask her to tell me about it.

But I don't.

I'm not sure I'm ready to know.

And I don't think she's ready to tell me.

"There's no 'kind of' about it, Ivy."

We share a look before mutually breaking eye contact and enjoying each other's company without another word spoken between us the rest of the night.

~

MOM flashes across my phone screen as I'm leaving the Arnold Sports Complex after getting reamed out again with the rest of the team about our last game. My body aches from a shitty night's sleep from being in an uncomfortable position that left a knot in my neck and a tweak in my shoulder. Ivy was using me as her own personal pillow, and I refused to move because everything about the way her body was wrapped around me felt like old times.

"Hey, Mom. It's not Wednesday."

With my packed schedule this semester, we agreed on Wednesday calls since I could carve out time easier for my parents. Mom asks me if I'm eating enough, seeing anyone, and keeping up with my grades, and Dad asks about football. By the time I hang up, two hours have usually gone by because Mom steals the phone back and hounds me about proper nutrition and getting enough sleep since I'm always on the go.

"I can't just check up on my baby?"

Scratching the back of my neck, I tip my chin at a few passing guys from one of my classes. "I never said that. I'm just surprised."

"You shouldn't be. Break is coming up in a couple weeks and your father wants to know about plans since you've got a game that week. Are you coming here to have a late Thanksgiving, or should we come to you?"

I open up one of the glass doors to the building holding my calculus class and blow out a long breath. "Didn't you say Grandma was supposed to come over for Thanksgiving? There's no sense of you coming here if she is. She hates traveling."

As soon as she starts laughing, I know what she's thinking about. "You just don't want your grandmother causing another scene. I swear, the people we sat by in the stands last time were two seconds from getting security involved."

From what Dad says, Grandma was ready to help DJ's grandma, Meadow, fight the guys a few rows over who were cheering on our competition after a penalty should've been called. Meadow is a bad influence, but I don't think my grandma has ever had a better time at a game than when they were plotting some guy's demise. "We don't need any repeats, but that's not why. We're playing the Raiders, and it'd be too much of a pain for you guys to all come since it's an away game. Let's plan for a late get-together like we did last year."

Mom knows the history of my Wilson Reed days, and even though she was disappointed in what I did to contribute to my failed college plans, she's proud I picked myself up and tried again. Both my parents have been supportive since day one and I'm grateful for that. Not everyone can say the same.

"If it makes you feel better, your grandmother has plans already for Thanksgiving, so it'll just be us."

There's a brief pause that makes me feel bad for trying to derail their holiday plans, so I try making it up to her. "Maybe I could bring someone home with me if it's okay with you and Dad."

"A *girl* someone?"

I roll my eyes at her sudden chipper tone and stop outside the classroom, glancing at the time on my phone before pressing it back to my ear. "Yeah. A girl. Don't get your hopes up though. She'll probably refuse to come anyway."

"Why would she do that?"

A second passes.

Two.

A third, fourth, and fifth one.

"Aiden Joseph Griffith," she chides in a tone I haven't heard since I got into a fist fight in high school. "What did you do to the poor girl that would make her not to want to come with you? And who is she? Are you dating? How come I'm only hearing about this now? Does that mean it's becoming seri—"

My fingers rake through my hair at her rapid inquisition, debating my options. I've held off telling her this long, but if Thanksgiving could include Ivy, then she deserves to be reunited with one of her biggest fans. "It's Ivy Underwood."

Now she's silent.

Gripping the back of my neck, I turn on the people entering the room to avoid their curious stares. "I didn't want to mention it before, but she started at Lindon this fall."

A small breath comes from the other end of the phone. "I–I had no clue. Wow. Her parents…"

"I don't think much has changed between them," I reply grimly, clenching the phone tight in my hands. "Which is exactly why I doubt she'll want to come home with me considering her family is right there. I know for damn sure she has nowhere else to go though."

Mom's heart gets the best of her like it always does in situations like these. She's had a soft spot for Ivy since the day I invited her inside. Ivy's first bakeware set was bought for her birthday by my mother. For Christmas, Mom bought her recipe books. Ivy admitted she had to hide them because her mother didn't like her getting things from people, and I didn't realize until much later that it was because her family couldn't afford anything themselves. Birthdays were no more than a birthday card and song and Christmases were whatever they could scrape together for candy-stuffed stockings and a couple toys under the tree. "That poor girl. Nobody should spend a holiday alone, Aiden. What can we do?"

"There's nothing we *can* do. Look, I need to get to class, but I'll talk to her later. She's been staying with me and the guys for a little while. Maybe keep this to yourself for now, okay?"

"Aiden—"

"You know what Dad will say."

He'll tell me I need to focus on football, not women. He's not wrong, but Ivy isn't some coed I have class with or see at parties on occasion when I want a hookup, and they both know it. That's probably why Dad would worry I'd get distracted. You can't let people who mean nothing to you get inside your head because none of them matter.

Ivy does.

She always has.

Mom reluctantly agrees. "Fine. If she doesn't want to come here, I'll understand. We can figure something else out."

She'd want to?

As if she can read my mind, she says, "I never understood why her parents were so resigned with her. It always made me so angry. She was such a sweet girl, Aiden. You know how much I adored her. I doubt that's changed any, but time…it can certainly impact a person."

My jaw ticks. "For now, wait until I let you know what

she wants before you bring it up to Dad. And don't tell her parents. I know you still talk to them."

There's another momentary pause. "I ask about her, you know. But they never have anything much to say. Some people don't deserve to be parents. I know I shouldn't say it, but it's true. They're those people. Ivy is all I talk about in passing because somebody needs to ask about her in this town since they're adamant on acting like she doesn't exist."

I don't know what to say to that. There's no denying I agree with her. Her parents were shitty ones at best. I only give them partial credit for trying with Porter, but that doesn't dismiss the fact that they gave up on Ivy. Who the fuck does that?

"I'm glad she has you again, baby boy. She needs someone in her corner. That was always you for her, and I'm glad it's no different now. Fate has a funny way of reminding us what's important in life, doesn't it?"

Squeezing my neck before nodding a few times, I click my tongue. "I'll talk to you later, yeah?"

"I love you, Aiden."

"Love you too."

When I click the End button, I stare at the blank screen for a minute before sliding it into my back pocket and heading inside as the professor goes through attendance.

I already know what Ivy is going to say when I tell her about Thanksgiving, which means I need to convince her—tell her to think of herself for once. But I feel for her situation. If I were in her shoes, I wouldn't want to go back to that place either.

Someone bumps my arm, and I look up to see Caleb looking at me with pinched brows. He mouths, *You good?*

I can only manage to nod, paying attention to the lesson

and telling myself I'll figure shit out with Ivy when I get home. But the infectious woman with a fiery personality consumes me like always.

Some people grow from the chaos because that's how they survive, and others thrive in it because chaos is all they know.

Ivy does both.

But being a survivor doesn't mean she'll want to come back to the house that holds most of our memories, and the more I think about it, the more I realize I'm not sure I want that either. We're building new ones together that could mean ten times more if she'll let them.

This is why I'm Chaos, she once said.

I don't mind if she spreads her mayhem around me because I think it's one of the things I missed most about her.

When I glance up again, I see Caleb smirking at me. I lift my middle finger enough for him to see, and he has to clear his throat to fight off the chuckle that escapes his lips.

Fucker.

Chapter Fourteen

AIDEN

By the time I get home from Everly's, it's pitch-black and quiet. Most of the guys are off doing their own thing, and Ivy is already curled up on her side of our bed. Christ. *Our* bed.

Dropping my shit onto the desk in the corner, I peel off my sweaty shirt and dig through my dresser for new clothes. "You're in bed early."

The bedding shuffles. "It's not that early." A moment passes. "I was tired but wanted to wait for you to get back. Caleb said you were mentoring someone tonight when I was making some dinner."

I huff out a noise, tired from the long day and sore from the rough practices we've been having. "What else did he tell you?"

Silence greets me as I collect the rest of my things. When I turn on my heels, she's sitting against the headboard and watching me with hesitation.

Lowering my clothes, I ask, "What?"

Her tongue runs across her bottom lip. "I don't talk to

him that much. I made dinner and some dessert for everyone and then I came downstairs after. There are peanut butter energy balls on the counter up there. I tried following a healthier recipe knowing you guys probably have to watch what you eat."

Fuck me. "You can talk to him however much you want, Ivy. Caleb's a good guy. He just has loose lips. Worse than DJ sometimes, which says a lot. If the guys weren't chill, I wouldn't live here. Doesn't mean I'd trust those fuckers if you decide to hang out with them though."

A small smile threatens to move her lips upward at the corners. "Worried your friends will like me more than they like you?"

I walk toward the door, gripping the edge before giving her a once-over. It isn't until then that I realize she's wearing one of my shirts. It may not be my jersey, but the sight still goes right to my dick. "I know they will. There's no competition."

Blinking back her surprise, she grips the blanket in her fists and then flattens out the wrinkled material. "Oh."

I snort at her dismal reply, not gracing her with one in return as I walk to the bathroom to get ready for bed. I'm hungry and need to grab something before settling in, but the stronger hunger gnawing at the pit of my stomach isn't for food.

Deciding on just a pair of boxers and a T-shirt, I throw my clothes in the hamper and head back to my room. She's on her side facing the door, her eyes trained on me when I enter and not leaving as I click the lock into place, turn off the light, and walk over to my side of the mattress. Her attention brands itself to my skin, and the feeling is nothing like when other girls follow my every move.

"I talked to my mom today," I tell her cautiously, pulling the blanket back.

A few seconds pass. "Yeah?"

Humming, I settle my back against the pile of pillows. "I told her about you."

I can hear a couple guys raising hell upstairs, someone shouting outside, and a car going by with their radio blasting.

Glancing in her direction, I clear my throat when she makes no effort to reply. "I know you're not sleeping, Chaos."

She rolls over to look at me. "Why would you tell her about me? Why now?"

"Because you're sleeping with me."

Not that I can tell in the darkness, but she's undoubtedly scowling. "You let your mother think we're fucking?"

My cock twitches, but I settle it down despite her lips forming my favorite word. "Not exactly. I'm sure that would make Thanksgiving awkward when we go."

"Come again?"

"You know my mom. She has a heart of gold and won't let anyone celebrate alone. So no. I didn't tell her we were screwing. I'm not a liar, and I like to avoid having that sort of conversation with my parents." This isn't how I wanted to broach the topic, but it's now or never. "Before you tell me no, hear me out."

"Absolutely not."

When she throws the covers off her, I grab her wrist before she can bolt from bed. "No. I'm not done talking."

She tries and fails to jerk away. "And I don't like being grabbed, but you obviously haven't gotten the memo."

Instantly, I let her go, and she doesn't expect the sudden change. Her body nearly topples from the bed, but I capture and steady her. "In my defense, you usually need to be stopped whenever I decide to manhandle you."

176

"That's not true."

"Oh yeah. I'm sure you would have had a wonderful sleepover with *Remi*. He wouldn't have touched you at all. Perfect fucking gentleman, that one."

"Fuck off."

"Don't think so, Chaos."

She makes a noise and gets out of bed. "I don't even know how we got onto this topic. Forget about that asshole. I was never planning on sleeping with him. It's not my problem that you don't seem to believe it."

This is going nowhere. "Come to Thanksgiving with me. Don't try bullshitting me into believing you have other plans because I'll call you out on it."

There are footsteps nearing the door and I'm halfway out of bed, thinking she's leaving, when the light flicks back on. I blink rapidly to adapt to the sudden change before seeing her unamused expression. "Who says I don't have plans? Maybe I'm going to Bea's."

I sit back down, leg bent and propped on the mattress with the other foot on the floor, ready to push off the bed in case she tries leaving. "If you had her to go to, which you could if you weren't so damn independent, then you would have never even entertained the idea of leaving with him."

She has no response to that because it's obvious that I'm right.

"You don't want to go home, and I can't even pretend to understand. Your parents suck. You don't talk to Porter." I stop for a moment and eye her. "You don't, do you? You haven't said a word about him. You don't say anything about any of them. I have no idea what to think when it comes to you and your family."

Her eyes go to the wall where a few random pictures

hang of me and my family. I've caught her looking at them more than once since she started staying here.

Every time I've tried bringing up her family, she changes the subject. But something is different tonight, and I'm thankful she says, "I looked him up online once. Found his Facebook. But Mom and Dad...they weren't worth my time when I realized the feeling was mutual. Why chase after people and give them effort when it's never going to be returned?"

Interest flares in my chest. "And? Did you reach out to Porter? You always looked after him. I...I did too, after you left. Wanted to make sure he was going to be okay with them."

She walks over to the farthest photo of me and my old dog Captain, who passed away a year ago, her fingers lifting to touch his image. "I didn't have a reliable phone or anything at the time, so I didn't bother sending him a message. I wasn't sure when I'd be able to go back online or text him. Eventually, I stopped bothering to go on because there was no reason. I wasn't sure he'd even want to talk to me or what our parents told him after I left."

I let out a disbelieving breath. "No reason, huh?" Scrubbing a palm across the side of my face, I ask, "Did you look me up? I tried searching for you. Never found anything."

Hesitation takes hold of her tongue. "I had a fake name. Didn't want Mom and Dad finding me, not that I think they would have tried. And yes, I looked you up every time I had a computer nearby. Most of the phones I kept didn't have internet. They were prepaid junk. Cheap, you know? The one you gave me fell into a mud puddle and stopped working, and I didn't exactly have easy access to money then.

But I'd go to public libraries and use their computers for a while until they closed and had to ask me to leave. Your mom tags you in a lot of photos. I got to see your sports stats and the selfies Judd and the other douchebags you hung out with always took. You never smiled in any of them. You always looked annoyed." Her shoulders lift as if it doesn't matter, but those details mean everything to me. Because she cared enough to look, which is more than I thought she felt. "It was nice to see that you were doing well enough though."

"And what? No message? No indication that you were okay? Did you not expect to extend me the same courtesy you got?"

"It didn't matter, Aiden. There was no way I could have told you where I was because there was nothing you could have done about my circumstances. Not without leaving everything you worked for behind. And what if you did? Then we both would have been struggling."

"Don't." I stand and prowl over to her. "I thought you knew that you mattered. *It* matters. *We* matter. Every time you shit on yourself and the past, it feels like you're shitting on whatever the hell was going on with us then and what is now. I may not have had the resources back then, but you have no damn idea what one little message from you could have done for me."

"I…" Her eyes drop. "I'm sorry."

"Your apology doesn't do me much good now, Chaos. I spent a long time feeling guilty over not convincing you to stay. I should have tried harder."

"This is what I mean." Her finger gestures between us. "This right here is why I don't talk about it. We can't change the past. You trying to get me to stay with your family until you were blue in the face wouldn't have changed my mind.

And do you really think my parents would have been fine with me being next door? Mom hated it every time I talked about how much I loved you and your family. She hated our cooking lessons and our outdoor explorations. She couldn't stand that I was happier there than with them. I made my choice and I have to live with it, so you do too. That's how life works."

"If I told Mom about the situation—"

"Then what?" Ivy snaps, tossing her hands in the air like she always does when she's angry. She talks with them, her gestures never making any sense. "I love your mom, Aiden. I've always been jealous mine couldn't have been like her, but that's not the hand I was dealt. And thinking about how I despised my own parents enough to ruin my life has made me realize that I could have had worse. They could have hit me, and they never did. They could have pulled me into their arguments, but they didn't. I know there are kids out there who *wish* they could have been in my shoes, who would have been talked down to and condescended to and made to feel like shit, and what does that say about me?"

I don't reply. What good would it do, telling her that verbal abuse is still abuse? That emotional abuse is still abuse? She knows that even if she downplays it. She spent years going through it. She doesn't need me to remind her of everything she ran from.

She palms her face for a moment before brushing hair behind her ears. "I don't like to talk about them because it makes me realize how good I actually had it. My life didn't go to shit until I decided to up and leave. And Mom tried telling me that. I told her over and over that I'd run away, and she always said I'd come back because I had it better than I thought I did. But I was a prideful brat who thought

I could do better for myself. I really thought I could handle whatever life through at me because it'd be better than being the verbal punching bag at home whenever they were miserable." She drops her head, her hair falling to shield her face as she takes a deep breath. "She gave me a bus ticket."

My brows pinch. "Who did? Your mom?"

Ivy nods slowly. "I was supposed to go to Roserio where my grandma lived. Mom told me that living with Gertie might be for the best, and I thought it was her way of getting rid of me once and for all. Mom and Dad would spend so much money on Porter like they knew he had a future, and it made me feel like I..." Her voice gets rough. "Anyway, I traded in the bus ticket for one to Ridgeway because it was the farthest I could go without having to pay for a different pass. I left a note, Aiden, before I came to see you. I don't know if anybody told you, but I told them I would prove to them I could make a future for myself without their help. I'd get a GED and go to college and make something of myself like they knew Porter would. And I knew the moment I put it under my pillow for them to find that I'd never be able to show my face again if I failed because they'd tell me they were right."

All I can do is blink at the girl whose eyes turn glassy the deeper her admission goes.

When she lifts her gaze, her bottom lip trembles. "I'm the reason they never looked for me. I'm the reason I felt like giving up. The doctor at the hospital was right." Her hand curves around her arm, thumb trailing up and down the scar. "It was a cry for help, but I knew...I knew they wouldn't come. I wouldn't have wanted them to anyway, because then I'd have to face the two biggest critics in my life."

"Ivy," I whisper hoarsely, shaking my head at the revelation. "They could have still looked harder. They *should have.*

You can't take all the blame in this. They're your fucking parents. You're *their* responsibility no matter what goddamn letter you wrote them."

"I'm the one who left."

"And you're back. You got a GED. You made it to Lindon. You didn't fail. You had setbacks. Some rough, shitty fucking setbacks, but they didn't stop you. When are you going to give yourself credit?"

"I can't go back there."

"You can if you want to."

She won't meet my eyes as she releases a shaky breath. "I don't want to. What would they say? Nothing I'd want to hear, that's for sure."

I ask, "What do you want?"

Her lips part.

Close.

Part again. "What do you mean?"

"What. Do. You. Want?" Every word is said with concise clarity as I pierce her with my gaze until she can't look away even if she wanted to. "Because I know what I want."

Her head tilts up, chin high and eyes full of challenge. "And what is that? What do you want that makes you so different from the other guys I've been with, since you're so insistent that you're not like any of them?"

Stepping into her until she's pinned between me and the wall, I lift my hand to her cheek and brush my fingertips against her skin. Moving a piece of fallen blue hair behind her ear, I soak in the familiar scent of my shampoo that she's been using from my shower. I love seeing her in my clothes, smelling like me, taking over my space. I've never felt as territorial as I do right now. "I invited you to Thanksgiving. Can you say the same for the others?"

No reply.

"I sleep beside you in bed without touching you no matter how bad I want to. Your curves, your ass, it's all right there every fucking night tormenting me, but I never give in because I know damn well if I get a handful, it'll be because you want me to. Have any of the others refrained? Held back? Showed you an *ounce* of that respect?"

My nose grazes hers until I hear her sharp exhale against my jaw.

"I've told my teammates to back the hell off because I may not be able to touch you, but that doesn't mean any of them can. If the other guys gave a shit about you, they would have staked their claim. But they didn't."

Her hot breath caresses my parted lips as I hover mine over hers.

"I did," I whisper, dragging my hand up the back of her neck until my fingers are tangled in her hair. "And no matter how many times you say you don't want to be claimed by anyone, we both know that's bullshit. You were always mine, Chaos. All these years don't change the fact that it's always been me and you. Even when you didn't know it. Nobody else had a chance. So that's what I want. You. Not just your body, but you. Your personality. Your mind. Your problems. Your goddamn companionship. Because that's what I've missed since the day I watched you disappear into the night. I don't just regret letting you walk away. I regret never telling you how I felt. Stop trying to push me away. It won't work anymore." My fingers tighten in her hair, pulling her head back by the tresses tangled in my fingers so her eyes lock with mine. "I'll ask again. What do you want, Ivy?"

Something snaps inside her, and she shows me her answer by crushing her lips against mine.

Chapter Fifteen

IVY

MY CONTROL DISAPPEARS AND all there is in this moment is Aiden. It doesn't stop that pang of worry in the pit of my stomach from making an appearance, knowing this will change everything between us. The final move. Yet it's hard to let that absorb when all I can really think about is his mouth on mine, his hands gripping my hips, and his body pressing me against the wall until I'm wrapping my long legs around his waist. When his hands slide to palm my ass, covered only by my thin panties, there's a silent alarm bell going off in the back of my mind that reminds me Aiden is leaving soon.

But I've lived the last few years believing that there aren't such things as regrets because every decision made, no matter the outcome, is a lesson learned. And all the other guys who have kissed me with a purpose, touched me with a destination, and taken me to bed with a plan have never done so with as much passion as Aiden Griffith is right now.

When he leaves, I know I'll be okay.

Because I'll have no choice but to be.

All I focus on now is that I'm *safe*.

He turns around and walks us to the bed, our frantic lips never breaking as my back hits the mattress. I part my thighs to make room for him to settle between, and he continues torturing me with his full lips. I've been kissed by a lot of men, but none of them compare to the boy who's trying to inhale the memories we share as if this is the only way to remind himself they exist.

His tongue traces the inner seam of my lips before tasting mine—our lips clashing and teeth clattering in a show of dominance before I'm flipping us over to straddle him.

"Do you want this?" I ask him, pulling far enough away to talk without touching the mouth that greedily follows mine for more.

"Do *you*?" His breath is coming just as fast as mine, his chest rising and falling rapidly under my palms as they rest on his pecs.

The heat building hotter and hotter between my legs is nothing compared to the ache as I grind my hips down on his hard cock, proving just how badly I want this. "Why don't you find out for yourself?" I challenge, sliding my hands under his shirt and rolling my hips. Between his boxers and my panties, there's little barrier keeping me from the part of him that I desperately want inside me.

He groans and grabs the hem of the shirt I stole before peeling it off me and tossing it onto the floor. His eyes instantly take in my full breasts on display, his hands moving up the curves of my body before cupping them in his hands and squeezing with a groan. "You're going to fucking kill me, Ivy. When the hell did you get so goddamn sexy?" His thumbs tweak my nipples before he sits up and takes one of them into his mouth and suckles before drawing back enough to add, "You were always beautiful, but this…"

Biting down on my bottom lip to suppress the surprise from his soft compliment, I arch my chest into him to absorb the feeling of his mouth and hands taking over every sensation racing through me. I never considered myself very vain when I was younger, but I knew I was pretty. I just never knew *he* thought I was.

I moan his name under my breath when he tugs my nipple with his teeth before switching to the other, guiding his hand to knead its twin. My fingers go to his hair, massaging his scalp, pushing his mouth harder against me, as I begin moving my hips and feel the wetness pool with the need to have him naked.

"Shirt," is all I manage to rasp, pawing at the material covering his hard-earned muscles. He pulls away, the sound of my breast popping from his mouth the only noise between us besides my heavy panting, his hand moving to tug the shirt off in one go, and he disposes of it with what he's already stripped off me.

Our hands become frenzied as they coast against each other's bare skin—mapping out every curve, muscle, freckle, and stretch mark. I've never been self-conscious when stripping down with other guys. Most of them only had one end game in mind and could care less that my stomach jiggles and thighs shake in certain positions. With Aiden, there's a strange sense of yearning for him to find me as sexy as he says I am—a girl without imperfections despite me being a shell full of them. His gaze makes me feel as confident as I've learned to be over the past few weeks with him. As beautiful as he says I am no matter what I've gone through.

I believe him.

Trust him.

There's always been something raw about letting someone see you naked. They're not just seeing your body but the smallest details that make you who you are.

Your past marred by scars.

Your present wrapped in skin.

Your future highlighted in small smiles and hopeful eyes.

His hands find my hips.

Mine find his biceps.

His squeeze my thighs.

Mine coast across his sculpted abs.

When his fingers dance along the top of my panties and trail down, down, down until they're barely brushing my covered slit, I mewl out an incoherent plea for him to touch me.

Aiden always knows what I need.

Moving aside the cheap material, he strokes me up and down, torturously slow. The pad of his thumb rubs my clit in circles until I'm moving my hips to find the friction I need and writhing when one of his fingers slips inside, quickly followed by another. There's no need to beg because his digits start pumping in and out of me, causing me to grip his shoulders and begin lifting my hips to ride it out.

"Aiden, please." Bending forward, I bury my face in his neck and breathe in the soap and sweat on his skin as I ride his hand like I would his cock. I nip his neck. "Need you."

He helps me lower my panties and his boxers down so we're both free, the air in the room thick with anticipation as it brushes where I'm wettest. "Condom," he grates breathily as I wrap a hand around his large girth and pump the hardened steel in my hand.

I pause only for a moment, remembering the last time we were in this situation. I want to tell him it'll be fine, lie and say I'm on the pill because I need to feel him inside me with no barrier, but we have to be smart. And no matter how beautiful the shaft in my hand is as it twitches and grows with every stroke of my palm, I know neither of us needs any surprises in the future.

Aiden reaches for his nightstand and pulls out a foil packet, his breath hitching as I help him roll the latex on. I notice the slight shake to his hands and assume it's in anticipation—an uninhibited need that's mutual as I rise and line the head of him up to my entrance and slowly, slowly, slowly sink down.

"*Fuuuck.*" The garbled word from him sounds pained as I take him fully and circle my hips to find the perfect spot that sets my nerves on fire. He stretches me in the most blissful way, his fingertips digging into my ass as I lift and repeat the movement, soaking in his length as I take every inch of him where I need him most. My hands hold on to his shoulders as I ride him slowly until he's shaking his head. "Too much. Too damn much."

I'm not sure what he means until his head drops back and the tendons in his neck tighten as his bottom half shoots up to fill me deeper and—

"*Jesus Christ*," he barks out, holding my hips down so we're pressed so close together I can feel him twitch and stiffen inside me. Once his hips settle, his breathing becomes heavier and I'm staring wide-eyed at him until he finally looks at me again with flushed cheeks.

"Did you just…?" I already know the answer, but the way his face reddens only confirms it.

His throat bobs, and there's something oddly…vulnerable in the glazed blue color that I look into, first one eye, then the other, before he looks away. "I haven't done this before."

I blink, then replay his words.

"Say that again?" I whisper slowly, sure I misheard him.

His jaw ticks. "I've never..." One of his hands rises to the back of his neck, squeezing it once and making the muscles in his arms pop. The tattoos I've admired when he shows them off shift, the Captain America shield moving as if to guard him and his shocking admission. "Shit, Ivy. You know what I mean. I haven't had sex until now. Okay?"

Stunned silent, all I can do is stare.

Oh my God.

I just took my best friend's virginity.

Finally formulating my thoughts, I choke out, "That can't be true. What about Sydney? Or, I mean, there have to have been other girls. Penelope from high school! I've heard people talk around campus. You're...*you.*"

There's a ghost of a smile on his lips despite the heated skin under his cheeks giving away his embarrassment. I never knew someone like Aiden—someone strong, confident, with the world ahead of him—could be this vulnerable. "I have no clue what Penny has to do with this, and I don't know if I want to have this conversation while my dick is still inside you." More blinking, then a garbled gasp as he rolls his hips upward experimentally until he's sinking further inside. I clench around him and let out a tiny breath as he hesitantly moves. "I'm not done, promise. Not sure I'm going to be able to stop now that I've realized what I've been missing this whole time."

Before I can reply, I'm on my back with Aiden thrusting into me slow and hard with a heady groan that vibrates our damp chests where they're pressed together. "Aiden, are you sure—*oh.*" He rests his forearms on either side of my head and starts jackknifing into me with an urgency that I can't truly fathom, his eyes getting darker and dilated with lust as he takes me.

My body arches as he grabs one of my legs and bends it forward, giving him better access to hit something that sparks a feeling few people have ever unlocked with me during sex, and I'm shaking my head, pinching my eyes closed, as the sound of his cock entering me fills the bedroom.

"You cannot be a virgin." My breathless, doubtful declaration has him chuckling as he trails kisses down my neck before biting into the base of my throat. "If you've never had sex before now, you obviously watch a lot of porn to know how to—*oh god.*"

His muffled laugh against my skin has me wrapping my arms around his neck and meeting his thrusts eagerly as I hold on for dear life.

I feel him move deeper.

Harder.

Needier.

He moves like he's lost in the feeling, like there's nothing else. Nothing to lose and everything to gain. And when I find myself back on top and riding his dick, I can't help but look at his lust-filled eyes and slick skin damp with sweat and fully understand what's going on right now as I feel my spine tingle and tummy tighten.

Aiden Griffith waited for me.

He let me go back then.

He didn't tell anyone for days.

And he waited.

I can feel the tingling sensation building higher and higher as his cock slides into me repeatedly. But it isn't only the way his pubic bone is brushing my clit in the rapid succession that brings my orgasm to its brink but rather all the ways we got here. How he helped me. How he cared about me. How he *respected* me. What a foreign word.

Respect.

When my legs start shaking and giving out, Aiden doesn't let us lose the rhythm. His strong hands grip me, using my spent body to fuck himself until we reach the peak.

And when we get to the edge, I dive off headfirst into an abyss.

Chanting his name, I clench around him and explode in a burst of emotions, memories, and feelings that have been pent up for so long.

The first day I met Aiden.

The first time I climbed into his window.

The first time I hid in his closet...his bed.

All of it comes rushing back as my body succumbs to the things he's done to it.

Collapsing on his body for I'm not sure how long, I finally manage to whisper, "You waited."

Instead of confirming it, he pulls out, peels off the condom, puts on a new one, and makes sure neither of us says another word the rest of the night, with me taking lead every single time our bodies come together.

Chapter Sixteen

AIDEN

MOM USED TO SAY that telling the truth and making someone upset is always better than telling a lie to make them smile. I'm not sure where she got the quote from, but it taunts me as I replay my night with Ivy.

I didn't mean to lie to her.

You waited.

I didn't wait the way she thinks. There was no romantic gesture making me stop from taking things further with the few girls I screwed around with before she showed up.

There was only football.

The sport dictated my life for years, especially after she left. It served as a distraction that turned into an obsession. I worked my ass off to get accepted to Wilson Reed University and play for the Raiders. As one of the best Division I schools, I knew my career would be guaranteed if I showed the team and spectators what I could do. My grades were some of the best at the school, my reputation solid, and my stats strong.

Dad's constant reminder not to distract myself with women, booze, and partying had stuck in my head long enough to prove what I was worth to them, but after a while, some of my teammates wore me down.

Like Jacob Mahone.

Mahone was one of the best starting tight ends for the Wilson Reed Raiders and damn good at what he did. I was always mesmerized every time I watched him play the field, running faster than a guy his size and stature should, and barely being taken down even when he had someone twice his weight on him. He was a powerhouse, and having him take me under his wing made me feel confident that I could get better from his guidance.

The problem with the Raiders is that once they have a team they trust, they don't like outsiders coming in and messing up their dynamic. Especially not ones who come in as freshmen and soak up the spotlight from everyone who matters.

I usually ignored the attention from the coach and cameras, nodding along to whatever I was told to do, and left it at that—go to practice, go to games, kick ass with my team, and not once focus on what the news would say about me. If I let the sportscasters' remarks go to my head then, I would have gotten cocky and forgotten that the only way to rise to the top is with hard work. Not luck.

I didn't start the first few games, but the second Coach Thompson put me in to test me, there was no taking me out again.

I had no reason to believe that anyone on the Raiders had bad intentions when they insisted on taking me out on the town to blow off steam.

"See what wearing our jersey can get you, Griffith," they'd always tell me. We'd barhop on occasion, hit up house parties where people idolized us, and soak up the attention from guys and girls alike. I only drank if Mahone and the others did, and usually never before game days.

"One drink won't kill you," Mahone had constantly pushed, until saying no felt like an act of betrayal against the team. Except one drink turned into two, then three, because they'd keep passing them over. One weekend of drinking turned into another. House party after house party with the guys became a common occurrence. Girls would hold on to both arms and leave lipstick on my clothes and skin, and the guys would all take pictures as a reminder of what the good life was like as a Wilson Reed athlete.

But I'd be the only hungover player to show up for practice despite being outdrunk by everyone else. I'd get drilled hard by Coach Thompson until I'd hurl on the sidelines and get hounded by the guys who recorded it because they thought it was hilarious. My grades started slipping because every time I tried staying in to study, someone would show up at my door and drag me out again.

The life I was molding for myself slowly started falling apart right in front of my eyes as pictures of me from parties started surfacing on social media and getting me the opposite kind of attention than the college wanted.

Coach Thompson warned me with the kind of stern, fatherly look my own dad gave me when he made a point. "Be better, son. We can't have anyone on the team slacking. Doesn't matter how good you are. I don't give anyone special treatment here."

I promised to focus.

But Mahone got his way in the long run.

The day I was kicked off the Raiders for failing a handful of classes and showing up on the field fucked up one too many times, the guy I trusted to help me slapped me on the shoulder with a seedy smirk and said, "Better luck at your next school, Griffith. Good luck ever starting again after this year."

Mahone's friends laughed and watched me walk from the turf, not one of them giving a shit that they'd ruined my chances. Their amusement still echoes in my head every time I think about the parties they'd bring me to and the women they'd force on my lap like I was supposed to follow suit with everyone else.

Don't be a pussy, Griffith.

Trust us on this one.

We got your back.

I should have known better than to believe someone with as much to lose as Mahone did would offer me any help. I don't like thinking the worst in people because it gets you nowhere in life. But thinking the best of them usually leads to nothing but mistrust and disappointment.

When my parents found out the news, Dad told me his drawn-out version of "I told you so" and Mom gave me a tight hug and told me everything would be okay.

Lindon U wanted me, even if their reputation was nothing like Wilson Reed's was, and it was a start. A fresh one.

It took an entire semester of me ignoring most of the Dragons outside the field before Caleb managed to earn some of my trust. All it took was a simple "heard the Raiders are assholes anyway" to make me laugh, slap his hand, and agree to move in with a few of the others the following semester. DJ wormed his way in after that with his constant persistence, and everyone else on the team slowly followed in some form.

I may not be close with a lot of the guys, but they're nothing like the Raiders—not threatened by competition or challenges. Coach Pearce may think that being selfish is how you get to your goals, but I couldn't do it without my team backing me every game.

None of this may have been what I planned when I submitted my college applications in high school, but Lindon was where I needed to be. I just didn't know how much until the day I saw Ivy again.

So the only thing I really waited for was a chance to prove myself again—my talent, skill, and loyalty to the game.

Not Ivy, but only because I had no idea if I'd ever see her again. Hoping I would was only going to distract me from what I set out to do. What I always told her I'd do with my life.

I didn't wait *for* her.

I waited *because* of her.

She left and I needed an outlet.

She left and I needed *something*.

And that was football.

It was a future.

Silence is all she's awarded with when I creep out of bed with extra precision not to wake her. I could leave a note, send her a text, but I can't put to words the feelings over what we'd done. Nothing I could write would be enough.

You waited.

I didn't, and it's hard to admit that when I'm not sure she'd understand. Because football means the world to me, and after everything she's gone through, the last thing I want is for her to feel second best.

But it's all I can give right now.

I meant what I said.

I want her.

But I want football too.

~

I knock on Coach Pearce's door and catch his attention from the paperwork he's looking over. It's only when I see movement in the corner of the room that I realize he's not alone. Chet Wilkins, formerly two-time Superbowl-winning New York Jets quarterback, is standing in a suit by the trophy case.

"Come on in, son," Coach says, pushing up from his desk. "I'm sure you know who this is, so I'll skip the formalities. Wilkins and I go way back to when I was a rookie for the Jets."

I knew Coach had some experience on a pro team. One season with them and he suffered a shattered ankle that ended his career.

Clearing my throat, I nod at Coach and look to his friend. "Hello, sir. Real nice to meet you. I'm a big fan."

Wilkins chuckles, walking over and stretching his hand to shake mine. "Likewise, Aiden. Bill here has been talking about you for some time. I've been keeping an eye out on your games. You're one hell of a player."

Hearing that from someone like him makes pride swell in my chest. I stand straighter and give him another nod, making him grin in amusement.

Coach intervenes. "Wilkins is a scout for the Buffalo's team. We've been talking for a while, and it could be a route for you."

I stop at the seat in front of his desk, dropping my bag onto it. "You mean the Buffalo Bills?"

Wilkins nods, leaning against the wall with his arms crossed. "I know a few people who are probably going to reach out shortly, so I wanted first dibs. Suppose that's the plus side to dealing with this cranky asshole all these years." His chin gestures toward Coach with a mischievous smirk on his face that only widens as Coach grunts. "Heard Mass, Jersey, and a few others may be interested too. Wouldn't surprise me if they try snatching you up with a hefty contract that some of the other teams can't offer."

Holy shit. "Mass as in New England?"

Coach makes a noise. "What other one is there? Won't lie, son. Might not be your best option in the long run. It's obviously a strong team, but I think your talents could take a lesser one to the top. You'd be famous for making a name for someone else."

"Or losing with the rest of them," I refute.

Wilkins laughs. "He's not wrong, Bill."

Coach scrubs his face with a palm and levels with me. "They drafted Jacob Mahone. Kid has the kind of stats that will make him the next Gronkowski if he plays the way he did for the Raiders."

"Funny. I've been told the same thing."

"I'm not saying it to piss you off," he returns. "Stating facts, that's all. With the big names leaving other teams, it opens up spots for your talent to shine. That's all I'm getting at."

"Buffalo has talked about you extensively," Wilkins tells me. "They've seen what you can do here and what you did at Wilson Reed. There's no doubt you've got what it takes to take a team to championships like you've done for the Dragons. You don't get into fights, you stay out of the drama, and you're dedicated to getting better. That's more than a lot of prospects, especially your age, can say."

"And," Coach adds, "it's more than people can say for Mahone. He may be a fierce competitor, but he'll get himself into trouble soon enough with that mouth and personality of his. Wallace is going down the same path. Ruined potential as far as I'm concerned if he doesn't get his act together soon."

Both men nod, leaving me blowing out a breath and sinking into the chair. "What does that mean for me? We talked about the combine next year."

Coach hums. "I was filling Wilkins in on your plan to take a leave of absence so you can focus on training. There will be multiple scouts watching for you. Your game is improving with every competitor we crush out on the field. I have no doubt you'll be saying goodbye to this school for good after winter finals."

My nostrils twitch over that. I may not love school, but Mom has always wanted me to get a degree. She understands what this opportunity could mean for me though. If Dad hasn't drilled it into her head, dozens of other people—Grandma included—have reminded her that I could make a name for myself without a mundane piece of paper signed and stamped by the college like it means something.

I look to Wilkins. "You think I could be first pick with the Bills?"

His lips stretch. "Hell, kid. I think you could be first pick with anyone. Not many people can do what you can out there. That takes sacrifice and loyalty to the game."

Sacrifice.

Ivy's face pops into mind, and I have to push it away for the time being. As if he knows what I'm thinking, Coach says, "I've reminded him what his priorities are this close to the combine. He knows what's most important. Knows not to get distracted."

I look to the ground, jaw tight.

Wilkins walks over to me, putting a hand on my shoulder. "There are going to be perks no matter who chooses you and who you sign a contract with. But consider New York. You're from here. You've got family around. You can bring the team to a lot of victories. Any team would be lucky to have you though."

After leaving the office, my head fills with about a thousand different thoughts that are hard to sort. The tornado of what-ifs and worries leave me mentally drained, and I'm grateful I have class to force me to focus on something other than my future football career and the girl I left naked in my bed.

What is it that Dad says? *Oh, right.*

It's not really a dream if you don't sacrifice anything for it.

Chapter Seventeen

IVY

THE SOFT MUMBLINGS OF other students gathered at the tables in the library fill the otherwise quiet space as I tap my pen against my notebook and stare at the row of unoccupied computers. Glancing down at my phone screen and staring at the last text I sent that was left unanswered, I swallow my doubt and push back my chair.

I'm usually the one who leaves the rumpled bed without another word and doesn't look back, so I tell myself it's just my bruised ego getting to me. Karma. I've never been the girl who waits for a guy to text her back, and I don't want to start now.

Logging into one of the school's computers, I pull up the old social media site that I haven't used in a long time. I'm not sure why my talk with Aiden stirred a need to do this or why waking up alone left a hole in my chest that I feel the need to mend on my own, but the temptation for change is too much to ignore.

Aiden's always been the person to make me want *more*,

make me want *better*. And I'm the only person who can make it happen.

The second I'm on the website, my fingers only hesitate a moment before typing in the name I've thought about more times than I can count.

There he is.

Porter Underwood.

His account is private, but the profile picture is undoubtedly him in… "A football uniform?" My eyes narrow as I study the image, running my fingertips over Haven Falls High's name on the jersey plastered to him.

Porter still plays like Mom and Dad said he would all those years ago.

"Ivy?" someone calls from behind me.

I turn quickly to see Raine walking toward me with a smile on her face. A few of the girls from the house are with her, all glancing in our direction as they settle at a table nearby. Most of them look away, but one—Hannah—is still watching closely with interest in her eyes. Besides Raine, the petite brunette currently staring was the only other person I didn't totally dislike. We rarely spoke, but there was always the slightest flinch whenever Sydney said something rude to me that made me think she couldn't be *that* bad if she didn't approve of their leader's cattiness.

"Hey," Raine greets.

"Hi."

Her eyes go to the screen, her lips stretching a little more. "Who's that? He's handsome."

I want to roll my eyes, but I don't. She's not wrong. My little brother doesn't look so little anymore. He's grown into his big ears, and he's filled out based on the way his gear fits him. Mom used to say that if he grew into his feet, he'd tower over every single one of us someday.

Sighing, I murmur, "He's my brother."

I'm sure if I looked, I'd see some form of surprise on my former housemate's face. Since moving, I see her at Aiden's place frequently, but I don't say much. When she knows I'm downstairs, she'll break away from Caleb to say hi. Sometimes we'll watch TV. Other times we'll do homework together after asking each other how our weeks have been. Raine is sweet for putting in an effort, yet my tongue remains lead in my mouth when my brain pushes me to make conversation with her.

"I can see it now." She points toward his eyes, which are the same bright shade of unique honey brown as mine. Everyone used to say it's where the similarities stopped in both looks in personality. Porter was the spoiled younger child, and I was the bitter older one.

I guess nobody was wrong in that assessment, but it didn't stop me from being irritated over the commentary when no one knew the reasons I had to be bitter.

I don't want to see your face again.

My heart threatens to crack further, but I hold it together the best way I can. Those words propelled me to act—to run.

"I didn't know he played," I admit. It's a whisper to the air, yet Raine still hears as I examine the computer screen. His hair isn't nearly as curly as it was but cut short and styled with either gel or sweat. He always loved talking about football with Aiden. He looked up to our neighbor just like I always did.

"You don't stay in touch?"

Licking my bottom lip and wincing at the slice of pain over how chapped they are from the cold weather, I shake my head. "I don't talk to anyone in my family. It's...uh, complicated." My attention shifts back to her. "I want to reach out though. Maybe give him my number if I work up the courage to."

The softness on her face returns. "I think that's a great idea. I'm sure he'll look forward to hearing from you."

I swallow my doubt. "Yeah."

If I were in Porter's shoes, I'm not sure I'd feel the same. The night I left home, I cracked his bedroom door open slowly to see his sleeping form in bed. I walked in, pulled the blanket up to tuck him in like I used to help Mom do, and whispered, "Good luck."

Someone calls Raine's name, causing her to look over her shoulder and lift a finger up in wait. When she turns back to me, I'm not sure why I blurt, "Can I ask you something?" but I do.

Her eyebrows practically dart up to her hairline. "Of course. Sure."

Rubbing my thighs with the heels of my palms, I stifle a small sigh. "Has Aiden been happy? I mean, like, really happy. Before I..."

She blinks slowly, then a knowing smile creeps up at the corners of her lips as she drops her gaze to the floor for a moment to collect herself. "Aiden has always been serious about everything since he got here. Caleb could barely get a word out of him at first. Some of the guys thought he was mute or stuck up until my boyfriend managed to crack his shell. When you showed up..." Her shoulders lift. "Caleb mentioned that you two knew each other from when you were younger. I think it's great that you both wound up here even if it was by random luck. Aiden's dedication to building his future probably produces some happiness, but personally,

I think he deserves more of it. Sports can only get people so much, you know?"

"Money makes people happy."

"But *people* are the biggest source of it," she counters pointedly.

I press my lips together for a moment. "I think people can also cause the most pain in the long run, especially the people closest to you."

For a few heartbeats, she's quiet. "That's a sad way to look at it. But I guess you're not wrong. The people we care about most have the power to hurt us the worst." Not expecting her agreement, my eyes go to hers. She adds, "But that doesn't mean they do. A lot of times, people use that as an excuse to not even try."

This time, I'm the one staring down at my ratty winter boots. When I saw the first thin coat of white powder on the ground, I muttered the whole time I laced them up.

Raine clears her throat. "I came downstairs one night after Aiden moved you in, but you weren't on the couch."

Defense kicks in. "So?"

Her eyes brighten, but the rest of her expression is casual. "So try with him. I think it'd be good for the both of you if you let things play out without thinking too much. He's never let anyone in his life, shown so much interest in one person, as he has with you. That means something. And I know it's probably complicated with the draft and his future. I'm not sure what I'd do if Caleb decided he wanted to go pro. But if there's anyone who can figure it out, it's you."

"You don't know me, Raine."

"I know you're the most stubborn, headstrong, and independent person I've ever met. I'm a little jealous of you, to be honest."

I gape at her.

She laughs. "I am. I love my life, but sometimes I wonder what it'd be like to be on my own and be a badass like you are. You're so…intense, but in a good way, you know? Driven like you're always trying to prove something. It's kind of motivating. I love Caleb, and I'm happy with how things are, so I wouldn't change a thing. But you and Aiden are different. There's something about you that seems…certain. Aiden's a good guy too. Stubborn but good. I think he's met his match with you." Silence greets her statement, so she nods over the conversation's end. "I hope you hear from your brother. It'd be good to talk to family for the holidays. I'll see you around. We could try grabbing food sometime again if you want."

When I nod, I watch her turn and start walking toward her friends but then stop and look back at me again, nibbling her bottom lip.

"Hey, Ivy? There's something I think you should know. I heard some of the girls talking at the house after what happened with you, and it wasn't really Syd's idea to kick you out. I mean, sure, she didn't really like you for some reason, but she doesn't like many people. Um, anyway…it was Aiden who convinced her to make you move."

My eyes widen and something heavy unfurrows in my chest cavity. "What?"

Her lips rub together at my sharp tone, her eyes sharper with awareness like she regrets saying anything. "He was looking out for you. I don't blame him. You shouldn't have had to stay in the dingy basement. You would have gotten sick again. It was a sweet gesture."

Anger takes over the shock at him intervening in my living situation, boiling in my stomach. He knows better than anyone how much finding my own place meant to me. It wasn't ideal, but it was mine. Somewhere I didn't have to open my legs to secure. "Looking out for me," I repeat dryly, knee bouncing. "Wow."

"Don't be angry at him," she tries convincing me, a pleading expression on her face. "Aiden is always going to look out for the people he loves. There's nothing wrong with that. You're better off at the football house anyway."

Too late.

"Don't tell Caleb I know," I tell her distantly, my skin tightening as I run my palms over the sleeve covering the deepest scar. "I think this is a conversation Aiden is going to have to have with me without any warning first."

She winces but nods. "Okay. Um…" Her eyes go back to the group waiting for her. "Don't kill him. Even if you'd survive behind bars, it's not worth it."

When she finally leaves me alone, I take a few deep breaths before turning back to the computer and staring at my brother's picture for way longer than is probably considered normal. He looks happy, well cared for. Isn't that what I've always wanted?

There's no brushing off the minor bitterness swirling deep down in the pit of my stomach knowing that means our parents *tried* with him. Why not me? I'm not sure thinking about it is worth it after all this time.

Sometimes people don't need reasons to be bad. That's just who they are. Maybe knowing Porter is okay, that he's working toward his own future, that'll be good enough. It'll have to be.

The message I send him is short.

I exclude my phone number.

A girl can only take so many hits before she stops getting

207

back up, and I'm not sure what it'd do to me if I wait for a text message that never comes.

~

Some of the football team is home when I walk down the basement stairs. I hear their loud footsteps and booming voices, something crashing followed by varied laughter, and it makes me *angry*. I've been in a mood all day, replaying Raine's words over and over and letting them simmer with every passing minute.

I thought Aiden understood how much doing things on *my terms* meant to me. Nobody controlled my life anymore. It was me making the decisions. Where to live. Who to talk to. Who to *sleep with*. But here we are, at a house that *Aiden* lives in with *his* friends after *he* got me kicked out of the one place I'd secured for myself.

When I walk into the basement to find both the common room and Aiden's empty, I walk upstairs to see if he's there.

It's rare I spend time with the others because I don't like being in anyone's way. The guys are always nice if I'm in the kitchen grabbing food or making them something as payment for letting me stay—greeting me with head nods or a small "hi" or "hey," shooting me polite smiles, or if they're DJ, tackle hugging me because he has no sense of personal space. Some of them will thank me for whatever I leave on the counter or fridge for them to eat, and once in a while, I'll get requests of certain things to make next.

Despite my protests, Aiden makes us come up and join them for random movie nights, and unlike when the girls did it at the house, it's never that bad. Maybe because my former childhood friend would always be pressed against me, his entire side plastered against mine, and his tense personality warning away anyone from paying us much attention. It always feels safe with him. Comfortable. Effortless.

That sense of safety should be enough for me not to cause a scene right now, but I guess I have my parents' temper after all.

"Where is Aiden?" I ask Justin, the first poor soul I see.

He stops what he's doing, peeling off his coat and boots and nearly falling when he narrowly avoids stepping on his bum knee, and blinks at me. "He's in the living room with the guys, I think."

I walk past him, ignoring DJ and the blond—Skylar—he's been hanging around lately when he tries saying something to me in the hall about making more carrot cake, and enter the large den where the remaining few Dragons players are surrounding the TV and watching some sort of game footage.

Aiden is planted on the love seat off to the side, instantly turning his head in my direction before I can say a word.

It's always been like that.

Since the day we first met, his eyes would find me no matter where I was, how many people were around us, or how loud things were even when I was silent. At night, he'd stir from bed when I lifted his window and crawled over the pane as quietly as possible. He'd follow me to the fort even if I never asked him to.

Aiden always knows.

Senses.

It's unnerving.

"We need to talk," I inform him, crossing my arms over my chest and ignoring the looks I get from his buddies.

I think I hear a murmured "Aw, shit" from one of them

and Caleb say, "Here we go," but I don't bother giving them a look. If Raine kept her word, not even the team's running back knows what storm is brewing inside me.

Aiden stands and walks around the guys, someone mumbling the *Jaws* theme song while others join in, which makes me want to smack them all, before the six-five tight end stops in front of my tense body. "Are you okay?"

Am I okay? I snort. "That's one hell of a question, Griffith."

More noises from the peanut gallery behind us leave Aiden threading his fingers with mine before tugging me along with him toward the basement door. My heart *thump, thump, thumps* loudly in my chest as little tingles shoot up from our joined palms.

A lump of unspoken feelings forms in my throat, making it hard to swallow. I have to reach in deep, pushing the way his hand fits against mine out of the way, and remember why we're having this conversation.

I slip my palm from his despite how much I enjoy the warmth and scratchiness of his calluses from all the work he does with his hands. Distractions while having this talk aren't what I need, so I take a few steps back to distance myself from the way he smells and how his hard body towers over me like an open invitation to wrap my legs around him.

"You got me kicked out."

He stares.

"You *made* Sydney kick me out."

His jaw ticks.

"Are you really going to stand there and not say a fucking word? I can't believe you would tell her to do something like that! Did you not think I'd find out? Did you not care? Did—"

"Why the hell are you angry for leaving that shithole when you have somewhere ten times better to sleep?"

That makes me scoff, the frustration flowing through my veins. "Oh, and I suppose it's better because you're here? You need to get your ego in check, buddy."

His nostrils flare as he steps forward, fists clenching and unclenching. "Because there are walls that don't have mold, ceilings that aren't leaking, and people who aren't trying to scratch your eyes out or get into your pants every two goddamn seconds. That's why."

"You're kidding, right? You can't really say that anymore considering where your cock was, so don't play the Saint Aiden angle like you're better than the others who wanted in my pants. You got what you wanted."

Another step forward. "Is that what this is about? We slept together and I had to leave early for campus? It isn't like I ditched you considering you've been living here *in my bed* for weeks now. I didn't use you. I didn't touch you then or make any move that indicated that's why I brought you here. Try again."

"This isn't about that!" I yell. "And you're such an asshole for even thinking it is. You told somebody to *kick me out* of the place I was staying. A place I got *by myself*. Somewhere I could stay that didn't involve me having to suck somebody's dick just to get a few hours of sleep. That's screwed up, Aiden! Admit it. Own up to it for once instead of trying to play the goddamn superhero. That shield on your arm doesn't actually make you Steve Rogers."

The door opens from the top of the stairway and footsteps hesitantly descend, halting the conversation. When Caleb pops up, he's rubbing the back of his neck and clearing his throat. "Hey, so...er, the guys are sort of eavesdropping at the top of the stairs and they're hearing everything you're saying. Yelling doesn't really help if you want this kept between you two. Thought I'd warn you."

Aiden gives his red-faced friend a terse nod before Caleb disappears again, exchanging words with the people I now know are getting a free show at the top of the stairs.

"Your friends know my big secret now. I'm sure they'll love my company even more whenever they see me, thinking about exactly what I'm willing to do for some sleep and a slice of pizza." I look away, hiding the way my cheeks heat. I don't want to be embarrassed for what had to be done in the past. Aiden's words are pinned in my mind.

You're a survivor.

So why don't I feel like one?

He finally speaks up again. "We're not going to get anywhere if we're yelling. And the guys won't do or say a damn thing about what they heard. I'll make sure of it."

"I don't care if they do," I lie.

He eyes me knowingly.

"Why did you do it?" I ask him.

"To get you out of there."

"What if I didn't want that?"

"You don't want charity," he corrects, tone not allowing for any argument. "But that hasn't stopped you from sleeping in my bed every night. I don't force you there. I didn't force you to kiss me or make you spread your legs. We both wanted it. You being here is no hardship for anyone, least of all you. If anything, you're the one with something to gain."

I glare over his dry sentiment. "Considering you lost your virginity"—I make sure my voice is loud enough for our audience upstairs—"to me, I'd say I'm not the only one who's gaining something from this arrangement. Whether I

212

opened my thighs for you or not isn't the deciding factor. I'm allowed to be pissed off that you made a decision for me that wasn't yours to make. Not when you knew what it meant to me to have control, and you still took it away."

One more step and we're facing off. "You can keep telling yourself that all you want, sweetheart, but you'll have to admit you like being here eventually."

I say nothing.

Neither does he.

It goes on for a long stretch of time until I hear someone from upstairs say, "Do you think they're making out?"

Then another person says, "Was Griffith really a fucking virgin?"

I grin. He remains stoic.

Eventually, I look him in the eyes and quietly say, "I need control, Aiden. Not the illusion of it. Without control I…" I sniff back tears and feel my ducts burn from the weakness trying to escape me. "Sometimes I wish that the blade would have done what it was supposed to when I put it through my skin two years ago. We could have avoided all this…anger. Uncertainty. At least then I would have controlled my fate instead of letting it control me."

His Adam's apple bobs. "Don't say that. It didn't work because you weren't meant to succumb to those demons. Not then. Not now. Especially not when I'm back in your life again."

I try stopping my jaw from quivering, my bottom lip trembling as I force out, "You can't stop the voices in my head, Aiden. Especially not when you're gone. We're on borrowed time. Maybe we always were."

His large palm cups my cheek, and without thinking, I lean into it. "But that doesn't mean I can't try, Ivy. The reason I finally decided to talk to you that day in Bea's is because I was done waiting for you to. I didn't want to leave knowing I didn't even try to regain what we had. Let me help you. Let me try to do something. This doesn't have to be goodbye. We have options. *You* still have a choice, and I'm *asking you* to choose me."

I close my eyes.

He releases a breath.

It's completely silent upstairs.

Chapter Eighteen

AIDEN

WE WIND UP MOLDED together as I wrap my arms around her as tightly as possible, like I can suffocate the monsters that live in her mind. Her cheek rests against my drumming heartbeat, one of my hands cradling the back of her head. "How many times have you thought that?"

Her tone is throaty. "Too many."

"Have you hurt yourself again?" I try keeping my tone even, but the hardness leaks through. Chaos has been fidgety lately, always tugging on her shirtsleeves, always running her fingers over the scars I know she hides. It's made me nervous, like at any moment, I'll find blood on the sheets or stains on her clothing.

When she says nothing, my throat thickens with a need to know.

"Have you hurt yourself again, Ivy? You need to tell me so we can do something about it."

Her body locks in my hold, but I don't let her shut down. My fingers thread through her hair, combing the locks gently. Eventually, her quiet voice breaks the screaming thoughts swirling around in my skull. "No."

I let myself breathe.

Until, "But I've wanted to."

Drawing back and tipping her chin up to meet my eyes, I search her distant expression. The colored orbs staring at me aren't focused and they're glassy from an urge I'll never be able to understand. "What can I do?"

She shakes her head, staying quiet as her jaw quivers under my fingers.

My fingers tighten on her chin, not letting her do this. "What do you need from me?"

A tear escapes one of her eyes and trails slowly down her face. I capture it with my thumb, watching as more follow suit. "To let me have even the slightest control no matter how bad you think you know better. I know you want to help. To fix things. But you can't. I'm the only person who can do something about my life, Aiden. You need to accept that or you *will* lose me."

I let out a strangled breath, knowing it's not that easy. "Baby, I don't know how to do that." She tries looking away, but I won't let her break eye contact as she lets it out. "But I'll try the best I can. I'm sorry. Caleb and Raine would talk about how horrible the house was and you've had enough of that shit in the past. You deserve to be someplace where people want you. *I* want you here. I want to protect you when I couldn't before. It's going to be hard to go against that nature."

She attempts to move from my grasp, but I refuse to let her block me from experiencing this together.

She's human.

And she hates it.

"I'll help you feel better," I vow, sliding my hands down her sides as I lower to my knees in front of her. Her shaky breath releases sharply as I find the waistband of her leggings and steadily pull them down, revealing a scrap of white lace underneath.

"Aiden—"

"Shh."

Pulling the material away from her center, I lean forward and press a kiss against her bare skin, skimming the seam of her lips.

A noise rises from her throat as her hands find my head, fingertips digging into my scalp as I part her and brush another kiss closer to where both of us want to be.

This wouldn't be the first time I've gone down on a girl, but it'll be the first time it matters. It won't be a show that some random jersey chaser puts on to make me feel good about what I'm doing but something for the woman towering over me to remember after it's done. I've never liked fake people like the chicks I messed with before, and the tears still dampening Chaos's face as I trace my tongue along her folds tell me this is as real as she can get.

Caressing the smooth skin between her thighs, I murmur, "You shave."

Her voice wavers when she croaks, "I—I wax. I don't..." There's a brief pause, a sharp breath with every stroke of my lips and tongue against her clit. "I don't always trust myself with a r-razor."

Rewarding the honesty the best way I can, I flatten my tongue against her clit and stroke the seam of her to gather the arousal quickly building with one of my fingers. The tip of my finger grazes her wet opening before moving back upward to the bundle of nerves my tongue is working. She moans out my name and digs her fingertips into my scalp harder until there's a bite of pain, but I don't stop sucking her as I work my finger inside.

Her hips arch forward, her legs shaking slightly, until I grab ahold of one of her thighs to steady her. She begins moving to the pace I set, rolling her pelvis forward until my face is full of her soaked pussy.

The rapid pants of mumbled words are all I hear as I lap her with my tongue and coax her body into giving her the release it needs, clearing her head of thoughts and her chest of feelings it doesn't need to hold on to.

The determination to give her that freedom has my mouth and fingers working her faster and harder until she throws a leg over my shoulder to open herself up to me more and ride the wave that takes over.

I pull back enough to grab ahold of her and walk us backward to the couch, lying on my back. She falls with me, her eyes glazed over as I gesture for her to come closer, until she repositions over my face. My palms grip her inner thighs, fingers wrapping around what I can of her legs, which straddle my face as I lift up and continue giving her everything I can.

Her hands keep my face pressed against her as she comes silently riding me, the fingers I move to get her off quicker being clenched as they milk her orgasm. I take everything she gives me, tasting her, memorizing her, until her body stills completely.

Pulling out my fingers, I kiss her one last time before putting her panties back in place and watching her slide off me.

When I stand, I wipe my mouth off with the back of my hand and help pull her leggings back up, taking the flush of her cheeks as a victory.

We stare at each for a moment, her breath steadily going back to normal as a palm slides down the front of me. I stop her as she hovers over the obvious erection in my jeans. "Only you."

Her throat bobs as she swallows, fingers squeezing me once before letting go. I'm about to say something when she reveals, "I messaged Porter today." Her sudden exclamation leaves me silent, causing her to shift from one foot to another, her flushed face turning pink. "I need to know he's okay." My mouth opens to reply when she cuts me off. "He plays football at the high school."

This time, I nod. "I know. Mom and Dad sometimes bring him up when I'm home. He's good from what I hear. Quarterback of the team."

Her head bobs once, lost in the confirmation.

"He's doing fine," I tell her. I'm not sure that's what she wants to hear though. "But it's okay if you don't want that."

Her eyes snap to mine, narrowed and ready to lash. "Why wouldn't I? I've always wanted the best for my little brother. I—" She stops herself, averting her eyes.

"I know you have. I know that better than anybody, don't you think?" I take her hand and squeeze it. "But sometimes that grates on people. You can't always be the punching bag so others miss the hits, and that's what you were to your parents, just so he wouldn't have to deal with it. That's a lot for anybody to deal with for as long as you did."

Ivy has nothing to say to that.

I decide to prod. "Do you want a relationship with him?"

"Like I said, I want to know he's okay. I need to know because…"

I wait for her to finish, the seconds ticking by and her mouth parting and closing with no words escaping the fullness of them. "Chaos?"

Her eyelids pinch together as she withdraws her hand. "Please stop calling me that." The pain in her tone makes me study her even closer, her eye twitching and lips weighing heavily at the corners. "I need to know he's okay because I'm not, and one of us should be."

When her voice cracks, I swallow back the urge to clock everyone who made her feel that way in their fucking faces.

Ivy is a living, breathing oxymoron.

Chaotic and selfless.

She puts her guard back up and looks at the door leading outside, her next move obvious as she takes a step away from me.

I do nothing to stop her with every inch she puts between us. "I don't want to be Chaos anymore" is all she leaves me with, her face and tone devoid of any shred of emotion.

When she leaves, I don't follow no matter how bad I want to. I give her the control she pleaded for and wait until the door closes behind her before sitting down on the couch.

I think about Chet Wilkins and drop my face into my hands with a heavy sigh. "What the fuck am I doing?"

Chapter Nineteen

IVY

IT'S BEEN OVER A week of avoiding Aiden at the house, and he's made it too easy. Every night, I fall asleep on the couch, hoping he'll get the hint, and every morning, I wake up in his bed after he carries me there. The difference is that he's never with me—his body heat gone from the sheets, leaving me with cold cotton when I open my eyes and turn to his empty side of the mattress.

When I creep out of his bedroom this morning, I find his body draped uncomfortably across the cushions of the small couch. I'm halfway out of the room when I double back with a drop of my head to cover him with a blanket. He doesn't have anywhere to be on Sundays, unlike me, so he should sleep in as long as he can.

He disappeared for a few days with Caleb and DJ, and the only text I got from him about it was *be back soon*. And while I didn't deserve any further explanation, the guys remaining upstairs knew I was anxious when they'd come down hesitantly to ask if I wanted to hang out and watch TV or join them for dinner when they ordered delivery. Aiden must have asked them to make me feel included.

Three days of no Aiden should have been a relief, a break from his concern over what I admitted, yet I was out of my mind wondering if I'd finally chased him away like I tried doing from the start.

I barely get to the stairs when I hear a gruff "thank you" coming from the couch. Glancing over my shoulder, I see Aiden's arm still draped over his eyes and his body in the same contorted position as before.

Swallowing, I whisper, "Go back to sleep."

There's a humming noise coming from the big brute as I go up the main set of stairs. When I walk into the kitchen, Caleb and Raine are sitting at the table and DJ is putting together food at the counter.

"Good morning," Raine greets first, smiling up from the plate of eggs in front of her.

DJ turns to me, arms open. "Morning. How about a hug to start the day?"

Caleb throws something at his teammate and DJ smacks it away right before it hits his chest. "Knock it off, bro."

"I'm just being a good roommate."

I grab my favorite Starbucks drink from the fridge, which magically started appearing shortly after I moved in. "Do you hug all your roommates?"

Raine giggles. "That'd be interesting."

DJ looks offended. "I happen to give damn good hugs. The guys would be lucky to receive one."

"To receive, huh?" Caleb glances at the blond, whose cheeks tint at the insinuation his teammate makes. "Didn't know you were so generous, Danny Boy."

Turning to DJ, I ask, "Danny?"

He grumbles at Caleb. "Yeah, Danny."

"Short for Daniel," Raine pipes in.

"Huh." I uncap my drink and take a sip.

Danny decides to ignore all of us. "Do you want some breakfast before you go to work? I make a mean omelet."

Both Raine and Caleb nod.

"How do you know I'm working?"

Caleb laughs. "You do realize we had to go to Bea's every single Sunday with Aiden, right? It took us a couple of visits before we realized why he was so insistent on going when he only used to go there every once in a while."

Raine bites back a smile. "It's true. When Caleb told me that it was you Aiden was going to see, I almost couldn't believe it."

A blush creeps under my cheeks that I try hiding from everybody. "Oh, well…"

DJ's arm drops over my shoulder, tugging me into his side. "The guys all fucked with him after it was obvious he was drooling over you."

The running back chuckles. "It's hard not to when your friend goes from zero to one hundred in no time flat. Dude never parties, drinks, or lets any of the girls lure him into a room alone. Then you show up and he threatens to punch us in the nuts if we look at you wrong."

A loud laugh bursts from DJ. "Remember what he said to Brady? Get this, Ives. Justin didn't know your man had already claimed you and said something at the bakery one day. We all thought we'd get kicked out when Griff got all up in his face and threatened to cut off his dick and shove it down his throat."

My eyes widen as I look to Caleb for confirmation. He nods in agreement, stretching his legs out and stealing

Raine's coffee. "Dude is serious about a lot of things, and you shot to the top the second he saw you."

Throat tightening, I cap my drink and quickly grab my coat from the hall outside the kitchen. "As interesting as this talk is, I should get going. Thanks for the breakfast offer though."

Caleb quickly stands. "Let me drive you. We got some snow overnight and I doubt it'd be a nice walk since the town sucks at clearing the sidewalks before noon."

I try refusing, but he's already grabbing his keys and gesturing toward the door. We're walking toward his truck when I say, "You don't have to do this."

"I know." I'm buckling in and sitting on my hands to warm them from the cold cab when he starts up the vehicle and turns to me. "I can't tell you where we went, so don't ask."

"I…" Well, okay, I *was* going to ask. "I hope wherever you went was relaxing for him. He deserves it."

A noise rises from the driver's seat. "He can't be distracted for the game coming up. The Raiders did him in. It'll be hard for him even if he won't admit it."

Instantly, my gaze drops to my lap as if I'm about to get the same talk their coach already delivered.

"He got screwed over at Wilson Reed," he explains. "He'll tell you it was his fault, but they were basically hazing the guy. I told him he could have filed a lawsuit against the school and probably won. You know, petitioned to stay on the team based on wrongful acts from the upperclassmen on the Raiders. But you know him. He didn't want to fight it. Said something about it being a losing battle. I don't know." He shakes his head at the thought. "They gave up something good, but their fuckup was great for the Dragons. It's going to be a game of vengeance out there, but he needs his head in the game. He can't be worrying about whether you're okay or what he can do to fix it when he can't even do that for himself."

I stare down at the dirt, pine needles, and other things on the carpeted floor as he backs out of the driveway. "I know that. I've told him to stop worrying about me, but he won't listen. *You* know him too. He always puts others first even when we don't want him to."

"From what Aiden says, that's not too far off from what people say about you."

I want to roll my eyes at that, but when I think about it, I realize he may not be totally off. I never like to compare myself to anyone, least of all Aiden, but we both want what's best for each other. I'm not sure I can fault him for everything he's done for me, no matter how much I want to.

Caleb's sigh is one I take as agreement.

"I heard there'd be blood on the field because of his transfer here," I remark timidly, knowing this is probably the longest conversation we've had, since I usually bow out before he can get to know me any better.

That earns a small snort from him. "If there is, it wouldn't come from Aiden. He's a big guy, sure, but he's not a violent one. You'd know that if you took him up on his thousands of offers to attend one of the home games. DJ on the other hand…"

My nose scrunches. "DJ?"

"Kid may be an animal-loving flirt, but he can be vicious out there. We have to reel him in sometimes. Don't let the smile fool you."

I can't help but grin to myself. "His smile never fooled me before."

"Probably a good thing," Caleb remarks nonchalantly.

"Just because Griff isn't a violent player doesn't mean he won't beat someone for looking at you the wrong way. DJ was right about the Brady thing. Aiden never had beef with anybody, but we all thought shit was going down that day our captain said something."

The skin on the back of my neck tingles and rises until it settles under my cheeks. It's hard opening up to anybody when I've only ever really let Aiden in when we were younger. Trying to talk to his friend is new territory. "For the record, I want to be there for him. But we haven't been talking after…um, the other night. Then you guys left, and I'm not asking for details, but I haven't known what to say or do to make it better. I know he's trying to give me what I asked for, but it's driving me nuts."

He's quiet for a moment, contemplative as he waves at someone passing by in the other lane. "The guys all have a lot of respect for Aiden. If he asks us not to say something, we don't. We give him space because he works better without being crowded. And we protect what's important to him because we all get that he'd do the same for any of us. You'll get through whatever the hell has been eating at you guys, but go easy on him. He's put a lot of time into football and school, and as much as I want him to put that same effort into you, into being happy, I know something has to give first."

I know what he's getting at, and I squirm in discomfort over it. Everyone wants me to let him shine as if I'm trying to dirty him somehow, but I've been his biggest fan since day one. I was there for him when he came home from all the football games I was never allowed to go to because Mom wanted me home. I soaked in every single detail about his victories even if I didn't understand them. I was there to tell him to research the best schools that could get him to the pros faster because I knew he wanted to do what he loved for as long as he could. He never cared about the fame or the money or anything else.

It's always been the game.

"If I wanted to apologize to him about avoiding him and support him at the game on Friday..."

His friend looks at me as he slows down near the bakery. "I don't think you'll need to grovel for long if that's what you're asking. And he's been trying to get you to a game since he finally got the balls to talk to you, so it's not like he'd throw a fit if you showed up. Especially not at that one. He'll need plenty of supporters to handle his own demons when he steps onto that turf." While his truck idles at the curb, Caleb shifts his body toward mine and rests an arm on the steering wheel. "Listen, Griff is my friend. He barely talks to any of us lately without biting our heads off. I'm not saying that's your fault. We all know he's his own worst enemy and doesn't make things easy for himself. But that's what worries me. You guys are too similar. One of you needs to cave. So give the guy a break, would you? It's officially Thanksgiving break now, and Aiden could definitely use a vacation from giving himself to everybody else. He's wearing himself thin, so change that."

"I didn't mean to cause a rift at the house. I never wanted to move in to begin with because I always complicate things like this."

"We don't mind," he tells me.

"Because Aiden *told* you not to mind."

He shakes his head. "Nah. Raine and I knew you were a laid-back chick since the day we met you. And the guys like you because you're not afraid to talk back or put DJ in his place when he oversteps. You don't care what people think of you and it's refreshing. Most girls who wind up at our house are the opposite because they want to be front and center. And let's be real. You feed the guys, so they'll almost always come back like stray animals wanting more."

I don't reply because I don't want to hear about all the women who probably visited Aiden in the past. Not that it could have been too often knowing what I do about him now.

Caleb clears his throat like he knows where my mind went. "Yeah, well, guess after your guys' talk, it's pretty obvious he kept to himself when some of the jersey chasers found their way inside. So…"

I open the door, not wanting to have this talk with him. "Thanks for the ride."

Before I close the door, he says, "Coach has a soft spot for Griff. I know he talked to you a while back and I'm glad you said whatever you did to him. Coach Pearce is a great guy, but he's so busy building a beast on the field he forgets that there are certain things that Aiden is capable of balancing off it too. I doubt Coach'll care too much if Aiden drives to the game instead of bussing with us. Might be good to have some headspace to prepare for whatever will happen out there."

I don't say anything.

He adds, "Might be good for him to have you beside him, because it won't be easy going back to the place that let him go so easily."

It's hard to swallow as I acknowledge his comment with a short nod before walking toward the bakery.

Would it be better for him?

Something tells me driving to the college that didn't

want him with the girl who left him behind will produce the opposite results.

He can't be distracted.

I don't want to see your face.

My fingers ball into a fist and release when I walk in and see Elena's bubbly face. "Out of your head," I tell myself.

Another day.

Another front.

But the itch under my skin still remains.

"Head in the game."

Chapter Twenty

AIDEN

I'M TOSSING THE FOOTBALL up in the air and catching it when Ivy shows up at the doorway of my bedroom. Clenching the ball in my hands, I examine her Bea's Bakery shirt and tight ripped jeans, both absent of the sugar and coffee stains usually caked on when she gets home. "You're back early."

She hesitates for a moment before walking in, eyes going from me to the mess of papers and books I left scattered on the desk and floor out of frustration. "Bea let me leave early because it was slow. Are you having trouble with your project?"

I shake my head, tossing the ball again and staring at the ceiling. "You've barely said a word to me in days and you want to talk about school?"

She's quiet as she walks over and sits on the edge of the bed, picking at the lint on the blanket. "No, not really. I don't even like school." Her shoulders droop slightly. "My parents never hit me," she says quietly, causing me to catch the ball and raise my brows at the random admission I already knew.

Sitting up, I lean against the headboard and remain silent while she stares at her twisted hands that fidget on her lap.

"Do you remember that one time I knocked on your window and you had to help me in because I was crying so bad I couldn't climb in myself?"

The memory hits me hard. Her tear-stained face and shaking hands struggled to grip the windowpane, and she was trying to swallow her sobs so my parents wouldn't hear as I helped her inside. "I remember," I grit out, jaw ticking over the path of memory lane I still struggle with revisiting. "I asked what happened and you could barely say a word. We—"

"Ended up falling asleep on your bed once I calmed down and never talked about it," she finishes for me, nodding slowly. "You told me as long as I came to you, I didn't have to say anything. All that mattered was that we had each other like we promised we would."

I swallow down the rise of emotion that tries working its way up my throat.

"I'm not asking you to give me that out all the time, Aiden, just on the things I already struggle with. I'm sorry for walking away and ignoring you when you were trying to help, but I'm not used to you being so demanding. Before, you were a lot…"

Cocking my head, I wait for her to finish enlightening me on who I was back then.

"Er, softer isn't the right word, but more…patient. And I get that it's probably because we went from seeing each other every day to being apart for years but—"

"That's not why," I cut her off.

Her face scrunches. "It's not?"

Dropping the ball onto the mattress beside me, I cross

my arms over my chest. "I may have been patient back then, but it didn't mean I wanted to be. Every time you'd come into my room and didn't tell me what happened, it drove me fucking nuts. But I knew if I asked, you'd probably brush it off like it was nothing, and that would have made me angrier. I took your silence, but I never accepted it."

She blinks at me. "Oh."

My lips flatten into a grim line at her response. "The reason why I want to know things now is because we're older, we're away from the place that made you crawl into my bed crying, and we have a chance to fix it. I'm not saying you can talk it out and forget all the reasons that made you want to leave home. I'll never understand that because I've never been in your shoes. I may have heard your parents fight. Hell, the whole neighborhood did."

She winces at the fact.

"But pretending like that part of you doesn't exist means you can't move on from it. Holding on to the shame you feel for not swallowing your pride and going home when you knew you couldn't do it by yourself isn't going to get you anywhere. Trust me, the only way to stop letting shit take over your life is to face it head-on. *That's* when you can find more than a scrap of the control you need."

She squirms on the bed, drawing her legs up to cross under her. "Like your game on Friday? People say it'll be an interesting one. Are you going to face Wilson Reed head-on?"

I scoff. "I'm sure people have said that, especially if you've been talking to Caleb again. The Raiders had every right to kick me off their team. It's just a game." The last bit is a lie, and she sees through it.

"Doesn't mean it can't hurt." Her refutation doesn't soak in, so she tries a new method that has my chest tightening.

"You wouldn't like it if I said the guys had a right to treat me like shit just because I stepped into their homes."

"Don't," I warn.

"So," she presses, "you can't say what happened there doesn't hurt you. I know they're a good school. Elena babbles about the pro players that have come from there. You used to talk about Wilson Reed when we were younger. Even if you're making a future right where you are, it's okay to admit you care about how you got here. I know how much getting into that school would have meant to you, and I'm sorry I wasn't there to celebrate when you got the acceptance letter or comfort you when everything happened."

"I couldn't care less about them," I insist, trying to drill it into her stubborn head. "Our situations don't compare. Don't you get it by now? If they made an exception for me, if I put up a fight like my parents wanted me to, I wouldn't have come here. We never would have seen each other again."

Her eyes go back to her lap. "You don't know that for sure."

"At the risk of you being pissed off and walking out again"—she doesn't hide the slight flinch from me—"I *know* it's true. How else would we have seen each other? You wouldn't go back home on your own, you admitted that already. I tried looking you up online but you said you had a fake name so nobody could find you. Tell me how else we would have met up? Because I've got nothing."

"I…" Her voice fades before she clears it and picks her head up to look at me. "I would have found you. It would be hard not to with your name plastered everywhere as a big hotshot football player."

Her attempt to lighten the mood only sours mine more. "It would have taken me going pro for you to come out of the woodwork?"

Ivy's eyes round as they snap up to meet mine. "What? No. I mean, yes, but only because it would have been easier to get in touch. You've talked about going to the NFL since you first tried out for youth football. It isn't like whatever this is between us is based on what your future holds."

I blow out a frustrated breath. "I've had people from high school reach out once they heard my chances at going pro, and it never gets any easier to deal with. It's a big reason why I keep to myself. I can't get in trouble or risk my shot at what I've worked so hard for, and nobody can use me."

She frowns. "I bet that's difficult."

All I do is shake my head.

"If it makes you feel any better, I would have still found a way. Even if you weren't on billboards or in Doritos commercials wearing some famous team's jersey."

A small grin cracks on my face. "You remember."

She nudges me with her leg, a matching smile teasing her lips. "That we used to make up random commercials for Doritos and pretend you were their newest poster boy? Yeah. I remember that well."

We both get a laugh over the old memories of us perching ourselves in front of my mother's video camera and acting out a scene. Ivy always told me to keep it under sixty seconds and would make me do it over again if I went over.

Once the nostalgia wears off, the reality sinks back in. We lose the smiles and watch each other with wariness.

It's me who says, "I may be a demanding prick these days, but it's because I want what's best for you. Is that so bad?"

She bites her bottom lip and slowly shakes her head. "I guess not."

"Then why do you fight me?"

"A lot of reasons. Do I really deserve you treating me

with respect? Sometimes it feels like I should have a worse life than I already do for making the choices I have. It's fight or flight for me, Aiden. It always has been."

"You don't have to do either here."

I can tell she wants to argue but something in her mind tells her not to. Instead, she says, "The day you had to help me into your room was the first day I'd ever thought about hurting myself. I heard Mom telling somebody on the phone that she thought about packing up and leaving. I don't know who she was talking to, but she said something about not being sure if she'd take us. When she found out I overheard, she tried telling me it was because she'd have to find a job and get her own money before she could support Porter and me. But there was something in her eyes that made me feel like she was lying. I'd felt like a burden before whenever she'd say how much she wished she weren't stuck at home with us or married or how much she wished she'd gotten an education to have a different life for herself.

"I guess I thought if I hurt myself, maybe she would feel differently. Be motherly. Feel bad about all the times she wanted a different life because she was stuck with two kids. It wasn't like she was cold to me my whole life. She'd take care of me when I was sick, make my favorite food for my birthdays if they had the money, and buy me things whenever she could. But the moments she and Dad were at each other's throats, it was like she was a different person. I remember her telling me once that love changes people, and I never understood why she let it. There are so many things that could have made them better. They could have sold the store or split up or *something*. I mean, no kid wants to see their parents get divorced, but it's better than them constantly being visited by the cops when their fights get too loud and making their kids feel like part of the problem."

The first time the lights from the cop car lit up my house after the Underwoods moved in next door, I'd asked Mom if everything was okay with Ivy. We hadn't known each other long at that point, but I knew cops showing up usually wasn't a good sign. Mom was holding the phone to her chest with a frown on her face as she looked out the window, her eyes focused on the large bay window that lined up with their living room. When she glanced down at me, she rubbed my shoulder and told me to go back to bed after saying, "Ivy is fine, sweetie. Her parents just need a little guidance, that's all."

And I believed her.

Until it happened again.

And again.

And again, until I saw her father being put into the back of one of the cop cars.

When I made the pact with Ivy, I wanted her to know she could always come to me whenever she needed someone. It took one more fight between her parents for her to tap on my window after dark and make a spot for herself in my closet.

I promised her I'd never speak a word to either Mom or Dad about her frequent sleepovers, but I think they knew. Mom would give me extra food and a knowing look or leave one or two more blankets on my bed. But we never discussed it, so I kept the charade up.

"I didn't hurt myself until after I left." Her voice breaks me from the red and blue memories, dissolving them until her face comes back into view. "That day I was at the hospital was a wakeup call for me. I could find another way. I thought it'd be better if I left. There were…things that were said to me out of anger, things that couldn't be taken back. Sometimes Mom would apologize, but most times she pretended it never happened or acted like she wasn't serious. Those sorts of things build and build and build, collecting under your skin and in your soul until you can't take it anymore. Sometimes the emotions won't come out on their own and you need to do something about it. It started with my thighs for me. A tiny cut here and there. Then it got worse with each day that went by after leaving that letter and realizing there was no looking back."

My fists clench until there's a bite of pain in the centers of my palms from where my fingernails dig in. "You always had a home with us. If you didn't want to go back to your parents, I could have convinced my parents to find a space for you at my place."

"Don't do that," she tells me gravely. "I already told you that you can't wish for things to be different. None of us get a do-over button in life. I used to stay up at night wondering what would happen if I went home and begged for forgiveness, but nothing would have changed. My parents would be angry, maybe angrier, and they'd fight and make me feel worthless all over again. If I wasn't a burden then, leaving and causing a scene like that would have made me a big one if I'd gone back. I'd be the chaos in their lives like they said I was."

My lips part. "What?"

Her tongue dips out for a moment in contemplation before nodding. "Mom was on edge about everything and I kept asking for money and attention, things Porter seemed to get so easily from them. And I'll always remember Mom saying, 'I don't need all this extra chaos right now, Ivy. And that's all you are.' And that wasn't the first time she'd indicated

I was the chaos in her life. She'd said it when I was little and would do something stupid like draw on the walls or accidently knock something over when I was playing. She'd be upset with Dad and say things to me that I remember to this day." When she sees my face, she frowns but manages to reason with me. "The thing is, I sort of get it. When our emotions run high, we say things we don't mean. I like to be by myself when I'm upset because I've seen firsthand what our emotions can do to us if we're not careful.

"Either way, it started feeling like I was the chaos she said I was, even if all I wanted was for everyone to get along. I stopped remembering what it felt like to hear them talking instead of fighting. I wasn't able to remember when Dad would come home. Sometimes he'd just be there, and the only reason I'd know is because they'd find something to argue about. He avoided her when she'd suggest selling the store, she'd get upset when he ignored her, I'd fail at making it better, and it'd start all over another day. It's why I don't like being called Chaos. I tried making a joke out of it, like I could embrace what I was, but it stopped being funny when I realized Mom might be right."

Even though I shake my head in disagreement, there aren't words to tell her that isn't true. She'll always believe her version of things, and nobody will convince her otherwise.

I remember Mom and Dad coming back home after I told them Ivy ran away. Mom's eyes were red, but she tried hiding them from me, and Dad patted my back and shook his head when Mom disappeared into their room as if to tell me to leave her alone. When he went in after her, I heard them talking, Mom's wavering voice asking Dad, "How can they just send her away, John? She has a life and friends here, and they act like they don't care."

I never understood what they meant. Ivy told me she was getting on a bus and finding something better for herself.

Come with me.

Three words that haunt me still.

But not as much as the two I replied with.

I can't.

Ivy picks at the skin along her nails, focusing solely on them instead of looking anywhere else. Definitely not at me. "I'm always going to be screwed up because of the decisions I made, Aiden. There's no getting rid of what I've done. There's no forgetting the nightmares I wake up from or the memories I get trapped in. The feelings deep inside me are engraved in my soul. I'll never fully be better. This is…it's a lifetime of battles ahead of me, and I don't want to make anyone suffer by watching me figure out if I want to live or die when it all becomes too much. Even if I never want to remember my choices, I don't necessarily regret them, because I wouldn't be who I am today if I didn't experience what I did. Does that mean I'm proud of succumbing to my weakness? To my thoughts? No. But I have to remind myself that I want to live more than I want to die—that I have reasons to now when I didn't before."

Clicking my tongue, I rub the back of my neck and heft out a sigh. "Damn, Ivy. That's… You make it hard to be pissed at you."

When I glance back at her, she's trying not to grin, and I'm glad the thick tension has dissipated slightly. "You used to tell me that all the time."

I grumble, "Some shit never changes."

Unwinding her legs, she stretches them out beside mine. "About the game this weekend… If I wanted to attend, who do I need to blow to get a ride?"

My face shadows over. "Not funny."

She cracks a grin. "I think so." Before I counter her, she's moving forward and tracing the elastic waistband of my basketball shorts with one of her fingers. "I find myself free and interested in seeing how bad these Raiders are compared to the Dragons now that we have you. I'm sure they'll be kicking themselves for letting you go."

All it takes is her pulling down my shorts and blowing on the tip of my engorged cock for me to groan, "I'll drive us."

And the only response I get back is her lips wrapping around me until words no longer matter.

Chapter Twenty-One

IVY

THE CLOUD OF FLOUR comes out of nowhere as I'm stirring the dough, pausing to blink at the mess covering me. "Did you just…?"

I look over at Aiden—who's sporting the *I love to rub my meat* apron that DJ got him after he, Caleb, and Justin all saw their tight end helping me cook dinner—and see an unconvincing look of innocence on his face.

When he asked where I was going earlier, I told him I wanted to make some cookies. It was a way to procrastinate from doing homework, which still sits untouched in my backpack on the couch downstairs. I didn't think he'd follow, much less tie the apron around himself, but he's been letting me guide him through the recipe like his mom used to do for me.

"I'm not cleaning that up," I tell him, fighting a smile when I put the bowl down and wipe off the flour remnants from my shirt. It's impossible to look clean considering it's pure black with a mostly faded logo on it from some old soda corporation. It was a cheap thrift store find, already broken in with holes, so I guess a little flour won't kill it.

"We'll make DJ do it."

From the other room where said DJ is studying with a few of the guys for some sports class they take together, we hear, "No, you won't, Betty Crocker."

I laugh and return to the thick dough, pulling some out with the spoon and grinning at Aiden. "Remember when we used to get into fights about who'd get to lick the spoon?"

He steals the spoon from me and brings it to his mouth. "Don't act like it was any competition. My mom always let you have it. I think she loved you more than me."

I grab the wooden utensil back. "Don't put it in your mouth! I still need to use it to stir in the chocolate chips."

Another remark comes from the peanut gallery perched in the other room in the form of a "that's what she said" joke that spawns a fit of laughter among the guys.

I roll my eyes but grin as Aiden snorts at his roommate's cliché quip. It's not too far off considering where my mouth usually is every morning if Aiden hasn't already left for the gym. Seeing his face contort with pleasure as I suck him off is one of my favorite ways to start the day, and it always gets better when he flips me around, spreads my legs, and shows me the same kind of attention.

I turn toward the kitchen door. "None of you are getting these cookies if you don't shut up and study."

I feel a set of eyes on me. "Isn't that a little hypocritical considering you're doing anything in your power not to do schoolwork?"

All I do is shrug and pick up the bag of my favorite chocolate chips from the counter. When I struggle to open them, Aiden takes the bag and gets the job done with those bulging, inked muscles currently on display in the plain white tee he's wearing.

I grumble, "Show-off," causing him to snicker as I bump him with my shoulder and slowly pour the chips in. "I'm surprised the guys are doing work at all since it's break."

"Their professor decided to have an exam first thing after break ends, so they figured they'd get studying in now before they all leave after the game this weekend to head home to see family."

We haven't discussed more about Thanksgiving since he brought it up last time, and I'm grateful. It isn't like I want to avoid the topic completely, but I haven't figured out how I feel about it. Emily Griffith was the mother I always wanted, and her husband, John, was the stoic yet supportive father I wanted mine to be like too. But being around them will cause a lot of tension. Would they like me now? Would they see me as a threat to Aiden like everyone else does? Would they ask questions about what I've done to get by? They'd have no reason to want me around their son if they knew what I did.

I wouldn't want my kid around someone like me either, no matter how much I've worked on myself—bettered myself.

And the thing is, I'd hate for Aiden to feel like he has to choose between me and his parents. He chose his life before—his future career and his family. I'm not sure what he'd choose this time, but I have a feeling it'd be different. Am I ready for that? To let him in fully? To let *him* make that choice for himself?

A broad shoulder nudges my arm. "Out of your head, Underwood. You're doing that nose-scrunching thing when you think too hard."

I relax my face and sigh. "That sucks they have a test when they come back," I cop out, relieved when he hums out an agreement instead of questioning my thoughts.

I'm surprised when Aiden comes up behind me, putting one hand over mine where it holds the spoon and the other covering the one that holds the bowl in place. I settle into his back without a second thought, letting him take over stirring the chocolate chips in until they start disappearing into the sugary mixture.

"Why are you helping me anyway?" I ask, voice quiet so we can have a private moment without one of the others commenting. They're usually respectful anyway, giving us space and only teasing when the moment is right. But sometimes Aiden will shoot them all looks if he and I are together upstairs and his arm hooks around my waist or his hand slides into the back pocket of my jeans, as if he's challenging them to comment.

They never do.

They just accept what is.

So why haven't I accepted this is real? That it's actually happening?

His arms tighten around me. "Because baking makes you happy, and I like seeing you that way. And I enjoy spending time with you even when you're scowling at everyone."

I go to refute the statement but stop myself, knowing my resting bitch face is top notch. All the guys tease me about it. Even Justin admitted he was shocked I was a "cool chick" after getting to know me better because I always looked two seconds away from murdering someone in class.

"You must keep really bad company if I'm the only person you enjoy spending time with," I tease, twisting to look up at him with a smirk.

He's already looking down at me. "You do get me off like no other."

I elbow him as hard as I can, which is still a weak attempt

at bodily harm on someone who has, like, two percent total body fat. "Asshole."

He chuckles above me, focusing back on the dough we're working on. "I'm fucking with you, Ivy. Don't make me say it."

"Say what?"

I feel his nose nestle against the top of my head, then his lips press against the crown of my skull. "That I like you."

Thump, thump, thump.

"That I want to see where this goes," he adds, lips peppering another kiss against me.

Thumpthump, thumpthump.

"That I hope you'll give me a shot."

I close my eyes and feel one of his arms hook around me and hug me to him. For the longest time, we're quiet. I'm about to answer him, tell him how much I like spending time with him too, even if its downstairs doing homework or listening to sports, when DJ walks into the room.

"Ugh. Get a room." He winks at us and walks over to the fridge, grabbing an energy drink. "But not before finishing the cookies." Aiden is probably glaring at him, because DJ smirks and says, "What? Your girl knows how to bake. I plan to take full advantage while she's around. Oh, don't give me that look. You know what I mean." When he turns his focus to me, his eyes roll. "You need to give this guy a break and reassure him he doesn't need to worry about me stealing you away. I mean, I'm a catch, but I don't think you can handle me."

The man embracing me snorts dryly. "I think we both know it's the other way around, Bridges. Get out of here."

He never corrects DJ, or anyone, when they call me his girl.

His.

Girl.

But then again, I don't either.

Chapter Twenty-Two

IVY

THE SWEAT COVERING MY palms doesn't go away even with three passes of them over my denim-clad thighs. My eyes focus on the scenery and speeding cars we pass on the interstate as I listen to the soft sound of music crooning from the speakers of Aiden's truck. The distraction is enough to stop focusing on the destination.

"Out of your head, Underwood," Aiden tells me for the millionth time, reaching over and taking one of my hands in his. I don't remember getting sick of those words until recently. It's like I've taken up permanent residence in my head whether I like it or not. I wince at how clammy my palm is and try pulling away before he notices, but he threads our fingers and keeps them held tightly together between us like he doesn't care. "It's not going to get you anywhere. Plus, the child locks are on so you can't make a run for it."

I gape at him like he's insane. "We're going ninety on a four-lane interstate with homicidal drivers weaving in and out of traffic around us."

"Not like you haven't tried escaping a moving vehicle before" is his smart remark, which makes me glower even if it's true.

Sinking into the seat, I rest back on the headrest and study our linked hands from the corner of my eye. "You never used to touch me this much when we were younger."

A sound rises from his throat and his fingers twitch around mine. "I didn't know if you wanted me to. Things were complicated then."

My eyebrows quirk, a nervous bubble of laughter escaping my lips. "And they're not now? If anything, we're the dictionary definition of complicated these days."

"Why?"

Is he serious? There's an endless list of reasons that pop into my head. "Because I ran away from home, slept with who knows how many men for shelter, sliced myself up like a Thanksgiving turkey, and corrupted you by taking your virginity."

The grip he has on the steering wheel turns his fingers white. "You didn't 'take' anything, Ivy. I willingly gave you that. I don't even want to address the other shit because we've already talked about it. You did what you had to."

I say nothing, swallowing down the anxiety creeping up my throat.

"Your favorite color is purple, isn't it?"

I blink. "What?"

"I never understood why because your room was pink, you only wear dark colors, and I don't think you own one purple item. But you always said it was your favorite."

I think of the red and blue cop lights for a moment. Something beautiful was created from the constant chaos and I resonated with that. The purple tones would flicker and flash through the bottom of my bedroom closet whenever they'd arrive.

He goes on, "You're still obsessed with caffeine but only drink those overpriced, nasty-ass Starbucks drinks they sell at gas stations and the Stop 'n' Shop." Aiden looks at me for the quickest second before focusing back on the road. "Your eye twitches when you're irritated, like it is right now. You wear your emotions on your face, you pretend to be a bitch so people don't talk to you, and you dye your hair because…well, honestly, I don't know why you do that. You used to love how much the color was a mixture of your parents. You said it was like you got a little of both of them, but the good parts."

Wincing at the words I'd used so long ago, my hand goes lax in his to stop from fighting his persistence. I blow out a sigh. "That makes me sound like I thought they were awful all my life. They were just…intense." Shaking my head, I stare out the window. "Most of that is observations anyone could make, you know. Even DJ if he spent time paying attention to people instead of flirting with them."

"You trying to tell me all your hookups knew even one of those things about you? Something tells me they had one thing on their mind, and it wasn't your favorite color."

"Do you really want to know about them?" I take his silence as an obvious answer. "Didn't think so. For the record, you're probably right. I didn't even know half their names, so why would they know anything about me? But before you get all high and mighty for making a point, we both know it wasn't the same with them. It was a place to stay."

My eyes drift to the reflection in the sideview mirror, which shows silver-white hair with red streaks to replace my faded blue thanks to Elena's help. Once she found out I was taking the day off to go to the Wilson Reed game, she'd insisted on our school colors.

I touch one of the pin-straight ends of my hair and tug lightly. I've damaged the strands from all the chemicals I've put in it over the years. One day, I'll be comfortable enough to go back to my natural color and stop messing with it to give it time to heal. "I dye my hair because it's one of the few things I can do for myself."

He squeezes my hand. "It's control," he states in understanding. "It looks good."

"School spirit," I mock, trying to look as excited as Lena did when she saw the finished product. "According to Lena I need to have a lot of it since I refuse to hold a sign professing my undying love for you or Lindon." His long silence nips at me until I'm shifting in the seat. "Don't be weird about it."

All he offers is, "What?"

"What I said."

"About...?"

My eyes narrow. "Seriously?" I see the corners of his lips curve. "You're an ass," I mumble.

"But you tolerate it. You always have when it comes to me and the shit I say."

I flick his hand, but it doesn't budge from where it locks with mine. "That's because you were a lot nicer when we were younger. Now you're just..."

"Yes?"

"A pain in the ass."

He smirks. "Been called worse."

"I have no doubt about that. I'm sure your mom has been on the giving end of those remarks because she's always been good at calling you out on your bullshit."

We let the traffic and radio fill the quiet space between us for a few drawn-out moments before I close my eyes and say, "I loved you a lot back then. More than I should have. You weren't just a safe place for me to run to. You were... everything."

A second passes. Two.

Then, "Ivy."

"It's okay," I tell him quickly, not willing to hear him. "I was sure you didn't feel the same way. I figured that what I felt was probably infatuation. I doubt I'd know what real love was even if it smacked me upside the head."

"That's not true."

I point out the obvious to him. "My parents didn't love me."

He's silent, as if contemplating an argument but not willing to voice it.

"Maybe they did," I relent, heavy doubt weighing down my words. How many times did I choose to be optimistic because it was better than believing the worst? Glass half-full instead of glass half-empty. "Everyone says love is better shown in people's actions, not words. I don't even remember the last time Mom and Dad told me they loved me, much less showed it."

Aiden takes a deep breath. "People express love in a lot of different ways. If they didn't tell you, maybe they showed you in ways hard to accept."

"By fighting? By not bothering to change for me and Porter?"

"By letting you leave."

My eyes scan his serious face, trying to figure out where his mind is. That's when something hits me...

He let me leave too. He let me climb out his window

after the longest hug we'd ever shared and watched me disappear.

He'd given me time to get to a better place. My parents didn't love me.

But Aiden…

I'm not sure how I find my voice, but eventually I reel in my thoughts and inhale a small breath to relieve my stinging lungs. "Is that your way of saying you loved me, Aiden?"

The hand tucked around mine squeezes again but doesn't release like before. He holds on like he needs to, like he's afraid I'll go somewhere if he doesn't. "I never stopped, Ivy. Just because you left didn't mean I could forget what we'd been through. All those times we'd meet in the woods or explore the town or hang out in my room until you had to go home and check on Porter. We always found our way back to each other. When you left, I focused on perfecting football and being the best at the game to distract myself from everything."

I lick my lips. "And?"

He gives me another glance, eyes barely roaming over my stricken face, before turning back to the road and saying, "And look where it brought me. Right back here to you."

It's not an *I love you.*

But it's so much more.

The words I want to say back are stuck to my tongue, clinging on for dear life. I want to tell him I'm glad he's back in my life and about the way my limbs buzz and heart races and lips always want to stretch into a stupid smile when he's around. Fear holds the words captive in my mouth like a rope lassoing and pulling them back down my throat until I'm choking on them.

When Aiden realizes I have nothing to say, he turns

the radio up, unthreads our fingers, and white knuckles the wheel with both hands.

Tell him, I demand.

In the silence are answers left unspoken between us, but it's nearly impossible to discern which ones we want to hear and which we convince ourselves to.

I'm not even sure how to sort fact from fiction anymore because I'm so used to self-sabotaging myself before anyone else can.

Tell him, the voice in my head repeats.

But tell him *what*?

That I'll miss him when he leaves?

That I'll be waiting for him?

I'm not sure he even wants me to.

So I settle on saying nothing.

Nothing at all.

~

Aiden sets our things down on the couch in the middle of the huge hotel room, unfazed by the expensive-looking furniture we're surrounded by. According to Coach Pearce, who met us in the lobby, all the players are bunking together in one of these massive rooms except us. Someone pulled his attention away as we got our keys, but I felt the middle-aged man's eyes on me, except there was something oddly praising about the way they flitted over me, unlike at the bakery. I can't tell if it's because he appreciates the guts it took for me to stand up to him or because he thinks he's got a stronger hold on Aiden than I do.

Fighting for Aiden's attention isn't a competition, but I have a feeling the man staring at me wouldn't like the results if he's used to winning.

I'm examining the beautiful view out the windows by the queen bed when Aiden reemerges from the bathroom. "Coach wants all the guys to meet in the lobby soon." His tone is distant as he digs through his bag and pulls out a jersey. I think he's about to exchange it for the sweatshirt he's wearing, but instead he tosses it at me. I barely catch it when he says, "You have ten minutes to get ready."

I blink. "What? I thought I'd stay—"

"You'll have company to show you where to sit." His no-arguing attitude makes me start to scowl. "Don't give me that look. You may not like it, but it's what's what you need right now. Maybe you'll even thank me later."

Dread threatens to suffocate me, wrapping around my heart and trailing up to my windpipe. "What does that mean?"

He gestures toward the jersey. "Put that on and maybe I'll tell you."

The material wrinkles in my clenched hands as I watch him walk toward the door. "You know I need more than that."

Aiden's spine straightens, his hand letting go of the doorknob to turn and face me with anger across his shadowed features. "That's your problem, Ivy. You refuse to let anybody try convincing you your needs can change. But you said you wanted to do better. Put on the goddamn jersey and *trust me*."

He doesn't offer me any room to reply before storming out and slamming the door shut behind him. The picture on the wall rattles with his exit, leaving me gaping at the empty space.

My eyes drop down to the jersey.

I'd asked him to trust me before.

"If you can't come with me, then you have to let me go," I *whisper, burying my face in his neck and squeezing him as hard as*

I can. His arms are like a hook around my waist, anchoring me to the bedroom I've spent more time sleeping in than my own. "Trust me, Aiden. I've got this."

Sighing in defeat, I slide the red jersey on over my long-sleeved shirt and watch it drop to midthigh on me. I flatten my palms along the slick material and turn toward the large mirror on the wall perched over the dresser.

Number 89 is plastered in big white letters on the front, and when I turn to glance at the back, my lips waver at the bold GRIFFITH across the back.

I'm remembering all the times I wished Aiden would have offered me his team jersey in high school, knowing it would have meant something. The girls who tried worming their way into my good graces would beg me to convince him to let them wear it "in support" at the games they attended. But I knew better. They wanted to date him, to claim him, to hang on his arm. And I never liked that, so I'd always find a reason not to tell him about their interest. It wasn't like he didn't already know girls wanted to be with him. Sometimes I'd even wonder why he didn't take up offers to go to parties or dates when they'd ask him. Instead, I'd soak up how he'd tell me he preferred staying in with me. I don't know if it was a lie, but I liked to believe it wasn't.

Sitting on the edge of the bed, I pull at the shirt and blow out an exhausted breath. He was always the better one of us two, always good to me and willing to absorb my drama whenever I brought it to him. His family treated me with respect even though they knew who my parents were, and they never made me feel unwelcome even if I struggled to make conversation.

Aiden made that pact in the old war fort behind our houses knowing it wasn't for his benefit. It was for mine.

Which is why it's important now more than ever for me to follow that pact like he's always done for me. To be there for him during his big moment because it'd mean everything to him.

A knock at the door has me staring from the new shirt covering my body to the wood separating me and who I assume is Aiden. My first response is always to avoid the problem and pretend it doesn't exist, but he won't let me do that anymore if our conversation was any indication of what's to come.

I expect a mountain of a man standing behind the door when I open it, not a curly-haired dirty blond with dark-brown highlights and hesitant honey-colored eyes pointed at me. The same ones I'd seen online when I searched his name not that long ago.

Oh my God.

"Porter?" I whisper, stepping back in shock as I stare at my not-so-little brother. He towers over me now, something I'm not accustomed to. I look him over, waiting for him to disappear like a figment of my imagination.

It takes him a few seconds, but he slowly nods and shoves his hands into the pockets of his jeans. One of the knees has a rip in it that looks artfully done, and he's wearing a pair of sneakers that look exactly like another pair of Nikes he loved in the past. His favorite brand—always expensive but...him. "Yeah, it's me."

His voice is deeper, the baby fat on his face long gone and, in its place, a narrow jawline and enviable cheekbones all clean of scruff except for a little peach fuzz over his top lip. Those eyes haven't changed, and I start to wonder if mine show as much emotion as his.

No wonder Aiden can read me so well.

"What are you doing here? How…?" My eyes pop open as I take another step backward into the room as panic seeps in. "Are Mom and Dad with you?"

Skin itching at the thought of what I may have to face, I think back to all the times Mom would tell me to go to my room. Or how often Dad would ignore me because he was too tired to deal with whatever conversation I wanted to have with him when he came home from work. And Porter… I have no idea what my brother thinks of me. Not then. Not now. Sometimes I'd wonder if he wished that I would have just let our parents argue without butting in. There would have been less drama that way. I'd be invisible but still *there*. For him. For Aiden.

You can't change the past, that voice inside my head reminds me for the billionth time.

"He didn't tell you?" is my brother's response, face paling over the revelation.

I slowly shake my head in confusion.

"It's just me and…" He glances down the hall and shifts his weight from one foot to the other. "I didn't know Aiden didn't say anything. I came to see the game with his parents. They brought me so I could see you."

It's hard to swallow knowing Mrs. Griffith is here. She's the only other person besides Aiden that I idolized.

"I lied to Mom and Dad," he admits sheepishly, cheeks turning from white to pink in a microsecond. He always did that if he felt bad, blushed. "They think I'm staying at a friend's house for the weekend."

Friend's house. He has a friend. That's…good. Really good. For a long time, he'd mostly hang out with Aiden and me whenever I'd try getting out of the house. He'd have boys on his sports teams he'd talk to, but none that he invited over.

Mom and Dad didn't like entertaining anyone. That would mean people would see how imperfect they really were.

Blowing out a breath, I wipe my hands down the front of the shirt and nod to myself over the admission. Porter's eyes go to the jersey I'm wearing and his lips twitch, leveling again without giving me a solid reaction of what he's thinking.

"Will they... Will you get into trouble? If they find out you lied, I mean. I don't want you to—"

"Stop," he cuts me off quickly, pain in his eyes as he steps forward. "It'll be okay. I mean, yeah, they'd be upset, but it wouldn't be the end of the world. I, uh..."

My heart clenches at his hesitation, and I realize I need to be the person I wasn't to him before. "You can tell me," I reassure him. "I can take it. If you're angry or upset..."

His eyes go back to the hallway, looking anywhere but at me. I get it. I'm nothing like I used to be either and have no clue what to say or what not to. "Ivy, I'm not sure angry or upset quite covers what's happening in my head right now."

I run my tongue across my bottom lip, the faint taste of my bright-red lipstick hitting my taste buds as I glance at the carpet. "That's fair."

His sigh is heavy. "It's not because of what you probably think. Listen, Aiden said some...things he wants left between us. His parents are chill people and agreed to drive me here to see you and the game when Aiden suggested it."

My heart thuds. "You wanted to see me?" *When did Aiden suggest it?* "But you never replied to my message."

"Your account was gone before I could," he explains quickly. Porter starts taking a step toward me but second-guesses and ends up taking one backward instead. "I did try, Ivy. It took me a couple days to see it, and I'll be honest, I wasn't sure if I was going to respond. But then Aiden showed up at one of my practices at school."

"He *what*?" Heart thudding in my chest, I shake my head.

My brother winces. "Shit. Listen, that doesn't matter. He thought it'd be good if we had a chance to talk, so he got me a ticket. Plus, er, well, I'm being scouted by the Raiders, so I want to see what they've got going for them before I make up my mind. But I did try to respond, honest."

Eye twitching, I wrap my arms around myself and swallow my opinion on the school matter. It isn't me who has anything against the well-known university, but I can't help but feel bitter in Aiden's defense. I wouldn't want Porter to go through what Aiden did.

"I deleted my Facebook account the other day," I say sheepishly. I'd checked to see if he'd seen my message, and when I saw he hadn't, anxiety got the better of me. Instead of obsessing or waiting for the moment his message was marked as "seen" without so much as a reply, I deactivated my account and told myself I did all I could.

Porter shifts on his feet when a couple doors open down the hall and deep voices echo. "I think the team is getting ready to leave. Mrs. Griffith told me to come get you. She wanted to come with me, but her husband said to give us some space since it's been a while."

Been a while. I refrain from commenting on that understatement when DJ and Matt stop by my door and eye Porter.

Matt asks, "Is this kid giving you trouble? We don't mind helping out if he is. Aiden would want us to, or we'd get our asses handed to us."

Porter's eyes round at the way the two men crowd his space. "I'm, er—She's—"

DJ chuckles and smacks Porter. "Nice to see you again, kid. Glad you decided to come after all."

What the hell? "How do you know—" I stop when DJ shoots me an apologetic smile.

"I promised I wouldn't say anything," he tells me, and that's when I realize where their trip was to. Haven Falls. Aiden, Caleb, and DJ went to my hometown. *Our* hometown.

I sigh. "Matt, this is my brother. Stop scaring him. Aiden, and apparently DJ and Caleb, thought it'd be good to surprise me."

Matt snickers. "You don't seem like the type to like surprises."

Porter scratches his jaw. "She never did."

Squeezing my torso, I murmur, "That's because the surprises I had growing up were never good ones." They're all quiet, making me feel bad for making things awkward. I focus solely on my brother when I say, "Let me grab my stuff and then we can go."

"Are you coming with us?" DJ inquires.

"Aiden's parents are taking us" is all I offer for explanation before disappearing into the room and grabbing my phone and my bag from the bed. The small crossbody purse is nothing special, but it holds what little money I have, Chapstick I'm bound to lose by the end of the trip, and my ID cards that are heavily outdated.

When I'm back, it's just Porter and DJ left. "Where'd Matt go?"

I get a shrug from the blond. "Told him I'd make sure you got down there okay. I haven't seen Aiden's 'rents in a while."

My brows rise as I close the door behind us and follow

DJ and my brother down the long hallway toward the elevators at the end. "You mean since your not-so-mysterious boys' trip, like, a week ago?"

He presses the button and snorts as the doors open for us. "You didn't need to know, Ives."

I grumble my disagreement.

"They come to a lot of our games. Big supporters of Griff's. His mom gets into it, and his dad—" He stops himself. "Well, he's a good guy but he's intense. Wants the best for Aiden and sometimes shows it in a tough love kind of way."

That grabs my attention. Aiden's father has always been a big fan, helping him train and learn the playbooks when he played in high school. But he always meant well. "Do they not get along?"

"Nah, that's not it." DJ hits the ground floor button and turns to Porter and I, who are leaning against the opposite wall. "They get along fine. His dad definitely bothers him sometimes with how hard he pushes him, but it keeps Aiden on track."

"Mr. Griffith seems cool," my brother intervenes, giving me a one-shoulder shrug. "We talked football the whole way here."

DJ looks to him. "What position do you play again?"

Porter clears his throat, looking almost shy over the question. "Quarterback."

"Ah, big shot. You a leader then?"

Something about his questions makes me snap. "Can you stop with the inquiry, DJ?"

Porter instantly drops his eyes to the floor as we descend to the ground level. DJ presses his lips together and nods, not looking surprised over my reaction.

Shoulders tensing, I glance between the two boys trapped in the little box with me and realize I'm not being fair. I don't know Porter—his likes, who he's become—and I have nothing to contribute. Having someone else get to know him better before me makes the itch come back under my skin, the pressure that I want to ignore. "I'm sorry," I say to both of them.

It's Porter who bumps my arm with his, offering me a small smile when I shift my eyes upward. "I get it. This isn't easy for me either."

DJ remains uncharacteristically quiet across from us, letting us have a moment. I'm not sure how many we'll get before I mess everything up.

Biting on the inside of my cheek, I move my hand down to Porter's and link our palms. For a moment, he freezes, but eventually he melts into my touch and squeezes right back.

When the door opens to the lobby, neither of us lets go, and the people who greet us at the very bottom instantly smile when they see us walk out hand in hand.

"Ivy," a voice belonging to a familiar dark-haired, bright-eyed woman calls out to me. It's hard to breathe when Mrs. Griffith gives me a once-over with a big smile. Her hair is streaked with more white than I remember, and the corners of her lips and eyes are wrinkled from years of laughter that I remember being so fond of hearing. "I am so happy to see you, sweetie."

She envelopes me in a tight hug, and only then does Porter let go of me. I'm frozen, telling myself to lift my arms and return the hug like I used to. I lived for her warmth and happiness and am slammed with the cinnamon and sugar scent wafting from her from all the time she must still spend baking.

"Hi, Mrs. Griffith," I offer weakly, hooking an arm around her back.

She squeezes me tighter despite my lackluster attempt at a reunited front. "Oh, Ivy. I'll never get you to call me Emily, will I? You're as stubborn as I remember."

I pull away first, managing a smile that she returns easily. "Yeah. Aiden likes to remind me about that."

Her hands go to my shoulders, rubbing lightly until the friction warms me. "You're still beautiful too. I'm sure my son has told you that plenty of times as well."

Before I can control myself, heat gathers in my cheeks. "Er..."

"Emily," Mr. Griffith calls out from a few feet away. His baritone voice has my eyes shifting to him for a moment. "We should get going or we'll be late."

There's something unreadable in his eyes as they study me carefully. His hair has gone almost completely white, a far cry from the dirty blond he used to be, and his eyes are hazel green and hardened from life and experience. I recognize the silent warning in them that I've gotten from others surrounding Aiden and already know this may not play out like my old friend thinks it will.

I know what disapproval and fear look like because I've seen and felt both plenty of times when I look in the mirror. John Griffith is showing me his feelings with one single head nod in greeting.

"Hi," I greet him, picking my head up as if his guarded eyes don't affect me.

Porter sidles up beside me. "You good?"

I swallow, the lie slipping off my tongue effortlessly because I've caused him enough problems by putting myself first. "Of course. Ready to go?"

His head cocks as if he's contemplating my honesty, but he doesn't say anything other than a short, "Yeah."

The second mother to me, the one who I used to pretend was mine when I needed someone maternal to praise and comfort me, guides me, my brother, and her husband out with a hand at the small of my back.

She leans in when we fall back from the others and whispers, "I've always believed that the best things in life come after some of our toughest trials. I don't know what's happened over the past few years, Ivy, but I have no doubt you're stronger than ever. But Aiden..."

I try to calm my racing heart, but it does nothing to steady the heavy thumping in my chest that always comes with Aiden's name being mentioned.

"Aiden has some trials left to face." When I meet her eyes, mine are shy and laden with confusion as she rubs my back. "Wait for him to sort it out like he did for you when you went to your grandmother's house. That's all I'm asking."

I say nothing in reply, her words twisting my mind with confusion until I realize she has no idea where I've been.

And maybe, to preserve what respect she still has left for me, it's better she doesn't.

Chapter Twenty-Three

AIDEN

I NEVER THOUGHT I'D step onto this turf again, listening to the rapid chant of Raiders fans filling the recently renovated stadium. The crowd is a mixture of gold and red, with my former team's colors taking up most of my periphery as I coast the crowd with my gaze to find the only people I care about from the sidelines.

Mom is holding a huge white sign with my number in big red letters, sporting college garb that matches the rest of my family. And while I always appreciate seeing them cheer me on at the games they attend, it's the long jersey that looks like a dress on Ivy's body that captures my attention the most.

Coach Pearce got my parents seats at the fifty-yard line like he always does, not realizing he'd be adding two more to the group until last minute. And when I told him one was for Ivy, he gave me a look before I shut him down saying, "You're my coach, not my father, and not me. You don't get to make decisions for me, and you don't get to speak to the people I care for with disrespect."

And to my surprise, he ensured I'd have the extra space for them and added, "Your girl reminded me a lot of the missus when she handed me my ass during our talk, son. Scared me to hell to know there's a clone of my Liza. All I can say is good luck. It may be you bringing home the big paychecks, but it's her who's going to wear the pants in that relationship."

If I didn't know he loved his wife so much, I might have taken that the wrong way. Instead, it made me chuckle. He slapped my back, I shook my head, and he hasn't said a word about Ivy since.

Ivy is listening to something her brother is saying, her arms crossed over her chest and a jacket that looks like my mother's draped over her shoulders for warmth.

When I decided to make the trek home with Caleb and DJ, I wasn't sure what I'd say when I showed up at the little white house I'd only been in a handful of times after meeting Ivy. She preferred hanging out at mine, away from her mother since she was always there. She'd feel bad about leaving Porter behind, so she'd always tell me she had to check on him if we got lost on one of our adventures, never wanting to leave him alone for too long. She liked teasing me about playing superhero, but she was no different when it came to her little brother.

It doesn't matter how many years separated them or what she thinks of herself for leaving him behind, she never stopped caring about what happened to her family. That's only proven in the way her arm moves to wrap around her brother's as she listens with rapt attention to whatever he's explaining to her as he points at something in the field.

"Griffith," Coach barks, pulling my attention away. Ivy's silence in the truck stung, but I tried not to take it personally.

I didn't say the three words I feel directly, so why should I expect her to when she's adamant she doesn't know what love is supposed to be like?

I wanted to tell her, *it feels like this*.

But would she run?

Turning on my heels, I face Coach with a nod of my helmeted head. "Coach."

He puts his hands on my shoulders, squeezing the pads protecting me. "The first quarter didn't look so good for us, but Wallace managed to get us on the board. That's something to work with out there. Are you going to be good for the second? We need your full attention if we're going to beat these assholes."

"I will, sir."

"Are you sure? Your head didn't look like it was in it. If we're going to turn this game around, you're going to need to put everything you've got out there."

"Absolutely. I'm positive." The word is bitter on my tongue, tasting of disbelief.

"The boys are talking a lot of smack out there, and DJ already got us a penalty for unnecessary roughness because of the shit talk. Last thing I need is getting a player ejected because they're letting petty bull crap creep under their skin. You're tough. Keep your head up out there if you want to beat them."

"Yes, Coach."

"I knew the second I saw you two together that Ivy has the capability of changing everything for you. You can drool over her after we beat these sons of bitches. Understand?"

My jaw ticks because I don't like him talking about her. I know he wants me to make the most out of the talent I have, but I hate how he minimizes everything and everybody else while doing it. "Understood, Coach."

He releases my shoulders and grabs the headpiece on my helmet, pulling me closer. "I didn't hear you. Are we going to take the Raiders down?"

My nostrils flare. "Yes, Coach," I say louder.

He lets go of my helmet and gives me one last look before clapping his hands and calling us together.

The cement feeling in my stomach only grows heavier with each passing quarter.

An interference call in the second.

A fifteen-yard penalty in the third.

Tripping.

I come face-to-face with one of the opposing defense players, who narrows his eyes at me. "I can see why they let you go," he says, trying to block my opening. Ignoring him doesn't get the message across, and he mimics every move I make with a sense of challenge that goes beyond the game. "What? Nothing to say. What they say about you must be true then. You're nothing but a pussy."

Grinding my teeth, I create an opening just as the ball comes soaring in my direction from Wallace. I'm running with as much speed as I can and avoiding the Raiders coming at me when I catch the ball and cradle it to my chest and make a break for the end zone.

I'm twenty yards away.

Fifteen.

Two guys are hot on my heels, one of them mere inches away when I push myself harder than I ever have before to get to the ten-yard line.

This touchdown would put us in the lead.

We'd win.

All the trash talk.

All the bullshit.

All the penalties.

It'd be worth it.

Five yards away—

Three—

A body slams into me with so much force, it's suddenly hard to breathe when my body collides with the turf. I bounce on impact and slide past another yard, watching the ball roll away from my body.

The buzzer goes off.

The final quarter ends.

The crowd goes fucking insane, a noise that's deafening when reality hits me as I lie sprawled across the ground.

Lindon Dragons lost.

Wilson Reed Raiders won.

The guy who took me down jumps up in time for his team to run over and celebrate with him, surrounding my spent body with poor sportsmanship. I turn my head and watch as two of my own team members run over with shadowed expressions on their faces as they push past the assholes gyrating their hips to help me up.

"You good?" Caleb asks, checking me over, helping me brush off pieces of the turf my shoulder pads dug up on the fall.

"No." My voice is almost unrecognizable between the noise of the Raiders fans cheering at their school's victory and my own acknowledgment that I let the university beat me for a second time.

I said this wasn't about facing my demons, but maybe if I'd been honest with myself, I could have put my all out there on the field.

Caleb drags DJ away from the Raiders grouping together and walks all of us over to the rest of the team. Wallace is shooting off at the mouth, Matt is throwing his helmet on the ground and yelling at one of the referees closest to him, and Coach and his assistant are making their way to us with unreadable expressions on their faces.

When I meet Coach's eyes, he only shakes his head at me as he tells us all to go to the locker room.

As we make our walk off the field, there's a mixture of boos that follow us from the Raiders fans. A few people direct their displeasure at some of us individually, and I'm not surprised to hear my name being the biggest target.

It's my friend who murmurs, "Ignore them. They're all dicks."

It may be true, but it doesn't roll off my shoulders as we pile into the locker room and wait for Coach's speech. But when he enters and says barely two sentences before telling us to clean up and get back to the bus to go to the hotel, we all know we fucked up.

Me the most.

The game that should have given me redemption gave me deprivation instead. And I fucking welcomed it by letting my eyes go to the stands one too many times to see how Ivy was taking the game.

How she clapped with my family.

Held the sign my mother made.

Laughed with her brother.

The water in the shower flows over me, refusing to wash away the feeling that remains stuck on my skin even after I change, grab my bag, and meet my family outside. Some of the guys pass me with a few pats on the shoulder, others murmur "next time" and "sorry, bro" as they head toward the bus Coach has ready for us.

My parents, Ivy, and Porter are all waiting for me with a few other families and significant others. Ivy and Porter are standing behind my parents, and it's Mom who approaches me first with a comforting smile.

"You played a good game," she tells me, hugging me lightly before letting go and looking over the side I fell on. "You're okay, right? Did someone check you over in the locker room to make sure nothing is broken?"

Dad sighs. "He's fine, Emily."

I nod. "I'm good."

The only thing busted is my ego, but I don't relay that information.

Porter walks up with a reluctant Ivy close beside him. "I think they should have gotten called out on a couple plays. They weren't playing fairly. Sorry, man."

The shrug I offer is tight. "It is what it is. Glad you could see it." My eyes move toward the silent one in the group, our gazes locking with something heavy in the air between us.

She clears her throat. "I'm sorry too."

I'm not sure she means about the game.

I nod once, walking over and pulling her into my arms. I don't care that my parents are watching or the people around us. None of them even come close to earning an ounce of the fucks I give about needing this woman in my arms right now. Leaning into her ear, I whisper, "Our hotel room in thirty."

She shivers, offering me a small nod before stepping back after I squeeze her tightly in goodbye.

When we depart, I don't look back when I join the guys on the bus. Caleb sits next to me, DJ in the seat in front of us, and all of them stay silent to give me time to process.

We win as a team and lose as one.

But none of them feel the same crushing defeat as I do right now, because a nagging feeling in the pit of my stomach is telling me I'm about to lose a lot more if I don't play my cards right.

The girl and the career before I actually have either.

~

When the hotel door opens, I'm still leaning over the bathroom sink after splashing water in my face to cool off, white knuckling the counter while the water runs. I don't bother telling Ivy where I am before she walks in and stops right behind me.

Two warm arms wrap around my naked torso, squeezing me in silence. A cheek rests between my shoulder blades, and a small breath escapes me as I reach forward and turn off the faucets.

Instead of talking, I turn around and tilt her chin up so she's looking me in the eye. There's an understanding between us as she nods a few times and raises on her toes to meet me halfway for a brief kiss. It lasts no more than a few seconds before I break it off and trail my hands down her sides until I'm peeling my jersey and her undershirt off at the same time. She unbuttons her jeans and lets me pull those and her panties off as she unhooks her bra and lets it fall to the floor until she's completely naked in front of me.

I study her body, mapping her curves with my eyes and feeling myself harden by the second with every swipe over her bare skin. She takes my hands and puts them to her chest, her full tits filling up my palms before she slowly trails my hands down her smooth stomach, over her navel, and leaves them gripping her hips.

Leaning forward, I close the distance and kiss her again, this time harder, needing her to taste how badly I want to get out of my head. She starts rubbing my chest, palming my pecs, and moving her hands down to my boxers to pull them down until my cock springs free.

The kiss continues, a game of give and take, before she moves us so her body bends over the sink with her back to me. She moves her hair over one of her shoulders and looks at me in the mirror. She leans forward so her supple ass is nearly brushing my erect cock, one of her hands snaking behind her and wrapping around my shaft, slowly pumping me.

I know I should stop this before it goes too far. I'm angry at the game results. Disappointed that we lost. Confused over what comes next. She deserves better than to be a distraction from those emotions, yet she plays along, coaxes me with languid yet skilled movements, reminding me who's really in control right now.

It sure as hell isn't me.

Groaning, I step toward her as she lines me up with her opening and pushes back until the tip of me is inside her. Choking down the noise rising up my throat, I watch her settle her forearms on the sink, biting her bottom lip and pushing into me further. When we lock eyes in the reflection, she gives me a small nod before I bottom out in one full thrust, my balls hitting her ass. "Fuck, baby. We should stop."

Her eyes close and her head drops forward as I withdraw and repeat the action with a little more confidence. "Don't. You need this."

You. Not her.

My hands grip her hips as I thrust inside her, the feeling of being clenched every single time driving me to go faster and harder until I'm grunting and listening to the way she moans with me.

Ivy's body shifts forward the harder I thrust, so I grip the wall with one hand and grab a fistful of her hair with my other. Her lips part as I bury myself inside her and circle my hips before jackknifing over and over and listening to the little containers of soap and lotion on the sink rattle with the impact of our slapping bodies against the hotel vanity.

"Touch yourself," I demand in a strangled voice, knowing I won't last long enough to get her off.

One of her hands disappears between her legs, and another sharp breath escapes her lips as I twitch inside her tight pussy. Grinding into her once, twice, a third time, I quickly pull out as she moans my name and absorb the sound of her orgasm, stroking myself until I come on my hand and her back.

Her body slumps forward as she breaths heavily, my come still slick on her pale skin. I grab the hand towel hanging beside the sink and wipe her off, then clean myself before throwing the balled-up cloth on the bottom of the tub.

She starts standing when I grab my boxers from the floor and slide them up my thighs, jaw ticking as I watch her hair shield her face from her reflection in the mirror.

"Never let me use you like that again," I growl, gathering her clothes and handing them to her with a hard expression on my face. "I shouldn't have fucking done that to you. Christ. You deserve better than that, remember?"

She steals a peek at me from under her lashes. "Is that your way of saying I can do better than you, Aiden?"

I swallow down the guilt trying to choke me. "It's me saying you can do better than what you think you deserve. Nobody should use your body like that."

Walking out of the bathroom, I stop a few feet away from the door when I hear, "You're wrong. I let people use me before because I didn't think I could do any better. I let you in because you needed me, and I wanted to help. There's a difference."

I turn to her, brows furrowed.

She's still naked, my jersey clenched in her palms and barely covering her naked breasts as she steps forward. Her dusky pink nipples peek through the thin material she's clinging to like it's her lifeline. "You needed something, and I gave it to you. I don't know much about love, but I'd like to think that's part of it. Don't make it less."

My eyes close as one of my hands swipe down the side of my face. "Ivy..."

"Don't make it less," she repeats, her tone pleading until it busts something inside me. "I can't take hearing that when I'm finally accepting what I've always felt about you. I want to be there for you if you'll let me. I don't know where that's going to lead us, but you can't backpedal because you feel bad after one bad day. We're both going to have a lot of them. So please, don't make this less."

I shake my head, her words smacking into me harder than they ever have. "Never."

She doesn't look like she believes me, so I walk back into the bathroom and make her look at me. My thumb brushes her flushed cheek and swollen bottom lip as I search her uncertain eyes, which are darker than normal and glazed with unfallen tears.

"Never."

Chapter Twenty-Four

IVY

INSTEAD OF STAYING WITH Aiden's parents at the small family-owned inn on the outskirts of Lindon, Porter stays on the couch downstairs at the football house. He's reluctant to agree, quiet when it's just us two alone after Aiden went upstairs to chill with the guys, but he sets his backpack down on the cushion between us and sits on the opposite end of the sofa from me.

My hands drag down my thighs as I watch him study the room like I did when Aiden first brought me here. His legs spread to get comfortable, his arms resting crossed over his chest, and when he finally looks at me, I don't expect him to ask, "Are you and Aiden a thing?"

Legs crisscrossing under me, I shove my hands into my lap and fight the blush that wants to creep under my skin. "Is that really what you want to talk about?"

He shrugs. "Seems like a good place to start considering he went through all the trouble to get me here."

Knowing he has a point, I give him the best answer I

can conjure. "I'm not sure what Aiden and I are right now. We're…" Like him, my shoulders lift slightly. "It's a work in progress, like a lot of things are in my life. I don't want to talk about that. We have years to catch up on. Things I should explain."

"You don't need to explain anything."

"How can you say that? I up and left. Do you not want to know why? Get closure?"

He averts his gaze, making me feel anxious for his reply. "Mom and Dad told everyone you went to live with Grandma Gertie."

My lips part, then quickly close.

Porter lets out a heavy sigh and then swipes his fingers through his hair. "I believed them for a while because I had no reason not to. You left and Mom and Dad seemed… I don't know, Ivy. They weren't okay, but they were quieter than I remember. It was sort of nice." We both make faces, him cringing with guilt and me twisting with hurt. "Shit, that sounds bad. Look, I'm not proud of the things I thought. I was pissed off at first that you didn't even say goodbye, but it was obvious that our parents were going to at least try to be decent after you went away."

Went away. My tongue clicks as I think about the letter I'd handwritten and stuffed under my pillow. I made sure a corner stuck out enough for them to notice when they finally realized that me, my bag, and my favorite clothes were all gone.

I told them I'd prove them wrong.

I told them I didn't need Gertie or them.

I told them not to look for me.

"They really made everyone believe I moved in with Grandma?"

A nod.

I want to be angry that they went with the lie so easily, and there's definitely a sense of heaviness threatening to bubble in my veins, but I focus on something else to beat those darker feelings down for the moment. "They were better after I was gone?"

His Adam's apple bobs. "Define better," he murmurs, repositioning so he's sitting straighter. "They still fought, but it was nowhere near as much. I'm not totally clueless. I know you were the reason I didn't have to deal with them for so long. I remember all the times you'd make sure I ate or you took the fall if I did something bad so I wouldn't get into trouble. You were always doing that for me even when I was a brat to you, and I still—"

His abrupt stop makes me lean forward in curiosity. "What, Porter? Say it."

His knee starts bouncing. "You were always making sure I was okay, and I was still angry at you for leaving. I know you weren't happy, but I wanted to be enough for you to stick around. We could have had each other. Had Aiden. I know he was your friend, but some of my favorite memories were all of us hanging out."

I stare at him, not knowing he felt that way at all. He'd always cling to Aiden and ask him questions about football, getting irritated if I'd butt in or change the topic. I'd remind him that Aiden was my friend first, not thinking about how that must have made Porter feel.

"I heard you tell Mom all the time how much it irritated you that they spent money on me for sports or other stuff when they wouldn't invest in any of your hobbies. Part of me should have been happy you were going to live with someone who probably had the time to get you what you wanted and needed, but it was like you didn't care what happened to me anymore when you disappeared. You left, and that meant Aiden wouldn't be around either. I lost both of you."

It's impossible to swallow or speak, so I don't even try. The guilt is tenfold in my stomach. Aiden said he checked in on Porter, but I know it wouldn't have been the same. Not like when it was us three against the world.

He drops his head backward onto the couch cushion. "I'm not angry anymore. Confused, maybe, but not angry." Picking up his head, he offers me a comforting look. "I overheard Mom talking to Dad about Gertie dying. Heart attack, I guess. Anyway, she said they'd have to figure out what to do. I thought they were talking about funeral arrangements and when they'd get you back home and settled in, but Mom said something I'll never forget."

My heart drums loudly, vibrating my ears.

And it nearly stops when he says, "Mom told Dad that you were right about something. That you were always better off on your own. And Dad didn't say anything. He didn't agree or disagree. He just sort of stared at her, shook his head, and left. He was always leaving, like he didn't want to be there anymore either. That was when I knew I didn't know the real story. They lied to me. To everyone."

I clench my teeth, holding back the emotion rising up my throat before grinding out a cold, "When?"

"When, what?"

My fingers ball into fists, hidden between my crossed legs, squeezing so hard it physically hurts. "When did Mom say that? When did Gertie die?"

Porter hesitates, his eyes trailing to think of the time frame. "A couple years ago now."

A couple… "When I was eighteen?"

There's a pause, then a single nod.

When I was eighteen.

When I was doing shady things for shelter.

When I was lying on a cold tile floor with cuts through my arms because I needed help and didn't know how I could ask for it after believing they'd never want me.

She thought I was better off.

Maybe she even believed it.

I want nothing more than to show my brother what *better off* looks like. The pink lifted scars on my skin will be a reminder of how my life turned out because she thought I could do better than her.

But Porter doesn't deserve that.

To see my weakness.

My anger.

It's not at him. It's at Mom. Always at her.

"Ivy?" he asks quietly, brows furrowing at my long silent streak.

I shake my head again, trying to gather my words and struggling to string together thoughts. Eventually, I blow out a breath. "I'm here and alive, aren't I?"

My little brother doesn't need to hold my choices against me or blame Mom for not trying harder.

After all, I told her I could do better.

And I *am* here.

And I *am* alive.

Even though I probably shouldn't be.

Even though I don't always want to be.

"So you and Aiden…?" his voice trails off, and I realize now why my answer matters to him so much.

He needs to know I'm okay.

Happy.

"We're figuring it out," I tell him softly, offering the best smile I can without showing the heavy emotion behind it. "It's difficult when he's probably going away soon. We haven't talked much about it."

I finally feel like I have my best friend back, and I don't want to say goodbye again. But I know it's not that simple. He's had the same dream his whole life, and he's so close to finally achieving it. Who am I to hold him back?

"Do you love him?" my brother asks.

No hesitation. "Yeah, I think I do."

I jerk when a hand comes down on mine, and when I look up, Porter is sitting in front of me with sheepish eyes, offering me what little comfort he can since we're practically strangers now. "I think Mom will be happy to know that. She's mentioned you a couple times, saying she hopes you're doing well. Talks about you when she's baking. Her cookies aren't as good as the ones you made. When I told her, that she started laughing until she cried, and when I tried to apologize, she told me not to."

I'm not sure why he's telling me this, and I'm afraid to read into the meaning of his little story, so I choose to brush it off.

"I'm sorry I didn't believe in you like you always did in me, Ivy. I wish I could go back and say something to Mom and Dad. Maybe if we talked to them about things, it could have been different."

"You have no reason to apologize and every right to be upset," I tell him. Because I *didn't* say goodbye.

In a way, he's right.

I didn't want to deal with him anymore.

Taking care of him.

Handling the fighting.

The toxic words.

She's better off on her own.

I could tell Porter the things Mom and Dad told me over the years—the reason I had enough and decided to leave. Where would that leave us? If they acted put together for him, no matter if it was real or fake, who am I to ruin any relationship he may have with them?

So instead of bringing up past demons that I'll never get rid of, burdening him with them, I choose to move forward.

"Tell me how you got onto the football team. All that advice you asked Aiden over the years must have panned out," I diverge, grateful he goes along with it.

Turns out my brother is a big fan of Aiden Griffith. And when the player in question comes downstairs hours later to check on us, he and Porter talk the game, my brother's high school stats, and where he wants to take his future, all while my old friend steals peeks at me midconversation.

I mouth "thank you" while sitting with the Starbucks drink he brought down with him, seeing my brother's face light up having somebody to talk to.

Aiden believed in me when I couldn't even believe in myself, giving me what I needed when I was sure I didn't need anybody.

Drawing my knees to my chest, I get lost in the words he demanded of me in the hotel room.

Trust me.

My heart expands, realizing I do.

And I wonder what he sees in my eyes when he catches me staring, unable to look away as the realization crashes into me.

I've never truly stopped loving Aiden Griffith either.

Chapter Twenty-Five

IVY

THE SUNDAY FOLLOWING THE game against Wilson Reed, the house clears out for Thanksgiving break. All the guys go home for what remains of the last week off before finals start in mere weeks, which means Aiden and I are officially on borrowed time.

Porter is sleeping on the couch when I wake up later than usual to see Aiden already out of bed. I sneak past my dozing brother, who still sleeps twisted up to the point he must hurt when he wakes up, and head upstairs in a pair of ratty pajama bottoms and a sweatshirt from Aiden's dresser.

I hear voices in the kitchen and know immediately who they belong to. Hesitating around the corner, I hear Emily Griffith murmur quietly as Aiden says, "…deal is. You and Coach Pearce seem to think I can't handle myself when it comes to her when I've done nothing but prove otherwise."

My body tenses as I press against the painted beige drywall, careful not to be seen. Bottom lip tucked into my mouth, I nibble nervously and keep my breathing as light as possible to hear their replies without giving myself away.

It's his father who speaks up. "I have nothing against the girl. We've always liked her. But what if she decides to walk away? You weren't yourself for months after she left, and now is not the time to let someone in when you've got a lot of people watching you."

"Is this about the Raiders game?"

"Aiden," his mother says lightly. "That game was not your fault. Nobody who saw it blames you for the outcome."

"Your mother is right," says his father. "You played strong out there and so did most of your team. The Raiders had an advantage being in their own territory and got away with too much. I know it was a hard hit for you, but the results of that game won't impact the interest you have from NFL scouts. ESPN is still showing the reels and talking about it, especially since Bill told them about the combine you were entering in a couple months."

The sound of Aiden huffing makes me frown. He and Porter had the sports channel on last night when they showed a replay of the game, and the reels weren't exactly in favor of the tight end in the kitchen. "They showed me getting tackled with seconds left of the game. The only thing they're talking about is the loss I handed my team."

I want to tell him to stop beating himself up over it, but then I'd be a hypocrite. We're all our own worst enemies.

His father turns the topic back around, and I don't feel any better about it since it involves me. "Do you at least see where I'm coming from about this?"

"You mean about you disapproving of my choice because it'll pull my head away from thinking about football twenty-four seven?" my best friend retorts sarcastically. "Last I checked, that was a good thing. Everyone needs a break."

"But—"

"I just got her back, Dad," Aiden states firmly, leaving no room for discussion. I have to press my lips together to hide a smile. "If you want me to succeed, you'll support me even if you don't agree. I'm not saying I'm going to put a ring on her finger anytime soon."

My eyes widen as I press my fingers forcefully against my mouth to muffle the noise nearly escaping me.

A tiny breath still releases when he adds, "But that doesn't mean I haven't thought about it for the future, if she'll consider it."

Oh my god.

My mind takes me back to all the notebook covers that had *Ivy Ann Griffith* written in choppy cursive across the inside. I was always terrified Aiden would find them, so I tore them all up and buried them in the garbage before I left Haven Falls.

It's Mrs. Griffith who decides to break the tension growing between her boys. "We love you, sweetie, and we'll have your back no matter what you choose. We always have."

There's a sigh that I can only imagine comes from his father. "She's a good girl. And it's impressive you both wound up here after all this time."

Swallowing, I recall the time his parents were talking over a picnic they invited me to. I asked them how they met, and Mr. Griffith got a little smile on his face and said, "We happened to be at the right place at the right time when neither of us should have been."

It still seems strange that someone as big and burly as Aiden's dad would believe in something like fate. But

I'll never forget what he said next, which I held on to all these years.

"When you meet the right person, it doesn't matter what happens, because fate will always bring you together." I remember thinking I wanted someone to look at me like he did his wife, like they couldn't stop. Like they were always surprised by the person no matter how well they knew them. "But it's your choices that will make them stay," he concluded.

Footsteps stomp up the basement stairs, leaving me wide-eyed and pushing away the memory.

"Ivy?" Porter calls out tiredly. "Aiden?" I turn to see my little brother surfacing at the top of the stairs. One of his hands rubs his eyes as he gives me a sleepy smile. "Why didn't you wake me up?"

"I just got up too," I tell him, not completely lying.

Aiden walks out of the kitchen and over to us, pressing a kiss against my temple and bumping the fist Porter holds out to him. My nose scrunches at the gesture, which they both grin at like they're already bros. "Want some coffee?" Aiden asks, pulling me toward the kitchen.

When I walk in, Mrs. Griffith shoots me a little smile and wink like she used to when she was in on a secret. "Good morning, Ivy. Porter. We were all talking this morning"— her smile twitches in amusement as she directs the statement at me—"and Aiden and his father were saying they'd go to the store to get the rest of the Thanksgiving ingredients we need to finish the meal."

I'm still reeling over them insisting we celebrate together here.

"The turkey is already thawing. I just need some more vegetables and other odds and ends that the boys don't seem to keep any of around here."

The tight end whose arm stays wrapped around my waist groans at his mother's scolding statement. "It's not like we order delivery every night. We eat here and it's healthy."

"That's because I cook for you guys," I point out, jabbing his side with my elbow until he drops his arm so I can walk over to the fancy coffee machine that DJ splurged on.

Aiden's mom sidles up beside me. "I was thinking you and I can make an apple pie together like old times. The recipe hasn't changed any. Porter can help the boys at the store so we can catch up a little. Have girl talk."

I can feel the rising tension in my stomach, but not as much as her offspring behind me. Aiden says, "Mom, I think it'd be better if Porter and Ivy spent more time tog—"

"I don't mind," my brother says, already perking up over the thought of spending time with Aiden.

When the man in question looks to me for reassurance, I nod. I've been wanting to talk to his mom since Friday, but I never found the time or courage to say what I felt needed to be said.

Porter and I spent all day yesterday together touring Lindon's campus, and he pretended to be interested even though I could tell he wasn't. We wound up at Bea's where he got to meet Bea and my cheery young coworker, and Lena found a new person to blush over when my brother walked in. Secretly, I'm glad he'll be going home because I'm not sure how I feel about the two sixteen-year-olds flirting.

Bea welcomed Porter with open arms, looking surprised I hadn't mentioned having a brother but not telling him that, and gave us free drinks and food despite my protests.

It was a good day full of idle conversation that wasn't too heavy. He likes rap music and has no interest in school and no idea what he'll major in at college. His main goal is almost identical to Aiden's. Play football.

And when I asked if it's what he wants to do because he loves it, he gave me a dumbfounded look that told me I was ridiculous for thinking he was forced into it. It's another reminder that our lives are different—he was shown support and even the tiniest bit of decency, where I wasn't. Even though I blame myself for some of my downfalls with Mom, I can hold on to the fact that she could have done better. She *should have*. I was her kid too.

When the guys all leave sometime later, I put on an old T-shirt and leggings I pulled from the dresser drawer Aiden gave me a couple weeks ago that I don't mind getting food on.

"Aiden says that you still bake," his mom says, smiling as I coat the counter with flour before placing the ball of dough down and pressing on it with the heel of my palm.

Grabbing a rolling pin she must have brought with her, since it's a brand I can't afford, I offer an easy nod. "It calms me down. Plus, it's the least I could do for the guys since they let me stay here. I've learned some new healthier recipes so all the baked goods don't interfere with their games and training."

She slices the apples carefully, the sound of the knife against the chopping board somehow peaceful to me, a sound of familiarity minus the bright-green kitchen and hot-pink stool I'm used to when baking something with her. "The bakery you work at seems lovely. I was surprised when Aiden said you were an undeclared major. I thought you had to claim one after freshman year."

I go to answer but pause as I begin rolling. I asked Aiden not to say anything about my past to his parents once he confirmed they didn't know what had happened. There are some things people don't need to know, especially the two people who always viewed me with high regard. The last thing I want them to find out is where I really spent the better part of the last four years. I'd rather keep up the lie my parents invested in than admit the gruesome truth. "I actually just started at the university this semester, so I'm only a freshman. There were things I had to figure out before I decided to give college a shot."

She begins tossing the apple slices in a bowl and collecting the spices for the mixture that will become the filling. "And do you like it?"

I stare at the dough I flatten like it'll give me the answer. "Honestly? Not really. The structure is nice. It keeps me on track, so I know where I need to be and when. But I've never been great at school, and not much has changed in that regard."

"What about baking?"

Pausing, I look to her. Her eyes are focused on the filling, not glancing at me once to see the confusion on my face. "What about it?"

She brushes off her hands and turns to me, a hand going to her aproned hip. "You enjoy it, and it calms you. School isn't for everyone, you know. I didn't attend college for more than a year because I realized I didn't belong there."

My lips part. "You didn't?"

Her smile is encouraging. "Tell me something, Ivy. Why do you want to go? It's what I had to ask myself to make my choice."

"I..." I think about my parents and bite down on the inside of my cheek as I go back to the dough, sprinkling my flour onto it. "To prove that I could, I guess. Maybe to stall until I figured out what else there was to do. I need a plan."

"To prove to who?"

This time, I don't answer.

"You owe me nothing, Ivy," she says, brushing my arm with her hand. "But I'd hate to see you go after something because you think it's what other people want. Aiden hasn't said a word about what's happened since you left Haven Falls, and he told me not to pry. I'll respect that because if you want to tell me, you will, and I hope someday you do. But until then, I'd like to offer you some free advice."

My grip on the rolling pin tightens, but I don't object to hearing what she has to say. I've always held on to every word she's given me.

"Above all else," she says softly, "choose happiness. Not anybody else's, but yours. Because at the end of the day, you'll find a lot more of it when you open yourself up to everything life has to offer when you're truly content with where you are in it."

My eyes burn with tears that I try batting away unsuccessfully. I make a gargled noise that has Mrs. Griffith dropping everything she's doing and pulling me into her.

"Oh, sweetie. I didn't mean to make you upset. I just want you to be happy. I want my baby boy to be happy. And if you both work at it, you can experience so much in this lifetime together."

I bury my face in her shoulder. "What if I'm not enough? What if I can't?"

Her fingers cradle the back of my head, combing through my hair as she shushes me lightly with her melodic voice. "If it's what you overheard my silly husband say, don't let it get to your head. You and Aiden have had something special since the day you met. Anyone could see it. And you know how my family is about fate. We're all believers that if it's meant to be, it'll find a way, just like you two found your way back to each other after all this time. Neither of you planned it, certainly not Aiden. Very few things in life are simply coincidences. Don't write this one off before you have a chance to explore it." When she pulls back, she wipes at my cheeks with her thumbs and examines one eye, then the other, and slowly smiles. "Or *have* you already explored it?"

My tear-stained face reddens with heat that she laughs at.

"Oh, Ivy. I know better than to believe my son is celibate."

I choke on my tears, knowing I'll have to add corrupting her son to the list of things I never want her finding out about.

By the time the boys get back, they all walk into the kitchen laughing and joking around about something while Mrs. Griffith and I finish cleaning up the mess we made. The pie is on the counter waiting to be put in the oven after everything else is cooked for the late Thanksgiving meal, and for the first time in too long, I'm excited for the holiday.

Normally the itchy feeling under my skin becomes tenfold this time of year, knowing I have nobody to celebrate with. Watching others enjoy it with their families becomes too much, and I never thought making the decision to come here—a last-minute one made simply after seeing an ad at a public library I went to hide out in for warmth one evening—would lead to this.

A family.

My brother.

My best friend.

Swallowing when I see them all together, I'm struck by how much I want this to continue: the laughter, baking, and smiles. I want to chase the happiness Aiden's mother wants so badly for her son and me, and I want to do that with my best friend by my side.

No matter where it takes us.

Even if it means leaving Lindon.

The moment of clarity is broken when Porter walks over to me, his face pale as he glances from his phone to me. "I'm sorry, Ivy. I didn't know they were tracking my phone."

It isn't hard to figure out who he means, especially when tires stop outside the house. Turning to Aiden and the others, I ask, "Are we expecting anybody else?"

Aiden shakes his head.

Porter apologizes again. "I didn't know. I thought they'd be busy—"

"It's fine," I rasp, hearing two different car doors close.

My breathing becomes rapid.

My chest hurts.

Suddenly, Aiden is in front of me, taking Porter's place. "Breathe, Ivy. Out of your head." When I don't finish our old pep talk, he grabs both my upper arms and makes me look at him with expressive, encouraging eyes. "Out of your head, Underwood."

There's knocking at the front door.

My heart drums.

My skin itches.

I swear the scars left on my arms are laughing at me as the knocks start again.

Tap, tap, tap.

"Ivy," my best friend says.

I let out a breath. "Head in the game."

~

A twig snapped under the weight of my sneaker as I hauled the heavy bag full of clothes and food over my shoulder and snuck over the property line to get to my best friend's window. For hours, I'd been thinking the same thing. *Tonight is the night.* I'd be lying if I said I wasn't terrified about leaving, but I knew it's time. It was overdue.

The soft glow of light coming from the bedroom that smelled like cinnamon and body spray didn't make me smile like normal, because I knew when I lifted the window and slipped inside, it'd be for the last time.

Stopping short of his bedroom window, my eyes went behind me to the house I escaped from and observed the black interior. Sometimes Mom got up in the middle of the night because of insomnia. I'd see her drinking tea in the kitchen or curled up on the couch when I was sneaking out, and there had been times I was certain she saw me. But she never said anything, and I never offered any details about my midnight adventures.

Dropping my bag onto the ground, my fingertips danced along the edge of the window and pushed up the wood. There was a shake to my arms as I hauled myself in and saw Aiden already sitting up in bed with a pile of pamphlets covering his bedding.

When I walked over, I picked up one of them to study the university listed. "Are these what you were called into the coach's office about?"

I dropped the one I was holding and picked up the gold-and-white paper he'd been staring hard at. Wilson Reed University. I'd heard him talk about this one before. One of his favorite players graduated from there.

His answer came after a thick sigh. "He thinks I should consider going to Miami. The Hurricanes have had NFL stars come from their teams the past few years. It never fails."

My face twisted as I moved some of the pamphlets out of the way to sit down. "You hate the heat. You'd be miserable there. And Dan Williams says that you could make it to the NFL no matter where you go."

He deadpanned at the mention of the sportscaster from our local news station, but he knew that Dan Williams wasn't the only one who'd made that point, even if Williams used to play for a big-time college team before getting injured. He knew the kind of talent my best friend has wasn't something people would overlook because of the college name on his jersey.

Every time Aiden's college prospects were brought up, it became all of Haven Falls' business because they wanted to gloat one day about how the great Aiden Griffith once called this town his home. But unlike them, they'd never be able to say they knew him as well as me.

"What do you think?" I pressed, passing him back the Wilson Reed information.

"What do *you* think?"

My eyes didn't lift from the scattered papers covering his red-and-white-plaid comforter. There was a tear on it from when I tried making a break for it after sleeping in too late. I tripped and grabbed the blanket for support, tearing the material, bolting out the window before his mother knew I was there.

Eventually, I told him the truth. "It doesn't matter what I think. This is your life. Your future. Have your parents weighed in? I know their opinions mean a lot to you."

"Your opinion means a lot too."

Nibbling the inside of my cheek, I slowly moved my eyes to his. He'd already watching me warily, knowing what I hadn't said. "It's time, Aiden."

He shook his head. "No."

"We talked about this. It's—"

"I'll talk to my mom," he said quickly, pushing the

pamphlets out of the way and sitting up straighter. "We can tell her what's been going on and figure something out."

"Aide—"

"Ivy," he cut me off. "Please? I need you here cheering me on like you always do. Maybe that's selfish, but this can work. I'm sure your parents wouldn't mind if you stayed here for a while until things got better."

Did he hear how that sounds? I frowned, dragging my hands through my hair before dropping them into my lap. "Don't you think they should mind, Aiden? Isn't that the problem?"

He was quiet, contemplative of his next counterattack. We'd been through this before, and every time, we ended up at the same place.

"It's time," I repeated softly.

He reached out. "Don't."

I blurted, "Come with me then."

One second passes.

Two.

Three.

With each passing silent second, I knew the answer to the question before he even parted those beautiful, full lips. Usually, the words passing through them are of comfort. Things that make me feel warm and fuzzy.

But now...

"I can't." A breath passed between us, a moment of clarity between our locked eyes. "I can't go with you, Ivy."

I blinked.

He blinked.

I wet my lips.

His jaw ticked.

"I can't stay here, Aiden." It's not a guilt trip or a way to convince him otherwise. We both have our minds set on our futures, and they look nothing alike. Standing up, I point at the Wilson Reed pamphlet and say, "You should go there. It's what you want. You always tell me to get out of my head, so it's your turn."

He gets to his feet with a pleading look in his blue eyes that dims them and part of my soul with them. "What are you going to do?"

I thought about the bus ticket Mom gave me that was tucked into the side pocket of my bag. "I'll figure it out, just like you will."

Stepping toward me, there was hesitation in his eyes like he wanted to have the same argument but knew there's no point. So instead, he wrapped me in a hug, his arms tightening their hold around me until our bodies are flush together.

We stayed like that for a little while longer.

My arms curled around his back, knowing this would be the last time. Maybe I'd sneak into one of his games when he was big time. Follow his career when they announced he'd made the league.

Aiden Griffith would go on to do great things. I just hoped I was half as lucky.

I wasn't sure who pulled away first. There was a mutual understanding between us when there was a few inches of space separating our bodies, his heat still caressing me as he scoped out my bootcut jeans with a little tear in the knee and inside thigh, white T-shirt, zip-up hoodie tied around my waist, and my ratty sneakers. I could sense the disapproval, the need to say something, anything, but not wanting to upset me.

I didn't want to leave him.

I didn't want to go to my grandma's.

But I didn't want to stay home either.

"Be careful," he told me with a rasp to his voice that he failed at hiding. Before I knew it, he was hugging me again, this one not lasting as long, and I wasn't sure if I was sad or grateful.

"If you can't come with me, then you have to let me go," I whispered, burying my face in his neck and squeezing him as hard as I could. His arms were like a hook around my waist, anchoring me to the bedroom I'd spent more time sleeping in than my own. "Trust me, Aiden. I've got this."

When he drew back, his lips skimmed my cheek and I sucked in a silent breath as my heart skipped in my chest. He straightened to his full height, already six one with more room to grow according to his father, and looked to the window.

He didn't' mention the sort of kiss.

He didn't say goodbye.

So neither did I.

"Head in the game," I told him with one foot out the window, the other still planted on his off-white carpet, stained from all the years of wear from him, Cap, and me.

I didn't allow myself to hear his response before sliding out, grabbing my bag, and offering him a wave as I fought the waver of my lips.

Tears blurred my vision as I faced forward and tuned out the two houses I was leaving behind.

Out of your head, Underwood.

~

Porter is still pale when Mr. Griffith greets the two people I haven't seen in over four years at the front door. My brother and I stand shoulder to shoulder, arms entwined by the elbow, with Aiden on my other side and his mother slightly in front of me as if they've formed a barrier between me and the past.

Thudthudthud.

It's almost impossible to hear what exchange happens between the two fathers as my heart gallops in its cage. My eyes lock on the wide-eyed woman who's gaping at her two children with utter shock across her face.

Mom looks nothing like I remember. Her copper hair is chopped short and graying, her face makeup free, her clothes worn and faded, and her eyes—the eyes that Porter and I get our color from—are hollow until she darts between my little brother and me. "Ivy?"

My father has hardly changed. His hard face is stoic as he stands by my mother, arms crossed in front of him like he's always on guard, waiting for something bad to happen. "Care to explain what's going on here?"

When his eyes rake over me, I notice the slightest raise in his dark eyebrows, the same brown his hair used to be before the obvious receding hairline took over. Looking at my parents, I remember the beautiful shade of copper brown my hair used to be with natural red highlights in the sunlight. Mom used to brush her fingers through it and tell me how jealous she was over it.

"Ivy?" Mom repeats, stepping toward me with a newfound hesitation in her tone.

Porter tightens his grip on me. "Before you start yelling, it was my idea to come here. Ivy had no clue, and when she found out I lied about where I'd be this weekend, she wasn't happy."

The choking noise my mother makes is almost in disbelief as she shakes her head, shock still the dominant feature on her face. When her lips part, I manage to refrain from

297

flinching over the unknown anticipation of what will escape them, but it all dies down when she closes them again as if she's incapable of giving me anything other than my name.

Four years.

And that's all I get.

Mrs. Griffith clears her throat, breaking the growing tension in the entryway. "Perhaps we should sit down? Aiden, this is your house. It's up to you."

Blue eyes swing to me, a silent conversation passing between us as I stand frozen between him and Porter. It's the same look I got the day I walked away from him, except now it's leading us to a very different outcome.

He nods once before turning to everyone else with a similar impassible expression like his father wears. "We can sit in the living room, but I don't want any fighting, or else those who initiate it will have to leave."

I'm not surprised it's my father who scoffs over the agreeable request. "Who are you to tell us what we can and cannot do about our son after he up and left, lying about where he was?"

"Sounds oddly familiar," Aiden returns straight-faced, a warning tone directed at my father. "Maybe you should watch your words, considering you've spent far more time trying to run a failing store all these years instead of giving a shit about your children. Including the one you let up and leave years ago."

Mrs. Griffith places a hand on Aiden's shoulder in silent warning, but it doesn't stop his shoulders from stiffening. "Let's sit."

Porter, Aiden, and I all sit on the couch together while my parents take the love seat to the side. Aiden's mother sits on the armchair while his father stands cross-armed and hyperaware of the darkening atmosphere beside her, a straight stance just like Aiden usually has when he's being cautious. They've always been more alike than Aiden liked to admit.

"First," Mr. Griffith says, "we apologize for bringing Porter here. We didn't know he lied about his whereabouts when we agreed to take him to the Raiders game at Wilson Reed to see Aiden and the Dragons play them."

Our parents' eyes shoot to my brother, and it's Mom's frazzled voice that says, "We told you that you couldn't go to that."

Porter sinks into the cushion. "I know, but when Aiden…" His eyes go to me, then to the tense body on the other side of me before looking back at Mom. "When Aiden invited me along, I couldn't say no. You and Dad were going to be working and never cared if I stayed at Jimmy's before, so I didn't think you'd mind now."

"You lied, Porter." It's been a long time since I've heard her stern, motherly tone. It's not as condescending when it's directed at my brother as it was at me. How many times did she simply dismiss me to my room by telling me she was over my dramatics when I was just being a kid? How often did she tell me to check on Porter when she didn't want to so she didn't have to be a mother at all? And *now* she chooses to be one after all this time? I don't get it.

Looking to Aiden and his parents, I force a smile to act like I'm fine and say, "Can I have a couple minutes with my family, please? I'd like to talk to them alone."

Aiden looks like he wants to tell me no, because he knows the look on my face is phony at best, but his mother pats his arm, and his father gives him a single nod before tipping his head toward the kitchen as if in quiet demand to follow them.

"If you need me," he whispers with reluctance, pecking my cheek, "you know where to find me."

Nodding absently, I watch the three of them walk into the other room before shifting back to my parents. This is the last place I want to be when they don't deserve these moments with me after all this time.

There's less evidence of the origins of my dark-brown hair from Dad when I give him a longer look, but the slight button nose I get from him is still there. The thinner lips and fuller face that I get from Mom still stand out on her as well. I'm not sure how long I study them or how long they let me before I realize I need to be the one who speaks up first. Like always, they never make the first move. Why should I expect them to be any different now?

I squeeze Porter's arm once as the only warning before I state my piece. "I reached out to Porter online."

Mom and Dad exchange a brief glance before turning to Porter for confirmation.

"She just said she wanted to talk," he tells them, nervously gawking between all of us. When he was little, he used to give me a hard time whenever Mom asked me to watch him. He'd throw tantrums and make a mess of his room or break something I'd either have to hide or take responsibility for, yet every night at the dinner table, his eyes would dart around at the rest of us like he couldn't figure out whose side to pick when obvious tension was there. And I couldn't understand why he wouldn't take mine after everything I did for him. He said he was angry at me for leaving, but it was mutual. I was angry at him for not trying to stand up for me like I did for him. "But it was my idea to come here. She had no clue about it."

Mom holds up her hand. "The problem at hand is that you lied."

Porter presses his lips together and nods.

The woman whose words still clench my heartstrings turns her focus to me. "I…" Her voice catches, forcing her to clear her throat and try again. "I'm trying to wrap my head around the fact that you're here—that you're here *together*. When Porter didn't come home, I thought the worst. I thought…"

My nostrils twitch with anger that I force back down, but it tries creeping up my throat regardless. When *Porter* doesn't come home, it's the end of the world. Go figure.

Dad remains silent, his eyes moving between me and his son as if he's trying to gather his thoughts. I want to ask him why he's not at the store, but I don't want to fuel the fire that's brewing between us already.

The room grows eerily quiet, blanketing us in threatened suffocation. "I reached out to Porter because I thought it was time. I needed to make sure he was okay."

Mom blinks back tears, head turning away as she tries collecting herself. She never liked people seeing her cry. Even at my final days at the house, after all the things she said to me out of emotion, she'd hide her tears behind closed doors.

Dad turns his eyes solely on me when he realizes Mom can't ask the question. "Why now? Why after all this time?"

"Dad," Porter cuts in.

Our father shakes his head. "I think we all deserve some answers, Porter."

Answers? They don't expect the harsh laugh that escapes me. Porter snorts over the noise, and Mom's startled gaze darts to me again with wide eyes. "That's a two-way street. I know I owe you a lot of them, but why don't we start with why you and Mom couldn't stop picking fights?"

Mom pales and Dad shifts to the edge of the couch

cushion. "Your mother and I have had a lot of problems, but we always did what we could to ensure you had a roof over your head. If you're insinuating—"

"Fred," Mom intervenes.

Unwrapping my arm from Porter, I stand my ground. "I know you guys kept a roof over our heads. We always had food. I'm not saying you were terrible parents. I've had to deal with the choices I made and know I messed up, but you should acknowledge your own part in it." I meet both their eyes as the words I've saved for years bubble out of me. "You never stopped fighting, not even when the cops showed up over and over again. Dad spent more time at the store than he did at home, and you, Mom, spent more time complaining about Dad than you did paying attention to anything else. You didn't give a shit about being a mother and certainly didn't give a shit about me. Remember all those times you told me I needed to stop being melodramatic when I told you I didn't like it when you two fought? Or whenever you'd lash out saying I needed to stop having a 'poor me' party whenever I called you out on being unfair to me and Porter? All I tried doing was being honest with you. Parents are supposed to appreciate that communication, not make their kids feel like fucking burdens for it."

Weeks before I'd made up my mind about packing my things and leaving, I'd gotten into a screaming match with Mom while Porter was at practice and Dad was at work. The cops had been there the night before, and some of the neighbors were talking, shooting scathing looks in our direction like we were cooking meth in our nonexistent basement. I'd had enough of being judged and finally told her to leave Dad to save the rest of us from being miserable.

"Does everything always have to be about you, Ivy? I swear,

I've never known someone who complained so damn much. Porter never acts out this way. Why can't you be more like him?"

The fact that she was too dense to see how differently we were treated still grates on me.

"I'm over your bullshit. I swear to God, Ivy. One more remark from you and you're gone. If you honestly think you have it so bad here, I'd like to see you try doing better. We both know you couldn't. Not without that boy and his mother next door backing you up. You don't have what it takes to survive out there, so you better be more grateful for the roof you have over your head here. Do you understand me?"

I'd understood too well.

I wasn't silent like Porter.

Submissive.

In the dark.

To my mother, I was a threat. Because I was willing to tell her what I thought.

She goes to speak, but I stop her. "It is not one person's fault. Dad was trying to keep the store afloat. You deserved to vent. We all had something to do with what happened, and I…" My eyes close for a moment. "I'm sorry for being too much for you to handle, but I'm not sorry for leaving. I'm not sorry for telling you how I felt back then. If I could go back, the only thing I would do differently is figure out how to make living next door work, even if it meant having to see you. Because in the end, you didn't want me there anyway. Since starting at Lindon and being around Aiden again, I've realized that I wanted to try to be the person he and his family always knew I was: a good one. I thought if I reached out to Porter, it'd be a first step in mending something between us, but I wasn't sure if he'd even give me a chance, and I wouldn't have blamed him if he didn't."

Mom stares right at me while Dad's eyes move to the blank TV screen. She doesn't want to talk and certainly doesn't want to hear what I have to say. She isn't looking for an apology and definitely has no intention of apologizing herself. People like her, like *them*, will never see anything they've done as wrong.

All Mom does is clear her throat and act like she's interested. "You go to Lindon? That's…" Her head nods, then shakes as if she's remembering the real point. "That's good, Ivy. But it was a long drive, and I think we should get Porter's things and go—"

I stand at the same time as she does. "That's it? I say my piece and you say you have to go? I'm *trying*. For once, I am trying to be a good person after years of not being one. It isn't like I asked you to come here. I didn't beg you to be in my life. I have made horrible choices, Mom. I have to live with the awful things I did to get by." Things I wish I could forget even if they make me who I am now. Tears leak down my face before I can stop them, my hand going to one of the scars covered by the sweatshirt sleeve, wanting to show her, to show all of them, but knowing they're not ready for what I'd done. "I know we'll never be okay, and I'm not asking to be. I don't want to be friends. I don't even care if we're family. Family isn't just blood-related anyway, which you've proven. I want *Porter* in my life, which is why I asked him to be. If you didn't give a fuck about me, you shouldn't have bothered coming here at all."

A shaky, broken breath escapes me as I say the words I know they need to hear. "If you want me to tell you that I was wrong about what I said in that letter, then fine. I couldn't do it on my own. But I survived anyway. I'm here." My voice is nothing but a croaked whimper by the last word, and suddenly two strong arms are pulling me backward into a hard body that smells like home to me.

I ease into Aiden as Porter stands from the couch and faces our parents. "I'm sorry that I lied, but I wanted to see Ivy, and I wasn't sure if you'd let me. You barely let me go anywhere besides Jimmy's house or school and practice. It's like you don't trust me even though I've never done anything to make you not."

To my surprise, Dad speaks first. "We trust you, Porter. It's just..." His eyes go to me, eyebrows flattened with an unspoken point.

They don't trust me.

"It's hard for us," Mom finishes for him, clearing her throat. "We're being cautious. We're...trying too."

Trying. What bullshit. Maybe they're trying for Porter, but that doesn't seem completely genuine either. "Don't be upset with him," I tell them again, frowning when my parents both let loose similar sighs of exhaustion.

"We're disappointed." My mother's admission doesn't direct it at either Porter or I, but I feel the two words in my soul, knowing they're more than likely not for my brother.

"You should tell her," Porter says, voice harder than I've heard it before. "Tell her what you've been talking about."

Dad eyes him. "Now is not the—"

Porter turns to me. "I wasn't going to say anything because I'm not sure if they'll go through with it, since they've talked about it before, but they've been talking about separating. If you ask me, it's about time. You're right, they should have never stayed together. They make everybody around them miserable."

Mom sucks in a breath. "Porter Lee Underwood! That is hardly appropriate to say, and it's none of your business."

He raises his hands. "Seriously, Mom? You're miserable. Dad is miserable. You gave Ivy the brunt of your frustrations, and the only reason you took it easy on me after she left was because *you* wouldn't be able to explain why another kid left if I decided I'd had it."

Dad's eyes grow wary. "That is enough."

Mom's hands go to her face for a moment before scraping back her frizzy hair. "He's right, Fred, and you know it. We have been over this time and time again, and nothing changes." Her hands drop to her sides as she addresses me and Porter. "Your father and I are serious this time. It should have happened a long time ago, and for what it's worth, I've known that for a while. But I'm supposed to hold everything together, and I thought I could do it when I couldn't." When our eyes meet, the burnt-gold color staring back at me captures all my attention when she says, "Letting you go after your insistence that you'd be better off made me believe it, because I was barely hanging on by a thread myself, Ivy. You have to understand, I thought sending you to Gertie's would have been better. I thought I'd figure out how to... That doesn't matter. Because I did none of the things I set out to do. The point is, who was I to think you couldn't achieve greatness just because I couldn't?"

Aiden's arms tighten around me as I stare at the woman in disbelief. My remaining tears start to dry, my face still damp and eyes still stinging, but for the first time maybe ever, I see her clearly.

A woman in pain.

A woman who gave up long before I did.

Still, that doesn't give her an excuse to treat people like shit just because she doesn't know how to handle her emotions.

I square my shoulders. "I'm not going to wish you the best or the worst, because I don't need that kind of bad karma in my life. But I do hope you figure yourself out, because you seriously need to get your life together."

Porter steps closer to me, taking my hand in his, showing his support without saying the words. He knows it's what I need. If nothing else, I can mend the relationship I broke with him. It's a start. It's something.

Mom steps closer, a hand extending, then lowering in doubt. "I think there are a lot of things we all need to work out in order to become a family, because we haven't been one in a very, very long time."

We never were. "I don't care what you and Dad do. I won't be part of the charade anymore. Like I said, it's Porter I want in my life. Not you. Not even if you finally divorce and realize how toxic you were together."

I feel Aiden's lips on the back of my head and feel a sense of relief—from his minor touch and at the peace I've made with myself for finally making up my mind about what I want. It's a small step forward, but it chips away at the many layers of ice coating the organ in my chest.

I don't know where any of us will go from here, but I'd like to think this moment is a step toward putting the pieces together again with Porter, even if they were never assembled right to begin with. Whatever relationship he chooses to keep having with our parents won't be any of my business as long as he sticks around.

A throat clears from behind us, and the Griffiths are both standing there. I'm not surprised when it's Mrs. Griffith who says, "We're celebrating Thanksgiving a little late this year, and we'll have plenty of food once lunch is ready. Porter, you're more than welcome to stay and join us."

Porter and I exchange a doubtful look before turning to our parents. As much as I want him to stay, I'm not sure he'll be allowed to since he's still under their supervision.

"I think it's best if we go," Dad tells us, voice low as he tips his head. "But the offer is appreciated. Porter?"

My brother presses into me. "I want to stay here for a little while longer. Just until—"

"You have school in the morning," Dad tells him firmly, a reminder that I take into consideration too. "And you can't miss practice. I'm sorry, but we need to leave."

He's not sorry about it at all.

Porter looks to me for help, and I want to tell him to stay, but I don't have that power. "We have each other's numbers now. We can talk. Text. Whatever you want. I promise, Porter. We'll grab food sometime soon."

His eyes go to the floor before he nods, but not before I see the guarded caution on his face that reminds me of myself when promises are made.

Aiden unwinds his arms from me and presses another chaste kiss to the back of my head before helping Porter get his things from downstairs.

Like my little brother, I'm afraid this is it, that after they close the door behind them, it'll be like this never happened. I don't mean to look to Mrs. Griffith for some sense of comfort, but I do. When Mom notices the exchange between me and Aiden's mom, there's a mixture of hurt and irritation that flashes in her eyes.

I don't care what she thinks or how she feels. I used to care too much. I've learned my lesson now not to give people more energy than they're willing to reciprocate.

My eyes go back to Mom. "I won't lose Porter. So you can still talk to him, maybe even find time to spend with him if you both want that," she reassures me, seeing the doubt etched into my features as I study her. "There's something I think you should know, Ivy. I got a call from St. Mary's Hospital one night. The nurse said she'd been concerned about why you were there, but she couldn't express any details. We were on our way when they called the next morning and said you'd left. Your father and I..." Her lips fold into each other as she collects herself. "Your father and I were going to come get you. Bring you home. But we couldn't find you anymore after that. You didn't have a credit card or phone or car to track, so we were back to square one until there was nothing we could do."

I stare at her, blindsided by the statement.

St. Mary's is the hospital in Vermont that I escaped from shortly after what I'd done. It was the beautiful, castle-like establishment I looked over my shoulder at as I ran into the night with a heavy feeling in my stomach that everything was going to change.

Whatever Mom says, I know it's too late.

Would have. Could have. Should have.

Mom's eyes don't go to my sleeves, which makes me think she still has no clue why I was there, no clue what I suffered through, what cries for help I made. She was so focused on her own misery that she'd never be able to focus on mine. Not even if she had come to get me from the hospital. We would have been stuck in the same endless cycle and probably wound up exactly where we are now.

I don't want that life.

I want happiness.

Porter stops at the door where Mom and Dad stand speaking in quiet tones to the Griffiths. He turns to me with a sad smile. "I was looking forward to that apple pie."

I roll my eyes at his weak attempt at lightening the mood. "I'll make you a fresh one sometime. I'm good in the kitchen."

"That's what Aiden says." Porter nudges my foot with his shoe, careful not to let his giant boot crush my bare toes. "Thank you for letting me crash here. I know your message wasn't an invite to barge into your life, but I'm glad I came."

"I'm glad you did too." I give him an awkward hug. "Although I'm sure the biggest reason you're glad you came was because of the boy crush you have on my boyfriend."

The second it's out there, my face blossoms with heat. I feel at least three different sets of eyes on me—my brother's amused ones, Mrs. Griffith's knowing ones, and Aiden's. His burn the hottest on my face, but I do what I can to avoid them.

My brother gives me an out, unfazed by my tease. "He was a bonus, but I think we needed this. I wasn't sure what I'd say, but your boyfriend"—his lips twitch into a little grin—"has a way of convincing people that it's not so much about the words that count."

Swallowing, I nod slowly.

It's the actions.

Letting out a tiny breath, I give Porter another hug, this one tighter, before opening the front door.

When they leave and it's just Aiden and I left in the living room, I turn and look up to see a smirk on his face. "Don't say it."

"Boyfriend, huh?"

I blush. "It just came out."

His parents are back in the kitchen finishing the meal preparations, so he leads me back to the couch. "I didn't mind it."

"But we haven't—"

"It's always been you, Ivy," he cuts me off confidently. "Why shouldn't we label it? We're always going to be friends, but we're also more than that. I don't want to see some other guy with his hands on you, so I might as well make my claim now."

Attention darting to the kitchen where something falls, I sink into the cushion. "I think you already made that claim a while ago," I inform him in no more than a murmur.

"So don't question me."

"Does this mean I'm your girlfriend?" He gives me a look like that's a stupid question, making me laugh. "Today was…a lot. More than I expected, that's for sure."

"You handled it better than I would have," he remarks. Not that I think it's true. He's more levelheaded than I ever have been.

"I don't think I want to stay here."

His brows pinch over the sudden topic change. "Where? The house?"

"In Lindon."

Slowly, he blinks. Once, twice… "Where do you want to go then?"

"Remember when you used to follow me into the woods knowing I'd wind up at that dilapidated fort? I never asked you to, but you'd do it anyway. Or when I'd walk to the ice cream shop on the other side of town alone when it was open during the summers to get their pistachio cones and you'd wind up there annoyed I'd walk by myself?"

"Because you needed me so you didn't get abducted," he replies dryly, his hand moving hair away from my face. His voice softens. "And because I wanted to be there with you."

"Exactly." I tug on the shirt he's wearing, picking a piece of hair off it and peeking at him through my lashes. "I want to be with you. Let's be real, Aiden. I never liked school

311

anyway. I'm not any good at it. But what I am good at is baking, and I can do that anywhere. And this isn't me saying I expect you to take care of me, because you know I won't allow it. I'll get a job. I enjoy working at Bea's, and there's got to be other places like it wherever you go."

"You're still processing everything that just happened with your parents. Don't you think you're being a little rash right now?"

"I'm being *real.*"

"Ivy, you can't—"

"I can," I inform him, leaning into him. "Because I want to. Remember what I asked before? Let me have some control. Let me make my own decisions."

He sighs in defeat. "Are you sure?"

"Out of your head, Griffith," I tease him, tugging on his shirt until he meets me halfway for a kiss. "Overthinking won't get you anywhere."

A sly, knowing smirk stretches his lips as he pecks me again. "Turning the tables, I see."

I simply shrug, waiting for the line.

When he realizes that, he chuckles. "My head is always in the game, Underwood."

Chapter Twenty-Six

AIDEN

RACHEL HOLLOWAY CONGRATULATES ME on finishing the semester with straight As, passes me my final transcript in case I'll ever need it to re-enroll in the future, and sends me on my way. I notice the way she quickly grabs her phone and blushes at whatever is on the screen, and I have an ugly feeling I know what it is considering it went off multiple times during our ten-minute meeting.

When I walk out of her office, I see Matt walking toward it. He smacks the hand I lift and bumps our shoulders together. "I bet you're happy to be done with this place. I'm jealous, man. I'm over it."

My brows raise as I gesture toward the athletic adviser's office he's obviously heading toward. "Word of advice, if you want to get out of here unscathed, you'll end whatever the hell that is. You know you're a good player. Train, focus, and you'll be invited to the next combine."

My teammate, who's usually the class clown with DJ, shoots me a displeased expression at the advice he'd be stupid to ignore. "No offense, but not all of us want to be miserable like you. Some of us go after what we want the second we know we want it."

"What do you want more?" I press. "Do you want football? A career out of it? Or do you want to risk everything for something that may not last? Be honest with yourself, Matt. You're a thrill seeker. You've always done dumb, risky shit because the idea of getting caught excites you for some damn reason."

His nostrils twitch before he eyes the office door that's wide open for a moment before turning back to me. "Mind your business. You got the life you wanted. I'm getting mine. I thought Ivy taught you not to butt into people's lives when your opinion isn't wanted."

My hands raise in surrender. It's not my problem and I've said my piece. That's the best I can do. "Fine, man. I'm just saying that you've got a lot going for you. I'd hate to see anything happen for something you might not be serious about. But you're right. It's not my business. I'll see you at the house."

I start walking away when he sighs. "You and your girl sticking around? I heard DJ saying something about you guys hanging out while you train with Coach in his free time now that the season is over. What else are you going to do? The combine isn't until February."

Coach Pearce knows some trainers who are going to push me to my limits to get me ready for the combine. I'm on a strict diet that Ivy has been helping with, even though half the shit I eat now is something a goddamn rabbit would consume, but I've already noticed results in my energy alone that the dietician said will get me prepared for when my training exercises begin after the New Year.

Rubbing the back of my neck, I nod. "We plan to stay at the house for a while and then spend some time in our hometown. She wants to spend some time with her brother. Catch up on life. Go to a few of his games before he graduates."

His brows go up. "Shit, yeah. Forgot that's how you know each other. Shouldn't surprise me, I guess. Not just anyone was going to catch your eye. Don't know if you know this, but you've got serious trust issues."

I snort at his sarcasm. "You a therapist now?"

He smirks, the tension between us gone like that. "Nah, just hella observant. DJ always said you would have had to have known Ivy for you to get all territorial over her. Plus, who the fuck hangs out at a bakery instead of sleeping in on the one day off a week we get?"

He has me there. But clearly it's worked out for the better. Ivy and I talked more about what comes next for us, and she's set on leaving the university. I can't be a hypocrite and convince her to get her degree when that isn't what she wants. If I'm not staying, I'm not going to tell her she should. We've spent enough time apart. We both agreed we'll figure it out as we go. Together.

"You're going back to the city for break, right?"

His hesitation makes me wish I hadn't asked, especially when his eyes dart back to the office I came from. "Er, yeah. For Christmas at least. My parents are doing a cruise to Alaska or some shit, so it'll give me time to do my own thing." He doesn't need to elaborate on what that is, and I know better than to ask. "Your girl going to be ready for what's coming your way? She said she officially put in her enrollment withdrawal, so it seems like she's serious."

"If anyone can manage, it's Ivy." She's at Bea's for her shift right now, telling Bea that she may be gone by the summertime. She was nervous telling her boss that after everything she's done for her, but I know Bea will be happy.

He glances down to the phone in his hand, lighting up with a name. All I see are the first two letters and decide it's my time to go. "I'll see you around, man."

I'm pushing the door open when he calls out, "Hey, thanks. You know, for the advice."

Nodding once, I head out and find Coach hanging up his phone as I approach his office. He waves me in before I can even knock, so I drop my shit into the chair and sit on the opposite one.

"Just got off the phone with Wilkins," he informs me as I stretch my legs out. "He said the Bills are still interested, but he has good sources that say the Patriots are going to try snatching you up based on how you present yourself in February. And before you say anything"—he eyes me as my lips part to speak—"I also heard they plan on making a spectacle of the tensions between you and Mahone. They won't want any problems between teammates, so they'll make sure it's understood you're on the same ground. No repeats of your time at Wilson Reed together."

My face drains of emotion, eyes narrowing. "That seems like bullshit. It's been years and they want to bring it up to make sure the media *doesn't* play on it?"

He leans back in his chair, tapping a pen against the playbook open in front of him. "A team like that will do whatever they can to make sure their reputation is clean. I have no doubt they'll offer you a pretty penny, son. Doesn't mean the monetary value is going to be worth your sanity if you sign their paper."

"I haven't even done the combine yet, so I'd rather not think about an offer." Or think about the selfish asshole who fucked me over at my first college. It led me to Ivy, which is the only positive thing from the experience.

"You doubting yourself?"

"No, Coach." If anything, I've never been more confident in myself. We lost against Wilson Reed, which still leaves a sour taste in my mouth, but I've got a lot more people on my side, including the girl who's always wanted to cheer me on no matter what I do with my life, and that's all I could ever ask. Whatever comes next will be something we can finally conquer together.

He studies me. "You change your mind about what you want then?"

"Absolutely not."

He gives one firm nod. "Good. Then don't go psyching yourself out before you've had a chance to prove to them what you can do. We both know you're good. Hell, you're better than every guy on the Dragons, and I'll confirm that on camera even if it pisses off the others."

"Probably shouldn't though."

The limp lift of his shoulders tells me he doesn't give a shit either way. "I believe in you, Aiden. I believe you can do great things and go far. I'm sure your family and your girl do too based on what I've seen. Having that support system is going to be real important for the next few years."

I huff out a laugh. "Now you're on board with me seeing someone if she gives me support?"

He shoots me a look. "The missus nearly bit my head off when she found out I'd gone to see your girl at her work. Won't be making that mistake again."

I don't bother hiding my grin.

He nods toward my bag. "You get everything you need from Rachel? She's adamant that you have what you need in case you decide to finish off your degree. I know some players choose to go back to school, but I highly doubt it'd be useful to you."

As much as I want to bring up Matt to him, I know it'd only cause more problems in the long run for everybody involved. So I keep my lips zipped, tell him Rachel got me everything I need, and then get dismissed.

My drive to the bakery is quiet, and when I see the brunette behind the counter handing a cup to an elderly man, I stop in my tracks. Ivy told me she was going to Elena's before work but wouldn't tell me why. When she looks up, there's a secret smile painted across those bright-red lips.

I approach after the last customer walks away with his order and lean across the counter. She stops me before I can steal a kiss, putting her finger against my mouth and pushing me away enough to meet my eyes.

"What? Afraid to be seen with me now?" I ask.

She thumbs my bottom lip. "*You* should be afraid to be seen with *me*. Haven't you heard? I'm a college dropout."

Reaching over, I flick a piece of her freshly dyed hair. It's a little darker than her natural shade but still beautiful. "I don't give a shit as long as you're happy. This looks good on you, by the way. What made you go back?"

She nibbles her lip. "It was time. If I'm going to do what makes me happy, I want a fresh start. No more hiding."

"The talk with Bea went well then?"

Her eyes go behind the counter briefly before she stands on her toes and presses a kiss to my lips. "Better than good. She told me I can stay as long as I'd like. She's even giving me some of her old recipes to practice making."

The woman in question comes out from the back, flour

covering her black apron and a big smile on her face. "She's forgetting the most important part of what I told her."

Ivy groans.

"I said I couldn't say no to her running away with you when the time came because she couldn't do any better if she tried."

I laugh as Ivy turns to the older woman with her arms crossed over her chest. "I'm not running away with him."

Bea's eyes change slightly. "You're right. I'd say you've done enough running in your lifetime. It's about time you settled, hmm?"

The comment makes me wonder just how long their talk was.

When I get Ivy's full attention, I say, "I'm going to Everly's for a while, then meeting up with Caleb later on. Told him we'd stop by toward closing to get you."

"You don't have to—"

I stop her there. "I don't have to do anything, but I want to. Plus, it's cold outside, there's ice everywhere, and you're insistent on not needing a car."

Her stance is the same. "I haven't driven in years and cars are expensive. I don't need one when I can walk places."

"Exactly. So we're picking you up."

She glares.

I shrug.

Bea laughs before disappearing into the back again.

"So do you want your usual?" she asks, shifting gears.

"Is that your way of saying you want half my bagel?"

"Are you going to keep insinuating you only ask for half of one because you knew I'd eat the other?"

All I say is, "The usual, please."

"Fine, but I'm putting *real* butter on it instead of that

nasty olive oil spread you like." She goes to work doing just that, passing me a coffee a few minutes later, then a bag with *half* an everything bagel a few minutes after that.

"Was that so hard?" I tease, passing her what I owe.

"I hate you sometimes."

She says it with a smirk, cementing what I've always known.

I lean in again, crowding her space. "I dare you to hate me, Ivy. We both know you don't. You couldn't even if you tried."

Because she loves me.

Even if she won't admit it yet.

Epilogue

IVY

"YOU HAVE NO IDEA what's going on, do you?" the woman with blue streaks in her blond hair muses. My hands have been curled tightly together as I watch Aiden fly across the field with three opposing players chasing after him and the ball he's cradling close to his chest.

The smile I offer is shy. "Is it that obvious?"

Her lips tilt upward, causing the blue paint on half her face crinkle. "You've looked lost this whole time, and maybe a little nauseous. I was wondering who you were here with since you don't seem that educated on the game."

An amused laugh bubbles from me because I *have* felt like I'm going to be sick whenever Aiden is nearly taken down. "You'd think I'd have it figured out after all the games I've been to by now, but you'd be wrong."

It's been over two years since we left Lindon, and my knowledge base for Aiden's game is still limited because I spend more time worried about him getting hurt than I do trying to figure out what's actually going on.

She laughs, holding out her hand. "At least you're honest. Most women pretend they know what's going on, but they're really only here to try getting attention from the players in hopes of going home with one of them. I'm Cassy, by the way."

"Ivy." Our eyes turn back to the field when a commotion stirs a few strangled gasps from the people around us.

Cassy sucks in a breath when Aiden jumps over a fallen player who must have failed at taking him out before twisting around another, barely avoiding a tackle, and diving into the end zone right as the buzzer goes off.

"Holy shit," my seatmate whispers in as much awe as I feel. The referee jogs over and gives the signals to someone before the scoreboard changes to appoint the New York Giants another six points. "We won. *We won!*"

The sea of blue-and-white people around us goes wild, jumping up and down and screaming out the number of the newest tight end on the team as he gets up and grabs the ball as other members of the Giants come running over and surround him in celebration.

"They may go to the Super Bowl if they keep this up," Cassy tells me, screaming over the others still celebrating the victory.

I nod along, trying to see over the crowd. Aiden and the others are walking off the field together, and I know I'll get a text within minutes of him getting safely back to the locker room to let me know where and when to meet him outside.

"So why are you here?" my seatmate asks as we collect our things.

A sly grin stretches across my face. "I'm hoping to go home with one of the players."

Her eyes widen and cheeks pinken as her gaze darts to

the jersey I'm wearing. It's brand new, with GRIFFITH printed on the back and 88 on the front. If he got his way, he would have had one custom made that said GRIFFITH'S HANDS OFF, but I told him I'd shred it before anyone saw it on me.

Something flashes over her face after she's done giving me a once-over. "What's your last name again?"

All I say before elbowing my way out of the row of seats is "I didn't tell you."

I was supposed to meet Porter here for the game, but he had a last-minute schedule change that made him have to stay on campus. Since the Giants went to Miami to play the Dolphins, it would have worked perfectly with Porter at the University of Miami. Aiden convinced him to accept the full scholarship that covered everything he'd need as long as he played for the Hurricanes while he attended. Mom and Dad wouldn't have to pay a dime, which is good considering their divorce was finalized last Valentine's Day. It's oddly appropriate for the cycle of things my family has done wrong to include a divorce on the day people are supposed to express love for each other.

I follow the directions I'm given via text and find myself in a concrete hallway with a few other significant others I've talked with before. Aiden told me I should stick with them, but I'm still no better at socializing than I was before, especially after dropping out of college once my first semester was done.

DJ took it the hardest since he had over a year left and wasn't planning on going into the draft. He managed to get my phone number before I moved to the New York metropolitan area after Aiden signed a contract with the Giants and still sends me random messages about his day—images of food he made, the cute blond he's completely obsessed with, romance book recommendations that they read together, and blurry pictures of his professor that he sneaks during class because he thinks the man looks like a clone of Snape from the *Harry Potter* movies.

"Hey, Ivy," Malissa Melburne greets, bouncing her two-year-old toddler in her arms. A diaper bag rests on the ground beside her, and a car carrier on the other. As soon as Aiden introduced me as his girlfriend to everyone, the amount of advice on what to wear and what not to, when to get married, and when to have babies started pouring out of the women I barely knew.

Admittedly, that's the biggest reason I don't sit with them if I can help it. I wouldn't have minded being the mute among them as I watched the game and let them think whatever they wanted of me, but having the added pressure of when best to move forward with Aiden so it doesn't impact his season doesn't help my anxiety any. I've gotten better, sought out help, but there are triggers that still make my skin itch with a desire to do something controllable.

And I do.

I call Aiden.

Then I call my therapist.

The apartment we settled into is a spacious three bedroom with a huge kitchen that Aiden told the Realtor was nonnegotiable. The free time I had after saying goodbye to Lindon was spent learning how to better my baking skills with the help of Aiden's mother and all the recipe books she got for me.

Things have been better with Porter too. He occasionally sends me bakeware and books using the money he's earning as a tutor on campus. I keep telling him not to waste his money on me, but he does it anyway. I think it's to annoy me, but I secretly like it.

With the help of Aiden, I've managed to earn a little money of my own from blogging about my baking adventures. My following is still minimal, only jumping in views whenever Aiden is involved in the little videos I post online, but it's enough to cover some of the smaller bills and the therapy sessions I've been attending.

"How's the baby?" I ask, wiggling my fingers at the little boy staring at me with his thumb in his mouth. He raises a hand and waves back, making me smile.

"He's good. Teething like crazy." She pecks his head and adjusts him. "Have you and Aiden thought about—"

"Oh, cut the girl some slack," another one of the wives says. It's the oldest one of us, who's shut down the women more than once on my behalf. For that reason, Penny is my favorite. "I know you would have waited to have Prince, but things happen. Let them live their lives."

Malissa grumbles under her breath, focusing back on her son and nobody else.

I give Penny a grateful smile, which she returns. "Nick loved those turnovers you sent over. I had to remind him that he had to save at least one for me."

Blushing, I shift from one foot to the other. "I can make more. I've thought about adding something different this time."

A woman a few feet down says, "You should try them with peaches."

"Peaches?" Penny remarks, scrunching her face.

"It's Don's favorite."

Baking for Aiden's team now is no different than it was in Lindon. I still get requests, and I still do the best I can do accommodate. They challenge me to change up traditional recipes with my own styles, which helps me in the long run when I decide they're good enough to post about on my blog.

Once the guys emerge, everyone goes their separate ways. Aiden walks over to me and drops an arm around my shoulder, pulling me into him for a tight hug. "Good game," I tell him.

"You say that every time."

I peer up at him, grinning. "Because I think they're all good. Say 'Thank you, Ivy.'"

"Thank you, Ivy," he obeys, rolling his eyes. When he hooks the same arm around my waist and walks me out toward the corridor that leads to where the players park, he asks, "Did anyone ask about us again?"

Apparently the guys are no different with him, saying most players don't stay with anyone as long as we have without making a commitment by now, but like me, he brushes it off.

"Malissa asked if I was going to pop out one of your babies anytime soon." He snorts at my choice of words. "Don't get me wrong, the act itself is definitely fun now that you know what to do with your dick, but I'm not ready for—"

"I've always known what to do with my dick," he refutes, eyeing me defensively even though he knows I'm teasing when I shoot him a wink. "And you never seem to mind when you're screaming my name and coming on my cock almost every night."

One of the stadium workers overhears and hides a laugh with a loud cleared throat as we pass him, making me smack Aiden's chest. "You did that on purpose."

He shrugs nonchalantly. "Maybe."

Once we're settled in his new Ford truck, with tinted

326

windows to hide us from the cameras that like to harass us on occasion, I see him turning to me as he presses the start button. "We might not be ready to be parents, but we could make other decisions."

My hand falters on the seat belt. "Like what?"

"Open the glove box."

Eyes darting in front of me, I hesitate only a moment before doing as he says, and I see a black box.

"Aiden…" My voice cracks as I brush my fingers over the square box before taking it out.

He puts the truck in drive and pulls out of the parking lot. "I'm not good with pretty words, Ivy. I tried thinking about how to do this in a romantic way, but we've never really been that way. This is more us."

"Are you… Is this what I think it is?" I'm afraid to lift the lid and see what's inside even though I already know.

We stop at the end of the lot where traffic passes by us. It's then he looks over, one hand gripping the steering wheel while the other reaches over and lifts the lid for me. "Let's get married."

Oh my God.

"Be my wife?" he asks, eyes combing over me as I stare at him in shock. The tender way he's looking at me invokes the same feeling as when he made a pact with me in our old fort hangout and the same feeling I got when I realized I loved the boy who'd wanted to be my friend so effortlessly, without any expectation or pressure.

Eventually, I manage to glance down at the beautiful gold ring that has a single diamond in the middle. It's not flashy or too fancy. It's simple. It's *me*.

"Let's get married," he says again, this time more casually as the truck moves forward into the road. "And then maybe down the line, you can pop out one or two of my kids when things are less crazy."

"One or two kids?" I squeak.

A shoulder lifts. "Or three."

"Three!" We've never talked about kids, but that doesn't mean I haven't thought about it. Before coming back into his life, I never thought I'd ever be a mom. But once we made things official, all of a sudden, I saw my future—a wedding, a house, and children. I saw it all for the first time—a chance to be the kind of mother mine never was.

All with Aiden right beside me.

"Is that a yes?"

"Is the three children negotiable?" I blurt, causing him to chuckle. "I mean, what'd my vagina ever do to you?"

A twinkle forms in those blue eyes as they give me a brief look. "It's done plenty for me and hopefully will do plenty more. We can talk about the number of kids we'll have later. Right now, I need an answer. Out of your head, Underwood. Yes or no?"

I let out a quick breath.

He wants to marry me.

He wants to have kids with me.

The single word response is the easiest one I've ever said. "Yes." I pick the ring out of its carrier and study it closer before slipping it onto my finger and shaking my head in awe of the piece of jewelry that looks like it's meant to be there. "But we're not having three kids. Two."

He pauses for a moment. "Fine."

"Fine."

"Good."

I smile to myself as I touch the ring. "I love you. You gave me back my life, Aiden."

He gave me a second chance.

My brother.

A future.

The truck slows in traffic. "You did that yourself, Ivy. Don't give me the credit when I don't deserve it."

I huff out a laugh. "You deserve more credit than you allow yourself. Even after all this time, you hate admitting that you're like my own personal superhero. Be honest, Aiden. We wouldn't be here if it weren't for you being willing to deal with all my bullshit."

He doesn't say anything, but I know he agrees with me even when he flashes me a skeptical look.

Our hands find each other, linking between us on the seat. One of his fingers settles on the ring as if he wants to make sure this is real.

Ivy Ann Griffith.

I laugh to myself.

Maybe I always knew it'd end like this.

READ ON FOR A SNEAK PEEK AT THE
NEXT BOOK IN THE LINDON U SERIES

BEG
YOU
TO
TRUST
ME

DANNY AND SKYLAR

LINDON U

B. CELESTE

Chapter One

SKYLAR

BAD DECISIONS TASTE LIKE rum, coke, and something metallic. A taste that reminds me of the time my older sisters dared me to see how many quarters I could fit into my mouth at once.

With fluttering eyelids and heavy limbs, I come to with a dry mouth and cloudy head, finding it hard to move in the soft sheets covering my chilled body. Sheets that don't feel as soft as the expensive, certified-organic cotton threads covering the twin mattress in my room.

The bed under my leaden limbs feels too lumpy, nothing like the thick, foam pad covering the school-supplied mattress on my raised frame.

One of my sticky eyelids peels open in confusion, vision blurry but able to take in the unfamiliar setup of the room. It's bigger and colder than the double I share with my freshman roommate Rebecca, and the furniture is nothing like the stuff I have.

It takes a few seconds, but I quickly realize the reality

of the situation. Bolting upright, I careen to the side when dizziness slams into me. The black sheet falls down my body, exposing the untied, wrinkled purple wrap shirt I borrowed from my friend Aliyah that's exposing the peach bra I'd slipped on underneath. I suck in a sharp breath when my eyes go to the empty spot beside me, then slowly to the side, where I see what's thrown onto the carpet.

Time stops.

Panic seeps into my rib cage.

I lift the sheet and shakily lower it once I see the naked skin it's covering, then glance back at the black leggings and panties in the middle of the floor. They're the only things I'd worn that were mine. The shirt, shoes, and new pushup bra were all from the girls I befriended who insisted I needed to dress up for the party they were dragging me to.

You'll have fun.

We won't let you out of our sight.

My recollection of the events beyond letting them play with my stubborn, black-dyed hair and telling me what makeup would look best on my tan skin is fuzzy.

Too fuzzy to put together how I got in a room I don't recognize with my pants off.

Doing a quick scan to double-check that I'm alone, I toss my legs over the side of the bed and wince at the ache between them. I bolt toward my clothing, worried someone will bust in. Tugging the panties up my legs, I stop when I glance down and see the small smears of blood on the insides of my thighs.

I stare.

Not breathing.

Not blinking.

Thud, thud, thud. The drumming between my head and

heart is in sync, demanding my attention as I stare at the red smattering my skin.

A moment or two later, I force myself to finish getting dressed with shaky hands.

Pressing an ear against the wooden door to see if I hear anyone outside it, I quietly turn the knob and creep out of the room with my borrowed black heels tucked in my hands and my heart lodged in the back of my throat.

I cringe at each creak of the floorboards under my bare feet as I tiptoe down the narrow hallway toward the wooden staircase. I don't know what time it is because my phone is dead, but the sun is out and blinding me, making the headache throbbing inside my temples ten times worse.

As I creep down the steps and toward the front door, I notice that there's no remnants of a party left. No plastic cups lying around, no food on the carpet, no weird boozy smells that I vaguely remember from the night before. The bits I do recall consist of a packed house that made me feel claustrophobic, loud music that made it impossible to hear what my friends were saying as I followed them into the mass of bodies, and the scent of cheap beer.

I'm almost to the door when I freeze midstep after hearing, "Who the hell are you?"

My body locks up from the deep voice behind me. I don't recognize it, not that that says much. I'm not familiar with most men around here, since my small circle of peers is made up of my roommate Rebecca and a few other girls—Deanna and Aliyah—I met during orientation a month before.

Footsteps come from somewhere else, stopping close by. A second voice, less deep and more amused, says, "Huh. I thought everyone did their walks of shame already. Sorry, big man."

I make myself look over my shoulder, but I don't know why. I'm met with two different faces. One boyish and clearly amused, if the mischievous glint in his blue eyes is any indication, and the other full of…nothing. No emotion. Nothing readable. The shorter of the two—though not by much—grins at me before scoping out my body in a once-over that makes me want to make a break for it.

If I were smart, I wouldn't let them stare and leer. The shorter one cocks his head until his messy blond hair flops over his forehead and lips kick up. He elbows his friend, who looks massive and far less enthused by my presence in comparison.

Both are built like athletes. Strong. Broad. Like they could take down another person their size or larger if they wanted to. Deanna said the party was at the football house.

We won't let you out of our sight is what Dee promised me.

How did I get separated from them?

"We didn't know anyone else was here," the taller, stoic-looking one tells me. His lips press into a firm line as he watches me, eyes narrowing. Accusatory.

I'm uncomfortable.

Hungover.

Confused.

It doesn't take much to figure out what exactly happened last night, and it makes me feel itchy. Dirty. My mouth feels dry as cotton, and I just want to go back to the dorms and take a long, hot shower.

We won't let you out of our sight.

But where are they now?

I swallow, stuttering through the nerves rising up my throat. "I–I…"

Unable to form proper words, I shake my head and dart

toward the door. I don't know where I'm going since it was dark out when we drove here, but I don't stop or look back either.

I walk fast, following the sidewalk and feeling the hot sun heating the pavement and burning my feet. I only get a few feet away before having to stop and empty the contents of my stomach into a bush.

When I stand up, I blink a few times to ward off the tears glazing my eyes, brush off my mouth with the back of my hand, and accept what happened last night.

I, Skylar Vivian Allen, lost my virginity at a party I didn't even want to go to. To a man I don't know. In a house I don't know.

Where my friends left me.

Freshman year at Lindon University is *not* off to a good start.

ABOUT THE AUTHOR

B. CELESTE IS A new adult and contemporary romance author who gives voices to raw, realistic characters with emotional storylines that tug on the heartstrings. She was born and raised in upstate New York, where she still resides with her four-legged feline sidekick, Oliver "Ollie" Queen. Her love for reading and writing began at an early age and only grew stronger after getting a BA in English and an MFA in English and creative writing. When she's not writing, she's working out, binge-watching reality game shows, and spending time with her friends and family.